CONDUIT

PARAGONS:
BOOK TWO

C. Steven Manley

CONDUIT: Paragons Book Two
Copyright © 2015 C. Steven Manley

Nightrunner Press

FIRST EDITION

ISBN: 0692539115

ISBN-13: 978-0692539118

Cover by C. Steven Manley and Jeremy Bronaugh

Copy Editing by Lynsey Morandin

Interior Formatting by Jeremy Bronaugh and Lynsey Morandin

For more information visit:
www.cstevenmanley.com
twitter.com/cstevenmanley
instagram.com/cstevenmanley

For Amy, Brittany, Jacob, and Julia Rose.

Thank you for putting up with a guy who's more comfortable in the worlds he imagines than the one he actually lives in. I love you all.

PROLOGUE

Jordan Screed ran for his life.

The cool night air rushed across his face and pounded in and out of his lungs as he moved. He sprinted through the forest with the speed of a frightened deer, leaping over brush and boulder that no normal human could possibly have vaulted. When he landed, he did so with a grace and agility that could have won him the gold medal in any Olympic competition.

Medals and competitions were the farthest thing from Jordan's mind, though. He raced through the night with no thought but escape. He could hear his pursuers coming for him, running in their awkward way, going around what he merely jumped over, crashing through the forest with no thought of stealth, and closing in from every side.

The clouds parted for a moment and silver-gray moonlight pierced the openings in the forest canopy. There was movement to his left; he saw a dozen or so human-shaped things running his way with a clumsy but effective stride. Jordan cursed and veered to the right, heading toward the tree line and the beach that lay beyond it.

The sounds of pursuit were all around him now, coming from every direction. He tried to pick up the pace but even he, one of the most powerful of the Awakened – a Paragon of the Fae bloodline – could only go so long before he needed to rest, and Jordan had been running for hours. He cursed at that and – not for the first time – told himself he would not stop so long as he was conscious. The moment he crossed the tree line, though, the decision was taken out of his hands.

Jordan stopped suddenly and actually slid a few feet in the soft loam before coming to a stop at the edge of a jagged stone cliff. The dark waters of the Atlantic Ocean spread out before him in a seascape of gray motion and ghostly whitecaps. Salt and sea life flavored the breeze coming up from the water and the sky was a mass of rolling, iron gray clouds that were occasionally tinged with silver by the full moon they struggled to hide. It was easily a seventy-foot drop to the narrow, rock-strewn beach below. Jordan was considering it when he heard them come up behind him. He turned around on tense legs, muscles coiled and ready to move if the need arose.

From the tree line, the dead emerged in a rough but complete half circle, surrounding him. There were dozens of them and they all bore the marks of what had killed them: stab wounds, sliced throats, and more vicious injuries that seemed to have come from claw or tooth. There was even the occasional bullet wound in their gray, black-veined flesh. When the ones with functional tracheas hissed or moaned at him, it was past teeth and tongues stained black and viscous.

They surrounded him, but held their ground. The scent of decaying meat joined the ocean's musk. Jordan suspected why and wasn't surprised when he saw the crowd part enough for his brother to walk into the half circle with him.

Carmine Screed was nearly a foot taller than his

brother and built like a professional basketball player. Long, lean muscles rippled beneath the loose shirt he wore and he moved with surprising grace for so large a man. His face was rugged with cold, defined features and an expression that spoke to perpetual apathy. Though lost in shadow, Jordan could almost see the dark blue of his brother's left eye assessing the situation without expression. Carmine's right eye, though, was another matter entirely.

It was a solid, oily black orb with no hint of a pupil or an iris. It had healed that way after a man named Israel Trent – another Paragon – had gouged it out during a fight a year earlier. Even though Carmine assured Jordan he could see out of it just fine, the thing always made Jordan feel uneasy. The facial tattoos that curved around that side of Carmine's face in jagged, Celtic lines did little to alleviate the feeling.

"Jordan," Carmine said, fixing his brother with both eyes, "why are you running?"

"Carmine, bro. Fight it, man."

"Why," Carmine said in a tone that Jordan knew was not his own, "are you running?"

"Because I'm not interested in joining your posse," Jordan said, stabbing a finger at the dead things surrounding his brother.

"But it's better," Carmine said. "You'll see. When you can hear her voice, you'll see."

"See what? Goddammit, Carmine! She's in your head, man! Literally in your head! You're letting a bitch run you, man! We're the Screeds! We don't do that!"

"It's not like that, Jordan. It's not what you think. We can do a beautiful thing with her."

Jordan pressed his palms hard against his forehead in frustration. "Fuck! Are you even listening to yourself, Carmine? Am I even talking to you?"

Carmine stared at his brother, his expression firm but

emotionless. Around him the dead shifted and stank.

"Bring him to me," Carmine said.

The dead surged forward.

Jordan turned toward the cliff and jumped.

CHAPTER ONE

Israel

Israel Trent watched as the New York City night lights flashed by outside the dark tinted limousine windows, painting the city in muted colors too numerous to count. Outside, people moved in groups or pairs through the chill autumn night intent on getting to their destinations. The crowd was a heavy one – it was Friday night, after all – but thinned somewhat as the limo made the turn onto Fifth Avenue.

"Israel," Olivia Warburton said from across the spacious passenger cabin, "are you paying attention?"

Israel tapped one gloved finger against the window and said, "I am. I'm paying attention to that guy with the big sign around his neck that says 'The end is near, just not near enough.' What do you think that even means?"

"I haven't got the first idea," Olivia said. "If you want to fret over New York's homeless population, though, do it later. You have more immediate concerns."

Israel turned from the window and faced his companions. Olivia Warburton sat across from him looking every bit the billionaire matron that she was. Silver-gray hair topped a face that was lined but still regal. Her eyes twinkled with intelligence and moved like a cat's, subtle and quick. Her dark, formal dress was accented with glittering jewelry that seemed perfectly at home on this woman's full frame. She accepted a crystal glass with two fingers of expensive whiskey in it from the man sitting next to her.

The man called Stone poured his own measure of rich, brown liquor and said, "Oh, leave the man alone, Olivia. He knows what he's into here." Stone was Olivia's closest confidant and right-hand man. In most matters, a word from him was the same as a word from her. The fact that he was barely five feet tall, built like a human-shaped pit bull, and bald as a billiards ball didn't seem to make any difference. He took a drink from the glass and smoothed his thick but neatly trimmed beard with his free hand. "It's bad enough you made us put on these penguin suits," he said, tugging at the collar of his tuxedo. "The least you can do is let the man enjoy the drive through the city."

"A Council of the Veil Conclave is a black tie event, Stone. You've been to enough of them to know that," Olivia said.

"I think you both look quite handsome," the fourth member of the group said from the seat beside Israel.

He looked over at Doctor Allison Brandt and, as he usually did, marveled at how striking she was. Her skin was lightly tanned and contrasted beautifully with the cream-colored evening gown she was wearing. Her creamy brown hair was pulled into a complicated bun over a lean face, distinguished nose, and full lips. She regarded Israel with her dark eyes and smiled as she said, "Yes. You both look very James Bond."

Stone grunted. "There hasn't been a black man as Bond, has there?"

"Then we're overdue," Allison said. "What do you think, Israel? Ever done any acting?"

Israel returned the smile and said, "No. Not since

about the sixth grade, anyway. My dad still has the pictures."

"How's he doing?"

Israel shrugged. Maxwell Trent was a full-time resident at one of the best Alzheimer's treatment facilities in the country. "He has more bad days than good. He doesn't remember me about half the time. Doesn't matter, though. He's still my Pop."

"If you people are finished," Olivia said, "I'd like to go over things one more time with Israel. He's going to be under a lot of scrutiny."

Israel held up his hands in mock surrender. "Fine. You got me, Sheriff. Ask your questions."

Olivia gave him a pointed look over the rim of her glass. "Don't be flippant, Israel."

"All right, Olivia. What would you like to discuss?"

"Tell me about the Council of the Veil."

Israel took a breath and said, "The Council of the Veil is an organization that was founded in the ninth century after the fall of the Roman Empire. The reason for its formation was to end the hunting and killing of individuals who were members of the genetically altered bloodlines that were forced upon early humans by extra-dimensional entities tens of thousands of years ago. Religious fervor of the time led to people blaming the bloodlines for Rome's fall, so the Council was originally established as a kind of Underground Railroad to hide and transport bloodlines to less hostile regions. The idea spread until every continent on Earth established its own version of the Council, but they all serve one purpose: to maintain a veil of secrecy surrounding the existence of the bloodlines so that they can live in peace and not be subjected to the prejudices and violence that non-bloodline humans have always shown toward them."

"You sound like a Wikipedia entry," Allison said.

Israel shrugged. "I'm a journalist; facts are facts."

"True," Olivia said, "but ancient history does us little good. Tell me about the Council you're about to meet."

"It governs the Veil surrounding the North American continent. It has six members called Delegates and a primary mediator called the Arcane. Five of the Delegates each represent one of the predominant North American bloodlines: Seraphim, Infernal, Fae, Lycan, and Magi. The sixth Delegate is considered to be the Human representative and is usually a member of the U.S. government since it's the most populous and powerful country on the continent. According to you, though, while their sole focus is the maintenance of the Veil, they still suffer from the same infighting and political power games that plague any government body."

"And if someone violates the Council's rules? If they tear the Veil and reveal the bloodline world to a human?"

"They are executed," Israel said. "Almost without exception." Israel remembered a time when the thought of someone being summarily killed would have angered him. Now, he just couldn't find the feeling.

He glanced at Allison and saw a momentary flicker of concern dull the usual shine in her eyes. Though harder to catch, Israel thought he saw something similar in Stone's expression.

"What?" Israel asked.

"Nothing, mate," Stone answered in his odd British-meets-Russian accent. "It's just they could very well turn that kind of attention on you. It worries us."

Israel looked back at Allison and she gave a quick nod and looked out her own window.

"They won't tonight," Olivia said. "I have assurances from the Arcane and several of the council members that all of the peacekeeping protocols will be enforced as usual. Speaking of which – Israel?"

"The Peacekeeping Accords state that anyone who brings a weapon into the Conclave or enacts any sort of violence during the Conclave will be imprisoned and judged as one who has torn the Veil. Any council member who sanctions or enacts violence or any similar act of aggression either directly or through an agent against any other member's agents or interests for a period that starts on sunrise the day before the Conclave and ends at sunset the day after the Conclave will be considered to have torn the Veil and will be treated accordingly." The answer was so reflexive that he barely looked away from Allison as he spoke.

"Good," Olivia said. "I'm glad all my quizzing has paid off. You're welcome."

"Right, then, that's all well and good," Stone said, "but they've never had a Paragon Necrophage stroll through the front door, have they?"

Necrophage. The word made Israel meet the older man's eyes for a moment. Tens of thousands of years ago, an unknown race with the ability to bridge the gap between multiversal dimensions had visited Earth and - for reasons Israel suspected mankind would never know - had used their advanced science to manipulate and change the DNA of early humans, altering them into creatures that were something more or less than they had been. Then they had abandoned Earth and their creations.

As the millennia rolled on, most of these creatures were hunted to extinction or died out through some other means. The ones that didn't thrived, but changed. As it turns out, human DNA is a resilient and assertive structure. So, very slowly, the changes wrought by the extra-dimensional visitors were pushed aside and overwritten by the base human DNA. They didn't just disappear, though. These altered strands were relegated to what scientists call Junk DNA, a part of the human genome that appears to have no function.

Under specific and rare circumstances, a small portion of the human population can have those ancient genetic traits reactivated. Anyone to whom this happens is considered to be Awakened and generally fits into one of the five predominate bloodlines: Fae, Seraphim, Mage, Lycan, and Infernal. Though the names evoke images of western myth and religion, it was a well-known fact among the bloodlines that most of those myths and legends were the result of normal humans telling stories to explain the ancient Awakened that they encountered.

Just as the five bloodlines inspired myths and legends, the sixth most common bloodline, the Necrophage, inspired horror and loathing. Vampires, zombies, revenants, ghouls, wights, mummies – they were all Necrophage and, save for the rarest of exceptions, all feared and hunted wherever they arose. The exception was the Paragon, an Awakened who was a perfect balance of base human genome and the genetically altered junk DNA.

Israel Trent, the first Paragon Necrophage in nearly six hundred years, was one such exception.

"They will abide by the law, Stone," Olivia said. "I expect you to do likewise. So, if you've got some kind of weapon tucked away in that tuxedo somewhere, leave it in the car. The last thing we need to do is start an incident."

Stone gave her a deep frown and downed his whiskey. He pulled a cigar case from inside his jacket, but immediately put it away when he saw Olivia's disapproving glare. "I don't like going in there with nothing but fists and harsh language, Olivia. My mate Israel here scares a lot of people. Scared people do stupid things."

"A visit from the Council Inquisitors scares them just as much. I'm confident the two fears will cancel each other out."

"Council secret police or not," Allison said, "if someone thinks he can get away with attacking Israel covertly, he will. I'm sorry, Olivia, but I'm with Stone on this one. We need to be prepared for anything."

"You know, I'm not exactly defenseless," Israel said.

"I've been working out." This earned him a smile from everyone. The truth was, Israel was stronger than any three world-class powerlifters combined and could run at a sprint for hours without tiring. Being a Necrophage meant that he was technically dead; he had no need to breathe and his heart did not circulate what passed for blood in his body in any detectable way. His sole need was for animal-based proteins. If he went for too long without them or used his prodigious strength for extended periods without fueling his body, then he reverted to a thing that was the stereotype of the mindless undead predator the world so feared and he would seek out meat instinctively and relentlessly. Any meat.

"Besides that," he said, patting the breast pocket of his tuxedo jacket, "I've got a few packs of Allison's super-jerky tucked away, so my appetite shouldn't be an issue."

"Don't call it that," Allison said with a critical smirk. "It's dehydrated and super concentrated beef protein."

Israel shrugged. "I have to call it something."

"Yes, but you're a writer. Surely you can do better than that."

Israel considered it. "Max-Snax? Protein Power Up? How about Concentrated Cow Bar?"

"Mighty Meat Stick?" Stone added.

"No, no, no, and hell no," Allison said, pointing at Stone on the last one.

Everyone shared another laugh as the limo pulled up into a short line of waiting cars outside the Empire State Building. The line was blocking the bulk of the right lane and they ignored the angry horn blaring from other motorists as they pulled around them. A few seconds of silence passed before Olivia said, "Stone? I'm waiting."

The bald man sighed and dug around the back of his waistband and came out with a thin, stiletto-style blade with a narrow handle. He dropped it on the seat between them. A moment later, he placed a palm-sized pistol beside it. "Happy?" he asked.

"Ecstatic. Is that all of it?"

"Only if you don't count my—"

"Stone." The warning in Olivia's tone was like getting tapped with a rubber mallet.

Stone nodded. "That's all, Olivia. You can relax."

"Not damned likely tonight," she muttered.

"You were willing to risk pissing off the Council that much just to watch my back? Stone, I'm touched, man," Israel said.

"Don't be," Stone said. "I didn't spend a year training you just to have some Seraphim zealot blow your brains out all over the bacon-wrapped shrimp. I'm protecting my time investment."

"Ah, that's sweet," Allison said. "I think he's man-crushing on you, Israel."

"I love you, too, Stone," Israel said, trying hard not to grin.

"You can both shut the hell up," Stone said.

They laughed together as the car rolled forward and stopped. Israel heard the trunk open as the doorman and driver pulled Olivia's wheelchair from the rear storage. A minute later, the street-side door opened and the driver helped Olivia into her chair with practiced efficiency. Stone, Allison, and then Israel climbed out and joined her on the sidewalk.

The Empire State Building rose up before them like the modern monolith that it was. Standing one hundred and two stories of art-deco artistry, it was still considered one of the seven marvels of the modern world. For a short time after the 9/11 attacks in 2001, it had regained its title as the tallest structure in New York City, but had been dethroned once more when One World Trade Center surpassed its height.

"Why here?" Israel asked Olivia. "Why not the World Trade Center?"

Olivia smiled. "Everyone watches the WTC because it's the go-to place these days. Remember, the Veil is about secrecy, so we tend to go to the places people don't notice as much and where it's easier to blend in. Trust me, though: This old building can still impress."

"Oh, fuck me," Stone grumbled suddenly. "Look who it is."

Israel looked up from where he had bent to speak with Olivia. When he saw the two men approaching him, his jaw involuntarily tightened. He knew if he had still possessed a pulse, it would have quickened.

Special Agent Hiro Namura of the Department of Genetic Research and Investigation walked toward the group with all the swagger he could fit into his slender five-foot, eight-inch frame. His taut face was lined with the stress of a lifetime of federal law enforcement work and his black, neatly trimmed hair was salted with gray. Despite his appearance, his words twanged with a South Texas accent.

"Well, well. If it ain't the stars of the show," Namura said. He walked up to Israel and stood far closer than was polite. Despite the height difference between them, Namura managed to look up at Israel in a way that made him feel like he was being looked down upon. "You keeping this thing fed, Warburton?" he said without looking away.

Before Olivia could reply, Israel said, "The 'thing' is standing right here. Why don't you ask him?"

"Oh, there's all sorts of things I'd like to ask you, monster-man. Preferably while you're strapped to a table with a pair of electrodes drilled into your head."

"Well, you could always have me declared a terrorist again. Oh, wait: You can't, can you? I forgot you got a Congressional spanking the last time you pulled that shit."

"Keep talking, 'phage. I'll get the last laugh. I always do."

Israel was about to reply when Olivia interrupted.

"What are you doing here, Agent Namura? I've never seen you at a Conclave before."

Namura turned his gaze on her. "Security for the new Human representative. The Senator thought it might be a good idea to have someone who knew the kinds of *things* that were going to be attending tonight. Agent Brindley and I are running point."

The man with Agent Namura had stood back from the group a few steps and was watching them with tight, alert eyes. John Brindley stood a few inches taller and more than a few years younger than his fellow agent. His sandy hair was slightly longer than Namura's and rustled in the breeze between the skyscrapers. His thin lips and pale face always seemed to be on the verge of smirking.

"Well," Allison said, doing her best to burn holes through him with her gaze, "you're really scraping the bottom of the ass-hat barrel if you had to bring him along."

"Fuck off, Allison," Brindley said.

Israel tensed but didn't move. John had once been one of them, a member of the Sentry Group and part of Olivia's inner circle. He'd been released from those roles when he'd revealed himself as a DGRI spy. His exit interview had involved getting tased. The memory always made Israel smile a little.

"Watch your mouth, boy," Stone said to Brindley.

"All of you, calm down this instant," Olivia snapped. "We are all subject to Conclave Law. I'm sure none of us wants the problems that would come with violating that."

"She's right, Brindley. Stand down," Namura said. "We'll have all the time in the world later." He gave Israel one more look up and down, shook his head, and then walked away. Brindley turned and joined him, taking a moment to show Israel's group his middle finger over his back.

Israel watched them go, his jaw tight. When he felt Allison's arm slip through his, he relaxed a little.

"Is it just me," she said, "or does Namura look and talk like a poorly conceived cartoon character?"

"It isn't just you," Olivia said.

Israel looked down at Allison and gave her a soft smile. "'Ass-hat barrel'?"

"Hush. I was in the moment."

"It's not too late to leg it," Stone said. "I know a great Irish Pub down on Water Street."

"No, Stone," Olivia said. "You in a pub is the last thing we need. This is our chosen road. We walk it."

With nothing else to say, they moved together toward the door.

CHAPTER TWO

After passing through a series of security scans and checkpoints where they were searched for weapons and contraband – Israel had no idea how Stone thought he would have been able to sneak his weapons in – they were ushered to a waiting private elevator with gold and black art deco-style doors that took them directly to the eighty-fifth floor. They stepped out of the elevator into a spacious balcony area that circled the room and overlooked the ballroom below with curved stairs leading down to his left and right. A total of seven banners were hanging from the balcony in heavy, vertical curtains of black and silver. Five of them were embroidered with five different symbols that Israel didn't recognize, while the sixth had the flags of the United States, Mexico, and Canada stitched onto it. The seventh banner was decorated with a combination of all of these within a circle. Israel walked to the brass and oak railing that circled the balcony area. When he looked out over the Conclave ballroom, his felt his eyes widen at the sight.

Hundreds of people in gowns and tuxedos milled about on the floor below. They walked between tables, laughing and calling out to old acquaintances and friends, introducing themselves to new ones, and generally doing what people do at fancy parties while wait staff with trays of drinks and finger foods wove among them. That, however, was where the similarity to any other event that Israel had ever been to ended.

In the far corner, there was a man who had taken off his tuxedo coat and was juggling handfuls of fire to the delight of a number of young women, one of whom had a mane of fine, violet feathers covering her scalp instead of hair. At one of the tables, two men were arm wrestling and laughing like old friends, but as they each strained against the other's strength, their faces began to change and take on the aspects of some kind of animal. Israel thought maybe it was a bear. At the small bar, a woman in a black tuxedo was balancing a dozen champagne flutes, each half full of sparkling gold liquid, one atop the other, on the tips of two fingers. At the urging of the crowd, she took a thirteenth glass from another woman who was standing nearby and tossed it straight up into the air and caught it atop the stack without spilling a drop from any glass. The gathered crowd applauded with delight.

All around the room, Israel saw things that just a short year ago he would have laughed off as ridiculous and impossible: men with reptilian tales; women with blood-red hair and short, black horns; another with eyes that sparkled with golden light. Now, though, he knew he was looking at people who spent their lives behind the Veil finally coming to a place where they didn't need to hide. This was, he realized, a place of solace for the attendees where they could put away their masks and costumes and, if only for the evening, be themselves without reservation or fear.

"Quite a sight, isn't it?" Allison said as she and the others joined him at the railing.

"Yes. Yes, it is. What's with the banners, though? What

are those symbols on them?"

Stone pointed in succession and said, "Fae, Lycan, Seraphim, Infernal, Mage, Human. Each bloodline has its own mark. I'm sure you can figure out the one with the flags. That last one with all the others on it is the Conclave banner. It represents the whole of the Awakened within the protective circle of the Veil."

"Wait a minute. You guys keep a whole floor of the Empire State Building complete with signatory banners set aside for parties? That doesn't seem all that covert."

"It isn't always like this," Olivia said. "If the Council was that foolish, there's no way they could have stayed this well-hidden for this long. Officially, this floor is in perpetual development for one business interest or another. It sits completely vacant the vast majority of the time since Conclaves are held very rarely these days. Anything that might hint at a bloodline or the Council is kept off-site and hidden. They only get pulled out and dusted off for events like this."

"Okay," Israel nodded, "I get it."

He studied the banner that Stone had indicated belonged to the Seraphim. The symbol on it was a diamond with two identical shapes coming off its center in swooping, angular curves. After a moment of studying it, he realized that it looked like a winged diamond. As he studied each of the symbols, he noticed they all drew off the central diamond shape, but had surrounding shapes that somehow evoked something of the bloodline they represented – forward-pointing horns for the Infernal, canine ears and teeth for the Lycan. He was puzzling over the Mage and Fae symbols when Stone said, "C'mon, mate. Let's try and stay a moving target, yeah?"

Israel looked up at his friend and followed his gaze to the floor below. The musicians still played and the waiters were still weaving among the crowd, but easily half the faces he could see were looking upward. Looking, he realized, at him. None of them looked particularly friendly or hostile, just cautious.

"Good idea," he said. "Because I think this is going to suck."

"Oh, it'll be fine," Allison said without much conviction. "Most of them know your name but not your face. They're just curious. The Leticia incident was big news behind the Veil."

Israel's jaw tightened at the mention of Leticia. The name referred to a tiny, now nonexistent Texas town that had been ground zero for a doomsday cult's attempt to bring their monstrous 'gods' into the world. He, Stone, and a woman named Erin Simms had been able to stop them, but at a high cost. Erin had been killed in the explosion that finally sealed the dimensional breach the cultists had opened.

He stepped away from the railing and joined his friends as they moved through the crowd and toward the stairs, Olivia's automatic wheelchair clearing a path for them. "Super," he said, suddenly very aware of the many sidelong glances he was getting, "I'm famous."

"I'd say more infamous," Olivia said. "Your heroics at Leticia aside, you're still a Paragon Necrophage and the last one of those who Awakened gave the Council from that era a real run for its money."

"Dracul," Israel said with more bitterness than he'd intended.

"Yes. Vlad the Impaler cast a long, long shadow," Olivia said, "and the Council's memory is no shorter. You acted as hero against the Progeny of the Inner Dark, but these people fear your very nature. To them, you're a contradiction of action and instinct. They don't know what to do with you."

"Leaving me alone works for me," Israel said.

"Ah, hell, Israel," a new voice said. "Where would the fun be in that?"

Israel looked at the newcomer and smiled. Carter Black – charter pilot, world-class scofflaw, and Mage – came strolling toward them in a crisp black tux. He carried a half-full glass of Scotch in one hand and had the other stuck into one pants pocket in a display of casual boredom that matched perfectly with his three-day beard and carefully tousled blond hair. He smiled as he removed his hand from his pocket and offered it to Israel. The two men shook hands with familiar ease.

Israel had met Carter during the Leticia incident, and in the ensuing year they had become friends. Carter would often fly the two of them and occasionally Stone down to Mexico for camping and fishing trips that doubled as survival training for Israel. Despite being born and raised in Chicago, Israel found he enjoyed the desert getaways.

"What the hell are you doing here, man?" Israel asked.

Carter returned his free hand to his pocket and shrugged. "Heard about your little coming out party and thought I'd come by and maybe stand behind you in case anybody gets any bad ideas."

"Yeah? They gave you an invitation for that?"

Carter shrugged and looked away for an uncomfortable moment. "Yeah, well," he said. "I know a guy."

"Know a guy?" Stone said in a mocking tone. "When do you not know a guy?"

"And a lovely good evening to you, Short-Round. Let's keep this on topic, shall we? As strict as the Council's Peace Accords are, I don't think any of us want some crack-pot who's binge-watched too much *Walking Dead* trying to take off Israel's head. Am I right?"

No one spoke and Carter nodded. "All right, then. Now, I may not be in your employ anymore, Mrs. Warburton," Carter said, "but you know my history and my training. For this auspicious event, I would like to offer you my services as a private security consultant and bodyguard for Mr. Trent. Since it's you, and because you are looking particularly lovely this evening, I will forgo my usual fee and do this free of charge in the hopes that one day I might recoup the same kindness."

"Oh, for—"

"Hush, Stone," Olivia said. Then, to Carter, "Favor for a favor, Carter? Is that it?"

Carter shrugged. "With full refusal rights should I ask too much. Truth is, I've grown kind of fond of our favorite Paragon here, and I'd hate to see him get hurt. Deal?" He extended his hand again.

Olivia smiled and said, "I suppose it never hurts to have a wild card in play. It's a deal. Welcome back to the Sentry Group, Carter. If only for the night."

Israel had rarely seen Olivia genuinely smile, but the expression she showed Carter was one of sincere fondness. Carter returned the same.

A series of chimes sounded through the massive room and everyone started moving toward the stairs in slow, casual groups. "Ten-minute warning," Olivia said. "We should find our table."

After negotiating the crowd and getting Olivia safely down the handicap ramp next to one of the stairways, Israel and the rest of the team found a table with a black placard and the words Sentry Group printed on it in raised silver letters. Like all the other tables, there were eight place settings with dishes and flatware that looked expensive enough to make a common burglar drool. At their table, though, the place setting facing the stage had no chair, and Olivia rolled her wheelchair into the empty space as though she had expected it to be vacant.

The others settled into their seats, Stone next to Olivia and Israel between Allison and Carter. The music stopped and the next few minutes passed with the sounds of hundreds of people conversing and rustling their way to their assigned places. On the stage, the musicians had cleared away their instruments and large, ornate, wooden chairs were being moved into place. There were seven in total, and Israel noticed each bore one of the same symbols as the banners that were hanging above them.

He glanced around the room and saw numerous near-by faces look quickly away. A few lingered and nodded in greeting before turning, but he didn't know any of them. One young woman with skin the color of a bad sunburn, orange cat's eyes, and hair as black as coal even went so far as to smile at him before returning her attention to her companions.

"She's an Infernal," Allison said, leaning toward him to speak over the din. "Actually, one of the more common manifestations of that bloodline's effect."

"I'd guessed that," Israel said. "I can see why her ancestors would have been mistaken for some kind of demon or something."

"Ignorance and fear gives birth to myth," Olivia said. "Myth evolves into history. It's the human way."

Israel was about to respond to that when the lights dimmed and seven electronic chimes sounded through the hall. By the time the seventh had echoed its last note, the room was silent.

A man walked onto the well-lit stage. He was dressed in a tuxedo so crisp and immaculate that it seemed to make every other suit in the room look rumpled. He appeared to be in his late fifties with dark hair that was streaked through with gray, but trimmed and managed with the kind of precision usually reserved for models and actors. He was familiar to Israel, but as he studied the perfectly shaved face and angular features, Israel couldn't place why. Heavy-framed, black glasses like Buddy Holly might have worn sat on his face as though they were welded there.

The man walked to the center of the stage and said, "I

am Xavier Black. I am Mage. I maintain the Veil." Then he walked to the chair with the cross-hatched diamond-within-diamond pattern that represented the Mage bloodline and sat down.

The moment Israel heard the man's name, he looked over at Carter and saw the same angular features mirrored on his friend's face. He leaned close and whispered, "You know a guy?"

Carter gave him half of a smile. "Daddy dearest," he said. "We're not what you'd call close. I'll tell you later."

The next person to take the stage was a woman more striking than any Israel had ever seen before. She stood an easy six feet tall and had hair so thick, rich, and blond that it seemed almost metallic. Those golden locks fell in a cascade around her lean and defined face and drew the eye over a body that Israel could not help but notice despite being technically dead.

"I am Marlina Kale. I am Seraphim. I maintain the Veil." She took the seat with the winged diamond symbol that Israel had seen earlier.

Four others came out and announced themselves in the same fashion: Emery Arberson, the Lycan representative, was a large man with tan skin and long, wavy hair and a beard tinged with gray. Israel recognized him as one of the men he had seen arm wrestling earlier. Harrison Jacks, who took the Infernal seat, was a small man with a big voice who sounded every bit the New York Italian that he was. Astrid Delacroix stood for the Fae bloodline. She was a dark-skinned woman with a voluptuous figure and full features that seemed to make her light Cajun accent all the more appealing. When the Human representative took the stage, Israel had to force himself not to gape at the instantly recognizable man.

Senator Phillip Michael Braxton was a second term Republican from the state of Missouri and more of a media darling than most politicians. Despite having some strongly conservative stands in an increasingly progressive political environment, Mr. Braxton had popularity numbers far above those of his contemporaries in Washington. His rugged good looks, disarming smile, and off the charts charisma coupled with a notable college football career made him very attractive to women and men alike. He was exactly the sort of politician that Israel's journalistic self did not trust for a hot second.

After the Senator had given his introduction and taken his seat, the final member of the Council took the stage. He was a tall man, well over six feet, and had a full head of thick, snow-white hair over features that looked like they belonged on a kind-hearted college professor. When he looked out over the crowd, his eyes seemed to take on a faint, silver radiance and a slight smile spread across his lips.

"I am Thomas Blackstone," he said, his voice carrying a slight but crisp British accent. "I am Mage. I am Arcane. I embody the Veil."

Applause rose up in the room and the Arcane let it go on for a moment before patting the air in front of him and calling for silence. Once it died away, he said, "Thank you. I want to welcome you all to this most auspicious of Conclaves. In the past we have always welcomed all of the Awakened within these halls: Revealed, Powers, and Enlightened Humans – it did not matter for none were turned away. Tonight, though, for the first time in centuries, it is the honor of this Conclave to welcome into its number a Paragon. Awakened of the Veil, I present Israel Trent!"

Israel had been surprised when the Arcane had announced his name so publicly, but he was doubly so when a spotlight – a damned spotlight! – lit up his seat. Ever since he had been Awakened, Israel had developed a problem with bright lights. His night vision was inhumanly good, but bright sunlight or direct lighting washed the world away in a flood of white that he couldn't penetrate. It didn't cause him any pain – very few things did anymore – but being blinded in a room full of potential enemies didn't do anything to reinforce his calm.

He felt Carter tense up next to him, alert and ready. Israel raised a hand to shield his eyes and said in low tones, "Olivia, what the hell?"

"I don't know," she said, her voice tense and on the edge of anger. "They didn't tell me about this."

There was a smattering of cautious applause that quickly died away. The spotlight faded and Israel's sight returned instantly. When he looked up at the Arcane, he saw the man looking down from the spotlight operator's position with a confused look on his face. His expression smoothed out quickly though, and he continued speaking.

"A Paragon in the modern era. Never since becoming Arcane did I imagine such a possibility. Thanks to Olivia Warburton and our Enlightened allies at the Sentry Group, Mr. Trent was able to realize his potential and just last year stopped a potentially devastating plot by–"

Xavier Black suddenly stood and shouted, "We have all heard about the Leticia incident, Arcane! What you seem to be glossing over is the matter of this man's bloodline. He may be a Paragon, but he is also a Necrophage, a threat to anyone who is exposed to his DNA, a man capable of raising an army of the dead as did Vlad Dracul before him!"

"Delegate Black, we are not here to hold this man accountable for the actions of another who is six centuries dead."

"Actually, Arcane," Astrid Delacroix, the Fae Delegate said, "I agree with Delegate Black. I recognize and appreciate the actions taken in Texas last year, but a Necrophage is a threat to all by its very nature."

"Thank you, Delegate Delacroix. As a Delegate of this august Council and a voice for the Mage bloodline, I call for the immediate arrest and incarceration of Israel Trent until such time as the extent of the threat he poses can be assessed!"

Israel stared at the stage, trying to read the faces of the Delegates. Stone spat out a curse behind him. Allison gasped in surprise.

Carter slapped Israel on the shoulder and said, "And here we go, brother. Buckle up."

CHAPTER THREE

The Delegates were shouting at one another. The bulk of the exchange seemed to be going on between the Arcane, Delegate Black, Delegate Delacroix, and Delegate Jacks. It was obvious the Arcane was standing against the call for Israel's arrest while the Fae and Mage Council members argued for it. The Infernal Delegate seemed to be trying to calm the proceedings down. Israel took his eyes off them and studied the other three faces on the stage.

Senator Braxton was taking in the argument with a calm expression, his lips ever so lightly curved into a smile that was amused, but calculating. Delegate Kale of the Seraphim watched the argument with an expression of half-contained boredom. When Israel's eyes swept over the Lycan representative, Emery Arberson, he found the man staring directly at him. Despite the stage lights and the darkness in the room beyond, Israel was sure that Arberson was watching him. Behind his heavy beard and thick eyebrows, the man's expression asked a simple question of Israel: "Now what are you going to do, kid?"

"Screw this noise," Israel said, standing up.

"Israel," Olivia said, "what are you doing?"

"I'm not going to stand here and watch a bunch of strangers argue over whether or not I'm a monster who needs to be caged, Olivia. If they have something to say *about* me, then they can say it *to* me."

"This might not be the best idea, Israel," Allison said.

Israel smiled at her. "It'll be all right," he said.

Carter stood up. "Hell, yeah, it will. This will be one of the first times one of these things didn't bore me to tears."

Stone gave Israel a deep sigh and rose from his chair.

Israel looked at Olivia. She was studying him as though he were leaving for an extended trip. Finally, she said, "Remember: no violence. Defend yourself if it comes to it, but do not start anything. You, too, Stone."

The three men turned and started making their way to the stage. A flutter of whispers arose from the tables around them as they moved. Stone and Carter both stayed behind and slightly to one side of Israel in order to better watch his back without seeming too aggressive. Israel approached the center of the stage and, instead of going to either end to walk up the short stairs to the raised platform, took two big steps and jumped. He rose ten feet into the air and cleared the horizontal distance to the stage with ease. When he landed, it was with a loud thud that cut short the Delegates' argument and drew every eye in the room to him. There were a few short, shocked gasps from the crowd, but everyone kept their seats. The Arcane turned and saw him, taking a surprised step back, but raised a hand to forestall the Council security that was already moving onto the stage.

Israel had landed with his knees bent and he straightened slowly to meet the shocked stares of the Council Delegates. Deciding to indulge himself a little, he took a second to smooth out his coat and cuffs. As he straightened his bow tie, he looked at Xavier Black and said, "The name's Trent. Israel Trent."

From somewhere off stage, Israel heard Carter laugh

out loud.

"Mr. Trent," the Arcane said, "welcome. You certainly know how to make an entrance."

"Oh, yes," Delegate Black said, stepping forward. "Very dramatic. Inquisitors, arrest this man."

"Ignore that," the Arcane snapped. Then he looked at Black and said in a quiet, angry whisper, "You're overstepping your authority and you know it, Xavier."

The Mage Delegate glared at the Arcane and then pointed at Israel. "What is he doing up here?"

"He," Israel said, "is standing right here and is more than capable of answering your questions, Mr. Black."

"That's Delegate Black to you."

Israel gave his head a slight nod and said, "Of course, Delegate. My apologies. I'm still getting a handle on the etiquette of life behind the Veil."

The Arcane stepped forward and offered his hand to Israel. "It's a pleasure to finally meet you, young man. Olivia has told me so much about you."

Israel shook the man's hand with his gloved one, careful as always not to squeeze too hard. "The pleasure's mine. She's done the same for you, Arcane."

The Infernal Delegate stepped forward and also offered his hand. "Name's Harry Jacks. Pleased to meet'cha. I read about that Texas thing. When I found out you were from Chi-town I was a little shocked. I figured only a New Yorker could throw a beating that epic on those Progeny stronzi."

Israel took the man's hand and said, "Thanks, I think." He raised his eyes and found Delegate Black glaring at him with firmly crossed arms. He ignored the man and let his eyes sweep across the other four delegates. Astrid Delacroix had returned to her seat and was watching him with wary eyes. Marlina Kale had lost her bored expression and was studying Israel like he was something she might like to order from a menu. Emery Arberson didn't look like he had moved, but had a grin on his face that radiated approval.

When Israel looked back, he saw that Senator Braxton had risen and was standing next to the Arcane, his hand extended in greeting. Israel took it and shook.

"Phil Braxton, Mr. Trent," the politician said. "It's a pleasure."

"Same here, Senator. I saw you speak once at a law enforcement convention in Chicago a couple of years back."

"Well, I hope I didn't stutter too much," the Senator said. His best campaign smile slid onto his face like it had a mind of its own.

"No, sir. As I recall, you were very well-received."

"If all of you are finished glad-handing the Necro-phage in our midst," Black said, "perhaps we can address the business of the threat he poses."

Israel was ready for this and spoke up before any of the other Delegates could respond. "Yes, Delegate Black, I think we should do that. Arcane, I didn't plan on being on stage tonight, but since I am I'd like to say a few things. With the Council's permission, of course."

The Arcane looked at Israel with curiosity twinkling in his eye and an amused smile on his lips. "I have no problem with that," he said.

"I do," Delegate Black said.

"Let the man talk, Xavier," Emery Arberson said, his voice carrying just a hint of a whiskey growl. "You get a lot more chances than he does."

"Yeah," Delegate Jacks said. "Say your piece, kiddo."

Senator Braxton looked at Israel. The smile was still in place, but there was a look in the man's eyes that was questioning. It was as though he were sizing up an opponent. "Absolutely, he should speak. This might be Conclave and Israel here might have some unique circumstances, but he was born an American and this is

American soil. Free speech is his right."

The Arcane said, "That's four of seven. The floor is yours, Mr. Trent."

Israel nodded his thanks and, instead of addressing the Council, turned toward the seated crowd. He heard an angry exhalation of air from Delegate Black and tried not to smile.

"The Mage Delegate is right," he said. "I am a threat." He paused for a moment and let that sink in and for the wave of murmurs to run through the crowd. "You see," he went on, "roughly a year ago I was kidnapped and imprisoned by the Progeny of the Inner Dark. Through sheer luck, one other person and myself managed to escape. What we saw down there Awakened us, and I became what I am now.

"I am a Paragon Necrophage. That means that while I can do things I never dreamed of outside of childhood fantasies, my blood and other tissues can infect humans and create the monsters that all of you fear, things that I thought only existed in Stephen King novels and George Romero movies until this happened to me. The fact that my existence makes the possibility of those fictions becoming reality is what makes me a threat.

"So, I wear gloves all the time. I keep my skin covered all the time. I avoid the general public as much as I possibly can. If I have to get on a crowded subway or elevator, I wear a surgical mask and glasses. I do everything I can to keep my problem from becoming someone else's because I have seen what I can become, what I can create, and it terrifies me. If I told you I hadn't considered finding a way to end it all in the last year, I would be lying.

"There are people, though, who wouldn't let me do that. Olivia Warburton and the Sentry Group have helped me – and are still helping me – come to grips with this existence. They have shown me that I can exist around my bloodline nature and still be useful. They have shown me that I am not a slave to my situation. Mostly, they have shown me that I am not the monster so many people assume me to be.

"I will not dishonor their faith in me. I will not dishonor the memory of my friend, Erin Simms, who walked out of that Progeny dungeon with me and died fighting them in Texas. Everyone wants to compare me to Vlad Dracul and the things he did. I've read the histories. I get why people would be so inclined. Tonight, though, before this Conclave and each one of you, I make this promise: I will use what I have become to protect people, to stand against anyone who would do harm to any Awakened, and to live up to the title 'Paragon.' If ever the day comes that I take steps down the road that Dracul chose to be more monster than man, I will make sure I am surrounded by people willing to put me down as I would deserve. That is my promise to the Awakened and humanity at large. That is the road I choose to walk."

There was silence in the hall for a long moment. Then, Israel saw Allison stand up and begin clapping, a wide smile on her face. Within moments, the action spread and there were hundreds of people on their feet. An enthusiastic whistle – Carter, Israel was sure – split the air.

Israel turned back to the Council and the collection of reactions aimed at him. The Arcane was the only Council member who had remained standing. He was a few feet behind Israel and looking at him with an expression of pleased approval. The others were watching him as well. They each sat in their respective seats – Israel had a hard time not thinking of the high-backed chairs as thrones – and looked at him with expressions that ranged from barely concealed hatred to excited amusement; Xavier Black generated the hate while Emery Arberson provided the amusement. Israel made a mental note to find out more about both of them.

Movement caught Israel's eye as the applause started

to fade. Agent Namura had come up on Senator Braxton's left and was whispering in his ear and showing him something on the screen of a smartphone. The Senator nodded, took the phone, and waved Namura off. The agent shot Israel a look that could have frozen running water before he stepped off stage and out of view. Braxton looked over whatever was on the phone a moment longer and then rose to join the Arcane.

They whispered for a few moments before the Arcane nodded and Senator Braxton stepped over to confer with the rest of the Delegates. The Arcane joined Israel closer to the edge of the stage.

"Arcane?" Israel said, keeping his voice low. "What's happening?"

"Just a moment, Israel," the Arcane said, equally hushed. He turned to the crowd and, raising his voice, said, "Citizens of the Veil, I can safely say that this has been the most eventful Conclave in decades."

There was a moment of soft laughter before he continued. "I think, though, that it is best if the Council adjourns to a quieter space to continue our deliberations. I see no sense in subjecting you to our disagreements. Rest assured, though, we are ever watchful and concerned with the maintenance of the Veil and the protection it provides you. Please, enjoy the rest of your evening."

The applause was lighter, more hesitant, but no one objected. The Arcane turned to Israel and said, "I'm going to send some of my men to collect Olivia. I need you to come with me."

"What's going on?"

"There is a situation nearby that needs tending to. The kind that could potentially lead to our exposure, not to mention a half a dozen or more deaths. Please, Israel, follow me."

He did.

The 86th floor of the Empire State Building was best known for being one of the two observation decks available to the public. It was a popular tourist destination, but as Israel looked out over the sparkling gold and silver lights of New York's nighttime skyline and the wide shadow of the Hudson River to the west, he wondered how many people got to see it like this. They were so far up that even his heightened senses couldn't hear the street noise below, but the sound of the cool night breeze moving around the building was like a whisper to him. He could smell the city below in faint, passing whiffs; the scent of the people he shared the balcony with was stronger.

The Arcane had taken him up one floor to the observation platform where they had been met by a woman wearing a plain, form-fitting black suit. She had immediately taken up a position next to the Arcane that was close enough to defend him, but far enough away so as not to crowd him. Now, her dark eyes watched Israel as though she were waiting for him to do something stupid. Instead, he decided to take in the view.

The other Delegates joined them in short order and each was immediately covered by one of the black-suited watchers. Israel knew these were Inquisitors: security and secret police force for the Council of the Veil and its Delegates. Israel looked them over in subtle glances. He had interviewed a couple of Secret Service agents back in Chicago once and these Inquisitors had the same no-nonsense bearing. They radiated a sense of discipline and controlled danger like the heat from a flame.

The doors to the observation deck opened and Olivia and Stone joined the group. No Inquisitor moved to protect them and Olivia didn't seem to notice. "Arcane, Delegates," she said. "What's happened?"

"I object to the presence of the Sentry Group in this matter," Delegate Black said, turning to the Arcane.

"Oh, stuff a sausage in it, Xavier," Arberson said. "The

audience is back inside; you can quit the grandstanding. Sentry's here because he–" Arberson pointed at Israel "is Sentry and he'll be an asset if things get rough."

"The Inquisitors can handle this situation, Arcane," Black said.

"Now, hang on a second, Mr. Black," Senator Braxton said. "That was a police officer who died. The DGRI have to have a presence in this since none of your people have any official standing."

"Fair enough," Black said, "but my objection to Sentry's presence stands."

"Excuse me, gentlemen? Down here?" Olivia said, waving from her wheelchair. "Would someone please explain to me what's happened so I can decide whether or not my group's presence is even an issue?"

Israel suppressed a smile. There were times he really enjoyed watching Olivia work.

"Olivia, apologies," the Arcane said. "There's something happening across the river in New Jersey. Over the last twelve hours, six young women have gone missing. About thirty minutes ago, two police officers encountered something the survivor described as 'monstrous.' Her partner was mutilated in the conflict."

Olivia cursed. "You think it was another micro-breach?"

"Possibly," Senator Braxton said. "It could also be an Awakened who went crazy when he changed or just doesn't understand what's happened to him. Details are sketchy, but if it is either of those, we need boots on the ground as of ten minutes ago."

"I understand," Olivia said, "but – and I can't believe I'm saying this – I see Delegate Black's point. Why do you need us? It seems pretty cut-and-dried."

"Solidarity," the Arcane said. "The Conclave turned into a bit of a sideshow–"

"More like the Xavier Black Show," Arberson said with

a scoff.

"Emery, you–" Black started.

"Silence!" the Arcane snapped, his gaze growing hard. "This is no time for your childishness. Neither was open Conclave, Xavier, and you damned well know it. I don't know who you paid off to pull that childish stunt with the spotlight, but I promise it won't be forgotten. There is a threat to the Veil and possibly six innocent lives before us, so focus on that and not your own self-serving nonsense."

Israel's eyebrows went up just a little. He could see why Olivia spoke so highly of this man.

"I suggest a joint operation," Senator Braxton said. "Two DGRI, two Sentry, and three Inquisitors. Word will spread behind the Veil that this action took place and it might go a long way toward repairing whatever lost confidence we caused tonight in the eyes of the citizenry. Plus, it will give Mr. Trent a chance to prove that his speech tonight wasn't just all talk."

Olivia and Stone looked at Israel. He shrugged and said, "I'm in. Let's go."

CHAPTER FOUR

Five minutes later, Israel and Stone were in the back of a dark gray panel van that was rolling into the Lincoln Tunnel on its way to Fairview, New Jersey. Though from the outside it looked like thousands of other delivery trucks you might see in the city on any given day, the back of this van was a rolling tactical response unit. Weapons and combat gear of every sort were neatly stowed in various compartments and on an assortment of hooks on the walls. Israel and Stone chose weapons and shrugged into vests and holsters as the truck bounced through the tunnel.

There had been a chorus of groans and light curses when Israel and Stone had seen Namura and Brindley show up as the DGRI portion of the response team. The two DGRI agents had made it very clear that they weren't happy with the arrangement either, but in the end had shrugged and gotten on with it. The Inquisitor portion of the team consisted of three men who watched the four newcomers struggling to don their gear while being jostled with critical eyes.

Israel tightened the last strap on his armored vest,

slipped a Glock 21 into a thigh holster, and then chose a Benelli M4 tactical shotgun from a weapons storage chest that doubled as a passenger bench. Once he had loaded eight shells into the weapon and another eight into the side saddle, he started tucking extra shells into his tactical vest. Satisfied, he settled the gun across his lap and sat down on the weapons bench to wait.

A few seconds later, Namura moved to the rear of the van and sat down across from Israel. He didn't speak at first, so Israel just stared at him and waited him out.

"That was slicker than a greased copperhead, what you did back there," he finally said.

"What are you talking about?" Israel said.

"That little soapbox moment you had back at the Conclave, turning your back on the Council and all. Slicker'n snot."

"Glad you enjoyed it," Israel said.

"Gotta say, you're a lot more eloquent than I would've given you credit for."

"Yeah, well, I'm a journalist. Words have always been kind of easy for me. Besides that, my Pop was in sales for most of his career so I guess it runs in the family."

Namura nodded. "That makes sense. That all they were, though? Just words?"

Israel leaned forward. "I meant every syllable. Say what's on your mind, Namura."

Namura leaned forward, getting inches from Israel's face. "Now see, that's the thing: I believe you. I believe you meant every word you said and your intentions are as pure as the driven snow. Thing is, you can't fight nature, even one as ass-backwards as yours. The day will come when the real you gets the upper hand and you just give in to your urges. On that day, when you slip up, Trent, I'm gonna do my damnedest to make sure I'm the one who puts you down like the abomination you are. Boom – just one to the head to scramble up all that nerve tissue you monsters need so bad and it's bye-bye, Necrophage."

They stayed that way for a few moments longer, eyes locked, neither blinking, inches from one another. Eventually Israel said, "You mind leaning a little closer, Namura? You smell really good."

The DGRI agent's eyes widened for the briefest of seconds, then relaxed. He gave the remark a soft laugh and then leaned back against the van's wall. Israel did the same.

They stayed that way for the rest of the trip to Fairview. Twenty minutes later, Brindley said, "We're about three minutes out, sir."

"All right, listen up" Namura said, his cop voice filling the space. "Because of the involvement with local law enforcement, I've been given command of this little field trip."

"Oh, balls," Stone said. "Say it isn't so."

"Put a lid on it, Stone," Namura barked. "Inquisitors, divide up as you see fit. I want two of you with Brindley and your third with me and Stone. Once we assess the details on site, I'll provide more orders. We're posing as FBI, so make sure your IDs are visible."

Stone spoke before Israel could. "What about Israel?"

"Mr. Trent will stay here as our communications link back to the Council and Sentry, as well as the liaison with the local PD. I hear he was once a journalist and words come easy to him, so he should be well-suited to the job."

"Namura, you ass–" Stone said

"Watch it!" Namura snapped. "The Council put me in charge and those are my orders. You have a problem, take it up with them."

Stone grumbled under his breath as he met Israel's eyes and shrugged as though he had something to apologize for. Israel shook his head at the man as if to say 'Not your fault.'

Brindley settled himself onto the seat next to Israel.

He slid a laptop with a reinforced case onto Israel's lap and said, "Here, this will link up with our comms via satellite. There's a map overlay and you'll be able to track us by icon. Think of it as Google Earth in real time."

"Fancy," Israel said.

"Just keep us informed if anything comes up we need to know about, but otherwise stay in the van and don't break comm silence. Namura's running this show, so he talks and we respond. Don't fuck it up."

"Wouldn't dream of it," Israel said.

The truck rumbled to a stop and Namura said, "Move out. Trent, stay put and keep your eyes on the monitor. If I need you to engage with the locals, I'll let you know. Otherwise, keep your spooky ass in the vehicle."

"Spooky? Seriously?" Israel said. "The Japanese Texan with the shit-kicker accent is going racial on me?"

"Just stay in the goddamned van, Trent," Namura said.

As they filed past him, Stone dropped a hand on Israel's shoulder and said, "Hang in there, mate. Guys like him always end up eating their words."

Israel nodded as the roll-up door opened and a flood of sensations filled the van. Emergency lights of every color flashed and strobed across his field of vision as the sounds of dozens of people moving, shouting, and talking on phones or radios washed over him. More than the sights and sounds, though, were the aromas. In the year since his transformation, Israel's senses had heightened to something comparable to a wolf's, but stronger. The enhanced sight and hearing were an adjustment, but he had discovered that the world contained far more scents than he had ever thought possible. At first it had been maddening, but now, after a year of learning to sort out and ignore the different smells, he'd reached a point where he could be among people without being distracted. It was like holding a conversation in a noisy crowd, but with his nose.

He flipped open the laptop. Namura and the rest of the team appeared as bright green dots with tiny call signs floating above them. He watched the actual people move away from the van and the dots move across the screen without so much as a flicker. He tapped a few keys until he had figured out the controls and zoomed in as far as he could. He enlarged the picture until he could make out the individual people moving around the van as though he were less than a hundred feet above them. His team was clustered around what looked to be a command station of some kind where he was certain Namura was making friends and influencing people.

He whistled softly and said, "Well, hello, Big Brother." He knew the government had satellites that could zoom in on earthbound details, but he had never seen it in action.

"Romero, this is Samurai. Come in." It was Namura's voice over the earbud Israel was wearing.

"Thank you for calling FBI Public Relations," Israel said. "How may I direct your call?"

"Stow the smartass and at least pretend you're a professional, Romero."

Israel sighed. As loathe as he was to admit it, he knew the DGRI man had a point. "Copy that, Samurai. What's your situation?"

"Unsub was last reported heading in the direction of the Fairview Cemetery. Local LEOs have been dispatched to the surrounding neighborhoods. Task force proceeding into cemetery."

"Copy, Samurai," Israel said. The link went dead and Israel watched as the green dots moved across an empty street and spread into a straight line formation that could sweep across the cemetery and leave very few stones unturned. Stone had taught him about search formations as part of his training with the Sentry group, but he had yet to put it into practice.

The van door was still open and Israel put the laptop down long enough to stand up and grab the worn canvas strap to pull the door closed and cut off some the noise. He could see the street the team had crossed and the cemetery beyond. The lights and sound grated against his senses. The scents of the urban environment and the people and all their various colognes and perfumes were a cloud in the night air. He had just tightened his grip on the strap and was ready to pull the door down when another scent, faint but lingering, cut through the miasma.

It was musky to the point of being sharp, like bad body odor cut with rotten meat. It smelled wrong. It wasn't just unpleasant, but out of place. It was, Israel realized, not human.

He stepped out of the van and inhaled the air, turning in place while trying not to look crazy while he did it. They had parked in what looked to be a small auto salvage lot that consisted of a single metal building and a half a dozen cars. He caught the scent again, acrid and offending, and found himself facing east, away from the cemetery and toward the rusting cars. Israel took a few steps in that direction and took a deep breath through his nose. It was faint, colored by rust and old tires, but the otherworldly stink was there, leading toward a stand of trees. Israel remembered from the satellite image he'd seen on the laptop that there was nothing but neighborhoods full of people beyond those trees. He turned west and walked toward the police line. The closer he got, the fainter the scent became. At first he thought it was just getting lost in all the olfactory noise, but decided it was actually weaker the closer he got to the cemetery.

Israel's jaw tightened. His orders were clear: Stay in the van and monitor the team and local cops. The team was in the wrong place, though – he was almost certain of that – and whatever this thing was, it didn't belong in his world. Facing it would likely be a death sentence for anyone it came across. He supposed it was a good thing that he was already dead.

Decision made, Israel popped out his earbud and returned to the van for his shotgun.

The scent was stronger the farther he got from the crowd of police and emergency responders. The FBI badge hung around his neck on a lanyard that bounced against his chest in time with his steps as he jogged down a crowded suburban street. His head was lifted slightly as he took long breaths through his nose. He didn't think he was following the exact path his quarry had taken. The scent was diffused, like it had drifted over to him from some-where else the same way the aroma of a distant neighbor's grill might catch your attention. It was distinct, but not precise. Besides that, he was pretty sure someone would have noticed someone – or something – running down the middle of the street carrying a teenage girl.

There were a few people out on porches or leaning against cars, but all of them seemed to be wise enough not to bother the man with the shotgun and the badge. He ignored the stares and disrespectful smirks he received and focused on his goal. The scent had changed some-what; while still acrid and offensive, there was another scent below that one now. It was the soft aroma of scented soap and delicate perfume. It was a scent that reminded Israel of first dates and awkward goodnight kisses. It was the scent of a girl stumbling into womanhood.

The scent vanished suddenly and he stopped, turning his head in quick motions trying to find it again. It only took a moment and he realized that whatever he was tracking had turned off its original route. He moved off the street toward a two-story house that was sitting silent and dark.

The darkness wasn't a problem for Israel; even in the

blackest night, he could see the world in shades of silver and gray that allowed him to move as confidently as a normal person on a sunny day. He moved up the short driveway to the front door. There was a closed single-car garage door to his right, but no sound came from within. To his left was a wrought iron gate leading between the tightly spaced houses and into the backyard. He pounded on the front door and announced himself as FBI. There was no response. He took another deep breath and caught another scent over that of his quarry. It was the scent of meat left out too long and the ripe tang of death.

His first instinct was to smash down the door, but he dismissed that notion almost immediately. He couldn't hear anything from inside, and whatever he was smelling was way beyond his help. He took a quick step off the porch and pulled open the wrought iron gate. He brought the Benelli to his shoulder just as Stone had drilled into him so many times and moved forward, his eyes tracking everything they passed through the ghost-ring sights.

The tight pathway opened into a backyard that was roughly the size three parking spaces side by side. At one time, it looked as though it had been a quaint and comfortable space despite its small size. Now, though, it was a mess. Part of the privacy fence was smashed into the yard and reduced to little more than a pile of boards and loose brick. The once comfortable outdoor furniture was overturned and mangled. The small concrete patio showed a starburst of cracks where something heavy had struck it, and the patio doors it butted up against were shattered inward. The stink of rotting meat was overwhelming beyond that portal. Israel went in anyway.

What was left of the home's occupant was all over the small living room. If Israel had to guess, he would say she had been an elderly woman who lived alone, judging from what parts of the room were still undisturbed. Whatever had killed her, though, had brutalized her with a bestial rage or glee that he thought only existed in horror movies.

His Necrophage nature kept him from getting nauseated anymore, but he could feel his repulsion mentally as well as anyone. He stepped out of the house and back into the backyard. All this destruction and anger – why hadn't anyone called the police? It would still be a day or two before the decay in the house grew strong enough to bother the neighbors, but surely someone had heard the attack. That kind of thing didn't go on quietly.

He was puzzling over that when his eyes swept over the ruined section of fence. The fence itself was comprised of wooden boards, but he could see a large number of bricks among the debris. His gaze tracked upward to the tops of the trees that grew in a neighbor's yard. There, above the treetop, was a huge, round brick structure that was easily fifty feet high. Israel realized he hadn't noticed it before because of the tree, but now rushed to the shattered fence. The base of the thing was just on the other side of the fence. It looked like a giant smokestack of some kind that came out of the ground. At the point where it met the fence, though, there was an eight-foot-tall hole that looked as though it had been battered from the inside out.

Israel thought it over and then cursed. He had hoped he could avoid this, but he needed to know what he was looking at. He slid the earbud back into place and immediately heard Namura calling for him. The anger in the man's voice was a hammer driving each word in.

"Copy, Samurai," Israel said. "Romero's back on the air."

"Dammit, Romero! Where have you been? Why'd you go off comm? I need satellite intel!"

"Yeah, about that. Not really in the van anymore."

"What? Where the hell are you?" The DGRI man sounded like he was about to start screaming.

"I'm at a house on McKinley Street just east of Henry

and Sixth. Maybe a half-mile from the cemetery. I'm looking at a huge brick smokestack or something. I need to know what it is."

"Why are you out of position, Trent? You were supposed to stay in the goddamned van!"

"Uhm, I think you mean 'Romero,' and I'm over here because you guys were going in the wrong direction."

"How the hell do you know that?"

Israel shrugged despite being alone. "The nose knows. Look, just tell me what this damn thing is."

"Romero, this is Arrowhead."

Israel recognized the call sign for one of the Inquisitors. "Copy, Arrowhead. You know something about this thing?"

"It's not a smokestack; it's a vent. The old Edgewater-Fairview rail tunnel runs under this whole area between the far west side of this cemetery and the Edgewater cliffs. The vent is a leftover from the days when the rail was still active through here. It's been out of service for decades, though. You think our kidnapper is hiding down there?"

"I do," Israel said. "I'm also sure that it's definitely a 'behind the Veil' kind of situation—" Israel stopped, listened. From the depths of the vent he heard what sounded like muffled pops and then a roar.

"Romero?" It was Stone's voice.

"Samurai, did the cops search the tunnel?"

"Negative. Their orders were to seal both ends, but not to enter."

"Yeah, well, I don't think they listen any better than I do. I'm hearing shots and less pleasant things from below. How deep does this thing go?"

"The tunnel's two hundred feet below surface streets, give or take," Arrowhead said.

Two hundred feet. Israel hadn't tried to jump that far before, but he had an idea. "I'm going down," he said.

"Negative, Romero," Namura snapped. "You hold position."

"Not going to happen," Israel said. "You guys try and catch up from the cemetery outlet. If you do, don't frickin' shoot me."

Israel reached up and removed the earbud before Namura could respond. There was nothing the government man could say to change his mind. Besides that, the gunfire from below was starting to sound wild and panicked.

Israel stuck his head into the opening and looked down. Even with his ability to see in the dark, he couldn't really make out any details at the bottom. Between the sounds from below and the otherworldly stink filling the space, though, he knew he was on the right track. He took a moment to sling the Benelli across his back and make sure it was secured and the safety was on. Ready, he focused on a spot on the far wall and jumped.

Besides all the soldiering skills Stone had been drilling into him – hand-to-hand combat, firearms, tactics, and the like – Israel had been exploring other ways to exploit his Necrophage abilities. One night after watching Casino Royale with Allison and Stone, he had gotten the idea to learn Parkour. After learning the basic moves, he had spent many late nights in downtown Atlanta practicing the vaults, jumps, rolls, and swinging techniques that were the core of the Parkour discipline. He quickly learned that when you didn't get tired, didn't feel pain, and were strong enough to jump four or five times farther than a normal person, you could take that discipline to the next level – and then the one beyond that.

Israel hit the far wall with his right leg and kicked at the same time. Bricks fractured and popped from the wall as his foot dug a shallow divot into the wall. This gave him a foothold for just a fraction of a second that allowed him to slow his downward momentum and push away from the wall. This propelled him toward the opposite wall where he repeated the process with his left leg. It took about a dozen of these fast, zig-zagging jumps before he dropped straight down into the abandoned train tunnel.

Water splashed up around his face and head as he landed and took the impact with his knees. It was still hard enough to crack bones, but he felt no pain. The damage started healing almost instantly, but Israel could feel the tingle of his hunger begin crawling through him with the exertion. He knew his body burned its energy the most when it had to repair itself, so, still kneeling in filthy water that covered his ankles, he quickly pulled one of Allison's protein bars from a pocket, tore it open with his teeth, and shoved the whole thing into his mouth. It tasted like the worst jerky in the history of jerky, but the hungry tingle faded in seconds.

He rose and unslung his Benelli as he took in his surroundings. The tunnel was about twenty feet tall at its arching peak. Mildewed bricks stinking of earthen rot covered the walls in a remarkably unbroken pattern considering their age. The water that pooled around his ankles was filthy and stagnant. Litter floated atop it and filled the tunnel with the evidence of decades of teenagers and indigents hiding from whatever authority they were trying to escape. Ancient, disintegrating railroad ties stuck out of the shallow water here and there, but there were no rails as they must have been removed and put to better use long ago.

The gunshots had stopped, but the smell of cordite and blood moved on the air from somewhere behind him. Israel brought the Benelli to his shoulder, released the safety, and started moving fast in that direction.

It didn't take long to find the bodies. There were four of them, all dressed in the bloody and tattered remains of Fairview Police Department uniforms. They were scattered around the tunnel like broken toys with limbs missing or bending in ways they were never meant to. There was no sign of any of their weapons, but the scent of gunfire was hanging in the air like the after effect of a thousand struck matches.

In the center of the tunnel, hunched over one of the bodies, was the thing that had wrought this destruction. It looked up at Israel with small, wide eyes that appeared ink black to Israel's dark-vision. It was massive – easily nine feet tall and thickly muscled under blemished, wart-strewn skin that sprouted tufts of hair in erratic places. Horns protruded from its head in what seemed a random pattern. Some thick, some thin, some long and some stubbed; they curved and twisted from the thing's head amid long, heavy strands of black hair. It sniffed the air with a broad, flat nose and growled from a mouth that was thick with too many blunt teeth and lips so deformed that they could never close properly. When it rose up and turned toward Israel, it did so on backwards-jointed legs as thick as telephone poles and held a man's severed leg in one massive hand. The uniform pant had been stripped from the thigh and it was plain to see where the thing had been feeding.

Israel tried to ignore the horrific sight and said, "Hey, what's up? Speak any English?"

The thing flung its meal aside and issued a challenging roar that filled Israel's nostrils with a fetid stink strong enough to wash away every other scent in the tunnel.

"Okay, then," Israel said. "Allow me to introduce myself."

He put the ghost-sights on the thing's massive chest and unloaded with the Benelli. Eight 12-gauge rounds of buckshot hammered into the monster's center mass in rapid succession, adding more cordite stink to the air and spent shotgun shells to the water's detritus. A thunderstorm of gunfire echoed through the dark tunnel as the thing staggered backward and fell with a loud splash that sent a tiny tsunami of stagnant water washing over Israel's ankles. He allowed himself a small smile that immediately vanished when he saw it start climbing back to its feet.

"Oh, shit," he muttered and quickly started slamming shells into his weapon. He managed to get five of them in before the monster came charging at him with black blood streaming down its chest and roaring like something straight out of Hell.

Israel darted to one side as the monster barreled past him and lashed out with one of its massive, clawed hands. Israel managed to avoid the blow by twisting out of the way, but stumbled and fell when his foot snagged on one of the old railroad ties. He rolled fast to his back when he hit the ground and leveled the Benelli at the monster. It was only just managing to stop its charge – nothing that big stopped on a dime – and was turning to run at Israel again, its vicious horns lowered and its arms tucked tight to its sides.

Israel emptied the shotgun again, the weapon's action spitting out the five shells in a matter of seconds. Between Israel's awkward firing angle and his target's movement, only two of the shots managed to connect. Both of these hit the thing in the legs, though, and it was enough to throw off its stride and send it pitching forward onto its face where it continued to tumble and slide toward Israel.

He rolled fast to one side as the thing collided with the tunnel wall. Israel scrambled to his feet as the monster started righting itself. He stepped back and reached for more shells, but misjudged the thing's reach. It hit him in the chest with a backhanded blow that sent him spinning through the air and face-first into the water and filth twenty feet down the tunnel. Israel hit the ground hard and slid through the muck much like the beast had done. He could feel his broken ribs grinding together, but there was no pain, just the pressure and the instability of the injury. More than that, he could feel the hunger beginning to crawl through him, but he didn't have time to do anything about it. Israel got to his feet and brought up the Benelli – the bent, cracked, and completely non-functioning Benelli.

Israel cursed and threw the broken weapon at the monster out of sheer frustration. His hand dropped for his Glock, but he decided against pulling it; if ten rounds of 12-gauge buckshot didn't stop the thing, the Glock was near to pointless.

The monster righted itself, horned head lowered, but eyes rolled up to meet Israel's in a challenge so primal Israel could feel it. The thing snorted hard through its flat nose and charged at him, rage driving it forward as it bellowed death for its opponent.

Israel, the hunger streaming through him like icy water, ran straight for the thing. When they were close enough, Israel leapt into the air and brought his legs up over his head in a high, gradual flip as the monster's arms closed on the empty air where his torso had been. Sailing over the thing's head, Israel reached out and caught one of the malformed horns with his left hand and used it as pivot point to twist himself onto the beast's shoulders. He locked his legs around the thing's neck and screamed, "Yippee ki-yay, motherfucker!"

The creature went berserk. Brick and dirt exploded from the walls where it collided with them as it charged down the tunnel at a breakneck, if staggering, speed. Israel picked out the straightest of the monster's horns and grabbed it with his right hand. He pulled and twisted at it, fighting against the creature's thrashing head and constant weaving as it ran. He strained and jerked, his teeth grinding together as he struggled against alien bone and sinew. Finally, with a hoarse victory cry, he felt the horn splinter and break free in his grip.

It wasn't as long as he had hoped and the broken end

was shredded and blunt, but it would do. Afraid of losing his grip, Israel leaned to his right and started stabbing the monster in the neck with every ounce of strength he could muster.

The creature staggered and stumbled, but kept moving, black blood fountaining out from wound after wound. Israel screamed a curse at the beast and pulled his blood-slicked weapon from the thing's neck. He raised it high and slammed it point-first into the monster's temple. The horn sunk deep into the thing's skull, piercing bone and flesh until it punctured the-fist sized brain.

It died instantly, its body going limp and falling face-first into the muck and ruin of the old tunnel. Israel rode it down and hit the tunnel floor, rolling along behind the dead monstrosity until they both came to a stop. He lay there for a moment, hunger filling him with ache to feed, scents and sounds coming to him with the perfect clarity of the born hunter. He rose, his mind an arena of instinct and reason, only to find himself facing six tactical lights aimed directly at him.

He knew what they were seeing. Black lips curled back in a snarl over dingy teeth, skin the color of cigarette ash, black veins creeping through a face that looked at the world with red-rimmed, oily black eyes. He knew how still he was – no breathing, no muscular twitches or swaying from fatigue, not so much as a blink. He knew all this because he had seen it himself once on a video and the memory of that is what kept the logical part of his mind intact and determined never to lose control.

"Israel?" Stone said from behind the lights. "Mate? You still with us?"

"Just..." his voice was a growling thing he hardly recognized as he reached into his vest pocket and removed one of the protein bars. "Just... a little hangry."

CHAPTER FIVE

"It was a minotaur," Allison said, "or, rather, the creature that inspired the minotaur myth."

They were back on the Sentry Group jet and had just left the ground in New York when she looked up from her iPad and made the announcement. Israel was completely healed now, having gone through all his emergency protein bars, and had even managed to get a shower and a change of clothes before boarding the plane. He was sitting across from Allison in a dark pair of slacks and a white polo shirt. Stone and Olivia were sitting in the seats on the opposite side of the cabin, but had them rotated to face their companions. Israel didn't know if that was strictly in compliance with FAA regulations, but figured it didn't matter; this was Olivia Warburton's, jet which meant it operated according to her rules.

The older woman leaned back into the rich, camel-colored leather and said, "My god, really? I've read about those, but never thought I'd live to see one."

"Me, too," Allison said. "There's no doubt, though. I compared it to the Histories and it's a perfect match in both description and behavior."

The Histories were the Council of the Veil's secret records of everything pertaining to the existence of the bloodlines dating back as far as they could reach. Israel had read bits and pieces, but not all of them. Allison, though, was a brilliant historian as well as a physician and biologist. She was considered the only non-bloodline expert on both the biology and history of the Awakened.

"What about the women?" Israel said. "Please tell me they didn't end up like those police officers."

"No," Stone said, "I was with the team that found them. That bloody thing had dug a pit in one of the drier parts of the tunnel and tossed them in it. One of the poor birds died, but the others survived. Damn beastie broke their legs so they couldn't run."

Israel tightened his jaw and shook his head. "And the officers?"

Stone shrugged. "They didn't follow orders. They were all relatively new to the badge and thought they were looking for a normal man. Poor bastards didn't stand a chance."

"Because they had a Veil over their eyes," Israel muttered.

"Because they didn't follow their orders," Olivia said, staring hard at him.

It was becoming an old disagreement between Israel and Olivia, but he didn't feel like getting into it, so he gave her a quiet nod and said, "Why did it collect the women like that?"

Allison cleared her throat and said, "Well, that's where the 'Ew, gross' part comes in. Thanks to you we didn't reach this point tonight, but in the Histories, whenever these things showed up, they collected women for some sort of mating cycle."

Israel balked at that. "You mean that thing was going to…"

Allison nodded. "With all of them apparently. The

corpse was hauled off by the DGRI, but I'm hoping to get a look at it later and figure out if there was something specific to its biology that causes this behavior or if it's a cultural or ritual thing it brought from its plane of origin."

Israel shook his head in disbelief. "It didn't seem smart enough to have much of a culture."

"You'd be surprised," Allison said. "The most primal of creatures can have social structures and even ritual behaviors, even if they are crude."

"I suggest," Olivia said, "we address the gorilla in the room. How did it end up in New Jersey?"

"I forwarded everything we've learned to Michelle. She's adding it to the data she's collected, but didn't say much. She was really excited, though. She wants to meet with us in the morning. I think she's got some results to share."

"I should hope so," Olivia said. "That woman's kept herself locked in her lab for... what? A month now?"

Allison nodded. "A little longer than that, actually. I told you, once she gets a theory in her head she goes into obsessive mode. There's always something worth waiting for at the end of it, though."

"Fair enough," Olivia said. "I, for one, have had enough for one day. Stone, I believe there's a bottle of Redbreast in the bar. Would you pour me a measure, please?"

"Of course," the bald man replied, "and a double for myself. Allison?"

Israel watched Allison wave a polite refusal without looking up from her reading. He wasn't offended that Stone didn't extend the offer to him. Since he had Awakened, his body rejected anything but meat and small amounts of water. He'd tried to get drunk once shortly after the Leticia incident and wound up regurgitating an expensive bottle of Scotch into one of Olivia's hot tubs, which had been subsequently quarantined, drained, and sterilized. The only thing that had made the experience bearable was the way Allison had laughed when he'd told her the story.

"Stop it," she said in a soft voice, not looking up from her iPad.

"What?" he said, knowing full well what she meant.

"Staring. I can feel it, Israel." Her eyes lifted to meet his and she said, "All of it."

He closed his eyes and said, "Sorry. I forget sometimes."

Allison nodded. "Me too."

They spent the rest of the flight making small talk and looking out the small windows at a night that hid far more than it revealed.

Silversky Estate was one of ten homes ranging from penthouse condominiums to sprawling ranches that Olivia Warburton kept around the world. It was about fifteen minutes outside Atlanta, Georgia, and bordered Panola Mountain State Park on the northern edge of its square mile area. While it contained a number of structures, Silversky Mansion was by far the largest and sat near the exact center of the property.

This was where Israel had been living for the last year, and while he had learned the names of the majority of the permanent staff, he had yet to memorize the mansion's layout; it was quite literally the size of a small luxury hotel.

He joined his companions from the night before in one of the larger chambers that doubled as a dining and meeting room as needs arose. It was decorated in the same combination of white, dark cream, and silver as the rest of the mansion. The floors were inlaid with geometric patterns of light and dark woods and were polished to perfection. A large walnut table with thick, ornate legs and a dozen chairs surrounding it dominated the room. In contrast to all of the natural wood tones and soft colors, someone had set up a very large touch screen monitor and a small variety of laptop computers near the room's back wall.

Allison, Stone, and Olivia were already seated at the table and enjoying a breakfast from the small but generous buffet set out before them. At the head of the table with her back to the touch screen was Dr. Michelle Brandt – physicist, mathematician, computer scientist, and one of the world's leading experts on multiversal theory. She looked exactly like Allison, but always carried herself with a more serious, businesslike manner. She was hunched over one of the laptops typing intently when Israel came in and was the only one who didn't look up to greet him.

Israel glanced a question at Allison and she just shrugged. Michelle was known for her ability to lose herself in her work, so Israel just smiled and busied himself piling a plate with scrambled eggs, bacon, ham, and sausage. He sat down next to Allison across the table from Stone and Olivia and started eating. He was nearly finished before Michelle looked up and said, "Oh, Israel. You're here. Why didn't you say something?"

"You looked busy," he said as he popped the last bit of bacon into his mouth. "And good morning."

Michelle looked at him as though he were speaking a foreign language for a moment and then said, "Oh, yeah. Sorry. Good morning."

The exchange brought subtle smiles to four of the faces in the room, but Michelle didn't seem to notice. "Okay," she said, "before we get started I need to ask you guys about last night's incident. Those pricks at the DGRI are being their usual uncooperative selves."

"Go ahead," Stone said. "We'll tell what we can."

"Super-duper. Okay, can you make a guess at how long the–" She paused, looked at Allison, and asked, "What are we calling this thing, Allie?"

"Minotaur," Allison said.

"No kidding?" Michelle said. "Wow. Okay. Any idea how long the minotaur was down there before it started causing trouble?"

"Let me think on that," Stone said as he looked at Israel. "What do you think, mate?"

Israel smiled and said, "Well, the women went missing over a period of roughly twelve hours, so there's a starting point. I imagine that pit you mentioned was pretty large if it was meant to hold six women captive, even injured ones. As big as it was, the minotaur would still have needed time to dig that. When we fought, it seemed to get fatigued, so let's assume a human rest cycle and maybe time to sneak a meal in. Roughest of estimates, I'd say a day and half. Two days, maybe."

"Right. Okay," Michelle said and started tapping at the laptop screen. After a minute of this, she said, "I'm going to broaden that out to a possibility of three to four days and collate with the other incidents since Leticia, then we'll let Pythia chew on that for a few minutes while I fill you guys in on what I've put together."

Pythia was the elaborate computer software Michelle had designed to collect and analyze data for the purpose of providing probable outcomes for any given situation. Given time, it could give a realistic expected outcome for anything from the percentage of car accidents on any given street to the winner of a presidential election. Israel and Stone had spent hours trying to get Michelle to apply Pythia's technology to the last Superbowl, but she had refused firmly and often.

"You said 'since Leticia,'" Israel said to Michelle. "What's that got to do with New Jersey?"

"Yeah, okay," Michelle said, grabbing an iPad from the table and standing up. "It's a lot to tell, but let's start with Leticia."

She tapped the pad a few times and a map of North

America appeared on the large monitor. After she had put the iPad down, she swiped her hands over the monitor until she had enlarged the map image to include most of the United States and a portion of Northern Mexico. She grabbed the iPad again and started tapping at it.

"Okay," she said, "Leticia was here." A red star appeared on the monitor and marked the southwest Texas town's location. "Now, I'm going to plot out all the breach events since Leticia – the 'micro-breaches,' as the DGRI has classified them. These represent breach events that were handled by the government, the Council, or us."

Nine bright green dots appeared scattered across the U.S. and one lit up near Saltillo, Mexico. Israel recognized the ones in Huntsville, Alabama; Asheville, North Carolina; and the Fairview, New Jersey, location from the previous night.

Stone laughed and said, "Remember Huntsville, mate? You still owe them a bowling alley."

Israel shook his head and said, "Man, that fire was not my fault."

"Focus, gentlemen," Olivia said. "Go on, Michelle."

Michelle nodded and said, "Okay, so nine events in a little less than twelve months. A lot, but by no means a cause for alarm. The DGRI and the Council wrote it off to an aftereffect of all the Inner Dark Energy that poured through the Leticia breach. I did, too, for a few months, but it started nagging at me."

"What did?" Israel asked.

"The breaches themselves," she said. "Okay, this is where it gets a little nutty, so try to bear with me. Israel, do you remember right after you Awakened and we tried to explain everything to you? Do you remember what I told you about the multiverse?"

"I'll never forget that. You told me that reality was like a kid's ball pit where each universe in the multiverse was one of the balls and where they butted up against one another there existed places to cross over if one had the technology to pull it off. The space between the balls where the curvature of the sphere left a kind of negative space was an infinite ocean of bizarre and theoretical energies we call the Inner Dark."

"Yes, perfect. So, my problem with the breaches was that the Leticia breach was a portal to the Inner Dark. See?"

Israel looked around. No one seemed to be following Michelle.

She said, "The things that are coming through – the minotaur, that snake thing in Huntsville, the tattooed creatures in Mexico – guys, these aren't creatures we have any record of ever crossing over from the ID. These things were from other worlds."

"So how does a portal to the Inner Dark cross dimensional barriers to bring extra-dimensional life here?" Israel asked.

"Exactly!" Michelle said, grinning. "Answer: It doesn't. A portal to the Inner Dark would have just dumped ID energy into this world and let anything that could fit crawl out. We know that nothing crawled out, and that excessive energy would have just incorporated itself into our ecosphere or floated off into space. The most we should have seen was a sharp uptick in the number of Awakened."

"Which we have," Olivia cut in. "I know for a fact the Council and the DGRI have both been stretched thin trying to deal with the number of newly Awakened show-ing up at hospitals and the like with no idea what's happened to them."

"Yes," Michelle said and tapped at her tablet. A mass of small white dots appeared on the large map. "And here they are. Nearly a hundred of them spread all throughout the country."

Israel studied the map. There was something about it that was raising his curiosity, but he couldn't quite place what.

"I came across an article online," Michelle said, "about a little town in Kansas called McPherson. It seems an entire eighteen wheeler full of corn just vanished into thin air – poof. It got me to thinking, so I made some calls and looked into it a little deeper. The truck left its loading point and should have arrived at its destination about forty minutes later, but just didn't show up. It was pretty much a straight shot and not a whole lot of ways to get lost, particularly when you consider the driver had been running that route for nearly ten years."

"So, what then?" Stone said. "Theft?"

Michelle shook her head. "Who would steal corn in Kansas? Doesn't make sense. I did a little more digging and found out a section of the asphalt on the same road the trucker was on was missing."

"The road was missing?" Allison said.

Michelle nodded and then tapped a button on her tablet again. Thirteen more dots appeared among all the others on the screen. These were bright orange and one of them was hovering over the Gulf of Mexico just south of eastern Louisiana. Michelle pointed at it and said, "U.S. Navy fighter jet on maneuvers – poof." She pointed at another point near Temple, Texas. "Small bus carrying elderly church-goers – poof. Thirteen total weird or inexplicable disappearances since the Leticia incident."

"So the Leticia breach wasn't what we thought it was," Olivia said.

"That was my first reaction, too," Michelle said, "but, no. Look at the map. See anything odd?"

Israel and Allison answered in unison. "It's a cone."

"Exactly," Michelle said. She tapped the pad again and two black lines appeared. They ran through the most outlying points – Trinidad; Colorado on the north; and Saltillo, Mexico, on the south – and continued through other points, gradually narrowing until they crossed in the

Atlantic Ocean somewhere off the coast of Maine.

"Exactly zero incidents outside these lines once you factor in the disappearances. What's better is that if you bisect the angle the lines make it goes straight through–"

"Leticia," Israel said in hushed voice.

Michelle nodded and a third black line appeared, cutting straight through where the town had once stood.

"Son of a bitch," Stone muttered.

"Why didn't anyone else catch this?" Olivia asked.

"The DGRI and the Council weren't looking for the disappearances. All they care about is keeping the Veil intact. People coming up missing aren't usually much of a threat to that."

Olivia nodded. "This is excellent, excellent work, Dr. Brandt. I still don't understand exactly what we're looking at here, though. How does this tie in to the micro-breaches?"

Michelle locked eyes with Israel. "Do you remember what else I said that day? About how the ball pit simile wasn't precisely accurate? How universes weren't rigid and comparing the multi-verse to a foam might be more accurate?"

Israel didn't recall that, but he nodded anyway to keep the scientist talking.

"Imagine a foam, like a Nerf ball or one of those memory foam mattresses. Imagine each bubble in the foam as one of the balls in the ball pit – a universe unto itself and the spaces between the Inner Dark. Let's say, for the sake of argument, that you were to prick the surface of our theoretical Nerf ball and then shove a needle through that opening. What would happen?"

Israel shrugged. "It would cut into the ball, leave a little hole."

"Not just a hole, but a deep channel, like a conduit that passes through all those bubbles in the Nerf's foam. A conduit that started in the Inner Dark and traveled through multiple universes. Think on that for second."

He did. It would explain why extra-dimensional creatures not native to the Inner Dark kept showing up. They were traveling down the theoretical conduit from their point of origin. "Okay," he said, "I see where you're going. The Progeny opened some kind of dimensional tunnel and things keep falling into and out of it. How and why?"

"The Progeny didn't do it," Allison said, her voice a whisper of hushed awe. "To do that, you would need the kind of energy that would allow you to manipulate space-time. You would have to be able to–" She looked up at her twin. Michelle nodded.

"What?" Israel said.

"Israel, you would need the kind of power that would allow you to teleport at will."

Despite not needing to breathe, Israel took a deep breath. "Erin," he whispered. "Michelle, are you saying she's still alive?"

Michelle nodded. "I can't be sure, Israel, but, yeah, I think so. I think that when she tried to teleport you guys out of that truck, she got you to safety, but she was pulled into the breach and through to... somewhere else. I think the fact that we keep having these micro-breaches is because she's still out there holding the conduit she left in her wake open somehow. If she was dead, I don't think it would be there. "

Israel tightened his jaw and studied the map. "We have to do something," he said. "Why is that a cone? Is that significant?"

"Have you ever seen a water hose attached to a high pressure spigot get turned on with no one holding the outlet end?" Michelle asked. "The spraying end whips around out of control. I think that's the best analogy I can give you for what's happened here; Erin's end is the spigot, ours is the hose."

"But why is it moving across the country?" Allison asked. "I mean, the intersection of the border lines is off the coast of Cape Cod. It seems like it should be centered over the Leticia site, if anything."

"I don't know. Rotation of the Earth, maybe? I don't have enough data for that. Regardless, that's not what concerns me the most."

"Let's hear what does," Olivia said.

"The narrowing. If you look at the timestamps of all the plotted incidents, you'll see the older ones are closer to Leticia and the newer ones are farther. It's like our water hose is getting shorter. Nature always seeks to return to equilibrium. I think the more time that passes, the closer we get to that conduit closing, assuming – and this is a huge assumption – that there is any way to get Erin back at all, it will completely vanish if that doorway closes."

"Then we need to get moving," Stone said, a hard look in his eyes. "Do you know exactly where we need to be?"

Michelle studied her iPad and said, "Pythia says there is a 92.3% probability that we will find the concentration point for the conduit's energy thirteen miles off the coast of Cape Cod. A place called Jasper Island."

They all looked at Olivia. She nodded and said, "Go."

CHAPTER SIX

Erin

A sharp clatter echoed through the fire-lit cave as the two combatants circled each other, wooden clubs blurring and striking against one another. Erin Simms backpedaled on bare feet and brought her hooked wooden club – called a Batla by its native creators – to a high guard position with her right hand. She moved with precision as she circled her opponent, careful to always maintain her balance and keeping the shorter wooden stick – the Jo – in a backhanded grip tight against her chest in her left hand. She kept moving, watching her sparring partner with a calculating eye.

He stood nearly a foot taller than Erin and returned her gaze through large, violet eyes that were slit vertically by gray pupils. His skin was a shade of golden amber that reminded Erin of maple syrup. Coal black hair hung in a mass of thin braids around his sharp, narrow face and when his wide, dark lips curled into a smile, showing rows of ivory white teeth with needle sharp incisors, it caused the thin slits of his nostrils to flair slightly below the narrow line of his nose. He moved his long, slender limbs in a fanciful maneuver of Batla and Jo that left him crouched low with his Batla raised high and behind him. The black tattoos that covered his body looked like onyx shadows on his skin.

Erin wrinkled her brow in irritation and said, "Stop showing off, Gratt'na."

The smile widened. "To display skill earned is not to cry oneself to the winds, little Sar'ha." His voice was smooth, like a strong breeze across a dry, sandy desert.

The pattern of tattoos that curved up from Erin's temples and behind her ears to gradually terminate in points at her jaw warmed as they translated his words into something her mind could understand. Even as effective as the magic – because she didn't know what else to call it – was, it didn't translate everything. Sar'ha had become a kind of nickname for her. As near as she could figure, it meant something like 'daughter of the farthest star.'

"Actually," Erin said as she took a quick step forward, spun, feinted, and returned to her guard position, "I think that's the definition of showing off."

"Sar'ha words cry truth," Barr'na, the aged and gray-skinned weapons master, said. "On this day, you train as a new Tarr calf, just learned to run."

"Truth," the fourth member of their group, Brinn'ha, said. "My brother Gratt'na moves uncertain on weak legs."

Gratt'na's eyes slid toward his sister and he held his arms open wide, the signal for sparring to cease. Erin relaxed and smiled as she watched Gratt'na turn and point one of his three thick fingers at Brinn'ha. She had seen this before and always enjoyed it.

"It may be," Gratt'na said, grinning, "that my sister Brinn'ha wishes to test the strength of my legs."

Brinn' ha, the same height and coloring as her brother, though with only half the number of tattoos, rose from her cross-legged seat on the cavern floor while simultaneously pulling Batla and Jo from her dark, Tarr-hide belt. Her braids, thicker than her brother's as she was the younger, swung about her face as she joined Erin in the center of the training circle. She nodded to Erin, who responded in kind and backed out of the circle. The story was that dozens of generations had trained the Batla and Jo in this cave, and the way the stone felt polished and smooth beneath her bare feet made Erin believe it.

Brother and sister faced one another from across the circle with smiles on their faces and arms crossed over their chests. They bowed their heads until they were staring at the floor and waited.

"Begin," Barr'na said, his voice crisp with understood authority.

Their heads snapped up and they sprang at one another. Batla twirled and swept while Jo stabbed out at perceived openings and then back to the ready position, close to the body. They spun like dancers and the music they made was the sound of wood against wood and flesh against stone.

Erin settled next to the Weaponmaster and crossed her legs, watching the two siblings playfully trying to bruise one another.

"Like this since child-time, they have been," Barr'na said. "Always for caring, but always for testing to be strongest."

"They love each other," Erin said, a soft smile on her lips, "but they are still brother and sister. I guess that's true in any universe."

"Just so," Barr'na said, "and as it is well to be."

Erin reached up and lightly scratched at the tattoos around her ears. Barr'na noticed and said, "The Marks of Understanding irritate at you?"

Erin shrugged. "Sometimes. Not as much as they did at first. I guess I'm getting used to them."

Barr'na nodded. "It is well that is so. The rest of your wellness is better in the same?"

Erin shrugged again. "I still get the headaches and the

dizziness, but they seem to be coming less frequently. Not nearly as bad as when I first arrived." She thought back to the wracking migraines and vomit-inducing vertigo that had swept over her daily during her first months in this world and shuddered inside.

Barr'na put one large, three-fingered hand on her shoulder. "From a turn of the cold time to the next turn of warmth beyond the cold have you been with the People of the Valley, Sar'ha. Healing, it is well to be."

Erin nodded and gently patted Barr'na's gray hand, noticing the specks of gold that scattered across it like freckles. In her world, people's hair turned gray as they aged. Here, it was the skin. Barr'na's hair was pitch black and so festooned with tight braids, beads, and bone ornaments that it rattled like a set of wind chimes when he moved. Erin knew the braids and decorations combined to announce his accomplishments and his place as an elder among the People of the Valley – or just the Valley People, as she thought of them – but she had never understood the system. She knew that as children, the Valley People kept their heads shaved regardless of gender until they reached puberty. Then, the hair was allowed to grow and the braiding and additions of ornamentation would begin.

A couple of months – by her best guess, anyway – after arriving, the Valley People had given her the tattoos that eased her communication with them and then collectively offered her a place among the tribe. She had accepted it with gratitude. Her old life – Earth, Las Vegas, Israel, and the Sentry Group – all of that was lost to her and she knew it. Someplace to call home, even among creatures so very different from her, was a welcome offer. The first thing they had done, though, was shave her head down to the bare scalp as a part of the initiation ritual. She hadn't minded at the time and had watched the bright red dyed strands of her hair fall away like dead needles in a pine grove. Later that same night, she had sat with the hair bundled into a braid in her hand and told her life story to the assembled elders and other members of the tribe who carried the Marks of Understanding. They had translated her tale of a tragic, abusive family life and the discovery of a true friend for others as she spoke. When the telling was done, she threw the red braid into a bonfire and said goodbye to her past. Consciously, at least, because her dreams were still of home and darker things.

Her hair had grown out eight inches or so since then, she guessed, and was pulled back by two thick braids that kept her bangs away from her eyes while the rest of her dark blond locks hung in loose waves beneath the braids. She had no ornaments in her hair except for two simple black beads that held the braids in place through some trick of hair-weaving that Erin didn't know or understand. She caught herself touching the beads as she remembered and put her hand back down. Looking backward was a habit she was trying to break.

Within the circle, Gratt'na let out a pained yelp as Brinn'ha scored a solid poke to his ribs with her Jo. She laughed over his pained exclamation and did a flourish that was almost identical to the one Gratt'na had shown off with to Erin. When Brinn'ha caught Erin's eye, she winked playfully. The wink was not a custom among the Valley People, but rather something Erin had taught Brinn'ha.

"Have you walked as the wind?" Barr'na asked. "Is it being healing in the same?"

Walked as the wind: That was what the Valley People called her ability to teleport from point to point. She had lost the ability entirely when she had first arrived, but as the migraines subsided, her power had slowly returned. She had expected her newfound tribe to react with fear and suspicion when she showed them what she could do; instead, she was treated as a gifted artist or hunter and even more closely embraced for her unique talent.

Back on Earth, she had been able to teleport thousands of miles and touch other things to send them wherever she wished. It was, in fact, using that power that she had come to suspect had brought her to the Valley People, though she had no idea how. She had discovered that her powers were far weaker here, though.

"I try every day," she said. "I can go maybe forty or fifty feet if I really concentrate. If I try to do that in succession, I can get about three repetitions in before I'm exhausted. If I try to touch something and Push it..." she shrugged. "Nothing. I can't even move a pebble."

Barr'na nodded. "Some has it healed, but not to its fullness."

"No," Erin said. "Not to its fullness. I think when I accidentally brought myself here, it injured me in some way. It... broke me, I guess. Broke my powers, at least. I didn't have them for long before that happened, so I can't say for sure. I really have next to no idea how they work."

"Not to be understanding," Barr'na said, "can lead to the fear choices. You do not make these, I see."

Erin shrugged. "It is what it is. It'll heal or it won't and there's really fuck-all I can do about it. I prefer to work with what I know and what I know is that I want to respect the tribe that has given me a home. I'll focus on that for now."

"You have given the right to us all times, Sar'ha. My wishing is for the tribe to show you in the sun and not only the only tribe night."

Erin nodded. Despite the Valley People's under-standing and acceptance of her, they were not the only people who inhabited this world. Hunters from other tribes, wanderers looking to trade, even a hedge mage looking to collect plants around the Valley People's settle-ment – they had all come at one time or another and each time Erin had stayed hidden while they remained. She wasn't sure how the world at large would react to an obvious alien walking among them, and the thought of the tribe suffering because of her was intolerable. As Barr'na had said, not understanding often led to decisions based in fear. In Erin's experience, those were always the worst possible ones.

"I prefer it that way," she said.

"I am for knowing why," Barr'na said. "I am not for the liking of it."

Erin smiled. Despite the odd speech patterns and the inhuman appearance, she had grown quite fond of the tribe and these three in particular. They had taken it upon themselves to give her a place to sleep, food to eat, and train her in the skills she needed to survive in the alien world. The Batla and Jo were only one of the things she had learned, but ranked as one of her favorites. It had served as a means to regain her strength as she had healed from the ordeal that had brought her here, as well as teach her some much needed self-defense methods. She felt leaner, stronger, and more capable than she ever had before despite never actually having to face anyone in real combat.

"Enough, Tarr-calves!" Barr'na said, snapping the end of his smoothly worn walking stick into the stone. "We are for finishing and preparation for green-coming festival. Weapons are for putting away."

Brinn'ha and Gratt'na stepped back from one another, arms spread wide. They sheathed their weapons as one, first Jo, then Batla, and then stepped forward smiling. They clasped both hands with one another and leaned in until their foreheads touched. Erin called this a Valley People hug.

She grabbed her darkly tanned Tarr-hide moccasins and pulled them up over her feet and shins. The Valley People all wore essentially the same outfit: long moccasins, loose pants, a long pullover top that was a mix of jacket and shirt that hung well below the waist, and a wide belt that kept the top snug and provided a handy place to secure tools or weapons. When Erin had arrived, the tribe had to custom-make her clothing as she was not as tall or long of limb as even the shortest adult among the Valley People. The light, sturdy leather had been stiff at first, but had not taken long to soften. Erin had reached a point where she had a difficult time remembering what other clothing felt like.

She rose to her feet in a smooth motion and joined her companions as they made their way out of the cavern. She paused at the mouth of the cavern and took in the view. Behind her, the mountain rose another two hundred feet or more in a massive, jagged wall of dark stone cut through with veins of milky white. Before her for another few hundred feet below, the valley spread out into a vista of turquoise grasses and narrow, gray trees with newly formed buds in every shade of green she could imagine. A brightly plumed, long-beaked bird the size of an Earth eagle glided through the air. Farther down the valley, herds of the thick-limbed and hairless Tarr grazed in contentment under their shepherd's watchful eye. The mountains rose on every side and in the middle of it all was the Valley People's home, a collection of sturdy structures built with light-colored logs that were hand-cut into easily stacked square columns and sealed with a mud mixture that was tough and durable.

The homes were arranged in a pattern that fanned out from the largest of the buildings, a long hall large enough to hold the whole tribe. This was the Elder's Hall and housed the tribe's ruling body, though it was open to any member of the tribe at any time. Erin watched, smiling as children played in the wide stream that flowed through the village while the adults piled wood for a bonfire and went about all the other tasks associated with preparing for one of the People's many celebrations of life and the seasons.

"Sar'ha!" Brinn'ha shouted from the trail. "Be for

joining us or be for staring at the winds?"

Erin took another last look. For some reason, she wanted to burn the image in her mind, burn it so that it left a beautiful scar on her memory. She shook off the feeling, though, and ran to join her friends.

CHAPTER SEVEN

Night came to the valley like a gentle mist falling slow and steady. As it grew darker, Erin busied herself helping Brinn'ha and Gratt'na lay out thin strips of Tarr meat and cleaning fish that had been butterflied open onto thick wooden racks. These would be leaned near enough to the fire that the smoke and heat would gently roast the flesh without catching the racks aflame. It was a kind of friendly competition among certain members of the tribe whose food would be most popular from festival to festival, and Gratt'na's passion for it shined through as he rubbed wild herbs into the fish.

"Not for being the second to Nonn'Ha again," he said as Erin handed him another freshly chopped handful of herbage. "Chaat leaf adds much for flavors."

The Chaat was a thin, wide-leafed plant that grew in only one somewhat isolated spot near the settlement. It had a sharp, earthy aroma that reminded Erin of horse dung and a flavor that was the equal of the scent. She kept that to herself, though, and encouraged Gratt'na's efforts. She knew how much he enjoyed these small contests. She couldn't help but think of it as *Iron Chef: Valley People*

Edition.

They were outside the cabin Erin shared with Gratt'na and Brinn'ha. It was the same cabin the siblings had grown up in before their parents had died in a Tarr stampede a few seasons before Erin had arrived. When she had needed a place to stay, the extra space they had made it the logical choice. Despite privacy being something of a scarcity, they had learned to get along and live together well.

The shadows were getting deeper as they worked and laughed, and Brinn'ha and Gratt'na bickered playfully. Finally, with the last of the meat secured to the racks and ready for smoking, they each took up two racks and joined the rest of the gathering tribe near the cooking fire. There would be two fires: a smaller one for cooking and a much larger one for dancing, telling stories, and general conversing. There was no equivalent for alcohol or recreational drugs in the Valley People culture. Erin had tried to explain the concept to Barr'na and some of the tribal elders once and they had scoffed at the very notion. The Valley People held the ability to observe and reason sacred. Anyone who willingly interfered with that was considered foolish in the extreme. Erin found the policy hard to argue.

Before long, night had enveloped the valley completely. The fires were fully ablaze and the tribe was well into the party. Stories were told, songs were sung, food and drink shared, and dances were performed in graceful, flowing movements by males and females alike. Children ran in and out of the firelight giggling and calling out with high-pitched squeals. Stars spread between the twin moons overhead and Erin sipped at a berry juice concoction that she favored while she watched the festivities.

Across from her, on the opposite side of the bonfire, she spotted a group of six of the smaller children. They were smiling in a way she had learned to recognize as shy, but she knew what they wanted. She pretended not to notice them and sipped at her drink as though nothing were out of the ordinary, but picked out a clear spot just behind them and focused on it.

She could feel the space between them in her mind. It was an acute sense of *here* and *there*. She focused on the space she had chosen with practiced ease until she could feel it fully and then mentally Pulled on it.

She disappeared from where she was standing, reappeared directly behind the children, and said, "Boo!"

She didn't know if the word translated to the Valley People's language – so many things didn't – but it had the desired effect regardless. They all jumped, squealed in delight, and went running in six different directions with laughter bubbling in their wake.

Nearby, some of the adults who had seen the exchange laughed as well and nodded at Erin in approval. She smiled in return and did a little curtsy – another thing that she wasn't sure translated, but seemed to garner the correct result.

It was a lovely and memorable night. Then, with one stabbing bolt of pain that started in her head and tore down her spine like a fillet knife through a fish, it all went to hell.

Erin cried out and arched her back. Her clay mug hit the ground and broke, red juice running like blood into the soil and sizzling against burning logs. Erin struggled to keep to her feet, but snapped forward suddenly as the muscles in her abdomen contracted hard. She hit the ground and twitched there in the dirt, pain wracking her body as her muscles contracted and relaxed in rapid, agonizing bursts. She could see the Valley People rushing around her, hear them shouting words that were distorted and incomprehensible. She rolled to her back just as Brinn'ha reached her and slid into the dirt next to her friend. Above and beyond her, the night sky was an ocean of glittering, opalescent stars.

The moment the breach occurred, Erin knew what it was. There was no sound to accompany it, nothing to draw the Valley People's attention from her, just a sudden and huge burst of sickly yellow light far above their heads. Despite the pain flooding through her, time seemed to freeze for an instant in the pale glow of that light. Erin could swear she felt it on her skin.

Then, there was a monstrous, whining roar as the light faded and what looked like a fireball came streaking through the night sky throwing off black smoke and bright lines of flaming debris. It wasn't a fireball, though, and as the tremors in her muscles abated, Erin realized what it was – an airplane. One of those sleek-looking military fighter planes that she had seen dozens of times in the movies. Her mouth fell slack as the plane spun and roared through the night sky.

The Valley People screamed in terror. Children clung crying to their parents and the Elders all hurried people to their homes, shouting for them to stay calm. This all registered as background noise to Erin, though, as she lay in the dirt and watched the flaming wreckage scream through the sky and disappear over one of the farther mountains. A second after it was out of sight, there was an explosion of sound that vibrated through her despite the distance. The Valley People who had not yet made it to their homes all gasped in shock.

Erin lay still, watching the trail of smoke that cut like a fading scar across the sky. She heard Brinn'ha calling her name, but couldn't find the strength to respond. She felt tears on her face – from the seizures, she told herself – but ignored them. The smell of the jet's passing was faint, but familiar – burning fuel, scorched rubber, chemically produced smoke. They were all things she knew, but also things she thought she had thrown away when she had watched a bright red braid of hair disintegrating in a fire.

She realized that she should have known better.

"Sar'ha," Barr'na said, his nostril slits flaring with worry, "if you are for knowing of the burning-screaming-thing that crossed the sky, be for the sharing of the known."

Erin was sitting on the floor against the back wall of her cabin. Brinn'ha and Gratt'na had half-carried her back through a crowd of terrified Valley People. Her strength was returning by slow degrees, but she wasn't quite ready to stand on her own yet. She sipped water from a fired clay cup and took slow, steadying breaths. Her face was half hidden in the shadows cast by the room's central fire pit, but she stayed where she was. Moving hurt.

"I recognized it," she said with reluctance. "I think it's from the same place I am."

"What such a beast is that being?" Gratt'na asked.

Erin shook her head. "It's not a beast. It's a machine. A flying machine. Like a tool we use to travel."

The three Valley People exchanged looks of confusion that crossed all language barriers.

"Not just traveling," Erin went on. "We use them to carry supplies long distances, put out really big fires, and watch the ground from far away. We also use them in wars to kill each other."

Barr'na pointed a crooked, gray finger at the door and the world beyond. "That was for being..." He let the question hang between them.

"That was the killing kind," Erin whispered.

Silence settled over the group for long moments. Then, Brinn'ha said, "How is it for being here?"

Erin shrugged. "I have no idea, Brinn," she said, dropping the 'ha honorific while they were in the privacy of their cabin. "I don't really understand how I got here, much less what happened out there."

"Burning," Gratt'na said. "Flying thing was for the

burning, not the using. Being destroyed in the burning."

Erin considered it. She had heard the explosion. Gratt'na surely had a point. A memory crept back to her, though. It was of an airman she had met back in the days before she had been Awakened and gained the power she now held. He was a young pilot stationed at Nellis Air Force Base who had taken a liking to her over all the other girls working in her brother's strip club and brothel. It was always just business for her in those days, but she got the impression he wanted to live out some *An Officer and a Gentleman* fantasy with her. He was one of the very few men she had ever known who was willing to pay for her time and just talk.

A lot of what he talked about was his life in the Air Force. He had loved flying and was never shy about telling her about this aircraft or that. She had listened dutifully because that was what she was being paid to do. One conversation that stood out for her, though, had been about the weapons fighter aircraft could carry. He had described in fair detail the amount of devastation just one rocket or missile could do and she remembered being awed by the description.

"It might not be that simple," she said, returning to the moment.

"How are you meaning, Sar'ha?" Barr'na said. "Gratt'na words cry truth. Flying thing was for the burning."

"Because not all of it will burn," Erin said. "And because it carries weapons, Barr'na. Terrible weapons."

"We are having weapons, Sar'ha," Brinn'ha said.

"Not like these," Erin said, shaking her head. "That jet can carry many, many weapons. Just one of those–" she held up a single finger to emphasize her point "–could level this entire village and kill all of the tribe. Just one."

"Not for being possible," Gratt'na said. "No weapon–"

"It's possible, Gratt!" Erin snapped. "My world is not

like yours. We create weapons like you create Chaat-Fish. We've made weapons that can kill thousands of people in the blink of an eye. We're really good at it and I'm telling you that it is very possible that something destructive could have made it through that crash."

"Such cannot be for the leaving," Barr'na said. "Such must be for the breaking. Or for the leaving in dark places."

Erin nodded. "Yeah, but we need to know for sure if anything dangerous is left. I'll leave when the sun comes up."

Brinn'ha and Gratt'na both started objecting at once. Barr'na let it go on for a moment while he studied Erin. Then he silenced the siblings with a single, stern word.

"You are for the finding of this thing from you-place," he said to Erin, "for the doing of what thing?"

Erin shrugged. "I'll know better when I get there. Collect anything that looks dangerous and drop it in a river or something. I don't know for sure. We just have to be sure that there isn't anything left that could threaten the tribe. I've got a better chance than any of you to recognize the dangerous stuff."

Barr'na considered it, then nodded his agreement. "The you-place-flying thing fell far to the other side of the sun-coming mountain. Long is the walking. What path are you for taking?"

Erin opened her mouth to respond, but realized that she had nothing to respond with. She had never traveled out of sight of the village. "You'll have to draw me a map, I guess," she said.

"Not for drawing of way-picture," Barr'na said. "A companion to be for showing the way is the right of things."

"I don't know if that's a good idea, Barr'na. If there are weapons left, it could be dangerous."

"You are for being of the Valley People, Sar'ha. Danger

for facing you is danger for facing we," Barr'na said. He turned to Brinn'ha and Gratt'na. "Where are you for standing?"

The siblings shared a look, a nod, and then faced Erin. "We stand with, Sar'ha. We stand with our heart-sister."

It was the clearest translation that she had ever gotten from the tattoos around her ears and when she heard it, a sob caught in her throat. Tears welled in her eyes and she was suddenly grateful for the heavy shadows.

"Then we are for the talking of it no more. The tribe will be for the preparing for you. You will be for the resting before the long-walk."

"Barr'na, I really–" Erin said.

"Enough, Sar'ha. For the talking no more. For the doing now. Your night is for the resting." With that, he turned and left the cabin.

As soon as he was gone, Brinn'ha said, "We are for knowing of the way, Sar'ha. Are you for the certain that this long-walk must be done?"

Erin nodded again. "Yes, Brinn. If there's anything left there that could end up hurting the tribe..." She let the thought fade and just said, "I couldn't live with myself if that happened."

"You were for the bringing of this you-place-thing?" Gratt'na asked.

"Gratt'na!" Brinn'ha said. "Sar'ha would not be for such!"

"No, he's right, Brinn," Erin said. "It's too much of a coincidence that I had that seizure and this thing just suddenly shows up. I swear to you both, though, I didn't want for this to happen. However I'm tied to it, I didn't choose it."

Gratt'na walked over and extended his hand to Erin. She took it and he pulled her to her feet like she weighed next to nothing. "Never," he said, "would I be for thinking that you would be for that choosing."

Erin met his large, dark eyes and nodded.

"Come," Brinn'ha said. "Barr'na words cry truth. We are for the resting. Long-walk will be for the testing of each of us."

"Are you guys sure you know where we need to go?" Erin asked.

"To the other side of the sun-coming mountain will be for the not-difficult. Then–" Brinn'ha shrugged.

"Then we will be for the looking-thinking. A way will be for the seeing."

Erin nodded. They bid each other a good rest and went to their respective beds. Erin lay silent and still on the thin, stacked Tarr-hide and grass mattress. She watched the shadows of the dying fire pit flicker and fade on the ceiling. For the first time in months, she thought of Earth and how different it was from this place. It occurred to her how very wrong it had seemed to watch that jet burning across the sky. It wasn't that the plane was in distress, but rather that it just didn't belong here. It didn't matter if it was from her world or not; its presence was an intrusion on a place with no need for it. She wanted it gone.

She would make it that way, she decided. They would find a cave or a lake and hide every scrap of metal and plastic she could find. Erase it from the surface of the world and fill in the crater if she could.

Then what, Erin? she thought. *If your fucked up DNA brought that thing here and you can't control it, do you really think they'll let you stay among them? What happens if you suddenly open a breach to the Inner Dark and let a flood of squidheads through? Do you want the tribe to end up like those people in Texas?*

The memory of the fight through the town of Leticia with Israel and Stone still made her tremble. No, there was no way she could risk that happening to the Valley People. If this wasn't just a random event, if there was some new aspect to her power that was beyond her ability to control, she would leave the tribe far behind rather than risk their safety.

   She rolled over and faced the wall. She felt the tears return to her eyes and didn't bother trying to fight them.

CHAPTER EIGHT

Israel

The Gulfstream G450 lifted off from the Atlanta International runway just as the clock ticked over to the five-thirty mark on Israel's smartphone. He thumbed off the display and slid it into the left inside pocket of his leather jacket. In the right-hand pocket was a wallet with a set of fake IDs identifying him as Vance Horton, a medical equipment salesman from St. Louis, Missouri. One of the things Stone had drilled into him without any mercy was the absolute value of anonymity. While Stone always seemed to prefer law enforcement credentials, Israel liked things a little more mundane. Over the last year, Israel had managed to set up a series of ten separate fake identities that he could switch between as he needed. It was very useful since the man the world knew as Israel Trent was legally dead and had been since the year before.

It had taken Michelle most of the day to tear down and pack up all the equipment she was sure she would need if her theory was correct. It had taken the remainder of the day to pack up the things she thought she might need. The delay in leaving had frustrated Israel, but he had waited as patiently as he'd been able to manage. Finally in the air, he settled back and tried to slow his mind by taking in his surroundings.

This wasn't the same jet they had taken to New York, but it was more than enough to get him, Stone, and Michelle to Jasper Island, Massachusetts, in a little over two hours. It was the third of Olivia's jets that he had flown on and, though it was the smallest, it boasted the same level of comfort and convenience that seemed to surround his ultra-rich employer. The seats were uphol-stered in an ivory-white leather that was flawlessly clean and matched the cabin walls as well as the couch that was against the bulkhead in the rear of the cabin. Stone was stretched out there listening to something through the earbuds attached to his phone. Michelle was sitting in a cluster of four seats mid-way between Israel and Stone.

He wasn't sure how they had ended up spread out like that, but he shrugged it off and took out his own phone again. A few quick taps and swipes and the Jasper Island briefing filled the small screen. He scanned the usual details: roughly eleven miles northeast of Cape Cod in the North Atlantic, 36.2 square miles, 269 feet above sea level at its highest point, home to a small town called Emberoak with a population just south of three thousand people. The population numbers caught his eye and he tapped a link. The screen took a moment to load and then he started reading again.

Four years earlier, the population of Jasper Island had hovered closer to the two-thousand mark, but then a tech company by the name of Darkarcher Gaming Sciences had come in and purchased a huge plot of land on the eastern part of the island. They started construction on a "design and idea realization center" almost immediately after that and had brought in state-of-the-art telecommunications and electrical infrastructure for the island. Just over a year later, even before the center was complete, DGS was the island's largest single employer and the reason anyone on that island had a cell phone that could actually get a signal. Since then, they had become a major player in the high-end computer components world.

Israel searched the web for a few minutes looking for more info on DGS, but could only come up with the standard press release fluff. He got up from his seat and joined Michelle mid-cabin, settling in across from her.

She looked up from her iPad as he approached and smiled for an instant, which was as much of a smile as he ever got out of her. "What's up, Mr. Trent?" she said.

She called him that sometimes. He didn't know why. He'd never heard her call Stone anything but Stone, and to his knowledge everyone else in Olivia's inner circle was first names only. Israel made a mental note to bring it up later and said, "Not much. Listen, what do you know about a tech company called Darkarcher Gaming Sciences?"

"DGS?" She shrugged. "They make good graphics cards, nice clock speeds, great standard processor and chipset integration despite being the only VGC on the market with a proprietary GPU setup, more than decent 3-D rendering stats. I haven't really looked into any of their next-gen tech, but I know they've been working with 3-D NAND and ultra-high throughput stuff, but I don't really pay much attention since I get all of my components through Sentry and it's all cutting edge. Why?"

Israel blinked and realized that had all summed up to Michelle saying, "Yes. I enjoy their products."

"I was wondering," he said, handing her his phone, "why they would build a big research facility way the hell out here in the North Atlantic. Why not Silicon Valley? Or Seattle? New York, Boston – hell, even Atlanta would make more sense than Jasper Island, Massachusetts."

Michelle took the phone and said, "This is *that* island? I'll be damned. How did I miss that?"

"I'm sure you were busy," Israel said.

She cut her eyes up at him, but didn't smile. "You'll be

really glad we have all that stuff when we need it," she said. "As for your question," she said, "Eric Murphy, the founder of DGS, is a very effective fruitcake."

"Excuse me?"

"He's a fruitcake, a nut-bar, three fries short of a Happy Meal, half-baked, cuckoo for Cocoa Puffs, more crackers than jacks, not quite right in the head, insane in the membrane–"

Israel held up a hand to stop her. "I get that part. What do you mean he's 'effective'?"

"It's kind of like being a functional alcoholic. You see it a lot with geniuses. He's prone to the crazy, but he still managed to build a billion-dollar tech company and design stuff that competes with the best in the world. He built his–" she raised her fingers into air quotes "'realization center' out in the north side of nowhere because he thinks that urban sprawl and pollution dampens the creative mind and kills spontaneity. He also thinks there are far too many distractions from pure thought in the modern world. Hence, the isolationist attitude toward his R&D center. Can't give him too much crap, though. Whatever he's doing seems to be working for him."

Israel grunted. "Guess so, but it still seems a little weird."

"Did you miss the 'prone to crazy' part? Supposedly he's in his late forties and already has arrangements to have his un-embalmed body hermetically sealed into a space-worthy coffin and launched in the direction of the most likely place advanced alien life might exist. He's gambling that they will have the technology to resurrect him."

Israel thought that over, shook his head just in case the thoughts had left any residual insanity behind, and said, "That has got to be a rumor."

Michelle shrugged. "No idea. But I know the guys who are designing exactly that kind of coffin."

"Coffins have designers?"

"Everything has a designer. Can't you tell by how pretty everything is?" The word 'pretty' was stiff with sarcasm.

Israel laughed. "So, you know anything else about Eric Murphy? All I can find is company line crap. Does he live on the island?"

She shook her head. "Nope. He likes to keep his distance from the R&D side of things. He believes that the presence of too intimidating an authority figure will disrupt the creative flow, so he doesn't show his face around there too often. I'm not sure where he lives year-round. Again – billionaire; I imagine he has more than a few choices."

Israel nodded. "Yeah, I suppose." He sat reading over the limited information he could find on the Internet concerning Darkarcher Gaming Sciences and its enigmatic founder. While he read, all the facts of the last few days started swirling through his mind like puzzle pieces that would sometimes connect and fall into place, but not nearly enough to create a picture yet. He sat thinking like that for a time before Michelle said, "Stop it."

He looked up. "Stop what?"

She kept her eyes on her iPad, but said, "Sitting so still like that. It's creepy. Make yourself breathe or blink or something."

Israel consciously drew in a breath and let it out. It was so easy to forget what he was when he was wrapped up in his thoughts. He had grown accustomed to the lack of normal bodily functions that came with his Necrophage nature; he didn't have to breathe or blink or even get up to relieve himself since his body so thoroughly absorbed the protein he consumed. He could sit for days in the same position with no need to shift position. The total absence of personal discomfort beyond those times the hunger was upon him gave Israel the ability to achieve a level of inactivity that unnerved other humans on an instinctive level. It was the perfect stillness of the uncompromising predator.

"Sorry," he said. "It's easy to forget sometimes."

"Yeah, you forget a lot of things sometimes."

He saw her close her eyes tight at that last statement, as though cursing herself. "Shit. Sorry," she said, "never mind."

"Oh, hell no," Israel said. "You don't get to be enigmatic now. If we have an issue I'm unaware of then throw it on the table. I need to know we're cool before we're on the ground."

"We're good, Israel. We're always good, but I promised Allie I'd keep my mouth shut. I just wish my mouth always consulted with me first."

"Allie?" Israel said. "What about her?"

"Nothing," Michelle said, a heavy frown coming to her face. "Look, I'm sorry, really. I'm totally cool with you and I totally have your back. This is just stupid, sentimental sister stuff and I promised I'd keep it to myself so, please, let it go."

Israel suspected he knew what was on her mind and realized he'd rather not get into it either. "Okay," he said. "So long as we're good."

Michelle nodded and gave him a thumbs up. Another minute passed in silence and she said, "So, do you want me to try and dig around for some data on Murphy? Do you think he's got something to do with the conduit?"

"Big-ass technology firm on the exact island Pythia says this thing is most likely heading for? Yeah, I'd have to say that's a fair place to start looking."

"Think it's the Progeny again?"

Israel shrugged. "No clue. I'll run it by Stone once we've landed and see what he thinks."

They sat in silence then, each busying themselves with their handheld devices and Israel making sure to keep air moving through his lungs and shift position slightly at random times. It wasn't long before they could hear Stone begin to snore from farther up the cabin and they shared a smile at the older man's rumbling breath.

They rode like that for well over an hour before Israel's sensitive hearing started picking up on the sound of rain against the jet's fuselage. He was just about to say something when the pilot's voice came from the overhead speakers.

"We are about ten minutes out from Jasper Island," he said, "but it looks like we're running into an unexpected weather cell. Why don't you folks go ahead and buckle up for safety while Dave and myself try and get us on the ground as gently as possible. Also, somebody please wake up Mr. Stone and repeat the message to him because I know from experience he can sleep through close-proximity thunder, so I doubt he heard a word of that."

"Keep talking like that, Stuart," Stone half-shouted without opening his eyes, "and I'll be forced to write a scathing letter to the airline's customer service department."

"Well, lo and behold," the pilot said. "I'm going to take your consciousness as a good omen. Buckle up and stow your gear, guys."

Stone got up and joined Israel and Michelle in the mid-cabin quartet of seats. He settled in next to Michelle and they all buckled their safety belts. Within seconds of doing so, the plane started shuddering as winds buffeted it from every direction. Rain pelted hard enough against the exterior that Israel was sure he could have heard it even without his heightened senses. The plane dropped in a lurching dip and leveled off just as quickly.

Michelle gripped the armrests of her chair until it looked like the leather would rip under her fingertips. "Well," she said, her voice strained with barely leashed anxiety, "this is fun."

"Hand-to-hand training is fun," Stone said. "Tough Mudders are fun. This is a roller coaster with no tracks. Not fun."

The plane shuddered. Israel looked out the window closest to his seat and saw the night beyond the rain-streaked glass. Heavy clouds whipped past the plane in dark grays and silvers in his night vision. There was no break in the cloud cover that he could see and flashes of lightning lit up the near distance, momentarily washing out his vision in a cloud of white.

The plane dipped and shuddered, banked and tilted. Israel kept watching the exterior. Another flash, this one closer, lit up his sight. Thunder boomed like invisible explosions. He noticed something he didn't like.

"Stone," he said, "the lightning."

"I see it," Stone said. "Usually comes with thunderstorms."

"No, smartass," Israel said. "It's getting closer."

"It's what?" Michelle shouted.

Israel pointed out the window just as the overhead speakers went live.

"Jasper Island tower, this is Gulfstream 2267. We are on approach and need instructions. Please respond, over!" There was only static and the storm for a moment. Then, "Godammit! Okay, everybody listen up. The storm is throwing off the instruments and the tower isn't responding so I'm taking us in low and–"

There was a booming crack and a blinding flash as the first bolt struck the plane. The speaker was filled with the sound of the pilot's curses and then nothing as the lights flickered and went dark. The plane shuddered into a dive and Israel could feel it lurching as the pilot and co-pilot struggled to regain control. The engines roared like beasts in agony with the strain. Over it all, Israel could smell smoke and the acrid stench of scorched wiring.

Another flash and boom overloaded his senses again

as a second bolt hit them. The jet banked hard and he felt it nose downward, engines still screaming, smoke starting to billow into the cabin. Even through the closed cockpit door and the cacophony of sound, Israel could hear the pilot screaming "Mayday! Mayday! Mayday!"

The plane nosed down, lurched up, and gradually nosed down again as it was whipped side to side like the storm was a cat playing with a Gulfstream-shaped mouse.

"Jasper Island, we are going down!" the pilot said. "Repeat, we are going down!"

Israel slapped one hand against his seatbelt and released the latch. He moved fast and crossed the short space between his seat and his friends' seats, inertia aiding him as the nosedive pushed him toward the rear of the plane. He collided with his companions' seats and spread his arms wide, clamping one hand on the back of Michelle's seat, another on the back of Stone's, and held on tight. He fought gravity and inertia and covered their bodies with as much of his as he could manage.

"Israel, what are–" Stone started to protest, but the rest of the words were lost under the sound of screaming engines, rushing air, and the deafening crack of another lightning bolt stabbing into the doomed aircraft.

CHAPTER NINE

The first thing he smelled as his consciousness returned to him was briny saltwater. Below that was the chemical reek of fuel and the sweet scent of flesh next to his face. The hunger was on him like a thirst that parched every cell in his body, but Israel pushed the feeling aside and focused on his surroundings.

There was smoke everywhere. Water splashed from somewhere behind him and smelled of old fish. Against his chest, he still held the two seats that his friends were strapped into. Israel could tell they were alive, though not conscious, by their scent. He let go of the seats and looked around.

Stuart had managed to bring the jet in at a slight angle near the shallows off the Jasper Island coast. Israel realized that his expert piloting was probably the only reason anyone had survived. Somehow, though, the Gulfstream had gotten spun around during the impact and was now pointing out to open sea. There was a huge break in the fuselage and the front of the plane was completely submerged, including the cockpit.

Israel splashed through the knee-deep water and dove

into the deeper water at the front of the aircraft. His night vision was blurred underwater, but it was enough to see by. He made his way to the cockpit door and wrenched it open. The pilot and co-pilot were both there, still strapped into their seats. He couldn't tell if it was the crash that had killed them or if they had drowned, but they were both far beyond help.

Israel moved back toward the mid-cabin seating. As he broke the surface of the deeper water, he felt the aircraft shift beneath his feet with a sharp, tearing crack. He watched as the rupture in the fuselage grew a foot wider and the water rose around his chest. He realized they must have come down on a drop-off of some sort and the water filling the nose was creating enough weight to break the already damaged plane in half. He looked up and saw black ocean already climbing up Stone's and Michelle's knees.

He rushed forward and shook Stone. "Wake up!" he snapped. "Come on, Stone, move your ass!"

The bald man's eyes rolled open and he looked around with a pained, groggy expression. "What–" he said. "Where the hell?"

"Shake it off," Israel said. "We have to go."

Stone's eyes widened as the situation flooded in on him. "Stuart!" he said. "We have to–"

"I tried," Israel said as he snapped Michelle's buckle free. "He's gone, man."

Stone shouted a curse and then doubled it when the plane shifted beneath them. Splinters of steel and fiberglass snapped into the water as the break widened.

Stone got up from his seat, the water coming all the way to the smaller man's armpits, and said, "Is Michelle all right?"

Israel pulled her from the seat and lifted her with one arm. His night vision showed him the blood pulsing through her major arteries in a kind of sepia tint beneath her silver and gray skin. "She's alive," he said, pushing aside the dark notions the sight of that coursing lifeblood inspired in his mind. "Can you see the break in the plane?"

Stone looked around for a moment, then said, "Got it. Let me—"

The plane shuddered and slid again. Stone staggered, went under for an instant, but then popped his head back up. "Go!" Israel said. "Through the break!"

Stone didn't argue or hesitate. As soon as they cleared the massive tear in the aircraft, they were both treading water. Rain pelted them like hard, cold stones that shattered against their skin and the sea splashed and churned as though it were in pain. Wind whipped the stinging rain into their faces and carried the sound of thunder every few seconds. Lightning lit up the sky between the thunderclaps and silhouetted roiling black clouds. Israel had grown up in the flatlands of Illinois; he was no stranger to thunderstorms. This was unlike anything he had ever seen before, though.

"I can't see, mate!" Stone shouted, spitting seawater at the end of it. "Which way?"

Israel looked around and spotted a small, rocky outcropping of land that stood out against the lashing waves. "There," he shouted, nodding toward the sliver of land.

"Where?" Stone shouted. "I can't see!"

Israel cursed and used the arm he was treading water with to reach out and grab Stone. He immediately sank beneath the surface but didn't worry; people who didn't need to breathe couldn't drown, after all. With one hand holding Stone and the other holding Michelle's head above water, he pushed them together. The waves and thrashing currents threw him around, but he managed to make it happen.

Stone seemed to get the idea instantly and grabbed Michelle in both arms and rolled onto his back with her on his chest so that they were both facing the furious sky. Israel took a firm grip on Stone's collar and started swimming. The water washed over them, pulled them under, and tossed them about, but Israel kicked and stroked with his free hand until they reached enough of a shallow area that they could walk, Stone carrying Michelle and Israel helping Stone stay on his feet in the shifting ocean sand. Once they were inland enough, Stone collapsed next to a set of large boulders. He coughed hard, but he managed to place Michelle on the soaked sand as gently as he could. Israel stepped away a few paces and spent some time purging water from his lungs and stomach. This done, he returned to Stone and shouted, "How is she?"

One of the standard issue items for all Sentry Group agents was a state-of-the-art smartphone that came with a thick, waterproof case rumored to be tough enough to stop small caliber bullets. Stone's had been in his pocket and he had it out now with the flashlight app active. He was shining it over Michelle's still form. There was a large gash across the hairline on the left side of her forehead. Blood poured from the wound, but was instantly washed away in the driving rain. Israel was grateful that the storm was bad enough that he could only catch the faintest whiffs of it.

The light clicked off and Stone held a hand over the cut, putting what pressure he could on it. "Pulse is strong, pupils are good, and she's breathing steady as near as I can tell in this shit," he shouted over the wind. There was a flash of lightning and Stone suddenly squinted at Israel.

"What?" Israel said.

"Turn around, mate. Show me your back."

Israel did as he was told. He saw the light come on again and heard Stone say, "Oh, bloody hell. Please tell me you've got some of Allison's Mighty Meat Sticks on you."

"I've got five or six," he said. "There's more on the plane. Why?"

"Because there's about a dozen rather large pieces of shrapnel sticking out of your back. You honestly can't feel that?"

Israel shrugged. "I've been too busy to notice."

Stone laughed at that. The sound of it carried through the storm's tumult. Israel found it to be rather comforting in spite of their circumstances. "Just leave them," he shouted. "Until the storm passes, at least."

"Hell, no," Stone said, returning to Michelle's side. "We don't need you leaking fluids around the bird here, and we damned sure don't need you going feral on us. Dig out one of your candy bars, mate; we're doing this now."

Stone lifted Michelle and propped her up as comfortably as he could manage to keep what water he could out of her face. Then he led Israel a short distance away, shouting "Just in case we make a mess!"

Israel nodded and knelt in the sand facing away from Stone. He took down one of the protein bars in three bites and opened a second, taking smaller bites from this one while Stone tugged and pulled at whatever assortment of things was lodged in Israel's back. Israel couldn't feel what Stone was doing as he worked, but his night vision showed him black lines of thin blood rolling down his sleeves and mixing with the rain to drip onto the rocky sand. Israel knew that without a protein-based body to exist in, the Necrophage DNA would break down in under a minute, so he wasn't concerned about contaminating the ocean.

The primary reason that Stone had been designated as Israel's partner was the fact that he was immune to Israel's Necrophage DNA. Stone was, in fact, not what could strictly be called human. Many years earlier, a much younger Olivia Warburton and a group of friends had discovered Stone in a secret prison run by a group of religious fanatics who were convinced that Stone was the gatekeeper to some twisted version of the Christian Heaven. They were utterly wrong about that and were, in fact, the reason he had been stranded on Earth.

"Just looks like pieces of the fuselage," Stone said. "Probably from that giant bloody hole in the cabin. I thought you'd lost your mind when you got up and grabbed us, but I suppose now I should thank you."

"No need. You'd have done the same."

"Wouldn't have helped, mate. I'm not as tall as you."

They both laughed as the storm raged around them and Israel's thin, dark blood dripped into the cold sea.

The storm continued for hours more. Stone sat huddled with Michelle, his jacket draped over them in what amounted to a pointless attempt at shelter. The woman was breathing in a steady rhythm and she moaned occasionally while her head rested against Stone's chest. Stone, for his part, seemed to have dozed off despite the lingering thunderstorm.

Israel stood in the steady rain and wondered at his friend's ability to sleep no matter what the circumstances. Stone had told him that he had learned at a young age that warriors should grab rest whenever the opportunity arose and it was a lesson that he'd learned well. It wasn't one Israel needed to embrace, though, since he didn't need to sleep anymore.

He flexed his abdomen and coughed up the last bit of saltwater from his lungs and spat it toward the surf, careful not to get any on the assortment of black and silver cases that were stacked on the sand next to him. While his friends slept, he had gone back into the water and swam to the crashed jet. Though mostly submerged, it seemed to have finally settled on the bottom. He'd swum into the cargo area to recover what gear he could find and discovered that one of the lightning strikes had started a fire in that area. A lot of the cases were warped or cracked from the heat and had filled with water. He had grabbed everything he could and dragged it back to the tiny island where he sat and waited on the storm to pass and his friends to rouse.

The sky was still gray, but the rain had subsided to the point of a steady downpour instead of the stinging deluge it had been. The clouds were still thick and gray overhead, but the worst of the storm seemed to have moved out into the Atlantic. Not like a storm normally would, though. Usually storms formed and moved across the Earth's surface by the dictation of whatever atmospheric circumstances it was subjected to. This storm, though, had moved away from Jasper Island in every direction until it formed a ring of black, lightning-filled fury that surrounded the island like a barricade. It was what Israel imagined being in the eye of a hurricane would be like, but there had been no indication of a hurricane anywhere when the jet had taken off. Israel didn't know what this storm was, but it was a long way from normal.

"Hey," Michelle said, her voice thick and drowsy. "How come we aren't dead?"

Israel looked back at his friends. Stone was blinking himself awake as well. "Stone's too stubborn to die and I'm already there," Israel said. "You just got lucky."

Michelle nodded and sat up, wincing. "My head really freaking hurts," she said.

"You took a nasty bump," Stone said. "Don't move around too quickly. Catch some of the rainwater to slake your thirst, if you can."

Michelle gave him a tiny nod and said, "Yeah, I'll just sit here for a minute and do that."

Stone rose and joined Israel. Israel nodded a silent question at Michelle and Stone returned the nod. "She needs a proper doctor," he said in a low voice, "but I think she's good for now. What's all this?" He gestured at the pile of equipment.

"What I could salvage from the crash. There was a fire

back there so a lot of it's damaged, but I got what I could. Damn good thing we hit the water, I think. There's a real good chance we all would've gotten roasted otherwise."

"I promise you that was Stuart's doing," Stone said. "He was a good man. Been flying for Sentry for nearly two decades. Flew me all over the bloody world."

"Sorry, man."

Stone looked to the sky and tightened his jaw. "He lived like a warrior and died a good death. I think he would've been satisfied with that. So what kind of shit-storm are we in now?"

"Well, I'm not sure about the shit part, but this storm is a weird one."

Israel pointed out the circling wall of clouds and shared his speculations about it. Stone nodded when he was finished and said, "You're right, there's no way Stuart would have flown near anything like this. No sane pilot would." He continued to study the wall of furious black and gray. "That is a lot of bloody lightning. More than could be natural, I think."

"Do you think it could be the conduit that's causing this?"

Stone shrugged. "No idea. I've never heard of weather coming through a breach, though."

"When Michelle's up to it, we'll run it by her."

Stone nodded. "Not sure when, but high tide will come with morning. I still can't see too well, but I'll bet my bar tab that this little island will be mostly under water when that happens. Any idea which way we need to go?"

Israel nodded. "It looks like the island proper is a few hundred yards in that direction. I saw a pretty rocky beach and a couple of small houses with boat docks, but I couldn't make out any real details. I thought I saw a light-house farther down the coast, but I can't be sure."

"You tried your phone?"

"First thing," Israel said. "Zero signal, even after the

storm let up. I looked for a sat-phone in all of this, but no joy."

Stone nodded. "They kept those in the cockpit."

"You want me to go back?"

Stone shook his head. "Don't bother; sea water's done for those. They weren't kept in watertight storage."

"Okay," Israel said, "let's go through all of this and see what we can salvage. As soon as there's enough light for you guys to see by, we'll make for the island. Maybe somebody in one of those houses has a landline we can use."

"I don't have a better plan," Stone said. "Let's get to it. How are you holding up?"

Israel knew what he meant. He wasn't worried about Israel being injured – the wounds in his back were fully healed over by now – but he was worried about the hunger. Israel nodded and said, "I'm good. I can feel it, but I'm solid. Most of my protein bars were slagged by the fire, but I managed to salvage a dozen. I'm going to ration them, so as long as I don't have to close another Leticia-sized breach I should be good."

Stone slapped him on the shoulder and said, "Good man. Let's see what we've got here."

They started opening cases and going through the salvaged gear. Most of what they had was the electronics gear that Michelle had spent all those hours selecting and now announced as useless either because of damage or because the components they worked in conjunction with were missing. By the time they had finished, there was enough light to see normally and the rain had slackened to a thick, spitting mist. They had managed to salvage two Glock 21 pistols, ten clips worth of spare ammunition, a laptop in a reinforced field case, five flashlights, a small backpack of first aid supplies – not all of which were usable – and an assortment of other electronic gear that Michelle said she might be able to assemble into something useful if she could find a place to work. They consolidated everything they could into as few cases as possible and left the rest.

"Hope there's some electricity over there," Michelle said, nodding toward the island. "My phone needs a charge in a bad way."

Israel glanced at his. The tiny battery icon was bright yellow and well below a third of its capacity. "Same here."

Water washed up around Israel's feet and he glanced toward the shore; Stone had been right about the tide. He looked back toward Jasper Island. Mist hung over the island like a gray shroud. Beyond the island, the black, lightning-thick ring of the storm stood like a prison wall. Israel focused on the nearest shoreline and pointed. "There," he said. "See that little stretch of beach at the bottom of that cliff? Between those two rock formations?"

The others looked where he was pointing and nodded.

"I can see the high tide line from here," he continued. "Swim for that and you'll have enough beach to stand on. I think I can see a path through the rocks heading up the cliff, too, but I'm not sure."

"What if it's not there?" Michelle asked.

"We'll deal with that then," Stone said. "We need to get on the main island."

"I'll grab all the gear," Israel said. "You guys start swimming and I'll meet you there. Don't wander off without me."

They nodded and splashed into the water. Israel watched until he saw them start to swim, trying to judge when the water got deep. He draped cases over his shoulders and neck by their straps. The few that didn't have straps he held in his hands or under his arms. When he was ready to go, he looked down at himself and smirked. "Look out world," he muttered, "here comes the bellhop from the black lagoon."

He shook his head and started walking.

CHAPTER TEN

Walking along the bottom of the ocean, Israel decided, was an enormous pain in the ass. Doing so while loaded down with equipment was even more so. It wasn't the weight so much – many of the cases seemed to float – but rather it was the fact that the ocean pushed and pulled his burden in a variety of directions that caused him to stagger and stumble when his footing was already tenuous at best. This wasn't the pristine sand of some tropical sport-diving location; the ocean floor off Jasper Island was rough, rocky, and seemed determined that it break at least one of his ankles. He trudged on, though, his father's voice in his head: "If you gotta go through Hell, son, the secret is to just keep going. You'll come out the other side eventually." He smiled to himself and wondered what his dad would say if he could see him now.

By the time he made it to shore, he was draped in a variety of sea plants and other detritus. He came out of the water slowly so he wouldn't fall, and found himself facing Michelle and Stone. The two Sentry agents were wearing grins far larger than Israel felt was appropriate. He wanted to tell them where they could put their grins, but there was too much water in his lungs.

He deposited the cases in a loose pile next to the waterline and went behind one of the stone outcroppings to cough up all the seawater. As he inhaled to cough the final time, a scent came to him. It was faint and fleeting, but it blew on the mist-heavy breeze like a half-heard whisper. It was the sickly sweet aroma of decaying flesh. Israel just shrugged and went back to his friends, guessing that any number of things could have died up and down the beach. He had just gotten the last of the seaweed off his jacket when Michelle said, "What now?"

"Find a way up this cliff and get to one of the houses we saw," Stone said. "Hopefully get our hands on a landline and contact Olivia."

Israel stared upward, judging the cliff's height. "No way I could jump that," he said. "I could climb it, though."

Stone shook his head. The motion flicked chilled water from his thick beard like a dog shaking itself. "Stay with us, mate. Don't exert yourself unless you have to. Let's do this like normal folks until we get a handle on the situation."

Israel agreed. If he tried to climb the rocks and slipped, which was very likely considering how wet everything was, then he'd fall and almost certainly break bones. His body would heal, but the energy cost could be enormous and he would use up his remaining protein bars in no time. Stone was right: It was better to do this the old fashioned way.

They gathered up their gear. Israel insisted Stone and Michelle take the pistols since he was more than able to defend himself without one. All Sentry Group employees who had even the slightest possibility of doing field work were trained to use the Glocks and were required to repeat that training annually. Michelle was no exception, and the way she handled the weapon as she checked the clip and slid it back into its waistband holster told Israel she had kept up her skills.

Israel ditched the case the weapons had come in and used its strap to tie some of the others into an easier-to-handle bundle. He looped his left hand through the strap and slung the cluster of items over his shoulder. Michelle had the case with the laptop and Stone had two cases, one over each shoulder in a double, cross-body carry that would still let him get to his sidearm.

"I hope you're right about this stuff coming in handy, Michelle," he said. "It's bloody heavy."

"I hadn't noticed," Israel said, smiling.

"Oh, shut up," Stone said. Then to Michelle he said, "What do you think you'll be able to do with it?"

"I'm hoping I can cannibalize some parts and get some kind of signal booster working. If I can get what I need, I might be able to punch a hole through that mess." She gestured toward the distant storm.

"That's why we can't get a signal? I didn't think weather screwed up modern cell phones," Israel said.

"It doesn't," Michelle said, frowning. "But that's the only thing I can think of. There's supposed to be a cell tower on this island. We should be getting some kind of signal. The fact that we're not..." She shrugged. "It could be a lot of things."

"Well," Stone said, "we aren't accomplishing a bloody thing standing here and I, for one, am ready to find a dry spot and a few dozen towels. Let's get moving."

So they went, weaving around salt-sprayed boulders and leaving footprints in the coarse, wet sand. It took them ten minutes of this before Stone spotted the narrow crease of a footpath that disappeared at a steep but manageable angle up and through the cliff face. They started up it at a slow, trudging pace. They took their time not only because of the steep angle, but also the plentiful and very loose stones that littered the path. Israel felt fine, but he could tell the wet, the cold, and the exertion were all beginning to take a heavy toll on his companions. Stone was in the front, followed by Michelle, with Israel bringing up the rear. Israel watched them both closely as they walked, ready to catch or carry them if they slipped and fell. It turned out to be all right, though, and they made it to the top without incident.

As soon as they reached the overlook, the breeze picked up slightly, swirling the mist in the gray morning light like the ghosts of gossamer-clad dancers. The mist was thick enough that Israel couldn't make out many details about the terrain, but he did see one of the houses he had spotted earlier a short walk away across a large, open yard. Stands of well-spaced trees filled the house's backyard, which Israel was certain ended at the cliff's edge. An unpaved driveway led to the house from a pitted asphalt road that disappeared into the mist in both directions. There were no vehicles that he could see either on the road or parked near the house.

Stone and Michelle didn't seem to notice any of this. They had stopped next to a sign that declared the path unsafe and closed to public traffic. Both were bent over slightly, breathing hard. Israel remembered that feeling, but couldn't decide if he missed it or not.

Stone glanced at the sign and grunted. "Leave it to me to pick the worst possible way up."

"We're here," Michelle said. "The rest doesn't matter now."

Israel pointed. "House is over there, but I don't see any people around or lights on."

Stone looked over and nodded. "Me neither. What about your sniffer?"

"Nothing really. This breeze is pretty stiff coming off the ocean, so mostly I just smell salt water and fish."

"Fair enough. Let's get to that house and find a bloody phone."

They collected their burdens again and started moving

toward the house. Israel noticed his friends' breath as they exhaled and realized it was colder than he thought. He considered giving Michelle his jacket, but dismissed the idea when he realized that the shrapnel had penetrated the leather in the back and he had bled – though 'oozed' might be a more apt description – into the fabric.

The blood he had left on the tiny spit of land they had sheltered on wasn't a worry because he knew it would wash out to sea and break down in a matter of seconds. What was soaked into his jacket, though, he was less certain about. He made a mental note to find some new clothes and burn what he was wearing.

Stone had taken the lead with Israel and Michelle a few steps behind him. They had gotten about a third of the way to the house when he slowed and held up a hand for them to stop. Israel saw Michelle start to ask a question and touched her arm, shaking his head; he'd worked with Stone enough to know when the older man wanted some quiet. As though to prove Israel's point, Stone dropped to one knee and place his left palm flat against the ground.

In Stone's home world, he had been something called a Stonecaller. Israel wasn't sure what that meant exactly, but it involved being tied to the land in some way that allowed Stone to manipulate the rock and soil. He didn't do it very often because it was physically taxing for him, but there were a few tricks he could pull off that were easier. Israel had seen this one before. It was something Stone would do if he wanted to see if they were being watched by someone from cover. It wouldn't help him locate someone in the house, but anyone with his feet on the ground had a fair chance of getting spotted.

Stone rose and eased the Glock from its holster. "We aren't alone," he said. "Something feels very wrong." He turned toward the fenced field and the trees that were across the road from the house. Mist hung heavy over the tall grasses.

The breeze shifted so that it was less from the ocean and more parallel to the coast.

Israel smelled it then – decay, the tang of raw meat, and the metallic sweetness of spilled blood. The mists moved gently with the shifting breeze and pulled away from the field like a curtain to reveal the figures standing there. Men, women, some older children – they were standing perfectly still, perfectly silent. Their clothes were wet and streaked with dark stains. Even from the distance, their bodies showed ragged wounds, some of which Israel was sure should have been fatal.

Michelle had drawn her weapon. She stared with wide eyes at the gathering in the field and said, "Are those–"

"Yes," Stone hissed. "Quiet now."

It was too late for that; the parting mist had revealed them. Heads filled with black eyes didn't so much turn in their direction as spasm that way. With jerky steps that seemed to loosen into a loping run, the things in the field came for them.

"Run, Michelle," Stone said. "Get to the house." He was calm, his voice clear and controlled.

"But–" she said.

"Go. We'll be right behind you."

They were moving faster now. Israel counted eleven of them. They were nearly to the split rail fence that separated the field from the road.

"You, too," Israel said to Stone as he dropped the bundle of cases.

"No, I'm with you."

"And if that house isn't clear?" Israel said. "This isn't what she does, man. She'll need you."

Stone hesitated, then said, "Bloody hell. Fine. Slow them down as much as you can, but, dammit, stay with us. Don't go too far into the dark."

Israel nodded and ran toward the field as Stone took off after Michelle.

Israel sprinted for the fence and reached it ahead of the oncoming monsters. With two quick jerks, he ripped one of the heavy, wooden cross rails from the fence and held it like a club, ready to swing and crush the first of the things that reached him. He watched them coming – black lips, staggering steps that seemed to cover more ground than they should, gray skin, black tongues squirming at the air as though tasting it. The most unnerving thing, he thought in the seconds before they were upon him, was how quiet they were. Not at all the hissing, moaning terrors from the movies, but rather as silent as the graves they had been denied. They came over him like a wave of raw meat and snapping teeth.

Then, they parted and ran right past him.

Israel had been ready to fight, ready to swing his club and defend his friends. Instead, he spent a moment in shocked silence as the crowd ignored him and leapt or fell over the fence on a direct path for Stone and Michelle.

Israel shook off his surprise, cursed, and swung his club at the last of the monsters as it clambered over the fence. He didn't pay attention to whether it was a male or a female, young or old. Stone had taught him that when fighting undead, you should only see a target. That made it easier.

The heavy wood hit the thing directly on top of the head. The skull shattered and folded around the makeshift weapon like a lump of clay around a potter's tool. All Necrophage, Israel included, depended on nervous tissue to function. Do enough damage to that and the undead in question was put down permanently. That was one of the few things the movies had gotten right. There was no scream or death rattle as Israel pulled his weapon free; the zombie simply slumped against the fence and stopped moving as its blackened brain matter ran down its face.

Israel didn't spare it a glance, though. He vaulted the fence and ran after the other undead. He held the club across his body as he ran. Even though he overtook the lumbering monsters easily enough, he didn't have the footing or leverage he needed to make the kinds of head-shots he knew would put them down. Instead, he poured on the speed until he was a few yards ahead of the pack and stopped suddenly, his hiking boots skidding on the gravel driveway.

He turned fast and swung his long club in a low, wide arch close to knee level. He knew he couldn't beat them down with blows to the head while they were on the move, so he figured he could slow them down first.

The club connected with legs and Israel heard bones snap as it did. Four of the creatures flipped forward in the air with the blows and went down on shattered legs. A fifth ran close to Israel and he sent it sprawling with a quick jab into its ribcage, but that one leapt quickly to its feet and kept moving toward Stone and Michelle.

Israel took a precious second to look at the four he had dropped and saw that their legs, either one or both, were twisted into unnatural angles with black bone showing through tears in their skin. Though they struggled to rise, the bones simply would not support them. They were re-duced to crawling on ripped, gray fingers toward their prey.

Israel took off after the remaining six; he could come back for these.

Israel poured on the speed. The first of the monsters had reached the front yard and was sprinting toward the steps leading up to the porch. Michelle and Stone both stood at the top of those steps in professional shooting stances. Two gunshots rang out as the attacker's head rup-tured and it skidded to a stop at the base of the steps.

Israel closed the distance with the one he had jabbed in the ribs as more shots rang out. He jumped into the air and came down behind and slightly to one side of the monster as he drove the end of the wooden rail into the back of the thing's head. His weight and momentum drove the club through the neck and into the meat at the base of the skull, forcing the creature face-first into the dirt where it spasmed and then grew still.

Israel looked up and saw the last of the creatures that was still running get one foot on the bottom step before a series of gunshots tore its head to ribbons.

Stone and Michelle both ejected their clips and loaded fresh ones, their eyes still scanning the yard. Even from where he was standing, Israel could see the barely controlled horror in Michelle's expression. She moved smoothly, though, and he thought she was holding it together pretty well.

Israel dropped the club and walked over to join his friends. He stopped at the bottom of the stairs among the bodies and looked up at them. "They ignored me," he said. "They thought I was one of them." It was harder to say than he thought it would be.

"You're no more like them than Michelle here is like a serial killer. You might be the same species, but you damn sure aren't the same kind of that species. Now, get your ass up here. We need to clear this house."

Israel gestured back over his shoulder. "I left a few crawling up the driveway. Save your ammo; I'll deal with it."

Without waiting for a reply, he returned to his work.

CHAPTER ELEVEN

Israel stared down at the last of the dead things. He had it pinned with his foot in the center of its back and the fence rail poised above it, ready to deliver the final stabbing blow. He hesitated, though, and watched it struggle, oblivious to anything but driving need to get to the living flesh that it could sense so very close by. It clawed at the ground, the only sound it made the scratching of exposed finger bone over hard-packed dirt. Israel studied the dead thing and wondered if the day would ever come when Stone would be standing over him, waiting to deliver the attack that would end him for good.

He shook the thought away, raised his weapon higher, and tensed for the killing stroke.

"Stop that!"

The words rode up his spine on a wave of prickling current. It startled him and he spun to face the speaker, but found only the empty, mist-shrouded yard. He looked around the area, searching for any sign of another person, but saw no one. The only sounds were the monster's scratching and the clatter Michelle and Stone made as they searched the house. He shook his head and went back to his task.

"I said to stop that!"

He whirled again, feeling that same prickle in his spine. This time, though, he realized that the words had not been on the air so much as in his head. It wasn't like hearing a voice – there was no pitch or timber that could mark it as male or female – but more like having words he didn't want to think shoved into his head.

"Who's there?" he said. "Show yourself."

"Show my– Wait. You aren't the one who talks – he's here. Who are you? What are you doing on my island?"

"Perfect," he said. "Now I'm going insane."

"I asked you a question. It's rude not to answer it. Who are you?"

"Fine," Israel said. "I'll play along with the voice in my head. First, though," he said and he put his foot in the center of the monster's back again and raised the fence rail, instantly bringing it down and ending the thing's struggling.

"I told you not to do that! Why would you do that to your brother?"

"My what?" Israel said. "Sorry, Voice, but that was not my brother. I'm one of those privileged only children."

Israel felt the prickle in his spine shift slightly and he didn't hear words this time, but felt a sense of confusion. Not his own, which was growing by the second all on its lonesome, but more like he was recognizing it on someone else's face.

"You aren't one of my clique. Who are you? You feel... familiar."

"You first. You say I'm rude, but you're the one getting into my head. That tops all other invasion of privacy records, I think."

"I don't have to tell you anything. This is my island. I make the rules here."

"Fine, but I'm not calling you 'Voice.' That's just too on

the mark. I think I'll call you..." Israel thought it over for a moment. "I know – Sybil. Not sure if you're a he, a she, or an it, but I'm going with Sybil."

"I don't like that name. Pick a different one."

"Nope. Sorry, Sybil. You're stuck with it. You had the chance to contribute, but you blew it. Besides, you're my hallucination so I can call you whatever I want."

"I am not a hallucination! Show me where you are and I'll send some of my clique to prove that!"

Israel opened his mouth to speak and then stopped. He didn't know much about mental illness or hallucinations, but it didn't seem like he should be able to make a voice in his head angry, much less have it threaten him. He started to wonder if this wasn't what he thought it was.

"What do you mean your 'clique'?" he asked.

"They're mine. My clique, like the one you just murdered. Why did you do that? I can talk to you – you're like them – but you're not the same. Who are you? You feel like the tall man, but different. You're–" The sensation under Israel's skin shifted again, this time to something like realization. *"Oh, god. It's you."*

Then, the prickling was gone. It vanished from his perceptions like steam into warm air. "Sybil?" Israel said. "Sybil? Come on, we were just getting to know each other."

He waited a full minute. There was no reply.

Israel dropped the splintered, bloody fence rail next to the corpse at his feet and jogged up to the porch. As he mounted the stairs, he yelled, "Hey, guys! Guess who's hearing voices now!"

"So let me get this straight," Michelle said, dropping her third damp towel onto the large coffee table, "we're on an island that's in the midst of a Necrophage infestation and you think a voice in your head is controlling them."

"Pretty much," Israel said from the window where he

had set up to watch the road. "And you can just say 'zombie.' It won't hurt my feelings."

"Good to know. I would really like a drink now."

"That's makes two of us," Stone said, "but whoever lived here was a teetotaler. Not so much as a beer in the fridge."

"Michelle, you think all of this has anything to do with the conduit?" Israel asked.

Michelle opened her mouth to speak, then closed it again. Her face took on the focused but relaxed expression that was the sure sign she had gone into her own head to think. The only thing that gave away the flurry of activity in her mind was the way her eyes flicked to and fro in their sockets. It always looked to Israel like she was sorting through thoughts or ideas and moving them around with those eyes.

"Okay," she said after a minute, her eyes still downcast and twitching, "is it possible that a micro-breach occurred on this island and let something Necrophagic in nature into our world where it started this outbreak? Yes. However, the possibility of that thing communicating in English and having enough of a mind to communicate at all, much less telepathically, is remote in the extreme, so we will discard that as improbable. More likely the outbreak is Earthly in origin and started on this island or some conveyance to this island prior to the storm hitting. Is the storm part of the outbreak or related in some tangential way? Possibly, but not immediately relevant, so put that aside for the moment.

"That leaves us with the supposition that the outbreak originated in the general area of the island, but does not offer an explanation for this 'Sybil' voice that Israel is hearing. Alternately, Israel could be going insane, but there is no other indication of that disease process, though we must take into account that the process may be altered by Israel's own Necrophage physiology. Put that aside as well. If proximity to the conduit released Inner Dark energy onto the island and an individual with the Necrophage bloodline was Awakened, he would have simply succumbed to the hunger like every other member of his species. Correction: every member except Israel. Is it possible that a second Necrophage Paragon has Awakened on the island? Possible, but improbable to the Nth degree. No, can't run with that. Fact: There is an unnatural storm surrounding this island. Fact: There is a zombie outbreak on this island. High probability: A transdimensional conduit is syncing up with this island for reasons and through mechanisms unknown. Probability: A newly Awakened individual is communicating with Israel through some unrecorded psychic means. Lesser probability: Israel is losing his grip on reality and hallucinating." Michelle kept looking down, her eyes darting about.

Israel and Stone shared a look. Israel shrugged and gestured for Stone to talk to her.

"So, Michelle," Stone said, "do you believe the conduit caused any of this?"

She looked up at Stone and said, "No. If it's related at all, it's only peripherally so. I think there's more than one thing going on here, I just don't have enough information to make a solid determination as to what those things could be."

"Seriously?" Israel said. "I get the Rain Man response, but that's all he gets?"

"What?" Michelle asked.

"Nothing, lass," Stone said, smiling. "You were just thinking out loud again."

"All right," Israel said, "let's assume for a minute that I'm not going crazy. Is there a bloodline that can read minds?"

"He– She? Sybil didn't read your mind," Michelle said.

"How's that?" Israel asked.

"You said Sybil kept asking your name, right? Well, if

she – or whatever – was reading your mind, she wouldn't have needed to ask. She could have just plucked the name out of your memory. That's one of the reasons I don't think you're losing it. This is really more Allie's specialty, but I don't think that hallucinations are usually that inquisitive. What Sybil did was telepathy – mind-to-mind communication. It's really a weaker form of what you're talking about. She could put thoughts into your head, but only get back what you want her to hear. Mind-reading typically refers to something a little more invasive where the reader can get at more hidden, deeper thoughts. Think of it as having a polite conversation versus being interrogated."

"Okay, I get the distinction, but my question stands: What bloodline can do this kind of thing?"

"I was in Italy back in the late eighties," Stone said. "I saw a Mage do what Michelle is talking about. That was a contact thing, though. She had to prepare the spell and touch the person we were questioning. It wasn't like what you're describing."

"Empathic sensitivities are not unheard of in the Infernal, Fae, and Seraphim bloodlines," Michelle said. "Straight up telepathy, though? I can't think of a single case."

"Is anybody else tired of never knowing what we're dealing with?" Israel said.

"That's the life, mate," Stone said with a grin. "And don't pretend for a moment that you don't love the puzzle. We all know better than that."

Israel shrugged. "Fair enough."

Somewhere in the back of the house, Israel heard a creak of wood. It was faint enough that he was sure Stone and Michelle were oblivious, but his hearing far surpassed theirs. He tilted his head, catching Stone's eye. The shorter man shot him a quizzical look, but Israel held up a finger in a twirling motion as a signal for them to continue talking. They did, but Israel had tuned them out, focusing on the sounds coming from the rear of the house. He left the window and walked as quietly as he could toward the doorway that led into the kitchen.

The house was an older one – wood throughout with walls separating every living space within instead of the more open concept of modern homes. He thought for a moment that the sound had just been the old wood taking one more creaking step toward eventual dilapidation, but when he heard another creak he knew better; that was the sound of someone taking a slow, planned step.

He gestured toward Stone, who joined him on the opposite side of the doorway. Michelle kept talking – something about getting a signal through the storm – but slowly drew her Glock. On a three count, Israel and Stone went smoothly into the kitchen with Israel in front and Stone behind and to his right, Glock up and ready.

Israel had expected to see another zombie. Instead, a man with a scoped hunting rifle turned on them from behind a kitchen island in a single, smooth movement and leveled the barrel directly at Israel's chest. His hair was little more than thick, blond stubble over his scalp. He wore a blue and gray uniform with an insignia Israel couldn't make out, but the badge on his chest was unmistakable.

"Jasper County Sheriff!" the man shouted. "Put the weapon down now!"

"Whoa, easy there, mate," Stone said. "I'm FBI. I'll put it away. My identification is in my back pocket." Stone slowly held his hands up and slid the pistol into its holster. With the same slow motions, he extracted the fake FBI credentials he had been carrying and held them up for the officer to see.

The man tilted his head slightly and looked the badge over from a distance. The rifle muzzle didn't so much as sway. "You don't sound like FBI," he said. "You sound

British."

"I am," Stone lied. "Born and raised. Used to work for London Metropolitan, but I got assigned to a joint FBI-Interpol task force. The Yanks liked my work and offered me a job here in the colonies. I was always a bit of a wanderer, so I took them up on it."

The officer looked him over. Then his eyes flicked to Israel. "And what are you? NSA?"

"I'm a salesman," Israel said. "Medical equipment. Name's Vance." It was the first time he had ever been forced to really use one of his false identities and the lies felt awkward on his tongue.

The officer nodded and lowered the rifle so that the muzzle was pointing away from anyone. As soon as he did, Stone raised a hand and shouted, "Put it away, Michelle. We're fine in here."

Israel looked out the kitchen window and saw Michelle in the backyard relaxing from a solid shooter's stance. The deputy looked out the window as well and said, "Son of a bitch."

"My partner," Stone said, nodding toward her.

"I'm Sheriff's Deputy Justin Wainwright," he said, a southern drawl evident in his voice now that he was relaxed. "Most folks just call me Bones, though."

"Interesting nickname," Israel said.

"Ain't it?" Bones said in a tone that forestalled any other questions on the matter. "Please tell me you're here about what's going on."

"Sorry, no," Stone said. "We were on a private flight that got caught in the storm. Plane's in the water off the coast there. We survived and made it to shore."

"Well, that's just damned lucky, ain't it? You get to survive a plane crash so that you can wash up on an island that's turned into Satan's playground."

"What's happening here?" Israel said. "I mean, from what we can tell there was no indication of any kind of storm in the area when we left the mainland. And the people we've come across are... well, I'm sure you know."

The back screen door slammed shut with a brittle rattle as Michelle came into the kitchen to join them. She looked at Bones and gave him a short, unsmiling nod in way of greeting. He returned it, but his eyes lingered for just a moment past the exchange.

"What's happening is a whole mess of 'hell if I know.' I'm still trying to get my head around the fact that dead folks are getting up and running around. Then that damn storm comes up outta nowhere–" The deputy laid the rifle on the bar in front of him, closed his eyes, and took a deep, shuddering breath. He was a large man, a few inches north of six feet tall, leanly muscled, and with features that were defined but still managed to be boyish. His uniform shirt was short-sleeved despite the cool temperatures. The bottom of a tattoo showed beneath the edge of the right sleeve, but Israel couldn't make out enough of it to tell what it was.

Bones' eyes slowly opened and he said, "Somebody please tell me how any of this could be real. I mean, there are rules, right? I always thought one of the biggest ones was 'dead is dead.'"

"Why don't you tell us what happened. Start with how you found us," Michelle said.

Bones nodded. "That's an easy one: gunfire. You folks made quite the ruckus coming ashore."

"We had a welcoming committee to deal with," Stone said.

"Yeah, I saw the mess out front. You're lucky. Just so you know, don't shoot unless you have to. They're attractted to the sound."

"Good to know," Israel said. "Thanks. So when did all this craziness start?"

"Two, maybe three days ago, I'd guess. They didn't come all at once in a big herd like in the movies. We started getting a lot of missing persons calls at first. Then 9-1-1 calls that were cut short. We'd investigate and find signs of a fight, blood, but no bodies. No signs of people at all. Then, night before last, they started coming in groups. They started with patrolling police officers. Then they hit the ferry station, the airport – made a right mess of that place. We're assuming they hit the Darkarcher facility too because we've lost public electricity, as well as all our comms to the mainland, and all of that was routed through DGS."

"Hang on," Stone said. "You say they took out–"

"Supply lines, communications, and defense capabil-ities, yeah. I'm a former Marine. Got two rotations through the sandbox under my belt. I know tactics when I see them and those deadheads were using them."

That hung in the air for a minute. Israel shared a glance with both Stone and Erin that was heavy with concern.

"Anyway, we lost a lot of people. A lot. Pretty much reduced Emberoak to a ghost town. Within a minute or two of dying, each one of those went from casualty to threat. Sheriff took charge when the mayor went down. By then, the police HQ had been overrun, so she got folks together and organized a defensive post up at the school. It's a big, brick thing that DGS built when they came to the island – sturdy, high roofs, running water, generators, good defensive position. So far it's stood."

"So what are you doing out and about?" Israel asked.

"I was a scout sniper back in the Corps. That means I'm a professional sneaky bastard. Once we were set up at the school, I decided to scout around and see if there were any survivors who might not be doing as well as us and find a way to bring them in."

"Any luck?"

Bones nodded. "Yeah, as a matter of fact. I've found two places so far where some neighbors had banned together and pooled their resources. They were pretty well-hidden with ammo and food, so I told them about the school and let them decide if they wanted to stay or go. They had vehicles, so if they want to make a run for it, they can. I was just leaving the second one when I heard y'all shootin' up the place. There're probably pockets like that scattered over the island."

"How many at the school?" Stone asked.

"Little over two hundred," Bones said.

Israel tightened his jaw. "Three thousand people live on this island, Stone."

"Not anymore," Bones said. "Interesting that you know that, Vance."

Israel mentally kicked himself. He was quickly deciding he didn't like the whole undercover thing. "Well, you know," he said to Bones with a shrug, "sales."

"Uh-huh," came the reply.

"Well, Deputy Wainwright," Stone said, "you've seen the lay of the land. What do you think our best move is from here?"

"I've got a vehicle stashed close by. Roads are relatively clear between here and the school. You say you're federal, you've got the badge, so you need to speak with Sheriff Holmes. Why don't you folks follow me and I'll give you a ride to the school."

"You read my mind, Marine," Stone said. "Your vehicle have room for what's left of our gear?"

Bones nodded. "It's a pickup. We can stow it in the back. What is all that stuff, anyway?"

"Lab equipment," Michelle said. "Forensic analysis stuff. We were on our way to DGS to talk about some tech upgrades."

"Uh-huh," Bones repeated.

"You don't sound convinced," Michelle said, meeting his eyes with a stare that could stop a bullet.

"Truth be told, I'm not. I think you're government, but

I know full well how easy lies can fall from the lips of government men. All I ask is that if y'all do know something about the hell that's come to this place, you speak up. There's a lot of good folks dead and worse here. I won't see them get dishonored any further by a mess of political bullshit."

Michelle studied him and then said, "Deputy, I swear to you, the moment I think I know something that could help save any living person on this island, I will share it."

Bones took a moment and let his gray eyes wash over the three of them. Finally, he said, "Hell, ain't like I can imagine it getting any worse. Grab your gear and let's get out of here."

CHAPTER TWELVE

It was about a five-minute walk to the spot where Bones had left his truck. Along the way, they didn't see any sign of the inhabitants of Jasper Island – living or otherwise. The misting rain continued to swirl in slow currents through the spotty stands of trees. Israel could see his companions' breath coalesce with each exhalation and he made a conscious effort to keep breathing himself for appearance's sake. He hoped that Bones wouldn't notice that his breath didn't fog up like everyone else's, but there was little he could do about it if that happened; he could control his breathing, not his body temperature.

The truck turned out to be an older, solid white Chevy Silverado with a diamond-shaped decal on each door. Each of the diamonds was divided into quarters and had four symbols for different academic disciplines in each section. A stylized ribbon below the diamond showed the words 'Darkarcher Institute for Primary Education' in black letters. Israel couldn't help but recall the diamond-shaped symbols he had seen back at the Conclave.

"It's a two-seater," Bones said. "You two agents ride in the back and Vance can keep me company in the front. It's not a long ride, but we'll need to take it easy so that we don't draw too much attention to ourselves. Big enough horde could be a problem even if we're moving."

Israel wasn't crazy about the seating arrangements and shot a glance at Stone, then Michelle. Before Stone could speak, Michelle said, "Good idea. Keep the civilian as much out of harm's way as you can."

Israel held her gaze for a second and then tightened his jaw. He was definitely starting to hate the undercover thing.

Bones nodded. "You two keep low in the truck's bed, out of sight. The deadheads tend to be slow to notice you unless they're close, but when they do, they come like a bad wind. Best not test our luck."

Israel put the bundle of gear in the truck bed and helped Michelle up. As soon as he saw Bones close the driver's door he said, "You sure about this? I'd feel better if you were up there."

"That's sweet, but I've got the gun and I've got Stone and I'm supposed to be a fed, remember? Now shut your chivalrous face and get in the truck."

"It's not chivalry," Israel said. "You're the best bet we have at figuring any of this out and fixing it. The last thing we need is for you to get tossed out of a speeding truck."

"I'll hang on," Michelle said. "Look, the reason we have fake IDs is to keep the Veil intact. You chose sales-man instead of badass federal agent. Now you have to play it out."

"She's right, mate," Stone added. Israel looked at him. Stone glanced at Michelle and gave Israel a reassuring nod.

Michelle didn't miss it. "Gosh, I just feel so damn protected."

"Hey," Bones said from the cab, "let's roll, folks."

Israel shook his head and got in the truck.

They'd been on the road for about two minutes when Bones said, "If you're a salesman, I'm Jean-Luc Picard."

Israel took his eyes off the mist-shrouded road. Bones was driving at a slow but steady pace through the heavy vapor. Israel thought he had seen some shapes moving out there, but nothing had come running for them out of the gray. "*Star Trek* reference?" he said. "I would've figured you for more of a Bruce Willis, action movie fan."

"See? That's it right there; takes a certain kind of personality to be the kind of salesman who does business with Darkarcher. They don't smart-ass like that. They're hungry and slick and want everybody to like them so they can move what they're selling. Smart-ass risks alienating people. You aren't like that. You watch. You listen."

Israel nodded. "What makes you think I'm doing business with Darkarcher?"

"No other reason to be here. Despite what public records might say, they own this island. Place would probably dry up and die without them. So, unless you were on your way to Nova Scotia, in which case you would have flown over or around that storm, you were coming here. I just can't figure out why."

"And you think I can help with that?"

"Hell, I'm sure as sin of that. Only question is: Will you?"

Israel was quiet for a time. The salesman thing obviously wasn't working for him. Finally, he said, "The name's real, but I'm a freelance journalist, not a salesman."

Bones looked at him. "No shit?"

Israel nodded. "No shit. Those two back there are some contacts of mine – friends, really – and they clued me in on this little excursion to Darkarcher. I've wanted to get inside that facility for a while, but couldn't get past the usual public relations barriers. Deal was I pose as their supplier for the equipment they were checking out and maybe get a look at what was on the drawing boards."

Bones thought it over. "That actually makes more sense. You three seemed to know each other a little better than the whole strangers on a plane story."

"Yeah, but look, man – don't spread it around. My friends are doing this on the down low. They could get in a lot of trouble if word gets out they let me tag along."

"I bet they could. Those are some good friends you've got there."

"The best. Can I count on you to keep it to yourself?"

Bones snorted a short laugh. "Look around you. I've – no, *we've* got bigger things on our plate than whatever widget you wanted to leak plans for on the Internet. Besides that, I think you getting into Darkarcher is off the table at this point."

Israel nodded. "Yeah, that's a given, I suppose."

"On the plus side," Bones said, "if you live through this shit you'll probably get one of those Pulitzer things."

Quiet descended as they rolled through the mist and cold. After a few minutes, Bones said, "Did Darkarcher cause all this? Were they doing something up there the townsfolk didn't know about? Something... weird?"

Israel took a moment to weigh his answer. "I honestly don't know, Bones, but I damn sure want to find out."

"Fair enough, but keep me in the loop. If there's somebody up there who needs to answer for this, then I want a piece of that bastard."

Israel met the other man's eyes and nodded.

"Oh, and for the record," Bones said, "Jean-Luc Picard was the smoothest dude to ever command any starship ever. Period."

Israel couldn't help but laugh as they rolled through the shadowed morning. The sound faded from the cabin and they continued in silence, Bones focused on the road ahead while Israel watched the trees to either side for any sign they had been noticed. The fabric of lies he had woven for Bones swirled through his mind like the mist outside the cabin. It was a plausible enough story, one he could play out better than the whole salesman thing since he actually was a journalist by training and trade. The name was still a lie, but he would just have to be careful to answer to it as naturally as he could. If Bones decided to push Stone or Michelle on his story and they balked, he could just play it off to them supporting the original lie.

Israel closed his eyes and shook his head in tiny, covert motions. Undercover sucked.

The trees started to thin and the breeze cleared away a lot of the mist, though it still hung over the island and the sky continued to spit at them with tiny droplets of rain. Bones drove the truck a little past the thinning trees and stopped. Ahead of them was a large, planned community with large houses of varying styles that stretched out along the road and faded into the mists farther on. Israel could see a little over two dozen houses with who knew how many beyond that. More importantly, there were figures standing stock still in nearly every yard, oblivious to the weather or anything else, it seemed.

Bones rolled down the window and Michelle and Stone dropped out of the pickup bed. They were both soaked and looked as miserable as anyone could as they gathered around the window. Michelle gave Israel a look that very clearly indicated how much she wanted to kick him in his warm, dry man parts. Israel just shrugged.

"Your reporter friend just filled me in on the real deal," Bones said. "Now that we're all on the same page, I'll give you a sitrep. That's Longbow Estates. DGS built the place as a compliment to the school, which happens to be on the other side of all that just over a mile from this position. The problem is the fact that there are about way too damn many deadheads between us and the school gates."

Israel heard what Bones had done there. By saying

Israel was a reporter but keeping how many facts he had actually shared vague, he had left room for Stone and Michelle to fill in the blanks that may or may not coincide with what Israel had told him. The man was still digging into their story, but Stone and Michelle were both trained to keep the biggest secret in the world. Israel knew Bones would need to do a lot more than dig if he wanted to crack them; he'd need a jackhammer and dynamite.

"Wait," Stone said. "You say the Estates is right next to the school?"

Bones nodded.

"And there're a few hundred survivors in the school? Why aren't the zombies swarming that place?"

"No idea," Bones replied. "It's weird. They just stand like that unless you get too close to them. The ones near the school – and there are plenty – just stare at the walls like they're waiting. This isn't like the movies, people. The way they took out our resources was planned and, if I didn't know better, I'd swear they're all just standing around waiting for an attack order from wherever. Which, all things considered, is way scarier to me than any movie I've ever seen."

Stone didn't say anything, but looked over the housing community with an intense expression that Israel had only seen once before – when they had been walking through an unnatural darkness in Leticia, Texas. Israel didn't like that expression. It meant that Stone was facing something he'd never seen before. Considering that he'd been living this life since before Israel had been born, the implications were less than comforting.

"How did you get past them before?" Michelle asked.

"I drove down that street like a bat coming straight outta Hell. They chased me, but they couldn't keep pace. I had quite the little fan club by the time they gave up."

"They gave up?" Stone said.

"Yep. Wandered back into the Estates. They're still

there, I'd imagine."

"What's behind the school?" Stone asked.

"Big lawn, bigger drop-off, and then a whole bunch of ocean."

"Why can't we just haul ass down the street again? Do what you did before, but in the other direction?" Michelle said.

"Because before I was leading them away from the school. This time we'd be leading them toward the school. I'd just as soon not do anything that might inspire them to swarm the place," Bones said.

"Any chance we could sneak around them?" Israel asked.

"All of us? I couldn't tell you for sure. You'd need to leave your gear behind. I'm not sure why you're still dragging all that shit around anyway. Darkarcher isn't seeing clients today."

"It's lab equipment," Michelle said. "Might help us figure out what's caused all this."

"If you say so," Bones replied, "but it's slowing you down."

"Terrain's pretty flat here," Stone said. "Not much in the way of tall grass. What if we took the truck off-road? Use the mist, keep our distance, take our time. Maybe we could get around the worst of them and come up to the back side of the school."

Bones thought it over. "We'd have to really watch our speed. Lots of rocks and things to get hung up on, but, yeah, that might be the safest bet. I don't know if there's a gate in the back wall or not, but that's not too big a problem. There's an older farmhouse a little ways behind us that opens up to a field we can cut across. We might have to dodge some goats. Think this shit affected them?"

They all shrugged.

"I hope not," Bones said. "Zombie goats might just be the last thing I could handle." He seemed to mull the plan over for a minute and then said, "I can't think of anything better. At least if we get seen with the truck, we'll have a better shot at outrunning them. I like those odds better than trying to sneak all of us past them or going so far around that we run across another group. Pile in – we'll head back to the goat farm."

The goat farm turned out to be a small house that was very similar to the one they had just left – a large barn and a barbed wire fenced area that was the size of a football field. All across it there were misshapen lumps of fur and unmoving flesh.

"Guess the deadheads got the goats after all," Bones said as they pulled up and stopped at the top of the driveway.

"You have an issue with goats?" Israel said with a smile.

"What? No, it's just– I don't know. They're just weird looking, you know? Besides, I ate some goat stew in Pakistan once and threw up for about two days straight. Just don't like them."

"Fair enough, I guess. I feel the same way about tequila," Israel said.

Now it was Bones' turn to laugh. "Jose Cuervo is a friend of mine. Hell, if I'd some of that in Pakistan, maybe whatever was in that goat wouldn't have jacked up my stomach."

There was a tap at the window. Stone looked in as Bones rolled it down. "Deputy," he said, "I suggest you and I clear the house and barn so we don't get any surprises while Agent Brandt and Mr. Horton drive over to the fence and get the gate opened. Are you okay with that?"

Bones agreed and got out of the truck. Israel shifted over and got behind the wheel. Bones had just finished pointing out where the gate into the goat pen was when the passenger door slammed as Michelle got into the truck. Without a word, she cranked up the heat and put her hands over the vents.

None of the men commented. Bones and Stone headed for the house and Israel put the truck into gear and rolled slowly toward the large gate. As soon as his window was up, Michelle said, "If you ever hear me say anything about wanting to get into the field more, remind me of this, would you? Because right now I hate everything."

"You can count on me," Israel said.

They reached the fence and Israel got out to open it. This done, he got back into the truck to wait. It took a couple of minutes for Stone and Bones to finish their work, so Israel used the time to fill Michelle in on the conversation with Bones and the way he had altered his cover story. She nodded, agreed that it sounded okay, but said little else. As soon as their companions returned, they got moving.

Crossing the field was easy enough as it was largely cleared of anything the truck couldn't easily traverse. Once they reached the far edge of the fence, though, it got more difficult. The grass beyond was taller and Israel could see large rocks hiding among the blades. It would make for slow going.

Bones insisted on getting back behind the wheel since he was used to the terrain and instructed Stone and Israel to walk a few feet ahead and warn him of hidden ditches or rocks that might be large enough to damage the truck's undercarriage.

Stone and Israel complied. Their first job was to pull up a couple of the steel bars that served as fence posts so the truck would have a spot to drive through. The thin bars were set into concrete and buried deep, but didn't prove much of challenge for Israel, though Stone did make a show of straining to give the other man a hand. While they worked, Israel quietly told Stone the same things he had shared with Michelle. Stone only nodded and said, "Fair enough, but we'll need to talk about this again later. Your

IDs need some work."

Israel agreed.

They walked on, moving at a reasonable walking pace, scanning the mist and the ground and telling Bones when he needed to change course, which didn't turn out to be all that often. Israel was starting to think that they were being a little too cautious. Before long, the backs of houses came into view like big, blocky mountains that were shrouded in mist and spitting rain. Behind the houses were dozens and dozens of zombies.

"Bloody hell," Stone whispered.

Israel only nodded. The dead hadn't noticed them – Israel thought they were still far enough away that they were relatively safe – but a loud noise would definitely get them a lot of attention that they did not want.

Stone gestured for Bones to make a sharp right turn so they could run parallel to the line of houses. Bones gave him a thumbs up from within the truck and made the turn. A hundred yards or so later, Stone whispered to Israel and pointed into the distance. Israel looked and got his first glimpse of the Darkarcher Institute for Primary Education.

It reminded Israel of pictures of Ivy League colleges he had seen in movies and on the Internet but on a smaller scale. There were multiple buildings, each of them two to three stories tall and built from lots of stone, brick, and intricate masonry. An eight-foot-tall brick wall surrounded the expansive grounds and Israel could see figures with rifles or shotguns peering out over the walls. He doubted the others could make out the people, so he whispered, "They've got sentries on the wall. I think they spotted us."

Stone was about to reply when his expression changed. He pointed toward the school and said, "What's that bloody thing?"

Even as Israel looked back, he felt it. It was a tingle in his eyes that quickly spread through his body. He turned in time to see a brilliant, silent flash of golden light that popped through the sky like an enormous flash bulb. At the same time, the pickup suddenly shot forward so fast and hard that Israel and Stone had to dive to one side to keep from getting hit.

Israel rolled instantly to his feet and came up just as the truck hit a large rock that wedged itself under the front end hard enough to lift the tires off the ground. He heard the muffled explosion of deploying airbags and sprinted for the truck.

Stone was on his feet and shouted, "Incoming on your six, mate!"

Israel reached the truck and looked over his shoulder. Already at least two dozen of the zombies were moving toward them with their awkward, clumsy gait, but they smoothed out and gained speed as they came. As Israel scanned the crowd, he saw that many others were following suit.

The driver's door opened and Bones staggered out. He had one hand over his eyes and blood was streaming from his nose in twin lines. "What the hell was that light?" he demanded. "It felt like somebody kicked me in the head."

Israel didn't have time to answer. He looked across the truck and saw Stone helping Michelle. She was waving him off and gave Israel a thumbs up.

"Was that what I think it was?" he said.

She nodded.

Israel cursed and looked toward the space where the light had been. Bones let out a curse of his own and grabbed his rifle from the truck's cab when he saw the incoming undead.

Israel was ignoring them. What he saw in the grass between them and the school held his full attention. He counted fourteen of them. They were standing up in the grass and looking around like some kind of gargantuan meerkats, front limbs hanging loose against their chests, their weight settled onto their haunches. That's where the resemblance ended, though. The largest of them stood an easy six feet tall and they were largely scaled, but with lines of bright red fur trailing from their elongated skulls over the crowns of their heads and down the ridged spines that comprised their backs and long, wide tails. Six solid crimson eyes ran down each side of their faces and sat above horned snouts with nostrils you could lose a golf ball in. The limbs that hung loose at their front had four thick digits that ended in hooked yellow claws.

The largest of them met eyes with Israel and roared, its mouth opening like the maw of a crocodile, yellow fangs streaming thick fluid in strings upon the ground. The rest of the pack followed suit and dropped to all fours, rushing toward the crippled truck.

Israel turned and saw the dead coming for them, perhaps a hundred strong. The others joined him, weapons in hand and barely restrained panic on their faces. "What the hell is going on?" Bones demanded.

"Look on the bright side," Israel said. "At least they aren't goats."

CHAPTER THIRTEEN

"Israel," Michelle said, "get the truck off that rock."

Stone and Israel both shot Michelle a shocked look. Stone opened his mouth to speak, but Michelle shouted him down. "We're going to have to tell him everything now anyway! Trust me, Israel! Move the truck!"

"Forget that," Bones said, raising his rifle and aiming. "It's going to take a winch and jack to get that thing free." A shot rang out. One of the charging zombies tumbled to the ground, tripping three others behind it.

"Israel!" Michelle yelled.

Israel cursed and ran to the front of the truck. He spared a quick second to examine the undercarriage, ignoring the hissing roar of the things that had fallen through the micro-breach. It looked as though the axle had wedged itself onto the rock, but Israel didn't see any fluids leaking or any obvious engine damage.

There was another rifle crack. Then, the sound of two Glocks firing in careful, measured pops. Israel's sensitive hearing picked up the sound of heavy, clawed paws slapping against the ground.

He crouched lower and got one shoulder under the

truck's front frame. Then he stood up with a soft grunt. Metal creaked, rock cracked, but the truck rose up with him and he pushed it backward and off the rock. The Glocks continued to fire as he lowered the front end to the ground. Bones was looking over his shoulder at Israel in slack-jawed amazement, his rifle momentarily forgotten.

"Get in," Israel shouted before Bones could say anything. Israel reached into the cabin and tore the deployed airbags free with about as much effort as it takes for a normal person to rip newspaper. He slid behind the driver's seat. Michelle got in the passenger side; Stone and Bones climbed into the back. As soon as they were in, Israel turned the key and watched as their death came for them from two sides.

The engine didn't start. It turned over, coughed, turned over again. The gunfire from the back grew more frantic. Everyone could hear the monsters' hiss now.

He turned the key again, pumping the gas pedal. The engine turned over, caught, and roared to life.

"Hold on!" he screamed and slapped the vehicle into reverse, trying hard to remember where the worst of the obstacles were from their walk to this point. He slammed on the accelerator and the truck rocketed backward. Bones and Stone had both been on their knees so they managed to stay in the truck, but they were pitched forward against the rear window with the sudden motion.

They had gotten twenty feet when two of the leading meerkat-things launched themselves into the air and came down claws-first in the spot the truck had just been. They both staggered, but quickly regained their footing and started for the truck again. They didn't get far.

The first of the zombies reached them in a blur of speed and silent, deadly intent. They threw themselves at the monsters with mindless need, teeth snapping and fingers clawing with no thought of self-preservation. The monsters responded in kind, claws flashing out to fling blood and viscera through the air, powerful jaws latching onto limbs and ripping them free of joints with almost no effort. More of the six-eyed monstrosities joined the fray. The undead kept coming, though, and soon the field was a mass of writhing bodies and unbridled carnage that made Israel glad he didn't dream anymore.

A group of the undead had changed course to pursue the truck and Israel said, "Back to the farm?"

"No," Michelle said, "head for the houses. The ground will be clearer there, but stick to the backyards and head for the school. Most of the other Necrophage are in the fight, so we shouldn't draw too many with us."

There was no time to argue the plan. Israel repeated his shout for the men in back to hang on and he cut the wheel toward the Estates and the oncoming zombies. He shifted into drive and gunned the engine. The truck fish-tailed in the wet grass, straightened, and shot forward just in time to hit the leading zombie head-on and plow him under the vehicle in a series of hard, wet thumps.

The others came behind it. They were spread out and didn't present so much of a roadblock as an obstacle course. Bodies collided with the fender and bounced off or tried to jump onto the truck only to lose their grip and roll off one side or the other. One of the undead managed to land in the truck's bed, but Stone and Bones made short work of it and threw it out behind them.

Despite all this, Israel kept his eyes on the terrain and tried to use his enhanced sight and reflexes to avoid obstacles on the ground. The rock had damaged the steer-ing, though, and the truck didn't respond as well as it should. It skidded and fishtailed as he struggled with the wheel and hoped against physics that the two men in the back wouldn't be thrown out.

They reached the closest yard and Israel cut the wheel hard to the right, bouncing through a small ditch as he did so. He heard grunts from the back, but a quick look in the rearview told him that both men were still there.

Michelle had been right – the land had been cleared for construction closer to the houses and Israel managed to accelerate without slowing to get around obstacles or through dips in the terrain. Despite a few more undead bouncing off the hood, within a minute they had crossed a wide yard and skidded onto the drive that lead to the school's front gates.

The gates were open and there were people gathered at either side of it – men, women, and some older teens, all with guns of some kind. As the truck grew closer, they opened fire. Israel heard a high-pitched buzz as a veritable swarm of bullets tore through the air and past the truck. In the rearview mirror, he saw the few remaining zombies jerk and fall under the barrage.

The truck barreled through the gate and Israel stood on the brake, screeching to a halt inches from a large fountain that boasted a statue of a man in a toga holding a large book. Israel checked on Michelle, who nodded that she was fine, and got out of the truck. "Stone, Bones. Are you guys–"

He didn't get to finish. Bones was already out of the truck and his big fist flashed in and caught Israel squarely across the jaw. There was no pain, no shock, but Israel took the blow and stepped back. The Deputy came in with his other fist for another punch, but Israel blocked that with a move that stopped the man's fist like he was punching an oak tree. With his other hand, he shoved Bones in the chest – not hard, but enough to stagger him back a few feet.

"Knock it off," he said, meeting the man's furious stare. "We don't want to go there."

"Who the hell are you, Israel? What do you know about all this?" Bones said his name like it was an accusation.

"Deputy," Stone said, "we need–"

"Deputy Wainwright," a woman's voice snapped, drowning out Stone's comment. "Stand down! What's going on here?"

Israel looked over the truck's bed at the speaker. She was tall – nearly six feet – and wore the sheriff's uniform as naturally as the graying blond hair that hung almost to her collar. The hair framed a face with a nose that was prominent without being distracting. Her full lips were pursed into a frown and her eyes took in the scene with unforgiving authority. The combat shotgun – a Mossberg 590, Israel thought – that she was carrying didn't hurt her commanding presence.

"Found these folks at Cal Thurman's place. Those two have badges, but I've already caught them lying to me twice."

"That so?" the sheriff said.

Stone stepped forward, holding out the ID for the sheriff to examine. "I'm Agent Stone," he lied, "that's Agent Brandt."

Israel watched as the sheriff took the ID from Stone and looked it over. He wasn't worried that it wouldn't pass inspection because it was technically a real FBI badge and ID. All their law enforcement credentials were issued to them through the DGRI from the issuing agencies with the understanding that the badge gave the bearer no real authority and was to be used only in situations where the Veil was in danger of being breached. If they had the means, the sheriff could check with the FBI and they would verify that the ID was real, but not much else.

She returned Stone's ID. "I'm Sheriff Holmes. Who's that one?" she said, nodding at Israel.

"We'll need to talk about that," Stone said. "Don't suppose you've managed to commandeer an office some-place, have you?"

"Well, his name's either Vance or Israel. They can't seem to decide," Bones said.

"Stow that crap, Bones. You'll get your say," the sheriff said. She stepped away from the truck and spent a minute giving two large men instructions on how to rearrange the sentry points. When she was done, she turned back and said, "Agents, bring your friend and follow me. You too, Bones." Without really waiting for any of them, she headed for the short, wide steps that led up to the school's main entrance. An engraved marble plaque above the doors read 'Administration' in thick block letters.

Inside, it looked like a militia checkpoint. There was a makeshift barricade set up just inside the door that could block access with little effort. Two very serious-looking men were posted there with what looked like a couple of pump action shotguns that were more suited to hunting than pitched combat. Still, though, if they decided no one was coming through those doors, odds were very good that is exactly what would happen.

The sheriff nodded to them as she passed and re-assured them that everything was under control outside. She led them past the barricade and into a room that served as the reception area. There, another pair – a man and a woman this time – were stacking food and other supplies against the far wall. The woman had a clipboard and seemed to be cataloging the goods.

"My compliments, Sheriff," Stone said. "Considering how quickly all this happened, you're very well-organized."

She stopped and faced the smaller man. "I'm retired Army. I've been a few bad places where bad things were happening. One thing I learned quick was that people with something to do are people who don't have time to panic. I set up this building as command and supply. The people who aren't combat ready or have other usable skills are all set up over in the gymnasium. We're making do. I took over the Administrator's office; come on in and we'll talk."

As they filed in, Michelle caught Israel's eye and whispered something far too low for anyone but him to hear.

He shook his head, not catching it, but then focused as she repeated it. It was faint, even to him, but he heard her clearly.

"The micro-breach Awakened Bones."

Israel did his best to keep his expression neutral, but couldn't help but give a mental sigh. Of course Bones had Awakened because there simply wasn't enough going on already. He thought over the events in the field and it did make sense; the breach had opened, the truck had suddenly shot forward, and then Bones had come out holding his hands over his eyes. What was it he had said? Something about being kicked in the head?

Israel thought back to the night it had happened to him and Erin. They had walked into a room with an ongoing breach – a small one – and they had both felt the light in their eyes as a kind of pressure rather than a glare. Later, he had learned that the sensation – Ocular Nerve Excitation, Allison had called it – was a dead giveaway for an Awakening event. Bones had seemed to be in pain, though, and that hadn't happened to him. He made a mental note to ask Michelle about that when he got the chance.

The five of them filed into the room and the sheriff closed the door. She was about to take a seat behind the wide desk which was cluttered with maps of the island bearing red circles and handwritten notes when she stopped suddenly and said to Bones, "Hey, your head's bleeding. Turn around."

"What?" Bones said, his hand going automatically to the back of his head. It came away with spots of red staining his fingertips. "Dammit," he said. "I hit my head while I was getting tossed around the back of that pickup. Didn't realize I was cut."

"Turn around and let me see," she said.

Bones complied and the movement brought the back of the man's head into Israel's line of sight. Bones was, indeed, bleeding. Through his shortly cropped hair, Israel could see a short but deep cut in the man's scalp just below the crown of his head. Blood was running in a thin, steady line from it now that they were out of the rain. The sight of the open wound and the tang of blood on the air sent a tiny shudder through Israel as the hunger rose up and took notice.

Israel noticed Stone staring at him. He nodded his understanding and pulled out one of the protein bars. He ate it in fast bites while the sheriff slipped on a pair of glasses she had pulled from her pocket and examined Bones' wound.

"Yeah," she said, "you need a couple of stitches. I want you here for this, though. Hang on." She opened the door again and leaned out. "Sarah," she said, "get somebody from medical up here. Deputy Wainwright needs some stitches. Not an emergency, but I'd like it done ASAP."

Israel heard a crisp "Yes, ma'am" from the outer office as the sheriff closed the door.

"Sheriff, I'd—" Stone started.

She held up a hand for him to wait. With tired motions, she moved behind the desk and sat down. She propped her feet up on the desk heedless of the maps and picked up a rubber band that was lying nearby. She stretched this between her left thumb and forefinger. She lightly hooked the stretched band with her right thumb and pulled it tight, letting it snap back with a tiny thrum. She thrummed the band twice more before she looked up at Bones and said, "Okay. First thing: Did you make it to DGS?"

Bones shook his head. "Came across two sets of survivors before I found Mulder, Scully, and the Lone Gunman, here. When I saw they were feds, I figured I'd better get them back to you."

She nodded.

Thrumm.

"Agent Stone," the sheriff said, "is it safe to assume you're in command of your group?"

"It is."

"Great, so I'm talking to you. Do you have the means to call for support from the mainland? We are completely cut off here unless you count the two-ways, but those don't do us any good for oversea comms."

Thrumm.

"I don't," Stone said, "but we managed to salvage some gear from the plane that crashed us here. Agent Brandt is an engineer. She thinks she might be able to cobble something together that will let her boost a signal."

"Not likely," the sheriff said. "I know a little something about comms from my days in the Army. Near as I can figure, the cell tower's been disabled or outright destroyed. Cobble together whatever you want, but there's just no signal to boost."

"Well, shit," Michelle muttered.

Israel looked at her. "You mean I hauled all that crap here for nothing?"

Michelle shrugged. "Looks like it."

Sheriff Holmes turned her attention back to Stone. "I didn't know the bureau had engineers."

Stone shrugged. "Bloody technology runs the world. We're trying to stay on top of it."

"What's that accent? British?"

"Mostly." Stone spent a moment retelling his fictional back story.

The sheriff listened in polite silence, nodded here and there, and thrummed her rubber band.

"So what's the FBI know about what's happening on my island, Agent? Before you answer, though, please assume that I know the first words out of your mouth are a lie and go with your second choice, which I hope will be the truth."

"Why would you assume he's lying?" Israel said.

The sheriff turned her gaze on Israel. The rubber band thrummed once more as she studied him. Back in his days as a crime reporter for the *Chicago Tribune*, Israel had known a lot of cops who could give a stare like that, a stare that made you start double-checking all your secrets because you just knew this person was going to get them out of you. He'd never seen one as good as Sheriff Holmes'.

"Why?" she said. "Because he's with the government and what's happening on this island reeks of government fuck-up. I've seen it before, but never like..." thrumm "... this."

"We want to help if we can," Stone said.

"Help? Agent Stone, three days ago this was a quiet little island winding down from the tourist season and getting ready to button up for the winter. Now? Now, we're a group of survivors trying very, very hard to live through a siege by a whole bunch of things that aren't supposed to fucking exist. And now, unless I've started hallucinating, we have whatever those lizard things are falling out of the damned sky! So, help? Yeah, you can help by telling me – telling *us* – what in the name of God is going on. Can you do that, Agent? Can any of you?" Her voice had risen, but still she pulled at the rubber band. Israel got the impression it helped to keep her focused.

Israel noticed Michelle watching the sheriff tug at the strip of rubber. She seemed disconnected, her face relaxed, but focused with an intensity that she only got when she was lost in her head. Her eyes flicked back and forth. He was about to say something when there was a soft knock at the office door.

"That must be our medic," Sheriff Holmes said. "You mind?" she asked, looking at Israel and nodding at the door.

Israel returned the nod, pulled open the door, and found himself face to face with Jordan Screed.

CHAPTER FOURTEEN
Erin

In the dream, Erin was running. She ran through a cold, bright, desert night. Her breath burned in and out of her lungs in frantic gasps. Behind her, the lights of Las Vegas glittered and shone, but not like the jewels that so many poets and songwriters had compared them to. No, this was not the opalescent sparkle of a cut and polished precious stone, but the dull sheen of moonlight off a thousand slick, wet teeth, the cold, excited gleam in a predator's eye. This was not the Las Vegas that entertained and fleeced tens of millions of people every year. No. Erin's Las Vegas was the one that ground up, consumed, and shat out lives like they were livestock, commodities to be used for profit and forgotten. That was her Vegas and it chased her through the dream like the unrelenting predator she knew it to be.

So, she ran – naked, feet bleeding from sharp stones and small, hidden cacti. Still she ran, stumbling and terrified. There were no thoughts of Paragons or of power, just the fear, the desperation, and the hopelessness of it all. She ran until she suddenly wasn't anymore.

It was always the same – the hand exploding up from the dirt to grip her thin ankle, the sudden fall to the rocky sand, trying to scramble away as the rest of the body clawed its way out of the hard-packed desert floor. It rose up over her, too clear in the dream-light and looked down at her with a sad, confused expression.

It had once been a man. It had once been her brother, Tiko. No longer, though. The handsome, roguish face was gray and misshapen by stones and gravel that had fused with it when she had murdered him by teleporting him deep into the earth. Fluid leaked from the places the stones broke through the skin. His eyes were warped, yellow where they were once white and oozing something that mixed with the dirt on his face and made it seem like he was crying muddy tears. He stood over her, naked and hideously ready as he had been so many times in her life.

He ran those muddy-teared eyes down her body and said in a voice that was thick with phlegm and gravel, "Hey, baby sister. Come show me how much you missed me."

That's when the screaming would start.

Erin's eyes snapped open as her body jerked on the cot. Her breath came in ragged gasps and she quickly settled back, turning her eyes to the cabin ceiling. It wasn't the first time she'd had the dream; she was sure it wouldn't be the last. For the thousandth time, she told herself that Tiko had it coming. Years of abuse and molestation and using vulnerable women for profit had earned him what she had done. It was true. Despite that, he had been her brother and she wasn't sure she would ever forgive herself.

She heard movement to one side and looked over to see Brinn'ha coming toward her in the dying firelight. The tall, flat-featured alien – though Erin realized she was the alien in this world – knelt next to the cot and said, "Sar'ha, heart-sister. Are you not for the resting?"

Erin shook her head.

"Are you for having the rest-seeings?"

It was a strange reality among the Valley People that they did not dream in the way humans did. They could have the waking hopes and aspirations for success or achievement that people from Erin's world often called dreams, but the idea of seeing uncontrollable mental pictures while resting was an unheard of phenomenon among them. After waking from this nightmare the third time, she had been quizzed by the elders on the experience. Many of them found it utterly amazing and sought to duplicate it through pre-rest meditations. Erin would trade places with them in a hot second.

"Yeah," she said. "Same one."

Brinn'ha flared her small nostril ridges and said, "I am for wanting this wrong-brother you slew to still live so that I might be for slaying him to save you such seeings."

"Don't say that, Brinn," Erin said. "It is what it is. I can handle it."

"I am for knowing that," she said. "This is not for meaning I wish that you must do so."

Erin smiled. "Well, what's done is done. No point in wishing for what we can't have."

"Truth. Are you for returning to the resting?"

Erin nodded. "I'll try; you do the same. I'm sorry if I woke you."

"Resting comes on stiff legs for me," she said. "I am for thinking of the coming long-walk. You are for being certain it is a thing we must do?"

"Yes. We need to know if anything dangerous was left after that plane crashed. We need to find it and dispose of it. Hide it away."

"I am for understanding this," Brinn'ha said. "There is something I am not for understanding, Sar'ha."

"What?"

"Why would Sar'ha's people build such mighty terrible weapons? Why would it be for the needing of them?"

Erin sighed and thought over her answer. "It's a very different place, Brinn'ha. There are so many people there that sometimes it seems like they outnumber the stars in the sky, so many people on one world with limited resources and spread out so far apart. Some of them hate what is different from what they believe to be true so they try to destroy the things and people different from them. Some people try to kill others to take what they have. Some people just enjoy killing. Either way, over time we've figured out lots of ways to get the killing done in bigger and bigger batches. That thing you saw is just a drop in the bucket."

Brinn'ha was silent for long minute. Finally, she said, "I am not for understanding such ways."

"Good. I don't ever want you to understand that. That's why we've got to get rid of that wreckage. I don't want anyone learning anything from it."

"I am for agreeing with this," Brinn'ha said. "Will you be for the returning to the you-place?"

Erin blinked at that. "What? I can't. I don't know how. You know that."

Brinn'ha studied her for a moment and then said, "That was truth for the before burning-roaring-flying-thing. For a full turning of seasons and more you have been of the tribe. Never before has there been a thing from the stars after you. Until the now. Change is the fire that will never burn out, Sar'ha. If this changing is a way for you to return to the you-place, it may be that you must be for the deciding."

Erin realized that she hadn't considered that. She had no doubt that she was tied to the breach that had brought the jet through; the seizure had proved that. The idea that the connection was somehow a way for her to get back to Earth, though, had not occurred to her. It had been many months since she'd given up any hope of that ever happening. Brinn'ha had a point; the idea deserved some consideration. "I don't know," she said.

"I am for understanding that truth," Brinn'ha said. "Sar'ha, be for the considering of this truth: Is the returning to the you-place a better truth than being of the tribe? We must rare be for fighting to protect our own and never are we for killing more than we must. The you-place truth sounds to not be for that. The you-place sounds... it sounds to be full of the fearing. The tribe is for the knowing, not the fearing. Are the Marks of Understanding for making my words clear?"

"They are," Erin said, a catch in her voice she didn't quite understand. "And I hear the truth in your words. I have to think on it, though, Brinn. I don't even know if it's a possibility."

Brinn'ha gave Erin an awkward bob of her head that approximated a nod. It was, like winking, one of the human mannerisms she had taught them. Brinn'ha rose and moved to return to her cot. She looked back and said, "I am for saying again: Change is the fire that will never burn out. It can warm our hands if we are for accepting it or sear our flesh if we are for fighting it. Always it is for the coming. Sleep well, Sar'ha. We will be for facing this change as a one."

Erin watched her go and settle onto her cot. She rolled to her back and closed her eyes, thinking on everything her friend had said. Eventually, sleep came to claim her.

The morning arrived on a cool, damp breeze and the sound of the tribe moving outside the cabin and talking in loud voices. The three would-be travelers rose and went about their morning routine. After a few minutes, they emerged from the cabin and found the assembled tribe, all of them, waiting outside the Elder's Hall. Barr'na stood at the forefront of the crowd with the other Elders. On a table before them were three fully prepared Tarr-hide packs that Erin thought resembled large duffel bags you could wear on your back with a single, diagonal strap across the chest. Before each pack was another wrapped bundle. These were smaller, long, and flat. The sun was rising over the mountains and cast the whole scene in fresh, golden light.

The whole thing had the feel of a ritual, but Erin had never seen this one. In truth, she thought this might be the first time she had ever seen anyone actually leave the tribe for any real length of time. Gratt'na touched her elbow and gestured for the three of them to approach the table that held the packs.

As they did so, Barr'na moved around to the front of the table to greet them. When they reached within a few steps of the Elder, Gratt'na tightened his grip just a little on Erin's elbow as a signal for her to stop. He released her and they all watched Barr'na.

"I am Elder Barr'na," he said with a voice that rose up for all to hear. "On this day of departing, I am for speaking for the Elders. I am for speaking for the tribe."

A short, soft chorus rose up from the tribe. "Barr'na is for speaking." The sudden translation of so many voices caused the marks around Erin's ears to grow warm with magic, but she did not flinch.

"A thing of the unknown has come," he continued, "but we are for the knowing and among us is a Walker of Worlds – Sar'ha. Sar'ha is for having the knowing of this thing, but not all of the knowing. Her knowing tells her that there is for having a chance-danger among the thing of the unknown. For the tribe, she is for seeking out the thing of the unknown and deciding if the chance danger is truth or not-truth. For the tribe, Sar'ha and her heart-siblings are for taking the long walk and finding truth."

Again, the chorus: "For the truth and the tribe, they

are for the departing."

Barr'na picked up the first pack with its smaller bundle and approached Brinn'ha. She accepted the pack, slung it over her shoulder, and took the smaller bundle from the Elder. They bent forward until their foreheads rested together and Barr'na whispered something Erin couldn't hear. He retrieved another pack and bundle, then repeated the process with Gratt'na. She could have eavesdropped on what he whispered, but felt it would be intrusive. She made an effort to ignore them.

With the third pack in-hand, this one slightly smaller to accommodate Erin's more petite human frame, Barr'na helped her slip the pack onto her back. He bent low to her, but did not touch his head to hers. He held out the smaller bundle and Erin took it from his long, gray fingers.

"Be for the opening of it," he said.

She unwrapped it carefully, though she knew from the feel and weight of it what was inside – a Batla and Jo lay in the carefully folded leather. These were not the practice weapons she had been using for the last year, though. It was the custom of the Valley People to award newly made weapons to warriors who were deemed ready to graduate from training to actively serving the tribe. The weapons Erin was holding were custom-carved and sized for her smaller grip, but she knew they were no less deadly than Brinn'ha's or Gratt'na's larger weapons. The wood was dark and smooth, polished and hardened through some process Erin didn't understand. The heavier end of the Batla was studded with small, sharp stones of milky white that were long enough to leave vicious cuts in an enemy's flesh. The Jo was not the short, blunt stick that she had used in training, but a double-edged dagger with a handle of the same dark wood as the Batla, wound with Tarr-hide strips for a better grip. The blade was the same milky stone that had been chipped and sharpened to a razor's edge against the black rocks that were the only thing that seemed able to grind down the lighter stones.

Erin stared at the weapons. She didn't know what to say.

"It was near to the giving before the unknown-thing was for the appearing. The Batla is for striking hard, the Jo is for the biting deep. I am for hoping they are never for the needing."

Erin nodded. Emotions swirled through her and robbed her of language.

"You were not for being born of the tribe," Barr'na whispered, "of the tribe you have become. Of the tribe you will always be, Sar'ha and Walker of Worlds."

Erin nodded again. A single tear dripped from her bowed head onto the milky, crystalline blade she held. "Thank you, Elder Barr'na," she managed to say in a choked voice.

He reached up with both hands and gave her arms an affectionate squeeze, then turned back to the tribe. "The giving is for being finished," he said. "Be for making a way for the takers-of-the-long-walk to be for departing."

As the tribe parted into two long columns, the three companions secured their new weapons to their Tarr-hide belts. Gratt'na took the lead since he was the one who knew the way, and walked down the corridor that the Valley People had made. As he went, he extended his arms and let the other members of the tribe brush their hands along his in gestures of farewell and safe wishes. Brinn'ha followed her brother, also with her arms extended.

There was a beauty in it, Erin thought, a sense of community and fellowship that she didn't think she had ever witnessed before. As she took her place among the travelers and felt hundreds of hands brush past her own, she could not help the tears that fell from her eyes. It wasn't the beauty of the ritual or the genuine sense of love she felt from these strange, alien faces she had come to see as friends that brought her to tears. No, Erin didn't cry at the beauty, but rather the dread she felt. She wept at the profound sadness that washed over her because she knew in that one moment that she would never see any of those faces again.

CHAPTER FIFTEEN

One of the things that Erin missed about Earth was going to the movies. When her life had been something that was more of an extension of her brother's existence than anything she could call her own, she had rarely gotten to see them. Tiko had hated novels, movies, and television – really any kind of fictional escapist entertainment. He had thought doing so made him sound intellectual. The truth was that he had rarely participated in a piece of fiction that he could keep up with. Erin, though, relished going to the movies.

Not just any movies, either. She liked the big, sweeping epic films. For her, a two-hour movie was a good start. She liked the ones that would pull her in and make her forget everything for hours on end. So, as she and her fellow travelers walked the length of the valley, she couldn't help but think of the films she had seen where the main characters had traveled great distances across wide, green landscapes. Peter Jackson's *Lord of the Rings* films replayed in her head along with scenes from Kevin Costner's *Dances with Wolves* and that old *Lawrence of Arabia* movie, though it was more sand than green. The steady, determined pace and resolute visage of the characters all replayed on the wide screen in her mind while snippets of uplifting soundtracks floated across her memory like audible ghosts.

By the time they had reached the end of their first day and stopped to make camp, though, Erin had decided that Hollywood could kiss her ass. There was no uplifting soundtrack, her feet were killing her, her calves felt like they might actually fall off her legs, and some kind of insect she had not encountered before had bitten her on the back of her neck, leaving behind a small welt that itched constantly. The movies had all made this stuff seem romantic and teeming with adventure. It wasn't. It sucked.

"We are for making the rest-place here," Gratt'na said. "Are you for being well, Sar'ha? You are for scratching at your neck like a Tarr with tiny-biters."

"Kind of feel that way," she replied. "Some damned thing bit my neck. Itches like crazy."

She saw Gratt'na's face tense at the word 'damned.' Profanities, curses, anything like that was not a part of Valley People speech and so did not translate through the Marks of Understanding. She had been forced to clean up her language since arriving or keep trying to explain why she was constantly referring to mating practices. "Sorry," she said. "Some insect bit me. It itches a lot."

"I am for thinking it was a Xanla-wing," Brinn'ha said. "It is not for the being harmful. I am for the having of a salve."

They settled in under the branches of a tall, narrow tree that reached skyward with growth on it that reminded Erin of cedar trees, but was much more dense and with a dark blue tinge to the foliage. Gratt'na went off to collect firewood while Brinn'ha applied a thick, strongly scented mixture of ground plants and congealed Tarr fat to the bite on Erin's neck. The smell was distracting, but the itching stopped almost immediately. Erin thanked Brinn'ha and had just dropped her pack to the ground when Gratt'na came rushing back without any firewood to show for his absence.

"Sar'ha," he said, "be for the following. There is an unknown-thing." Erin and Brinn'ha both followed Gratt'na as he jogged farther up the valley and turned into a small copse of the same type of tall trees that they had just taken shelter under. Erin noticed that there was damage to many of the trees – broken branches too thick to have been snapped by hand; thin, wiry leaves that were shredded in wide swaths; and bark that was torn from the wood beneath it. When Gratt'na stopped, she realized why.

The piece of wreckage was about five feet across and looked as though it had been ripped from the side of the aircraft by an explosion. The portions of it that weren't scorched black were the gray of a stormy sky, but carried no markings she could see. It looked as though it had spun through the trees like some kind ragged saw blade and torn up the vegetation as it passed before embedding itself into the soil. Erin approached it and saw that both Brinn'ha and Gratt'na had their hands resting on their weapons.

"It's okay," she said. "This part of it isn't dangerous. Think of it as a piece of its skin. Look around and see if there's any more of it."

They complied and Erin hooked her fingers under the edge of the metal. She realized that this was the first time she had touched anything that wasn't stone, wood, or leather in over a year. It was a fleeting but strange realization. Though the thing had some weight to it, it was far lighter than Erin had expected and she raised it up to reveal the back side of it with minimal effort. She held it there, examining it, looking for some kind of markings and found them almost immediately. Along the straighter of the edges, scorched but still legible, was a series of numbers and letters stamped into the metal. She held the thin piece of wreckage up with one hand and rubbed at the imprint with the other. The numbers didn't mean anything to her, but just beneath them in tiny letters were the words 'United States Navy.'

She had been looking for something she recognized, something she could read. The numbers had been enough, but the words were a confirmation she realized she hadn't really needed. Erin let the panel drop to the ground and stepped back, studying it and trying to sort out all the implications.

"Sar'ha," she heard Brinn'ha call to her, "there is being more."

Erin turned and joined her friends. Gratt'na was kneeling and examining the ground, but Erin did not see any more wreckage. "Where is it?" she asked.

"We are not for finding more of the skin of the unknown-thing," Brinn'ha said. "Gratt'na is for the finding of tracks. We are not for being the first to be here."

"What?" Erin said. She approached Gratt'na, but didn't bother looking around for whatever he was seeing. He had tried to show her how to recognize tracks, but unless they were blatantly obvious, she was useless. Instead, she scanned the ground and within moments found what she was looking for: a long, narrow divot in the grass.

"Fuck!" she said, forgetting and not really caring about the translation her friends would hear. "There was another piece in the ground here. Whoever came through got it. Gratt, which way are they going?"

"They are for following the same path as we," he said.

"So they're going for the crash site. Any idea who they are?"

"I am not for the sure-knowing," he said, "but in this season and in their number they are much as the Starless Tribe is for being."

The Starless Tribe. It had taken Erin some time to

realize that this was what the Valley People called bandits or raiders of some kind. She had never encountered them – Barr'na had told her the tribe was too strong to fear an attack – but she knew that they would typically try to sneak into smaller encampments in the dead of night to plunder what they could. They were thieves for the most part, it seemed, but they traveled in small bands and stories of much greater atrocities were not uncommon.

"Lovely," Erin said through gritted teeth. This was exactly what she had wanted to avoid, but she tried to take solace in the fact that even if there were still weapons that had survived the crash, it was unlikely the Starless could concoct a way to activate them or even know that they could. The best case scenario was that the Starless accidentally set something off that would provide a big enough boom to destroy the crash site as well as themselves; nothing dangerous left at the site, and one less wandering band of thieves – win-win.

Except she realized it really wasn't that simple. The tribe – this whole planet, so far as she knew – used no metal of any sort. Iron, steel, aluminum – they were all foreign concepts to the Valley People. They were a culture of wood, stone, and hide. If the Starless Tribe discovered the wreckage and figured a way to bend and shape the metals that made up the plane's body into weapons or shields or something, it could give them an edge that would allow them to attack settlements more openly, gather resources, and increase their power. If that happened, they might one day be a threat to the tribe.

"How long ago did they come through here, Gratt?" Erin asked.

"In the night," he said, "while we were for the resting."

A little less than a day, then. She looked toward the mountain that they were planning to pass through the following day. "They operate at night, right? Does that mean they rest during the day?"

164 | C. Steven Manley

"It may be for being truth," Gratt'na said. "I am not for knowing the Starless Tribe ways."

Erin cursed again. Frustrated, she reached out for the mountain with her senses, stretched her perceptions, and tried in desperation to find that sense of *there* so that she could Pull on it. If she could only do that, she could have them all to the crash site in a matter of minutes.

It was just so much harder than before. Her perceptions faltered after a few dozen feet and she exhaled a breath she didn't know she had been holding. It was like she was anchored or tethered somehow, like something was pulling away the power she knew she should have but just couldn't find.

"Sar'ha," Brinn'ha said, "do not be for the straining. Heed the warning of Barr'na. You would be for the self-hurting."

She nodded and kicked at the long divot in anger. "You're right," she said. "Gratt, any clue how many of the Starless there are?"

"Many," he said. "Many more than we."

"Of course there are," Erin said. "Any ideas? I mean, this is a problem, guys."

"We are for resting the small-time," Brinn'ha said. "Then we will be for the following of the Starless."

"Then for what if we are for the catching?" Gratt'na said. "They are still for being the many to we few."

"One problem at a time," Erin said. "Dammit! If I could just figure out what's wrong with my power, I could–"

"Do not be for the wasting of thought-strength, Sar'ha," Brinn'ha said. "Be for living seeking truth, not for accepting wanting truth."

Erin nodded. "Okay. Let's get a little rest, some food, and get back to it. How dangerous will it be to travel at night?"

"We must be for the great caution," Gratt'na said, "but

it is not for being a not-doing thing. I am still for thinking of what we do if we are for catching the Starless."

"Whatever it takes," Erin said. "Whatever it takes."

They didn't rest well or long. When the time came to break the camp and start moving again, Gratt'na muttered something about sleep being a weapon, but quieted when Brinn'ha hissed a warning at him. Erin heard the whole exchange, but didn't acknowledge any of it. Her sleep had been one anxious dream or portent of doom after another. She had uncontrollable mental flashes of the Valley People's settlements in flames or wild-eyed raiders cutting down the tribe with sharpened steel clubs and blades. In one of the dreams, a Tarr ran into the village with a bundle on its back. The bundle had exploded and Erin had seen the bloody destruction it wrought in the slow motion clarity that often came with dreaming.

She knew that was not a likely scenario. It took training and technology to set off the kinds of explosives the military used. Despite the dream, she thought that was the least of her worries. It was the wreckage that concerned her; there were too many chances for what was there to cause chaos.

A thought occurred to her: Did fighter pilots carry pistols? She didn't know, but the idea of a gun showing up in this world sent a current of cold dread through her veins. What if they did? What if this Starless Tribe found it, opened a bullet, discovered the gunpowder within and started trying to make it somehow? Could they do that? It had happened on Earth; why not here?

The dread intensified as she finished rolling the thin Tarr-hide she had slept on and stuffed it into her pack. She stood up, slung the pack over her shoulder, and faced her companions. With only a glance between them, they set off through the dark with Gratt'na in the lead.

The going was slow. They had decided against making any kind of torches because of the time it would take and the fact that they didn't really want any Starless looking back over their shoulders and spotting the light. A few hours into it, the sun started touching the tops of the surrounding mountains and revealed the rockier terrain they had entered. The ground was more of an upward slope there, and Erin could see the break in the mountainside looming ahead. From it, a wide, clear stream flowed over the rocks and through small pools.

Gratt'na saw her studying the mountain and said, "It is for being called Coldflow Passage. Always it is for being of the cold-season wind inside. During cold-season, it is for being a place of ice and treacherous footing."

"We can get through it okay now, though?" Erin asked.

"Truth," Gratt'na said.

"Be for the stopping," Brinn'ha said. "I am for having talk of this."

They stopped and Erin said, "What is it?"

"I am not for the thinking of passing through Coldflow Passage with closed eyes. Starless Tribes are for striking from the dark and the hidden places. They could be for the waiting within the Coldflow."

"Brinn'ha is for speaking truth. There is risk," Gratt'na said.

"Okay, so what do we do?"

"One of us is for going to try and to see if Starless wait to harm," Brinn'ha said.

Erin nodded. "I'll do it."

"Sar'ha," Gratt'na said, "we are for the having hunted far more than Sar'ha. To not be for being seen is our greater skill."

"No argument there," Erin said, "but you can't teleport; I can. Even if it's not what it used to be, I can still get far enough to get myself out of trouble. That means that, of the three of us, I have a better chance of surviving some kind of ambush."

The two Valley People were silent for a time. Then Brinn'ha said, "This is for being truth. I am not for liking it."

"Truth," Gratt'na said, agreeing with both his sisters' statements.

"Relax, guys. I've gotten across crowded strip clubs during dollar-beer biker nights without so much as a scratch or a tickle. I can handle this."

They were both staring at her with blank, confused expressions. They looked at each other, then back to Erin. It had been a while since she had said something that totally stumped them.

She smiled and said, "I'll be fine, guys. I've done worse."

"Be for the taking of time, Sar'ha, and for the using of stones for the hiding," Brinn'ha said.

"Also for the saving of your strength. Walk as the wind only if the need is for being great. Be for remembering how it steals your breath," Gratt'na added.

Erin opened her mouth to say "Thanks, Mom. Thanks, Dad," but bit back the sarcasm. The words would only confuse them and she knew their concern came from a genuine place. This was, after all, the first time they had set her loose in the world without being by her side. Instead, she smiled at them and said "I'll signal when I think it's clear. I'll be fine," and set off for the pass.

Rather than approach it directly, she circled out wide and came in at a steep angle that would provide her with some cover should there be any ill-intentioned Starless Tribe lurking inside. They would not have firearms, of course, and she had never seen a bow or arrow in this world, but they used leather slings that could propel stones hard enough to crack bone. There were also a lot of hunters she had seen who used short, narrow javelins that could puncture a body clear through in the hands of a skilled warrior. Erin had never really practiced with sling or javelin, but had seen the results of their use enough to give them the proper respect as weapons.

The mountain rose up over her in a thousand feet of dark, jagged shadows and sharp, gray edges. There were a hundred places to hide among those stones and ledges. Erin tried to watch them all as she crept to the passage opening. She was tempted to Pull to the other side to get a better view of the interior and confuse anyone who might be watching from the shadowed crevice. Gratt'na's warning came back to her, though, and she stayed her course.

As soon as she poked her head around the opening, a wash of cold air hit her in the face. It wasn't uncomfortable, but it was far colder than the air outside the passage. It reminded her of going into the cold rooms at the big warehouse stores back on Earth. The stream ran the length of the crevice, but there was plenty of room to walk on either side of the wide flow. She had expected the passage to be long and straight, a surgical slice through the mountain, but it wasn't; it curved and wound through the ancient rock. The stream cut deeper in some places and caused the uneven path on either side to rise and fall.

She saw the first Starless rise up from one of the depressions an instant before the second one – the closer one – struck.

CHAPTER SIXTEEN

Erin had spent the last year of her life learning to fight, hour after hour after hour in that cave with Barr'na and the others learning how to move and react. More than that, though, she had been learning to observe, to always be alert and prepared to respond to her surroundings. Not just with her eyes, but with all her senses. In the split second between the time she heard her attacker's foot slap stone and the moment his stone club would have crushed her skull, all that training saved her life.

The instant she heard the sound behind her, Erin focused on a spot behind and slightly higher than the attacker she was facing. As the axe fell, she Pulled. It was like blinking, but with an instantaneous sensation of wind rushing away from her. When she reappeared, she was positioned with her back to the Starless' back so that she wasn't facing either of them. She had planned on that, though, and spun around with her right foot only a moment behind her eyes and delivered a vicious side kick that landed between the surprised creature's shoulder blades. The blow sent him staggering toward his companion. His feet caught on the loose, slick stone and he pitched forward into the stream.

The one who had come up behind Erin was staring in disbelief at the empty space where the easy kill he had been expecting had just been standing. When his partner hit the water, the one with the axe looked up and saw Erin standing over them, Batla and Jo at the ready.

The axe clattered to the stones. The attacker tried to back away, tripped, and fell to rocky ground. "It is for being a demon," he screamed, "a mountain spirit!"

His partner had wiped the water from his eyes and was staring up at her in awe. He quickly averted his gaze. "Be not for the harming!" he cried. "We were not for the knowing of this spirit place!"

Erin stood over them, doing her best to glare at them with violence in her eyes. The truth, though, was that she was confused. In all the time she had spent among the Valley People, never once had she heard a member of the tribe refer to spirits or demons. She had assumed that belief in such supernatural things was just something that had never developed there, but now she wasn't so sure. Regardless, she knew she'd be a fool not to use the edge it gave her.

"Be quiet," she snapped. "Be quiet and answer my questions."

The two attackers quieted, but still watched her like prey watching a predator. They shared a glance that Erin read as confusion.

"Gorn'na," the axe wielder said, "I am not for understanding the demon's speaking. Are you for knowing it?"

The one called Gorn'na said, "I am not." Erin tilted her head slightly and examined his ears. No tattoos adorned them. She gave a mental curse, but kept the menace on her face. If these two didn't have the Marks of Understanding then that meant she could understand them but they could not do the same for her. She thought it over for a moment and then gestured at them with the blade of her Jo. "You," she said, stabbing her weapon toward Gorn'na, "and you," she said, repeating the gesture toward his companion, "stay." She pointed the blade at the ground.

It only took them a moment to get it and when they did, they both sat in silence with their eyes on the ground. Erin sighed and started yelling for Brinn'ha and Gratt'na. They must have already been on their way up because they answered almost immediately. They came on the scene, weapons out, and stopped short, obviously confused.

"They think I'm some kind of mountain demon or something," she said.

"Truth?" Brinn'ha said.

Erin nodded.

The siblings crossed the space between them and joined Erin. They stood next to her and looked down at the seated bandits, neither of whom had looked up at the newcomers. Erin took a moment and filled them in on the encounter.

"What are we for doing now?" Gratt'na asked, his voice low. "Starless are not for stopping the fight so much as bringing the fight."

"I am not for the killing of the not-defending," Brinn'ha said, matching her brother's tone.

"Of course we aren't going to kill them," Erin said. "Not unless they do something stupid. We need to talk to them and find out about the rest of their gang, why they're going after the wreckage, how many there are – that kind of thing. I need you guys to translate. They don't have Marks."

"They will not be for the free-talking," Brinn'ha said. "Starless are for being loyal to their tribe."

"That's okay," she said. "There was a great hero in my world named Luke Skywalker. He found himself in a situation like this once and used his adversaries' own beliefs against them. We can do the same." She didn't think that mentioning that Luke Skywalker was a fictional character or that his adversaries were little people and children in teddy bear costumes would do much to sell the plan. Besides that, she didn't have time to try and explain the concept of movies to them again.

"What are you for thinking, Sar'ha?" Brinn'ha asked.

She told them, not bothering to keep her own voice low. She tried to sound strong and in command. When she was done, Brinn'ha's face was pinched and tight, a sure sign that she didn't like something.

"On most days, I am not for spreading the not-truth," Brinn'ha said, "but our need is being strong."

"They are Starless," Gratt'na said, "they are for the fear-truth and not the found-truth. We would be for only speaking as they believe, not spreading the not-truth."

Erin didn't quite follow that so she just remained silent and watched the bandits.

"Truth," Brinn'ha said. "You should be for the speaking, Gratt'na. It is the truth of you."

Gratt'na said, "I will be for the speaking. Sar'ha, be for following the path of my words."

"You bet," she said.

Gratt'na stepped forward and spoke in a voice that was just loud enough to echo from the cold canyon walls. "You, who are being of the Starless Tribe," he said, "be for hearing my words."

Both the bandits raised their eyes, but looked at Erin rather than Gratt'na. She stood with her weapons in-hand and did her best to look menacing. The truth was she was starting to feel a little silly.

"Why are you for being here? You are for being the reason the great and fearsome Spirit of the Mountain is for rising. Why are you for doing the harm to those who are for seeking passage?"

"Be for mercy," the one called Gorn'na pleaded. "Be for begging your most hideous mountain spirit to be not for the harming!"

Erin's eyebrow shot up at the word 'hideous.'

"Be not for the begging and fear!" Gratt'na shouted. "Such are the things that are for offending my ruler-spirit. Be for the answering!"

Gorn'na's hands patted the air in front of him in a panicked rhythm. "I am for the answering, I am for the answering. Raff'na, Tarr Rider of the Cuts-in-the-Night Tribe, was for the ordering of we two to remain. He was for worrying of others who are for the claiming of the star-that-fell prize."

Erin heard a quiet hiss of displeasure from Brinn'ha at the mention of 'Tarr Rider' and she understood why. Tarr were, for the most part, as docile as the cows that Erin was accustomed to back on Earth. They did have a strong aversion to being ridden, however, and had to be beaten nearly to death before their spirits were broken enough to serve as a mount. Among the Valley People, Tarr were held in great respect and anyone willing to do such violence to one just so they didn't have to walk was considered the most pathetic kind of sadist.

"What prize are you for speaking of?" Gratt'na continued.

"Were you not for seeing? In the night? A great star was for breaking from the wide-black and falling to ground. There," Gorn'na said, pointing with one long finger farther down the pass.

"What is making your Tarr Rider for thinking he can claim such a prize? What is the number of the Cuts-in-the-Night Tribe that he is for thinking them equal to such a thing?"

"Our tribe is for being few," Gorn'na said. "We and a half score others, but we are for having a Starspeaker among us. Paar'ha, she is for being called. She is for claiming to have seen a vision of the fallen thing and the power that is for being at its place of coming to ground."

Erin didn't know what a 'Starspeaker' was. She

glanced at Brinn'ha and received a quick nod, indicating that her friend would fill her in.

"A Starspeaker among a Starless Tribe?" Gratt'na said. "You are for speaking the not-truth! Never is such a thing for happening!"

"What would you be for knowing of it, Valley Tribe Tarr-mater?" the other one said.

Within the space of two seconds, Erin teleported in front of the speaker, kicked him in the face, and teleported back. This left her a little out of breath, but it accomplished its purpose and set the captives to screaming again. Once they had settled down, she said, "Tell him not to talk to you like that or bad things will happen."

Gratt'na relayed the message and both the seated bandits patted the air before them, professing their apologies.

"Enough," Gratt'na said. "Be for the silence."

"Gratt," Erin said, "ask them what this Starspeaker is telling their leader that makes them think he can do anything with what they find."

Gratt'na turned back to the captives. "My ruler-spirit is for knowing what the Starspeaker is for having seen. What is for making her think your Tarr Rider equal to the prize? Be for speaking quick or be for firing the mountain-spirit anger!"

Erin suppressed a smile. Gratt'na was getting into his role.

"Paar'ha is for saying there is for being a rider on the star, a Walker of Worlds who will ally with the first of the tribes being for the finding. This Walker of Worlds is for having great power that can be for making a tribe powerful. This the Starspeaker has been for seeing."

"Holy shit," Erin whispered. "She knows about me."

Gratt'na gestured at the two bandits for them to remain seated. He walked up and joined his sister and Erin. "That is for being unexpected," he whispered.

"What the hell is a Starspeaker?" Erin asked.

"There are for being some among our kind who grow in years and become Starspeakers. There is a change that is for coming over them and they begin to see that which is for coming to pass, but has not yet. It is said they are for being to have speech with the stars that see all that was, is, and can be."

"She can predict the future," Erin said with a shake of her head. "Another damned Seer. Awesome."

"There are many who are for questioning this as not-truth, Sar'ha. There are many who are for thinking that such things are not for being possible and that Star-speakers are for being speakers of not-truth who do so with great skill."

"So, what? You're saying there's no such thing as magic? These Marks around my ears disagree with that."

Brinn'ha gave her friend a look that Erin thought was confused. "The Marks of Understanding are not for being impossible-truth, Sar'ha. They are found-truth. Found by those of the tribe who are for being the doing of a thing until the thing moves from question-truth to found-truth."

Erin thought that over. It occurred to her that she had just seen some marks on skin and some strange rituals and suddenly everything was magic. It wasn't to the Valley People, though. It was their technology. To them, a movie theater must seem like magic, whereas to Erin it just seemed like a matinee.

"Okay," she said. "So either this Paar'ha chick knows about me or she just got lucky and concocted the right lie. Either way, we've got to deal with the Starless."

"What are we for doing with these, mighty-mountain-spirit?" Gratt'na asked, smiling.

"Very funny," Erin said. "Let them go, but send them back the way we came. I don't want them getting ahead of us and warning their buddies."

Gratt'na turned to the captives. "Be for the standing,"

he bellowed.

They scrambled to their feet.

"Return to the valley," Gratt'na said. "Be for the staying of three days and nights, thinking on the violence you sought to be doing. On the fourth morning, you may be for passing through the Coldpass, but with no harm to any who would not be for harming you. Agree to this and be for going. Disagree and be for the drawing of my ruler-spirit's anger."

"Our Tarr Rider will be for seeking us," Gorn'na said. "His commanding was that we be for returning."

Erin vanished and then reappeared in front of the two Starless just out of arm's reach. She screwed her face into a snarl and let out a long, piercing scream in their faces.

Both captives turned and started running.

"You think they will cause the tribe any problems?" Erin asked once they were out of earshot.

"I am for thinking they do not wish to meet Elder Barr'na if they are for the trying," Gratt'na said.

"Truth," Erin said. She looked back at her friends standing on the slightly higher stones and looking at her with expectation on their flat but concerned faces. "Guys," she said, "go with them."

Brinn'ha and Gratt'na shared a look. Brinn'ha said, "Be for explaining, Sar'ha."

"I've got a bad feeling about this, Brinn. If this Star-speaker does know about me and I'm somehow responsible for that jet coming through into your world..." She swallowed back an inexplicable sob. "This is just starting to feel really big – bigger than just us. I don't want you two to get hurt. Go home. Go back to the tribe in case this goes tits up and you're needed there."

In near unison, both siblings said, "No."

"Guys, look–" Erin started.

"Be for the listening, Sar'ha," Brinn'ha snapped, an angry edge to her voice. "That we are all for ending is the all-truth. It is for being the truth of every people and every tribe. It is the all-truth. How we are for the being, the things we are for choosing and doing, are what are giving the all-truth meaning. We are for standing with our heart-sister, who is of the Valley People Tribe. If we are for facing our all-truth on the trail of that choosing, then that is for being the result of our choosing, not yours. We are for staying, Sar'ha, and we are not for the talking of it further."

Erin ignored the stray tear that fell from her eye – she blamed it on the mist that rose from the stream – and climbed up the larger stones until she was even with Gratt'na and Brinn'ha. She faced them, her expression somewhere between a smile and a frightened glare.

"Promise me," she said. "Promise me that if things get out of hand and I tell you to run that you will. Promise me you will run and you won't stop until you're home."

Brinn'ha and Gratt'na shared another look and then Brinn'ha said, "The promise is made."

Erin nodded and thanked her. They started moving again, carefully picking their way among the rocks and boulders, moving for the far end of the pass. They had been on the move for a few minutes when Gratt'na spoke.

"Sar'ha, I am for having a question."

"What is it?" Erin said.

"Can you be for explaining 'tits up'?"

Despite everything, Erin laughed.

CHAPTER SEVENTEEN

Israel

There was moment as the two men's eyes met, the briefest of instants when they could both see the realization come to the other's face and the memory of the last time they had met fast-forwarding through their mind's eye. Jordan holding Stone at gunpoint in a long-abandoned meat-packing plant in the Texas desert; Israel standing over Jordan's brother, who clutched a ruined and bleeding eye socket; the bullets tearing through Stone's body as Jordan betrayed the bargain they had made – all of this rushed through them both in the heartbeat it took before they started moving.

Jordan was the faster of the two, if only by a little. He flung the small first aid kit he had been carrying into Israel's face and jumped into a backwards flip that carried him ten feet from the larger man. He landed in a crouch and brought up a battered Colt 1911 in a single smooth motion, lining up a shot for Israel's head.

A year earlier, that might have worked. Israel, though, wasn't the same man he had been then. He had learned that hesitation and slow reactions were a great way to get yourself killed. He had trained hard to know when to think and when to move. Facing off against a Paragon like Jordan Screed was definitely a 'move your ass' situation.

He ducked under the surgical kit and tucked into a forward roll as Jordan's pistol boomed. Israel came out of the roll on his feet and delivered a lightning-fast kick to Jordan's wrist.

A second shot rang out and tore into the office's reception desk. Jordan managed to hold on to the pistol and launched himself out of his crouch high enough to plant both feet against Israel's chest. He kicked hard, using the other man's body as a springboard to do a second back flip that was designed to push Israel away and give Jordan time and distance for the headshot he needed.

Israel, though, didn't cooperate. His feet had been planted solidly enough that he hadn't moved an inch when Jordan kicked off of him. Israel saw the pistol coming up and leaned back and away from the shot. The pistol kicked in Jordan's hand and a bullet ripped away a section of the sheriff's doorframe.

Israel was on Jordan before he could squeeze the trigger again. He grabbed the man's gun hand and forced it down, squeezing hard. Another shot tore into the floor. Jordan reacted by executing some kind of sideways flip and roll combination Israel had never seen that effectively broke his grip despite his greater strength.

Jordan was free, but not without a price; the pistol clattered to the floor. He glanced at it and then bolted, moving like a cat for the door that led into the hall. Israel had seen that coming, though, and surged forward with his arms spread wide for a tackle.

He caught Jordan mid-leap and kept moving, carrying both of them into the closed door. They hit the heavy wood so hard that the hinges tore free of the frame, slamming the door into the hall and sending the already tense and terrified refugees scattering, fresh screams of surprise on their lips.

Israel was on top of Jordan. The other man was struggling like a pinned snake, but Israel positioned himself to bring his knee down on the other man's crotch like a hammer on an anvil.

Paragon or not, Jordan Screed was still a male animal with all the requisite plumbing. He grunted and tried to double up, but Israel didn't let him. He pinned Jordan's arms under his knees, rose up over him, and grabbed him by the front of his denim shirt. Holding him steady, Israel slammed his fist into the other man's face.

"That's for the people in Leticia!" he snarled.

His fist fell again.

"That's for Stone!" he said.

Again his fist, now trailing lines of blood through the air, fell.

"And that's for Erin, you twisted piece of shit!"

"Israel," Stone's voice snapped, "stop it! What in bloody–" Stone's eyes widened in surprise when he stepped into the hall and saw who Israel was kneeling on. Stone's pistol was already out and he leveled it at Screed's head. "Jordan Screed," he growled, "you're under arrest for acts of domestic terrorism and the murder of multiple Federal Agents."

"I don't think he can hear you right now, Agent," Bones said, moving over to stand next to Israel. He had gotten a large revolver from somewhere and had it pointed at Jordan.

It was true. Jordan's otherwise handsome face was a bloody mess that had already started to swell in numerous spots. His body was limp, unconscious but breathing.

Sheriff Holmes came and stood next to Stone. She had her shotgun in a relaxed grip, but pointed at Screed enough that there was little chance of her missing if she decided to shoot him. "Screed?" she said to Stone. "As in those two brothers who caused all that trouble in Texas last year?"

"One and the bloody same," Stone said. His voice was a low, dangerous rumble that Israel had never really heard before. He could understand it; Jordan had almost killed Stone the last time they'd seen each other.

"You're absolutely sure?" she said.

"I've got a copy of his digital file in my phone, Sheriff. You're welcome to look it over as soon as we get this bastard secured."

The sheriff nodded at Bones and he and Israel started securing Jordan's limp wrists behind his back with the deputy's handcuffs. Israel suggested they do the same to his ankles, but Bones balked at the idea. After a quick word with Stone, though, Sheriff Holmes tossed Israel her own set of cuffs and told her deputy to go along with it.

"In the interest of due diligence," she said to Stone, "how about showing me that file now."

Stone put his weapon away and pulled out his phone. He applied a few taps and swipes to the screen, then handed it to Sheriff Holmes. She looked it over, compared the pictures she saw to Jordan's face, swiped the screen a few more times, and then handed it back to Stone.

"Son of a bitch," she hissed. "On my island? In my town? Right under my damn nose? Is this the real reason you people are here?"

"Yes," Michelle said quickly, before Stone had a chance to answer, "at least partly. It's kind of complicated, Sheriff. Maybe we could get Screed locked up and then finish our conversation in your office?"

"Are they involved in what's happened to my island? Did they start this somehow?"

Michelle and Stone exchanged questioning glances. Stone shrugged. "That's actually a really good question," he said. "We don't know."

The sheriff nodded. "Sarah," she said over her shoulder, "isn't there a cleaning supply closet a couple of corridors over?"

"Yes, ma'am."

"All right, you and Clint go with Bones and–" She looked at Israel, her expression confused. "Who the hell are you, anyway?"

"My name's Israel Trent. Consider me a consulting investigator for Agent Stone."

"Uh huh. Sarah, you and Clint go with Bones and Mr. Trent. Get that closet completely cleared out, then secure this prisoner in the space. I'll round up a couple of guards for the door."

"Make sure they're not the sort to hesitate when it comes to shooting a man," Stone said. "Jordan Screed is the very definition of slippery."

Sheriff Holmes smiled. "I've got a couple of Vietnam vets in mind who would love a reason to ventilate a terrorist," she said. "They'll keep his ass locked down. In the meantime, let's wait in my office while the boys put away the trash. I want to hear more about the Screed brothers."

Once Stone had returned to the office with the sheriff and Michelle, Israel grabbed Jordan by the front of his shirt and hefted the unconscious man over his shoulder like he weighed no more than a toddler. When he saw Bones staring at him, he realized what he'd done and said, "He's lighter than he looks. Guess that's why he can jump around like that."

"Yeah," Bones said. "And back there in the field? The truck? Was that lighter than it looked, too?"

Israel shrugged, not sure what else to say.

"You still aren't telling me everything," Bones said.

"No, we're not, but we will."

"Why?"

He was about to answer when the sheriff's two assistants, Sarah and Clint, joined them in the hall. Israel mouthed the word 'later' to Bones and followed the assistants as they headed down the corridor. As they moved past the assembled survivors, Israel noticed no fewer than a dozen cell phones and tablet devices pointed in his direction, each almost certainly in camera mode. He cursed and made a note to mention this to Stone and Michelle. Nothing that was happening on Jasper Island needed to show up on the Internet.

They had waited while Clint and Sarah had cleared out the large closet that the sheriff had referred to and then deposited Jordan in heap on the floor. The man had never stirred. His face was a collection of bruises and bumps that were dark with dried blood, but he had seemed to be breathing easily enough. After making sure the two vets who were to be standing guard understood who they were watching, Bones and Israel had headed back to the office.

They were about halfway back when Bones told Sarah and Clint to go on without them. Once the two assistants had gotten back into the office, he turned to Israel and said, "Okay, it's later. Talk."

"Not here, man," Israel said, shaking his head.

"Why not?"

"Because damn near every person around us is walking around with a recording device in their pocket and what we need to talk about doesn't need to get recorded. Let me ask you something, though. Why did you wreck the truck? What happened?"

Bones shook his head and let out a short, sharp sigh. "I don't know. There was that light, the one right before the ferret lizards from Hell showed up. It was... I don't know. Uncomfortable."

"How so?" Israel asked.

"It was like getting kicked in the eyeballs, but not kicked. More like someone was pushing them into the back of my skull. It was so weird and sudden that my foot slipped off the brake and onto the gas. Bingo – instant wreck."

Israel remembered his own Awakening experience. It hadn't been as intense as Bones was describing, but the general sensation had been the same. "The same thing happened to me," he said. "I came up on something like what we saw out there and I felt what you're talking about. It changed me. That's–"

"Bones! Trent!" Sheriff Holmes shouted from the office door. "If you two are finished braiding each other's hair, we're waiting in here."

"On our way, Sheriff," Bones replied, starting for the door.

Israel stopped him. "Michelle is the best one to explain this," he said. "Get her alone, ask her about the ball pit. She'll know what it means. Until then, you can't tell anyone, not even the sheriff. I'm serious."

"Why not? You playing the 'national security' card?"

"For starters. Beyond that, it's just life and death."

"Today, gentlemen!" Sheriff Holmes said.

They started walking toward the office. The sheriff disappeared back into the doorway and Bones said, "Fine. I'll play along for now, but if there's something the sheriff needs to know, anything that can save even a single person who's still alive on this island, I will tell her. Make no damned mistake about that."

Israel nodded at that, but said nothing as they entered the sheriff's office. The door closed despite the bullet damage to the doorframe, though Bones did have to give it a hard pull before the latch clicked into place.

"Okay," Sheriff Holmes said from behind her desk once more. "That was exciting. Now let's get back to the part where you tell me what's going on without any of the usual 'that information is classified' bullshit."

Stone opened his mouth to answer, but Michelle spoke first. "Do you know how viruses work, Sheriff?"

She had returned to her relaxed position behind her

desk. The rubber band was back over her fingers, but she was stretching it absently while they talked instead of strumming at it. "Specifically? No. The general idea is that a person gets exposed and they get sick according to what kind of virus it is, right?"

"More or less," Michelle said. "As I'm sure you know from your military experience, weaponized pathogens, both viral and bacteriological, are a major concern. A while back, we got word that some highly funded domestic terror operations were trying to do black research into a new, highly infectious viral agent. Thing was, they were trying to make it undetectable by conventional means, either biochemical or microscopic – essentially an invisible but lethal viral agent. We had some data on the virus, but no equipment to study it with. The reason my colleagues and I were coming to DGS was to get some of their biomedical engineers to take a look at our computer models and see if there was a way to upgrade our tech to a level that could spot this thing. Before you ask, no, we did not bring any live samples onto the island, only computer mock-ups. Whatever's happening here, we didn't bring it."

Israel had to suppress a smile. The fiction rolled from Michelle's lips like a melody from a master musician. If she wasn't a genius, he was pretty sure she could make a living writing thrillers.

"What do you know about what's happening?"

"There is a strong possibility that the virus we're investigating caused it. I especially think that now that we've discovered Jordan Screed on the island," Michelle continued. "The Screeds aren't really true believers in any kind of ideology or cause, they're just the worst kind of hired help when it comes right down to it. They do, however, have a long laundry list of connections to zealots of every stripe, including the group that is developing this bug."

"Virus, walking dead – I can make that connection,"

the sheriff said, "but if you're telling me a flu bug put an impassable storm around this island and caused monsters to start dropping out of the sky then I'm not buying that."

"No, of course not," Michelle said. "If you recall, though, I said our bad guys were well-funded. What if – and I realize this is an enormous if – some of the funding, maybe even the research, came from DGS? I mean, that's a big facility over there. How much do we really know about what goes on inside? It could very well have ties to domestic terrorism and we just don't know it."

"That's a huge assumption," Bones said.

"I know," Michelle said. "But look at it: weather that should be impossible, things appearing out of nowhere, zombies? That all screams illegal research gone wrong to levels of comic book villainy to me. Where else on this island would you look for that kind of thing?"

Israel silently shook his head. The woman had a gift.

The sheriff thrummed the rubber band once. Israel noticed Michelle's eyes flick down to it and grow tight for just an instant, as though it were a problem she were trying to work out. "All right," Sheriff Holmes said, "let's say for a second I buy into this. What then? It's not like we can go kicking down DGS's front door and start arresting people for being mad scientists."

"Screed," Israel said, the name bitter on his tongue. "We start with him."

Stone nodded. "Yeah. If all this is coming out of DGS, then you can bet your bonnet whoever's up there has an exit strategy. We can interrogate him and find out what's what. Might be a way to get your people to safety."

Sheriff Holmes looked at Israel. "Meant to say you've got some moves there, young man. That little scrape seemed personal, though."

Israel didn't see any reason to candy coat it. "It was. Agent Stone and I were in Texas last year. I owed Jordan a little extra attention."

She nodded. "Fair enough." She seemed to consider the situation for a time, then said, "All right. That broom closet won't do for interrogation. I'll find a good spot and have it cleared. Then we'll talk to the man."

"Best to let us handle that," Stone said. "You've got your hands full with keeping your people calm."

"Oh, hell–"

"They're right, Sheriff," Bones said. "You need to be out here where folks can see you running things. I'll stick with them and make sure they stay honest."

The sheriff's expression softened a fraction. "Are you sure, Bones?"

Bones smiled. "It's cool, Jan. I got this."

She studied him for a moment and then nodded. "All right," she said, "take Clint and you guys–"

The rest of her words were lost to Israel as he was suddenly overcome by a sensation like thousands of ants crawling over his spinal cord and brain. He shuddered and clamped his eyes shut, trying hard not to let it show, but knew he was failing.

"Hi," Sybil's voice said. *"Your name's Israel Trent, and I know how to kill you now."*

CHAPTER EIGHTEEN

Israel muttered something that he hoped sounded like an excuse and rose from his seat. His eyes were still half closed against the tingle in his spine. He threw open the door and moved quickly into the outer office. The feeling intensified and he felt the words in his mind.

"Didn't you hear me? I know your name. Where are you? I can't tell."

"Get lost, Sybil," he hissed under his breath. "I'm busy." He moved into the hallway and wove among the small crowd, trying to find a place where he could find some measure of privacy. He spotted an empty corner next to a vending machine that someone had broken into. He leaned into the corner facing the wall and tried to look like he was resting.

"That's a lot of people. Where are you, Israel?"

"You're in my head," he said quietly. "You tell me."

"I can't. You aren't part of my clique, which I still don't understand, but that's okay. I talked to the tall one and he says that you're special, like him, even though you won't do what I say like he does. You should do what I say, Israel. Everybody who does what I say is happy."

"Kinda doubt that," Israel whispered. "Who's this tall man you keep talking about?"

"He asked me not to tell you. He said he wants it to be a surprise."

"Let me guess," Israel said, putting it together. "Bad attitude, big tattoo on his face, stupid last name that rhymes with 'weed'?"

The silence lasted longer than he thought it should. *"How did you know that?"*

Israel smiled. "Tell Carmine I ran into his brother. I've got him all tied up in a nice, dark closet. I'll be coming for him next."

"You have Jordan?"

"Oh, yeah. Cuffed and stuffed."

"Where are you, Israel? Tell me."

"Not a chance," he whispered.

"Tell me!"

The crawling sensation suddenly exploded into something more akin to pain than irritation. It went from scurrying and itching along his spine to something that felt more like burrowing and digging. He shuddered hard and, for just an instant, started to tell Sybil what she wanted to know. All of it. For one fleeting moment, it seemed like the most natural thing in the world to give her whatever she wanted and do whatever she said.

Israel ground his teeth and threw his will against the compulsion. It was washed away in the tide of his own determination and the feeling in his brain returned to something more tolerable.

"Nice try," he muttered.

There was no response other than a sense of angry frustration. Then, the crawling feeling was gone. It was as though someone, somewhere, had just flipped a switch.

Israel spent a minute collecting his thoughts and then turned from the corner where he had set himself. He found four faces studying him. Each held an expression of deep concern, but Bones and Sheriff Holmes looked more confused than anything.

"You all right, mate?" Stone said.

Israel nodded. "Yeah. Just a... migraine."

"You always talk to yourself when you have a migraine?" Bones asked.

"Sometimes, yeah," Israel said. "Look, I'm fine now. Let's get set up for Screed."

The sheriff's eyes lingered on Israel as she turned to Bones. "I think there are some study rooms in the library. Those should work, but make sure you keep that guy restrained. From what I saw when he tangled with Mr. Trent here, I imagine he'd be a bitch to catch if he gets loose. I'll be on the wall when you're ready to fill me in."

Bones nodded and they watched her walk away. As soon as she was out of sight, Bones gestured for the trio to follow him. Israel expected him to lead them to the library. Instead, though, he ushered them into an empty classroom and shut the door behind him. There was a loud click as he snapped the lock into place.

"All right," he said, looking at Michelle, "Mr. Migraine over there told me to ask you about a 'ball pit,' which sounds even stupider when I say it out loud. So, I reckon no one's leaving this room until you tell me what's what, and I mean right goddamned now."

So they did.

They told him everything about the secret history of the world: the multiverse, the presence of the Awakened among humanity, the DGRI, the Sentry Group – even the truth about what happened in Texas the previous year. Bones listened to it all with attentive stoicism. He stood, leaning against the door, arms folded, and took it all in, nodding occasionally and asking for clarification when he needed it. When they came back around to their presence on Jasper Island, he said, "And this conduit thing that opened from the– What did you call it? Breach? That's why those things popped in out of nowhere? From another... what? Planet? Reality?"

"Yes," Michelle said. "And the sudden burst of Inner Dark energies is what excited your ocular nerve and made your eyes feel so funky."

Bones smiled. "Funky. Good word."

Michelle smiled back, if only a little. "Point is, that's a dead giveaway for someone who's been newly Awakened."

"So I'm going to be like him now?" Bones said, nodding at Israel.

Israel tensed at that. They had kept his exact bloodline from Bones. Considering the Necrophage outbreak going on at the moment, it hadn't seemed wise to tell the deputy he was hanging out with a Paragon of that particular species.

"There's no way to tell in advance," Michelle said. "It all depends on your genetic legacy – your bloodline – and how strong it is in your genome. It could be as little as a cosmetic change to your appearance – what we call a Revealed – up to the level of full-blown Paragon – powers like the demi-gods of old or something in between. We won't know until it happens."

"And how long does that take?" Bones said.

"It was about a day for me," Israel said. "Twenty-four hours or so."

"His exposure was different than yours, though," Michelle said. "Israel walked into a room with a small breach that was active and ongoing. You were basically sucker punched by one. It's like the difference between walking out of the dark into lamplight and walking out of the dark into a professional grade camera flash. I don't know if the sudden intensity of your exposure will change the rate of your Awakening or not. You will Awaken, though. Accepting that now will ease the change when it comes."

Bones took that in, arms still folded tight across his

chest. He stared hard at Michelle, though not with any kind of anger in his expression. More than anything, he seemed to be trying to find some fault in her face or her eyes that would tell him this was all some kind of horrible prank. There was no such tell, of course, so he finally closed his eyes and shook his head in resignation.

"If you folks had just shown up out of the blue," he said, "if I hadn't seen the pure nightmare that I've seen in the last 48 hours, I'd call y'all crazy and tell you to go to hell. This shit is real, though, isn't it?"

No one spoke. No one needed to.

"Okay," Bones said, the word coming through a jaw tight with tension, "it is what it is. What kinds of changes should I look for? Is it gonna hurt?"

"Look for anything," Michelle said. "As far as pain..." She shrugged.

"Won't know until it happens. Got it," Bones said. "What about all the dead folks walking around, the necro-whatsits. You have any clue where they came from?"

"None," Stone said. "That and the storm. We weren't expecting any of that. I'll tell you this, though. These 'phage aren't acting properly. Something's different here."

"What do you mean?" Bones asked.

"Zombie Necrophage don't hold back. They aren't organized or rational. They're like sharks in a constant feeding frenzy. Every other 'phage infestation I've been part of was usually a total loss of life because the damn things don't stop until there's nothing left to kill. Here, though, they're different. The way they took the town, the fact that they basically have this school surrounded, but haven't swarmed it – it's not right. There's a big part of this we aren't seeing."

"I'll bet," Israel said, "that we've got some answers locked up in a supply closet down the hall. Let's find out what Jordan knows and see if we can't do something about all of this."

"While I wait to see what kind of monster I turn into," Bones said in a quiet voice.

The words hung in the air. Bones had his head lowered and seemed to be mentally wrestling with his new reality.

"For what it's worth," Israel said, "we're with you on this. No matter what happens, whatever changes come, we won't leave you hanging."

Bones was quiet. He finally looked up, met Israel's eyes, and nodded. "Good to know." He pushed off the door and said, "Screw this drama. Let's get some answers from Mr. Screed."

A half hour had passed by the time they had chosen one of the library's private study rooms and then brought Jordan to it. Israel and Bones cleared out the people who had settled there, assuring them it was temporary and necessary. Once the main doors were locked, the two men who had been guarding Jordan watched the door, and the blinds were drawn shut. They joined the others in their makeshift interrogation room.

The room had no exterior-facing windows, but did have one wall that was a large pane of thick glass that overlooked the rest of the library. A single fluorescent fixture lit the room in a bright wash of white light that stung Israel's eyes enough to make him wish he had his sunglasses. He had positioned himself in front of the glass pane to discourage any poorly conceived ideas that Jordan might come up with about escaping. Stone and Bones both stood between their prisoner and the door, while Michelle stood just behind them, well out of Jordan's reach. Jordan was propped up in one corner with his hands and ankles still cuffed and his head lolling to one side. He hadn't reacted once while they had moved him.

Israel had picked up on changes in the man's breathing that convinced him Jordan was awake, but pretending not to be. He was about to say so when Bones spoke up.

"Are you buying this shit, Agent Stone?" Bones asked.

"Not really, no," Stone replied.

"Me, neither. Did I mention I had some experience with field interrogation back in the sandbox?" Bones said.

"No, you did not."

"Well, I do. It's how I got my nickname. That's a different story, though. Point is, I had this Gunny – that's Gunnery Sergeant – who showed me a trick one time. See, we had picked up this well-known insurgent asshat who hadn't wanted to come along all peaceful like and wound up getting his bell rung a couple of times – kinda like our boy here. So, we bring him in to sweat him and he's all limp like a rag doll and shit and all us rank and file jarheads, we're thinking 'Oh, crap, we broke the guy. He's in a coma or something,' you know? Gunny, though, he ain't buying what the guy's selling. Not being the most patient guy to begin with, Gunny gets up from his chair all calm like and leaves the interrogation room. He's gone maybe ten minutes, right? Then he strolls back in like he's walking his dog on a sunny day, but he's carrying a full pot of coffee that he had freshly brewed just for the occasion. He took that pot and emptied it into the asshat's crotch. Full pot of steaming hot coffee all up in the man's tackle box.

"Well, that set the asshat to hollering like a stuck damn pig. Gunny, he turns to the rest of us and says, 'Ain't no man alive gonna sleep through his eggs getting hard boiled,'" Bones said. A fond laugh colored the story's last few words and Bones kicked the bottom of Jordan's foot hard enough to make the man's head bob. "What do you say, asshat? Should I go brew us up a pot and boil some sparrow's eggs?"

Jordan's eyes opened easily, bright and fully alert in his bruised and bloodied face. "That's a cute story, cop," he said as though he were bored. "You should write your memoirs or something. Oh, wait, you're not going to live long enough for that." He wriggled and shifted until he was sitting upright in the corner with his knees bent. His eyes swept over the room and settled on Michelle. "You guys didn't tell me you were bringing party favors," he said. "You'll need to uncuff me, though, if you want me to give her all the attention she deserves."

Israel took a step forward, but Bones beat him to it. He landed a kick into the man's ribs that Jordan could have easily avoided if he hadn't been bound. Air woofed out of the prisoner's lungs and he stared at Bones like he was a bug that needed to be squashed.

"You," Bones said in even tones, "should show a little more respect unless you're up for trying to breathe with a few broken ribs."

"I bet he could manage," Israel said.

Jordan turned his head to face Israel and, to Israel's surprise, grinned. "Israel mother-fucking-Trent," he said. "How've you been, man? You look good."

Israel didn't return the smile, but decided to play along. "Not bad. Spent some time in the hospital visiting with Stone after the last time I saw you. Then spent a lot of time looking for you and your shit for brains brother."

"Oh, yeah, that's right," Jordan said, turning his attention to Stone. "Nice to see you up and around, man. Seriously, your reputation doesn't lie – you are a tough son of a bitch. For the record, the whole shooting you thing wasn't personal. I just needed to distract Superfly over there so that Carmine and I could get away."

"It felt pretty personal," Stone growled.

"Wait," Bones said. "This guy shot you?"

Stone nodded, never taking his eyes off Jordan. "Three times, point blank, in the back."

Bones stared at Stone for a moment, then said, "Well, that's... Holy shit, I don't know what that is."

"It's history," Michelle said, taking a step forward, but still keeping Bones and Stone between herself and Screed. "We all have scores to settle with this man," she said, "but we have some more immediate concerns as well."

Jordan stared at her and said, "I recognize you from the Seer's files," he said. "You're one of those sisters, the twin geniuses who work for Sentry. Which one are you?"

"I'm the one who's going to brew the coffee if you try to jerk us around," she said. "What's happening on this island and you being here cannot be a coincidence. So why don't you start telling us what the hell is going on."

Jordan looked to Bones and then back at Michelle. "You sure about that, honey?"

"He knows," Israel said. "Just talk, man."

"Why? I mean, come on. What's in it for me? These accommodations aren't exactly five-star and, seriously, I've felt less hostility from prison guards. What good is telling you anything going to do me?"

"If we can use what you tell us to put an end to all this it might get you off this island wearing something other than a body bag," Israel said.

Jordan started laughing. It went on for a few seconds before Israel said, "What? What is so damned funny?"

Jordan stifled his laugh and said, "The fact that you think anybody is getting off this island alive is just precious. We're all done, man. All of us. There's no fucking way she's letting anybody on this island live."

"She?" Michelle said. "Who? Jordan, what did you and your brother do here?"

"Me and my—" Jordan bit back the rest of the statement. Anger and frustration flared on his face and he said, "Fine. You want to know what's going on? Ask your pet zombie over there." His head gestured toward Israel.

Bones' eyes followed just as quickly. "Pet what?" he said. "What's he talking about, Israel?"

"Oh, so the cop doesn't know everything. Figures,"

Jordan said.

"What the hell are you talking about, Screed?" Israel snapped.

"This!" Jordan shouted. "This is your fault! You! All of this, all those dead people, all of it, Trent! It's all on you!"

CHAPTER NINETEEN

The accusation hung in the air like the smoke from a gun. It was a long moment before anyone spoke again.

"You're going to need to explain that," Michelle said. "We've only been on this island for a few hours. All of this was already happening when we got here. How could any of this be our fault?"

"*His* fault," Jordan said, the words coming through gritted teeth. His eyes were focused on Israel and the lines of his face were creased with hatred. "His. Fault."

"You still need to explain that," Stone said.

"Yeah," Bones said, his eyes on Israel, "I'd like to hear that, too."

Israel noticed that Bones had dropped a hand onto his pistol, though he left it in the holster. He met the man's eyes and gave him a gentle nod of understanding.

Jordan kept staring at Israel and then, with a deep breath, said, "Okay. After the Texas thing, Carmine's eye was all fucked up thanks to him," he nodded at Israel again, "so we bandaged it up as best we could and took off. None of the cars were working, so we had to hike out in the dark – which sucked, let me tell you."

"Cry me a river," Stone said. "Get to the crunchy bits."

"Whatever, man. So, we finally get out of there about the time the big fireball goes off, which I assume was also Israel's doing, and suddenly everything lights up again. Phones, streetlights – everything. I figured that meant whatever the Seer was doing got shut down, which was cool with me because it meant I could call for an extraction. Problem was our handler was one of the people who wound up getting squidheaded when the breach first opened. Ricardo – kind of an asshole, but he always gave us a fair shake. Anyway, the only other contact number I had that was remotely tied to the Progeny was for an offshoot group we'd done some work for a few years back."

"Who?" Stone asked.

"Your mother," Jordan said. "It doesn't matter. Point is they said they'd get us out of there if we jumped ship from the Progeny and did some stuff for them again. We figured the Seer was getting flash-fried back in the desert, which pretty much fulfilled the contract we had and we weren't exactly in what you'd call a strong bargaining position, so we agreed. Half an hour later we're on a private helicopter headed for California. After that, a jet bound for this little vacation spot."

"Why would they bring you way up here?" Bones asked.

"Well, now, that was my question too, cop. I mean, what could they possibly have this far out of the way that they would need us for? At first I thought they were just stashing us out of sight until the heat died down. I mean, we were everywhere – *America's Most Wanted* in high-def and surround sound. Hell, they even seeded some look-alikes into transit hubs across the country to throw off the feds. Come to find out there was a little more to it."

"Stop there," Michelle said. "How long was this from the time you left Texas?"

Jordan shrugged. "A couple of days. Maybe three."

"And Carmine was still alive."

Jordan grinned. "Bitch, please. That Simms chick dropped him from who knows how high and he healed up from that no problem. Where is she, anyway? I've got some extra cash and thought she might give me–"

"Choose your next words with extreme caution," Israel said in a low, dangerous tone. His eyes met Jordan's and whatever the cuffed man saw there made him swallow and look away.

"You said there was more to it," Stone said. "How so?"

"Yeah, that's right. So, this group and the Progeny were one and the same way back when, but they had a falling out over the direction the group should go. They ended up parting company, but kept a close eye on each other. They've been working like that for a long time. These guys, though, they didn't know much about the Seer. We did. So, they brought us up here to lay low and spill what we knew."

"Let me guess," Israel said. "They had you hidden in the Darkarcher facility."

"Yep. Why the hell else would anybody come to this shithole island?"

"What's DGS got to do with any of this?" Bones asked.

Jordan laughed. "Man, you don't even know what's up with that place. It's a front. They've got the whole world thinking they're creating video cards and all that other electronic crack that people get hooked on – and they do – but that's not even close to the whole truth. The real work's underground on our side of the Veil."

"Like what exactly?" Michelle said.

"Well, as I understand it, that goes back to the break-up way back when. See, the Progeny was all about 'prophecy this' and 'worship that' – religious bullshit, y'know? The guys who really run Darkarcher, though, are a little more pragmatic. Where the Progeny think of the Inner Dark as a holy place where the masters of the universe live, the Darkarcher guys see a source of power that science and technology can exploit for fun and profit."

"Faith versus reason," Israel said. "That's an argument as old as man."

"If you say so," Jordan said. "All I know is that these guys were practically drooling at the idea of what the Seer was doing in Texas and the size of the breach there. Something about the amounts of energy released or some damn thing; I don't know for sure. They kept going on about not having much time or something – dissipation rates, stuff like that. We'd been here a couple of weeks when they came to us with some work."

"What?" Bones said. "They have an opening in the housekeeping staff?"

"Don't quit your day job, cop," Jordan said. "Anyway, they had my phone and had found a couple of the names that the Seer had given us, people we hadn't snatched yet. They wanted us to grab one."

Israel held up a hand for Jordan to stop, "Hang on. Why? What good is a potential Paragon to these people? And what does any of this have to do with you blaming me for what's happened on the island?"

"I'll get to that part," Jordan said. "As far as them wanting a Paragon, I asked them the same question you just asked. I mean, what good is somebody like that if they aren't Awakened, right? All they told me was that they had the means to jump start an Awakening, but only once. So they grilled us over and over again about the names the Seer gave us: Was there ever a failure to Awaken? Was there ever anyone who Awakened but didn't reach Paragon potential? Was there any way to predict the bloodline that would manifest? Stuff like that. Whatever they planned on doing, it was pretty clear they could only do it once and wanted to make sure they got it right."

"So what was the job?" Stone asked.

Jordan looked at Michelle. There was the faintest hint

of a smile on his lips. "Some femme in Arkansas," he said. "Nobody waitress in a nowhere little town with delusions of grandeur. We had to make arrangements to snatch her up and get her back here without drawing any attention. I wasn't crazy about the whole gig – we were still trending in the media – but the DGS folks hooked us up with some gadgets and injections that altered our facial structures enough to fool any recognition software. A little makeup covered Carmine's tattoos. Plus, he was wearing an eye-patch by then, so that helped a lot." Jordan's eyes cut into Israel again.

"I'm sure he'll make a great pirate," Israel said. "Get on with it."

Jordan scowled and said, "Point is, we were back in business. So, we did what we do and a week later we were back here unpacking a crate that held our mark – safe, sound, and sleeping like a baby."

Bones shook his head. "Wow," he said. "You are a real snake."

"Oh, stop," Jordan said, "my feelings. Seriously, though, I'm flipping you off behind my back."

"Let's try to keep this productive, Deputy," Stone said.

Bones nodded. "You're right. Sorry."

"This girl you kidnapped," Israel said. "What happened to her? Where is she?"

"Well, as far as I know, she's still at DGS. As for what happened to her, your guess is as good as mine."

"What the hell does that mean?" Bones said. "You were there with her. How you could not know what happened?"

"Did you miss the part about the real work being underground? I meant that literally, Sherlock. We weren't allowed to take the elevator to the basement levels, which is where they took her right after we delivered her. So, no, I don't have any idea what they did with her. The only thing I can tell you for sure is that whatever they did worked."

"How do you know that?" Israel asked.

"For starters, the people working with her said so. The day after she went downstairs, they were walking around like they'd won the lottery. They were talking about stable transdimensional energy flows and positive... attractant-somethings. A whole bunch of shit that was way over my head."

"Attractant vectors?" Michelle asked.

"Yeah, that was it. Anyway, they were all on top of the world because their little science experiment had been a success. Carmine and me, though, were a little worried we'd outstayed our usefulness. They said we were cool, though, and that they wanted to keep us around because if the thing they were doing with the girl kept working, they'd want more of them. Maybe even start adding names to the list. So we just chilled, waited for a few months to pass, started blending in with the locals. This place is far enough out that we weren't too worried about getting recognized so long as we avoided the cops. Besides that, hanging out at DGS was getting hella boring."

Stone glanced at Bones, who shrugged. "Folks live out here mostly to get away from the mainland. They tend to keep to their own. It doesn't surprise me no one spotted him."

"Go on," Israel said, nodding at Jordan.

"Well, that's the way it was – dull, but safe – until about a month ago," Jordan said. "That's when things started going sideways. I woke up in the middle of the night and Carmine was standing over my bed looking at me like he wasn't sure who I was. I asked him what the hell he was doing and he said he thought I'd gotten a woman into my room. Said he kept hearing one through the wall between our rooms. Needless to say there was no woman since we both had strict instructions from our employers to keep our hands off the DGS staff and the local ladies."

"Imagine that," Israel said, the cold returning to his voice. He'd spent a lot of time over the last year reading up on the Screed brothers; the majority of the disappearances and murders they were suspected or guilty of involved young women.

"Yeah," Jordan said, "I guess our reputations preceded us. Anyway, we were both behaving. DGS was our meal ticket and you never shit where you eat, right? Carmine, though, he started getting weird after that night. He quit talking to me, started talking to himself. He'd stare off into space for hours like he was listening to something only he could hear. About two weeks ago, he stopped leaving his room. Barely ate anything, wouldn't answer when I knocked. I thought for sure he was losing it."

"More so than usual, you mean?" Israel said.

This earned him another scowl from Jordan. "Yeah, a lot more than that, Trent," he said. "See, the whole time, this entire year, he's been wearing that eye-patch you fitted him for. I figured the eye hadn't grown back or hadn't healed right or something. He didn't like to talk about it, see, and he always said no when I tried to get him to show it to me. Wouldn't even let docs who were in the know about him being a Paragon look at it. Carmine's always been prone to vanity, so I figured it was just him dealing with a disfigurement, y'know? I thought that until about five nights ago." Jordan's eyes dropped at the memory. He grew quiet as though he were looking for the right way to tell the tale.

Stone didn't give him long. "Get to it, Screed."

Jordan looked up at him, nodded, and then made a point of looking directly at Israel. "I woke up again that night," he said. "It was about three in the morning and I heard something in the hall outside my room. I looked, and there was my little brother kneeling over some guy from the security staff. There were other people in the hall behind him, just standing and watching while a couple of guys held the guard down and Carmine—" Jordan faltered, swallowed hard, and then went on in a voice that seemed to struggle with itself. "He'd lost the eye patch and had a syringe and needle stuck into the eye that it had kept hidden. See, Trent, the eye was solid black. Just black. And dead. Like you. Whatever you did in Texas changed it somehow, and while I watched, he withdrew some kind of black fluid from his eye and injected it into that guard's neck. It was just a little, but enough, I guess, because the guard changed. He jerked and he shuddered and he changed into one of those things. Into one of you, Trent.

"That's when I really woke up, I guess. When Carmine looked up at me with that dead, black eye, I realized none of those people looked right. They were all 'phages, all gray and dead and looking hungry. Except for Carmine, though. He looked like he always did except for the eye thing. I asked him what the hell was happening and he just smiled and said I'd understand soon, that they had been on the way to my room when the guard had stumbled onto them. He said she would explain, that she would help me understand once I was in her clique."

"He said that?" Israel asked. "He said 'clique'?"

"Yeah, that's what he said," Jordan snapped, "but you're missing the point. This is your fault! If you hadn't done whatever the hell it was you did to him none of this would have happened! This is on you! This is—"

"What was her name?" Michelle said, stepping forward.

"What?" Jordan said.

"The woman you took in Arkansas. What was her name? See, I already know you're a sociopath. What I'm wondering, though, is whether or not you're so subhuman that you can destroy a random life without so much as getting the person's name."

"Susan Gunderson. She was a waitress at a Red Robin.

I had to memorize her file."

"Her file? That's all she was?"

"She was just another job."

Michelle nodded. "Like all the jobs you pulled for the Progeny?"

"Yeah, just like those. And they paid fucking good, let me tell you."

"I'm sure they did. Here's the thing, Jordan: If you and your brother had just left those people alone to live their lives in peace then you wouldn't have ever taken Israel and Erin and they wouldn't have Awakened, and none of you would have ended up in Texas where, incidentally, Carmine got far less than he deserved. See, what the two of you did made all this possible. You made Israel. So you know what? Fuck you and fuck your brother. This is your fault – yours and the Progeny's. And, for the record, no matter what kind of genetic wild card Israel got dealt, he is a more honorable and better man than you and your brother combined have ever been or ever will be."

Michelle had been steadily advancing on Jordan while she spoke, her hand on the holstered Glock. Stone placed a gentle hand on her shoulder before she got too close.

She looked at the stocky man and her features seemed to soften. He gave her a soft nod and she moved her hand from the weapon. She gave Jordan another withering look, which he returned in full measure, and stepped back to lean against the wall behind Stone and Bones.

"Then what?" Bones said.

"What the hell do you think?" Jordan said. "I ran like my ass was on fire and they chased me. I ran through the dark and the woods for miles before I finally had to jump off a cliff to get away from them."

"You did what now?" Bones said.

"I had to jump off a cliff. Guys like me can do stuff like that, cop," Bones said. "Uncuff me and I'll show you."

Bones chuckled. "Not going to happen, convict."

"Any 'phage I've ever seen would have followed you over the edge," Stone said. "These didn't?"

"No, they didn't," Jordan said. "I think – and don't ask me how because I don't fucking know – that the Gunderson bitch is holding them back somehow, controlling them. I got a chance to talk with Carmine before I went over the cliff and he was ordering them around like they were his gang or something. Only thing was it didn't sound like him. I mean, it was his voice, but the way he talked – no, that sounded more like her. I mean, she's a Paragon right? Maybe that's her thing, controlling deaders or something."

"How's that explain your brother?" Bones said.

Before Jordan could reply, Israel spoke up. "That one's on me," Israel said. "I'll give you the blow by blow later, but the bottom line is I tangled with Carmine in Texas and he had me on the ropes. I had a choice between infecting him with the Necrophage gene or getting my skull crushed; I chose to keep my skull. I'd thought it would kill him or that, if he turned, the Progeny would put him down. I damn sure didn't expect this."

"Nobody who gets infected lives," Stone said. "Not a one."

"Carmine Screed did," Jordan said, arrogant pride carrying the words.

"Not completely," Michelle said. "Maybe it's a by-product of his rapid healing ability. I don't know – the whole black eye thing, I've never heard of anything like that. Again, though, we're dealing with Paragons and we have precious little scientific data when it comes to their unique–"

There was a knock at the door. Everyone looked up as Mike Stapler, one of the guards the sheriff had chosen for Jordan, opened the door and stuck his head in. He was in his early sixties and had long gray hair pulled back into a ponytail from a thinning pate with a thick, neatly groomed beard that perfectly matched the shade of gray in his hair. He nodded to the room in general and said, "Sorry to interrupt. Bones, Sheriff wants you on the wall, said to bring the feds with you. Something's happening."

CHAPTER TWENTY

They left Mike and his partner watching over Jordan with strict instructions to shoot him if they had even the slightest provocation to do so. Israel made sure Jordan heard them talking so that the Paragon wouldn't get any ideas about trying to escape. Israel was reasonably sure Jordan could slip the cuffs off his wrists without much effort – there were reports of him doing that many times in the past – but the ankle cuffs were a different matter. He'd need a key or some serious tools to get out of those.

They followed Bones down the corridors past dozens of scared, angry, and confused faces, all of whom had taken up weapons and were heading for the doors that led outside. Israel had taken three steps into the iron-gray mist when he felt the prickle running through his spine and realized he'd been waiting for it. He stepped away from the crowd so he wouldn't draw any attention.

"Oh, good, you're already going outside. I guess your friends told you."

"Told me what?" Israel said. "What have you done, Susan?" There was a moment of shock from that, a sense of surprise.

"You know my name."

"Yeah. Jordan told me. He also told me what they did to you. I'm sorry you had to go through that."

"Spare me the school counselor speech, Israel. Carmine told me about you, about how you held him down and stuck your thumb in his eye. He said you'd lie about it, too, so don't bother trying to."

"Not to belabor the obvious, Susan, but I'm not the one who goes around kidnapping people. That's Jordan and your buddy Carmine's job."

"They only took me because they knew I wouldn't believe them if they told me how special I really was. They didn't hurt me, just made me sleep and brought me here so the people could wake me up. You try to keep people like me ignorant and normal. You don't want us to get woken up like you because you don't want anybody else to be as strong as you."

"And you believe him? The guy who jerked you out of your life and brought you here for them to do whatever it is they did to you?"

"They made me strong. That part hurt, but now I know how special I am. I know what I can really do. But none of that matters now, Israel. All that matters now is that you're going to bring Jordan to Carmine and me."

"Why would I do that?"

"You haven't seen yet? Look over the wall, Israel."

Another question formed on his lips, but Israel pushed it back and turned for the wall. The defenders had parked vehicles of every sort against it and were standing on them in a jagged line of bodies all peering out over the top of the ten-foot-high wall. He spotted an opening on the roof of an SUV and jogged over to it. A second later he was standing on the roof and staring out at the Jasper Island mist with a growing dread gnawing at his mind.

Late afternoon had come and what light had filtered through was growing darker by the moment. Despite that and the ever-present drifting fog, the figures clustered together were obvious. They stood a few hundred feet from the wall, a line of silent, staring monsters radiating hunger and menace. Undead, Necrophage, zombie – whatever name one might want to stick to them didn't matter in that moment. What mattered was that there were hundreds of them gathered and, in the distance, beyond the growing mob of dead, hundreds more crossing the landscape to join them. Israel remembered the population numbers he had read and whispered, "What are you doing, Susan?"

"That's my clique. I'm bringing them all to you, Israel. See, they want everybody to be part of the clique, too, but I keep telling them no. They know you guys are all hiding in that big school – they can smell you – but I keep telling them to stay away, to leave you alone. Not everybody wants to be part of my clique. They want to be part of the school clique and we should let them. So they do what I say and we get to live out here and they get to live in there."

"Okay," Israel said, still not entirely sure where it was going.

"You've got one hour to bring Jordan to us. A whole hour to get here. If you don't, I'll stop saying no. I'll just let them do whatever they want. I'm not sure how much fun that will be for the people in the school clique."

"Are you seriously controlling all of them?" Israel said. He knew there were potentially thousands of Necrophage on the island. If they swarmed the school it would be a slaughter.

"Them and that cool thunderstorm, Israel. See? I told you I was special, but you don't need to worry about what I'm doing. You've got one hour. If you've been talking to Jordan, then you know where to come. One hour starting right now."

The connection ended. Even before the crawling sensation vanished from his spine, he was back on the ground and calling out for Stone. He found him a few seconds later standing in a group with Bones, Michelle, and the sheriff. She looked up at his approach and said, "Trent. Good. Bones was just telling me you three have some experience with this kind of thing, as hard as I find that to believe. We need all the ideas we can get right now."

"We've got an hour," Israel said.

"What are you on about, mate?" Stone said, his voice tight with tension.

"It's the Gunderson woman; she made contact. This is all her, but somehow Carmine's got her convinced he's one of the good guys. I think she's got some kind of link with all the 'phages, but he's telling her what to do with it."

"How do you know that?" Bones asked.

"Things she said. Plus, look at the planned way they took out your communications and everything else; that's a move Carmine would make, not a Red Robin waitress from Little Rock.'"

"A what from where?" the sheriff said. "Who are we talking about? How did she make contact?"

"Susan Gunderson is a woman the Screed brothers abducted on behalf of a bunch of assholes running an off the books program at DGS," Israel said. "How she made contact and how she's doing this isn't really relevant at the moment. What is relevant is the fact that if I don't deliver Jordan to her and Carmine within the next hour she's going to cut the leash on those things and they're going to come over that wall like it's nothing but a speed bump."

"Hey, Trent, I'll decide what's relevant when it comes to my people's safety, got that? You're bringing me information that I have no way of checking and, frankly, it sounds ludicrous. You're asking me to believe that there's a single person out there somehow holding those things back? That's insane."

"Look around, Sheriff Holmes," Israel said. "Insane

has become the order of the day."

The sheriff stared him down for a minute, her blue eyes hard. Israel held the stare without blinking.

"Jan," Bones said. "We should listen to these folks."

"Yeah," the sheriff said, "and later you and I are going to talk about why you believe that. In the meantime, start moving everyone and everything into the gym. Trent's right about one thing: That wall won't even slow down a thousand of those things if they rush us. Bones, get all the supplies moved in ASAP, then pull the shooters from the wall. Use the vehicles to block the gym entrances. We barricade ourselves inside and make our stand there if it comes to that."

"That's a solid plan," Stone said. "We'll get Screed and–"

"No," the sheriff said. "That terrorist prick stays here restrained and under guard."

"Sheriff," Israel said, "you have–"

"I don't have to do a goddamned thing, Mr. Trent, except execute my duty to the best of my abilities. This nightmare started and you people came waltzing in here holding back way more than you're telling, then I find out I've got one of the most wanted criminals in the country camped out in my town, and now you're telling me I need to just let you take him and walk away with no other explanation than 'because we say so'? I don't think so, mister. Not on my watch. Screed stays here. He can die with the rest of us or, if by some miracle we survive this, he can get handed over to the Bureau when all this is over. Either way, you can't have him. Bones, you've got your orders. Make it happen." Before anyone else could reply, she turned and started giving orders to the people standing nearest them.

"Bones," Israel said. "C'mon, man, talk to her. I promise you I'm right about this. I swear."

Bones gave his head a slow shake. "The sheriff's a

woman of singular mind," he said, "and she is the sheriff. We'd all be dead or one of those things already if not for her. Frankly, guys, she's also got a point. I just met y'all, and the things you've told me are just unbelievable, but I know her. She gave me purpose when I was in a bad place. I owe her. I'm sorry, but I gotta follow her lead, and I suggest you do the same. Lord knows we could use the help." At that, he turned and headed back to the main building.

Israel watched him go, staring hard but without any anger in his eyes. He felt a hand on his shoulder and looked over to see Stone staring up at him.

"I know that look, mate. Think it through," the shorter man said.

"It's the right move," he said. "Pop always told me that when the chips were down, it was always better to ask for forgiveness than permission."

"Maybe, maybe not," Michelle said. "How do you know you can trust this woman?"

Israel shrugged. "I don't know," he said, "it's just a gut reaction. She doesn't have to give these people a chance. If she wanted, she could just order her goons out there to swarm the place, grab Jordan, and bring him to her, but she didn't do that. It's like she doesn't really want to hurt anyone else. She seems... I don't know... simple? Misled? Carmine's the wild card. He'd cut those things loose without a second thought and sit back to watch the show."

"Tell me everything she told you," Michelle said.

Israel filled her in on the exchange in short, thorough sentences. When he was done he could see her eyes darting about as she sorted through the new information. "That answers that," she muttered.

"Share with the class, Michelle," Stone said. "We're on a bit of a clock here, lass."

"The things Jordan told us," Michelle said, "and my theory about the conduit. Remember that? The reason we're here to begin with? Erin and her portal to wher-ever?"

Israel blinked at that. With everything they'd dis-covered, he'd nearly forgotten the whole reason for coming to the island. "What about it? What's Erin got to do with this?"

"I thought the fact that there was enough energy flowing through the conduit to fuel these microbreaches meant that Erin was alive at the other end holding the thing open somehow. Now, though, I don't know." She looked past Israel and Stone, focused on some point in space they couldn't pick out. Her eyes twitched back and forth.

"Michelle, please," Israel said.

Her attention snapped back and she said, "I don't know what kinds of things they have going on at DGS," she said, "but it's pretty obvious they've used Gunderson to hold open the portal that Erin created and now she's somehow learned to manipulate all that energy. But that would kill anyone – even a Paragon. The amount of energy you would have to draw to create and maintain a hurricane is, well, I can't do the math in my head and I can always do the math in my head."

Israel let that soak in for second. "So Erin could be dead after all?"

"I just don't know, Israel, but that is the highest pro-bability by a wide margin."

"Which is tragic," Stone said, "but in no way changes our current situation."

"Gunderson's the key," Michelle said, "to all of it. She controls it all, though I still can't fathom how exactly." Michelle gave her head a small shake before she could get swept up in her own thoughts again. "Regardless, shut her down and the conduit closes for good."

"Yeah," Israel said, "and right after that a thousand or so Necrophage turn this school into a buffet. Not to mention we have no idea what could happen to the weather if that storm comes apart."

"Oh," Michelle said. "Yeah. I guess there's that to consider, too."

"Do you think she can be reasoned with?" Stone said.

Israel considered it. "Maybe if I can get past her believing whatever line of crap Carmine fed her."

Israel heard it first – a muffled popping, shouts of alarm, frightened screams, and then what he thought might be breaking glass. It was coming from the administration building, the same building that housed the school library.

"Son of bitch," Israel said as he sprinted for the doors.

A minute later he was standing over the dead bodies of Mike and his partner. Mike had two bloody wounds in his chest and stared with wide eyes into the void. His partner looked to have had his neck broken with brutal efficiency.

Bones had come in just behind the Sentry team and he let out a vicious curse when he saw the bodies. He glared at Israel and Michelle but said nothing.

"No idea how he got loose," Stone said, "but the cuffs are on the floor, so I'm guessing he picked them somehow. He took a weapon and went out a window down the hall the hard way. He's long gone."

Israel took a long inhalation through his nose; Jordan's scent was strong even through the haze of cordite and blood. "Not for me," he said.

Stone nodded. "Thought you'd say that. The window's down the hall and to the right."

"You can't go after him," Bones said. "Those things out there will tear you apart just like they will him. Busting out like that was a damned fool thing to do."

Israel met Bones' eyes and said, "They won't come after me."

Bones stared at him for a long minute. "So you really are one of them?"

Israel shrugged. "Not exactly, but close enough that they won't attack me. Look, Michelle and Stone will stay here with you. I'm going to catch Screed and take him to DGS. If there's any luck at all left in the world, Gunderson will keep her word and pull back the dead so we can figure out another move. You need to get to the sheriff and fill her in, but don't tell her about me. Let her think what she wants."

"I'll come with you, mate," Stone said to Bones.

Israel nodded. "Michelle, please come with me. I need to ask you about what kind of set-up they might have at DGS."

"Get that wanker and get back here," Stone said. "This day isn't done by a long shot."

Israel and Michelle left the library and headed for the window Stone had indicated. Along the way, he asked Michelle what he might expect to find when he located Gunderson, but her information was either pure guesses or descriptions of technical equipment that might or might not be worth turning off.

"I should really just go with you," she said as they approached the shattered window.

"Not an option," Israel said.

"I know," she said, "it would just be easier. Don't you want a gun or something?"

Israel shook his head. "If I blow it, then you guys will need every weapon you can lay your hands on. I'll be fine without one." He hesitated and then met Michelle's eyes. "Look, if you get out of here and I don't, tell Allison I'm sorry I didn't make it back. Tell her–"

Israel stopped when he saw the expression on Michelle's face. It was a mixture of confusion and incredulity that he'd never seen from her before.

"Yeah, whatever," she said, shaking her head.

218 | C. Steven Manley

"Excuse me?" he said. "What's that about?"

"We're doing this now?" she said. "Why not! I've never had this argument with Allison at a good time, so now it is. You and Allison are a pair of idiots."

"What?"

"Idiots, lovestruck fools, hormone-saturated knuckle-heads. For two such intelligent people, when it comes to your relationship you've both got sand for brains. Let me ask you something, Israel: Did you kiss her goodbye? Have you held her hand? Done the nasty? Have you let her have a sip of your Coke on a hot day? Y'know, anything that a normal, intimate couple might do?"

Israel's jaw tightened and he reminded himself that he didn't hit women. "No," he said, "you know we can't do that. She'd get infected."

"Right, and that's where the sand for brains thing comes in. Look, man, I meant everything I said to Screed. You are a good, good man and it hurts me to think that I don't have the science to give you a normal life because I would love to see you and Allie together. I don't, though. No one does."

"She's working on a way to suppress—"

"Yeah, yeah, a way to suppress your infectious nature. She sang me that song. You know what? Maybe she could turn you white or Latino while she's at it because, honestly, that would be easier. She is talking about suppressing fundamental parts of your very genome that we don't even completely understand. Whole teams of researchers spend decades and millions of dollars trying to do things like that with no guarantee of success. She's one woman, albeit a brilliant one, working alone. Are you prepared to watch her spend the best years of her life trying to fix you? Which brings us to the aging thing: She is, you aren't. You're going to outlive her by many centuries assuming you can keep your head on your shoulders. Think on that for minute."

"Shit, I'm sorry I asked," Israel said.

"I know you are. Here's the bottom line: I love you both and would give up a lot for you to be happy together, but you can't, not in any normal way. If the two of you keep playing this stupid game where you pretend that you aren't what you are and she isn't what she is, then you've got nothing but heartbreak waiting for you down the road. I don't want to see that. Not for either of you."

Israel stared her down, but she didn't flinch. He'd thought of all this, of course, even discussed it with Allison, but never so bluntly. Something occurred to him and he said, "Wait a second. You ran this through Pythia, didn't you?"

Michelle looked away. "Maybe. That doesn't make the point any less valid."

"You did."

"It doesn't matter," she said, "just like this conversation isn't going to matter if you don't get going. I've no intention of dying on this island, so go get Screed and make sure we don't."

"We're going to revisit this," Israel said.

"I sure as hell hope so," Michelle said.

With that, Israel caught Jordan's scent and followed it into the mist.

CHAPTER TWENTY-ONE

Erin

It took longer to get through the pass than Erin thought it would. The short teleports had tired her somewhat, but the constant climbing over boulders and loose stones was nothing short of exhausting. They exited the Coldpass into a bright but quickly fading afternoon and stopped for a moment's rest, all of them breathing hard and massaging their fatigued legs.

It was the first time Erin had seen the world beyond the valley and it surprised her. Low hills covered in sparse patches of trees rolled into the distance where the vegetation grew steadily thicker until it condensed into a thick, dark forest of tall, narrow trees with thick leaves veined with dark blue lines. Other plants, many of which Erin was certain she'd never seen before, carpeted the hills in wide swaths of grassland and heavy patches of brush and bush. Some of the thinner groups of trees had long vines crawling up the trunks, and Erin though she could see smaller orbs of bright red hanging from them. Everything was green, but tinted slightly with other colors that seemed darker and richer than the plants on Earth.

Gratt'na noticed her looking and said, "They are for

being Nala-fruit," he said, gesturing toward the vines. "Very sweet in the mouth. Good for the eating."

"I wouldn't mind trying one or two of those about now," Erin said.

"A moment more for the resting," Brinn'ha said. "My legs shake as the trees in a bad wind."

Despite feeling like they needed to hurry, Erin couldn't argue the point. She sat rubbing her calves and taking in the scenery until Gratt'na said, "I am for the going on now."

Erin and Brinn'ha agreed and got back to their feet. The terrain was far more passable here, but their legs were still fatigued despite the short break. They moved slowly – far more than Erin was happy with – and reached the first grove of trees by the time the sun was well past its noon position. The grove was shaded and long shadows stretched back the way they had come. Erin stepped into the shadows and examined the Nala-fruit vines that covered the bases of the trees.

Their color reminded her of the Red Delicious apples she had enjoyed back home, but the resemblance ended with the color. They were thick, but not exactly round. They looked to Erin like small, smooth footballs roughly the size of her fist. Dark, narrow leaves hung stiffly from the point where the thick vine terminated into the fruit. The air around the plants was perfumed with a sweet aroma that Erin found reminiscent of something, but couldn't recall what.

Gratt'na reached up and snapped one of the fruits from its vine. He took a deep bite and Erin watched as his nose flaps flared with pleasure. "I am for the want of Nala-fruit to grow in the valley, but it will not."

"Why not?" Erin asked.

"None are for knowing," Brinn'ha said. "Many have been for the trying, but never are the roots for growing."

Erin shrugged and said, "They smell good."

"They are for tasting better than they are for smelling," Gratt'na said, gesturing toward the fruit. "Be for the taking."

Erin reached up and took one of the fruits. It snapped away from the vine without a sound. It felt heavy in her hand, thick and substantial. She held it up to her nose and inhaled. The scent was sweet with an acrid quality that she did not find at all unpleasant. It smelled, she thought, like smoked honey. She took a slow, deliberate bite and felt the firm flesh give way beneath her teeth. Juice burst in tiny droplets into her mouth and the flavor was like some alchemical mix of honey and really good beer. She chewed it slowly, enjoying the flavor and texture and then smiled at Gratt'na. "Not bad," she said.

"Truth," he agreed. "Not for the being bad at all. Be for taking a few in your pack for the having later."

Erin took another bite and then held the fruit in her mouth while she picked three more and stuck them in her pack. The fruit was very filling, and by the time she had finished she felt satisfied and somehow refreshed. Gratt'na and Brinn'ha were both chewing on their second piece of fruit when she said, "How much farther do you think we can get before dark?"

"If we are for hurrying," Gratt'na said, "we could reach the forest."

"Then we should get to hurrying," Erin said. A flush of energy ran through her and she smiled. Whatever was in the Nala-fruit made her feel like she was on a caffeine rush.

They started hiking again, Gratt'na and Brinn'ha absently tossing aside the pits of the Nala-fruit once they had finished. Erin watched one of them arch through the air and paused when, for just an instant, it seemed to freeze in mid-flight, hover, and then continue on its trajectory. She shook her head and kept walking. She was more tired than she thought.

The shadows grew longer as they walked. At one point Erin's head started feeling fuzzy and her instincts sent warning bells careening through her mind. In her life before waking up in the Progeny's dungeon and meeting Israel, Erin had done more than a few drugs. Whenever Tiko had caught her, though, he had beaten her thoroughly. He would scream at her that drugs were for weaklings and losers. He never commented on the fact that he could empty a fifth of anything in a few hours all by his lonesome or that girls who got hooked quickly lost their looks and, in his eyes, their income potential as prostitutes. He had, in his own twisted and brutal way, been doing her a favor by keeping her from getting addicted. Still, though, she'd had her share of highs and she knew damn well what it felt like when one was coming on. It felt exactly like she was feeling at that moment.

"Oh, shit," she muttered.

They all stopped walking. Brinn'ha looked at Erin, her brow twisted in confusion. "Sar'ha?" she said.

"You guys feel okay? Because I'm–"

Shadows suddenly lengthened at an impossible rate around them, swirling and reaching like living things. Erin blinked at a frantic rate as though she could somehow clear her eyes of the hallucination. She watched Brinn'ha's and Gratt'na's faces. They didn't react to the suddenly living shadows that moved around them, and in some back room of her mind Erin knew that meant something, but the significance was lost on her. She watched the shadows lengthen and grow darker until they snaked along the ground like inky streams.

"Sar'ha?" It was Brinn'ha again. This time the tone was more insistent, almost frightened.

Erin turned and saw her friend's concerned eyes watching. Erin wanted to smile at the expression she saw there. The movement froze on her lips, though, as she watched ink-black tendrils begin to slide up and over the back of Brinn'ha's face. They moved like quicksilver, sliding into her eyes, nose, and over her lips until they covered her face in a black, oily mask with eyes that glowed a dark violet and a mouth that was a gaping, oily maw. Horror had been building in Erin's throat and when she saw the two dozen or so black tentacles spring up from Brinn'ha's head and start whipping the air, she screamed long and loud.

Erin staggered back from the monster that had once been her friend. She fumbled for her weapons. Her back struck something and she spun, thinking to find herself facing another squidhead, thinking that through some impossible means she was going to be back in Leticia, Texas, facing hundreds of those glowing sets of eyes coming for her out of absolute darkness.

It wasn't that, though. It was Tiko. Not as he had been in life, but as he appeared in her nightmares – naked, reaching, hungry. She screamed again and staggered backward, flailing wildly with her Jo, staggering, stumbling, but staying on her feet. She spun again and skidded to a stop, her eyes growing wide at what she saw.

It was Israel. He was standing not ten feet from her. She vaguely noted that he was dressed in the same black hospital scrubs they had both been wearing the night they'd met. He smiled at her in that way he had – confident and reassuring. "Focus on the question," he said. "Focus and keep moving."

She felt tears in her eyes as she moved forward to embrace him, but slid suddenly to a halt as he changed. His normally chocolate-colored skin darkened and shifted to a dead gray. His lips turned the color of fresh tar and his mouth opened in snapping bursts that showed her a coal-black tongue and teeth that were stained by oily, black saliva. Brown eyes turned onyx fixed on her in a predatory gaze that drew another scream from her throat as Israel – this other Israel – moved toward her with a feral lunge that was driven by starving need. Still screaming, Erin turned and ran.

The squidhead that had been Brinn'ha was there. Her fist lashed out in a ruthless and efficient blow that knocked Erin to the ground. She hit hard and watched the shadows rise up in a midnight wave that swept her into unconsciousness.

Erin dreamed. She dreamed of stars that spun and danced across a black sky and then slowly fell into tall patterns that she recognized as a nighttime cityscape from back on Earth. She didn't know what city it was, but it glittered and sparkled with thousands of tiny lights that rose and fell in a familiar way that even in the dream made her long for home.

The lights shifted suddenly, shuddered as though by some geologic tremor and quickly streaked together into a shape. It was a man who glowed with silver-gold light like a silhouette in reverse. His head was bowed. When he spread his arms to the side as though in welcome, huge, glowing wings unfolded from his back and spread wide, flapping and carrying him aloft as though he weighed nothing. The light flared and suddenly her dreams started coming to her in rapid, momentary images.

Bald children rising from hospital beds; the winged man fighting in the street; people carrying signs and pressing against lines of police in riot gear; an elderly black man lying with his head at an unnatural angle; a city burning as an immense shadow lurched through it, leaving ruin in its wake; Israel, bloodied and screaming in rage – they all flashed through her mind and spun together until she saw herself standing in the rain among dozens of dead bodies with blood pooling at her feet like some kind of grotesque offering.

Her eyes snapped open at that and she gasped in a

deep, ragged breath. She was lying on the ground, staring up at the night sky. The twin moons, Frak'ta and Lat'ta, shone down and bathed the countryside in cool silver light. A fire crackled and glowed warm next to her. Brinn'ha rushed to Erin's side from where she had been sitting.

"Sar'ha," she said, "be not for the standing. Lay back. Be for the resting."

She didn't need to be told twice. Her head was pounding like she'd just woken up from a three-day drinking binge. She lay back on the Tarr-hide bedroll and closed her eyes. The images were still vivid in her mind and she muttered, "That was the worst trip in the history of really bad trips."

"What are you for meaning?" Gratt'na said.

"Never mind," she said. "Are you guys okay?"

"We are for asking that of you the more," Brinn'ha said. "What overcame you?"

"It had to be the fruit," she said. "Holy shit, that was bad."

"The Nala-fruit?" Gratt'na said. "Never has it been for having such a thing. It is for the eating alone."

"I'm not like you, Gratt," Erin said.

"Truth," Brinn'ha said. "It may for being that for you the Nala-fruit is for having the wrong-mind thing."

"Yeah. I think you're right," Erin said, trying hard not to sound sarcastic.

Gratt'na seemed to think this over and then said, "Sar'ha, I am for the asking of forgiveness. I did not–"

"Stop it," Erin said. "It's my fault for eating the whole damn thing instead of just trying a bite and seeing what happened. I've gotten too comfortable. Sometimes I forget my body isn't the same as yours."

Brinn'ha nodded and whispered, "Truth. We must be for the caution beyond the valley or what next we take for being safe may put Sar'ha on the path to the all-truth."

All-truth. Erin didn't understand why the marks around her ears translated the word 'death' that way, but they did and the meaning was clear. She swallowed hard and asked for some water. Brinn'ha produced some from a small Tarr-hide bag with a narrow opening that served as their canteen. Erin drank the bulk of it and then said, "How much time did we lose?"

"We are for being well into the night," Gratt'na said. "The Starless are for having traveled far."

Erin held back another curse. She felt stupid, like a teenager who had drunk too much trying to impress the older kids. The emotion was an irrational one, she knew, but it nagged at her all the same. She pushed the feelings aside and looked around. The sky was clear and the moons were casting a lot of light, enough that she could make out the ground beyond the fire's glow pretty well.

"It's a bright night," she said. "Do you guys think we could–" She turned and found her two companions standing there, packs on their backs, and Gratt'na kicking dirt over the fire.

"We are for knowing your mind, Sar'ha," Brinn'ha said. "Be for gathering your pack and let us be for the trail."

Erin smiled and started gathering up her bedroll. Within a minute, she had everything back in her pack and was slinging it over her shoulder.

"Are you for being certain of your wellness, Sar'ha?" Brinn'ha asked.

Erin nodded. "I'm okay. My head hurts a little, but I can manage." It was the understatement of her life, but she kept it off her face.

"Then let us be for the trail," Gratt'na said. "We must be for the slow walking. Even bright darkness conceals danger."

"Then lead the way," Erin said. "Brinn and I will follow behind you and keep our eyes on the distance in case there's anything to see."

They set off, Gratt'na in the lead, then Erin, then Brinn'ha. They moved carefully across the darkened landscape. Gratt'na led them around the more obvious obstacles and Erin and Brinn'ha watched the dim night around them. They watched for movement or light of any kind, anything that signaled the presence of some night predator or another. There was nothing to see, though, and it wasn't an hour later when they found themselves standing at the forest's tree line.

The forest canopy blocked a lot of the moonlight and they paused at the forest's edge and discussed whether or not it was wise to move forward. When Erin pointed out that if they could reach the Starless camp before sunrise they might catch most of them sleeping and unaware, urgency won out over wisdom.

It was slower going within the forest. The ground was relatively free of fallen trees and other debris, but there were many hidden roots and small plants that could trip them or tangle their feet. Moonlight broke through the canopy in thick beams of silver and highlighted the breath that puffed in small clouds from their lungs as it met air chilled by the late night. Erin looked through the trees and couldn't help but find a faint smile on her lips at the silent, shadowed beauty she saw there.

It felt as though they had been walking for hours when Gratt'na whispered "Stop" and crouched low, staring through the trees to his right. Erin and Brinn'ha followed his example and huddled close to him. Before they could ask, Gratt'na pointed to the right and slightly ahead.

Through the trees, the faint, golden-orange of firelight flickered. "Sar'ha," Gratt'na said. "Brinn'ha and I are for the stalking. You be for the waiting."

"Like hell," Erin said. "I—"

"You are not for having the hunter-step," Brinn'ha said, "and we are not for knowing if the fire we are seeing is for the Starless. Be for the waiting. We will return with the knowing."

Erin wanted to argue, wanted to point out that she could Pull over there if she wanted, but realized that wasn't really relevant. Even if she teleported, she still couldn't guarantee that she would do so silently once she reappeared. Of all the things that the Valley People had tried to teach her, stealth had come the hardest to her. She just didn't have the patience. Besides, her head was still pounding hard enough to be a distraction.

"Fine," she said. "Go."

Within a few seconds, they had disappeared into the shadows so thoroughly that even Erin lost track of them. She stayed there, crouching in the dark and the silence, fighting the compulsion to go after her friends. Her frustration was just about to get the better of her when she saw two shadows separate from the rest of the night and come trotting toward her in a low crouch.

"It's about damn time," she said.

"That is why you are not for having the hunter-step, Sar'ha," Brinn'ha said. "You must content your mind."

"So I've heard," she said. "What did you see?"

"We are for having found that which we seek," Gratt'na said. "The Starless are there – many of them for resting – and what is for being left of the you-world-thing."

"The Starless have collected much of it," Brinn'ha said, "but there are for being much larger pieces farther out from their fire."

"We can worry about the plane later. How many guys do they have?"

"It was as Gorn'na was for saying," Brinn'ha said. "A half score and their Starspeaker."

"You saw her?"

"Truth," Gratt'na said. "She and two Starless are not for resting, but for tending the fire and watching the dark."

Erin did a quick count in her head. Eleven total against the three of them, assuming the Starspeaker was a fighter.

"What do you guys think?" she asked.

"If we are surprising them," Brinn'ha said, "we could show many the all-truth before the others are for re-acting."

"Truth," Gratt'na said, "but we must be for flooding the soil with Starless blood."

"Truth," Brinn'ha said. "I am not for seeing another path."

Erin thought about it. "The Starspeaker knows about me, right?"

"Truth," Gratt'na said, "if we are for believing Gorn'na to be speaking truth."

Erin nodded. "Okay, so maybe we use that against them the same way we did those two jerks back in the Coldpass."

"What are you for planning, Sar'ha?" Brinn'ha said.

"Probably something really awesome," Erin said, "if it works. Really stupid if it doesn't."

CHAPTER TWENTY-TWO

Erin laid out her idea. Brinn and Gratt didn't entirely like it, but couldn't offer an alternative outside of a sneak attack and a risky fight that might or might not go their way. So they went along with it, but Erin had to admit that they had a point. As plans went, there wasn't much to it. It was something born more from lack of options than any kind of tactical insight.

Nonetheless, a few minutes later they had sneaked close enough to the camp that Erin could Pull herself to the middle of the site, but far enough away that she could remain hidden until she was ready to be seen. Gratt'na and Brinn'ha had moved in opposite directions away from Erin and were getting ready to cause the distraction that Erin hoped would set the stage for their tiny invasion of the Starless camp.

Erin studied the sleeping form that rested in a ragged circle around the fire. The leader was lying nearest the fire, reclining against a Tarr that was resting with its legs folded underneath its body, just as every other Tarr that Erin had ever seen did. The difference was that even in the dim light and over a considerable distance, Erin could make out the thick scars that crisscrossed the animal's sides and flanks. They were long, white slashes where none of the animal's short, dark hair grew. There were dozens of them and, for just a moment, Erin understood Brinn'ha's disgust toward whoever would torture an animal that way just for his own convenience. Killing the animals to survive was one thing, but what she saw there was just pointless cruelty.

She took her eyes off the sleeping Tarr and its master and watched the rest of the Starless. Seven others slept on thin hides or on the ground and two stood near the fire whispering to one another. A female Erin assumed to be Paar'ha the Starspeaker sat cross-legged near the two guards, but had her hands folded in her lap and her head bowed so that her chin rest against her chest. She was thin and wore a flimsy hide dress that hid very little of her skin that was so gray it was nearly black with age. White hair hung in thin, unkempt tangles around her face, and Erin couldn't make out her features. She figured the old Starspeaker was sleeping, but knew that it could be some kind of deception.

For the first time, she noticed none of the Starless had their hair made up in the tight braids that she was accustomed to. Each of them wore it loose and unkempt. It was time she had seen that and realized that she had been assuming that all the natives of this world were like the Valley People in the way they did things. She remembered the Nala-fruit and responded with a slight shiver. It seemed she had gotten into the habit of making a lot of assumptions. That was a habit she needed to break.

A deep warble that grew to a short screech echoed from the darkness on the far side of the camp and the guards quickly turned in that direction, raising their short, stone-tipped spears without being entirely sure why. Erin smiled.

One of the first things that a hunter of the Valley

People had to master was the hunting cries of a particular predatory flightless bird that supposedly roamed the wilds of the northern side of the valley. Erin had never seen one, but she assumed they were dangerous because the hunters of the Valley Tribe used that call to flush and route their prey effectively enough to stock ample provisions for the winter months.

Another warble, this one a slightly higher pitch, answered the first and there was the sound of something crashing through the brush outside the fire's light. A third cry cut the night, this one from another side of the camp, and the guards followed the sound. Paar'ha stirred, as did a few of the others, and another screech echoed through the dark. Erin waited for a minute while the sleeping Starless slowly roused and sat up, looking about in confusion.

Once half of them were looking around, she chose a spot that was in plain view of the drowsy raiders but far enough away from them that she could maneuver if they attacked. She drew her weapons, took a deep breath, and Pulled to the spot.

She appeared before them and the sound and movement from the shadows stopped instantly. A few of the men yelped in surprise and fear just as Gorn'na had done back in the Coldpass, and the two guards took a fast step back, leveling their spears and shouting in alarm. Erin lost most of what they said in the chorus of confused shouts and, by the time things had quieted, all the Starless were on their feet with weapons in their hands.

Paar'ha the Starspeaker did not rise, however. Instead she merely raised her head and fixed Erin with a level, assessing gaze that did nothing to otherwise change her posture. Erin met her eyes before Paar'ha looked over the assembled fighters, and for just an instant was certain she saw the Starspeaker's mouth quirk up into an ironic smile. It wasn't an expression she often saw on the face of the

Valley People or any of their race, but she would have sworn the Starspeaker was amused.

The Starless that had been resting against the Tarr stepped from the crowd and faced Erin. She hadn't realized it before since he had been so far away and reclining, but he was the largest example of his race that Erin had ever seen. Easily seven feet tall, bare-chested, and thick with muscle that showed through his heavily tattooed skin, he towered over Erin like the shadow of death and stared at her with eyes so devoid of any kind of emotion that she wondered if he was blind. Four jagged scars ran in parallel lines down the left side of his face and were broken up by the planes of his face. The lowest of the scars was an unbroken line that ended at what had once been a nostril flap, now torn away by whatever beast had given him those particular souvenirs.

He turned those passionless eyes on the Starspeaker and said, "Paar'ha, is this tiny thing for being the World-walker you are for having foretold?"

Paar'ha's eyes lingered on Erin. In a voice that crackled with phlegm and age she said, "Truth."

The scarred one snorted in something that bordered on disgust and took another step forward. "Worldwalker," he said, his voice gravel rough, "I am for being Raff'na, Elder of the Cuts in Night Tribe. I am for having the claiming of this star-that-fell and awaiting the prize that is for being mine by the doing."

Erin kept glaring at him and tried to look as menacing as she could in the face of someone who towered over her like a giant. His hair fell in straight, filthy strips around his head and she could not see if he bore any Marks of Understanding, but there were so many tattoos on his body that she thought it was a safe bet. Her angry eyes met his cold ones and she said, "Go away. This place is not for you."

Raff'na blinked, stared at her, then blinked again. "I

am for having been the first to discover the star-that-fell place. I am for being owed a prize. Paar'ha Starspeaker has spoken so and I am for having to see it done!"

Erin picked another spot far to one side near the edge of the firelight that looked reasonably safe and Pulled. She had figured out that if she started turning just before she Pulled then the momentum of the turn would continue as she reappeared. If she did it quick enough, it looked to anyone watching as though she just disappeared facing one direction and reappeared facing another. Brinn had told her it was kind of creepy – Erin's translation – and Erin was really hoping it was true. This entire plan hinged on the Starless being as superstitious as Gorn'na had been.

Another chorus of gasps rose when she reappeared and there was a moment of general rustling of dry grasses and worn leather as the men repositioned. Erin let it settle down and then shouted, "Paar'ha was wrong! This is not a prize or a fallen star. It is a dangerous thing that has no place here. It is a thing that will bring only fire and death to those who do not understand it. You, Raff'na of the Cuts in Night Tribe, do not understand it. Take your tribe and go. Go far from this place and do not return!"

Raff'na looked at his men, hesitant and frightened, then back at Erin. He pushed through the Starless, heading for his Tarr. Erin thought for one thrilling moment that the ploy had worked, that he was going to get on the beast and ride away. As usual, though, she should have known better. A few seconds later he was back. A heavy club with a long handle and a business end of black stone was resting over his shoulder in a familiar and easy manner. The stone was the size of Erin's head and looked like it had seen plenty of use.

Raff'na raised the weapon over his head like it didn't weigh anything and said, "I am for standing for the danger! I am for having the prize that is as the Starspeaker foretold!" There was a sudden clattering as the Starless started hitting their weapons together in a kind of tool-assisted applause.

Erin waited for it to settle down again, dreading every second. They were supposed to get scared and run away, not start cheering on their boss. As soon as it was silent, she said, "There is no prize here, Raff'na. The Starspeaker was wrong. Go find another prize in a different place."

"No," Raff'na said. "Paar'ha was for speaking of challenges and tests of will. I am for meeting the challenges and tests. I am for claiming the prize of the star-that-fell."

Erin cut her eyes towards the Starspeaker's and found them waiting. Paar'ha's eyes were the color of violent storm clouds. There was something in them, though – a challenge or a question, Erin couldn't be sure. It reminded her of the look an older stripper had given her once when she wondered whether or not the younger Erin was going to be the one to supplant her spot as the most popular woman on the stage. Erin held the gaze for a moment and then turned her attention back to Raff'na.

"This is no test, Raff'na," she said. "Nothing but trouble awaits you here. If you care for your tribe then go. Forget you were ever here."

"I am not for the going, Worldwalker," Raff'na said. "I am for having the prize and the power."

"There is no prize," Erin snapped. "You're not listening to me."

"A star is for having fallen," Raff'na said, more to his men than to Erin. "This is not a thing that happens with the ease of a blowing wind. It is for being great power that is for tearing a light from the sky. I am for claiming a part of that power, that prize, and I am for wondering why you, tiny thing–" he pointed his club at Erin, holding the heavy weapon parallel to the ground without so much as a tremble in his arm, "–are for having Cuts in Night Tribe go from this place. If you are for being Worldwalker, then it is for being your place to deliver this power."

"There is no power to give, Raff'na," Erin said.

"You are for walking-as-the-wind," Raff'na shouted. "Do not be for doing a thing of power and be for saying there is no power!"

Erin's jaw tightened. She met the Tarr Rider's cold eyes and saw nothing but resolve. Her plan, she realized, was as dead as disco.

"Unless," Raff'na said, "the power is not a thing for being given, but a thing that is for being taken."

"Don't go there, Raff'na," Erin said.

Raff'na hesitated, lowered his weapon and said, "Go where? Your words are for being strange."

Erin couldn't help but roll her eyes in frustration. "Oh, for fuck's sake, Raff'na! I can't share what I can do and fighting me for it won't grant it to you. Just go, please! There is nothing for you here."

Raff'na watched her for a long while, his dark eyes playing up and down her body, sizing her up as an opponent. Finally, he said, "You speak the not-truth, Worldwalker. I am for thinking that your words are being a test of my will and my want. I am for thinking that for the prize to be mine, Cuts in Night must feed the grass your blood."

Erin watched as the raiders raised their weapons in three-fingered hands. They seemed steadier now, more focused since their leader had given them a path to follow. Ten sets of eyes glared at her through the firelight.

"Don't do this, Raff'na," Erin said. "No one needs to die here."

"Oh, this night is for having blood, Worldwalker," Raff'na said. "Paar'ha is for having seen it as so. It is for being well, though. Your death will be a nothing thing, Worldwalker. You are not for being of this place and people. You are for being the vessel of power that is to be claimed and nothing more – even your hideous face is for having no use. A Tarr is for having more claim to life in this place than you."

Erin blinked at the words. They were like a verbal sucker punch that knocked her senseless for a moment. It had been a long time since anyone had said anything like that to her, referred to her as something useless except as a thing for other people to play with and then discard. For an instant, the old pain and fear flared through her belly and she remembered her old life on Earth. She kept it off her face, though, and just stared hard at Raff'na.

He gestured to either side with his club and the rest of Cuts in Night started fanning out to surround her. Raff'na took slow, measured steps toward Erin with his club held in a defensive grip in front of him. "Be not for fighting the Worldwalker, Cuts in Night! Her power is for being mine to claim."

Brinn had told Erin that the Starless were not properly trained warriors. They were little more than brutes who relied on surprise, what little actual technique they could pick up, and overwhelming force. The ones who were spreading out to surround her didn't concern Erin all that much; she knew that they would come across her companions any moment now. Raff'na, though, was a different matter.

He studied her, watched his stance, and didn't charge blindly forward like she had expected. His movements were practiced and smooth. He moved the way Brinn and Gratt did, like someone who had spent a lot of time honing his violent craft.

Erin felt her throat work in a nervous swallow and raised her weapons in a defensive posture of her own. She ignored the quiver in her belly, the ache in her head, and focused on quieting her mind. "Last chance, Raff'na. Call off your guys and we can all walk away."

"I am for thinking not, Worldwalker."

Erin nodded. "Okay. Don't say I didn't warn you."

Erin picked a spot behind Raff'na, started a high backhanded swing with her Batla, and Pulled. She reappeared halfway through the weapon's arc and expected it to crack Raff'na across the back of his head. The Tarr Rider had been expecting it, though, and had rolled forward as soon as Erin vanished so that her weapon missed, if only by a fraction of an inch.

Raff'na rolled to his feet and spun to face Erin, his club swinging in a wide arc over his head. Erin had misjudged just how long the weapon's shaft was and she had to take a fast step back to avoid the skull-crushing stone that cut the air inches from her face. Her feet moved with the sureness of long hours of sparring as she back-pedaled and then quickly stepped at an angle away from the club's arc so that she was out of Raff'na's direct line of sight.

The club was still cutting its circle through the air, so before Raff'na could adjust his stance, Erin used her smaller stature to her advantage and rolled beneath the weapon's trajectory and came up in a crouch next to Raff'na's legs. Like a striking snake, Erin stabbed out with her Jo and scored a hit on Raff'na's knee.

The Tarr Rider howled in pain, but managed to adjust his swing so that the club dipped into a lower arc that could have easily broken Erin into a bloody mess if she had been there. Instead, the club cut through empty air as Erin Pulled away. She reappeared well outside the weapon's range, stood, and then staggered as a wave of dizziness washed over her.

She was getting tired. Between the traveling and the fighting and using her power so much in the past day, her body was reaching the point of exhaustion. She took a deep breath and faced Raff'na, who had stopped his club swinging and was limping toward her with anger twisting his features and blood streaming down his leg.

She raised her weapons as he approached and surged forward suddenly, stabbing at her midsection with the club. Erin sidestepped the blow, but didn't expect it when Raff'na raised his good leg and kicked straight out at her. The blow hit Erin solidly in her sternum and knocked her off her feet. She landed flat on her back several feet from where she had been standing. Her chest was a sheet of knotted pain and she fought to draw air into her lungs.

It would have been the end of her. She was flat on the ground with a larger opponent whose reach far exceeded her own. All Raff'na had to do was bring the club down and crush her with it. The Tarr Rider, though, had misjudged the injury on his knee and, despite having landed his kick to Erin's chest, had fallen to the ground in the moment that all his weight was on his wounded leg.

Erin watched as he climbed to his feet. Behind him, she could see Gratt'na and Brinn'ha moving like spinning, slashing dancers through the other Starless raiders, who fought viciously, if not gracefully.

Erin drew in a gasping breath as Raff'na gained his footing and raised his club. She rolled to the side as the weapon smashed down, leaving a deep dent in the dirt where Erin's abdomen had been.

Erin ignored the agony in her chest and scrambled away on all fours as Raff'na kicked at her again, more carefully this time, and missed. Erin got to her feet and faced him, her Batla still in-hand, but her Jo lost somewhere in the forest grasses. Her eyes took in the melee going on at Raff'na's back and she said, "Your tribe is getting beaten, Raff'na. End this before anyone else has to die."

Raff'na was moving toward her with a pained gait. The skin beneath his wounded knee was a slick sheet of blood. The joint was already beginning to swell, and when he put weight on that leg, his face contorted in barely controlled agony. "I am not for the caring of Cuts in Night," he growled. "The prize and the power are for being mine. Many will be for coming to me when I am for having it. I will be for building a tribe that is for being the better of all tribes before. It will be for the killing and taking of all who are for standing against me."

Erin listened and then shook her head slowly. She realized that she had been among the simple, caring folk of the Valley People Tribe for so long that she had almost forgotten that there were people like Raff'na in the world – any world, it would seem. She had known lots of them over the years and they all shared one common trait: the self-centered certainty that they were the only ones who mattered and getting what they wanted trumped any other concern. Her brother, Carmine and Jordan Screed, John Brindley, her mother, and about a hundred nameless johns – all of them cared only for themselves and their desires and to hell with everything and everyone else.

The thought froze a cold knot in her aching chest and she felt her lips tighten over gritting teeth. The Screeds and their bosses within the Progeny were the reason she was trapped here, the reason she was so far from home and in such an alien place with such an uncertain future ahead of her. It was all their fault and this man, this alien called Raff'na, was just like them.

Raff'na stopped and studied her face for a moment. "Is that fear I am for seeing in your eyes, Worldwalker? Are you now for seeing your all-truth in the stone of my weapon?"

Erin met his eyes and slowly raised her Batla until it pointed at his face from the end of her fully extended arm. She ignored the pain and dizziness that was radiating through her body and said, "Not even close, bitch." Then she Pulled.

Apparently Raff'na had expected her to teleport behind him again because when she did reappear, he was already turning that direction. It didn't matter, though. Erin had judged the distance perfectly and materialized with her Batla in the same space as Raff'na's forehead.

She blinked at the sudden spray of fluid and gore as the weapon ruptured the Tarr Rider's skull from the inside out. His head warped into a grotesque parody of what it had been and his body slumped instantly to the ground where it contorted and convulsed for nearly a minute before growing still.

Erin watched it all, fighting exhaustion and dizziness and the urge to look away – warriors bore witness to their deeds, and carried their deeds with them in the light; cowards and Starless thieves looked away from their actions and denied them. That was what Elder Barr'na had taught her, and she fully intended to honor the lesson.

Erin looked up once Raff'na's body stopped twitching and she saw the rest of the tribe, the four still standing, staring wide-eyed at her along with Gratt'na and Brinn'ha. They seemed to have forgotten their own fight and very slowly started backing into the forest. Erin took a few steps in their direction and all four turned and ran.

Gratt'na and Brinn'ha watched her closely. Between the two of them, they were covered in dozens of cuts and other wounds. Gratt'na had a particularly bad cut that looked as though it had narrowly missed his left eye and would certainly leave him with a prominent scar. Despite this, they both stood with a steady stance, breathing hard and showing more concern than she had ever seen on their faces before.

"You guys okay?" she asked.

"We are for having wounds, but none that will not heal, I think," Brinn'ha said. "And you, Sar'ha? Are you for being well? What you did–"

"I won," Erin said. "And fuck him for making me do it."

Without waiting for a response, Erin turned and looked at Paar'ha. Sometime during the fight, the elderly Starspeaker had risen and was walking toward Erin with the help of a thick, crooked walking stick.

"I told Raff'na this night would see blood," she said in her rough voice. "He was for being too foolish to ask whose."

"Drop the fortune teller shit, lady," Erin said. "I'm–"

"I am for knowing who you are, A-rynn Se-iims. You are the one who has ripped a wound in the world. You are the one who will bring the all-truth to everything we see."

CHAPTER TWENTY-THREE

It was the first time Erin had heard a native of this world speak her name, or at least anything that remotely resembled it, and it took her back a step. She stared at the Starspeaker for a long moment and then said, "How?"

"Oh, little Worldwalker," Paar'ha said, "this place you are for having found yourself in is far larger and far more strange than you are for knowing. Though I call you Worldwalker, that is not for the whole of truth, is it?"

"What do you mean?"

"Worldwalker is for the meaning that you are for being one who chooses where you walk, chooses the path and the portal. Such a thing is not for leaving the cut in the world that you are for having left in your coming. I am for hearing your tale, A-rynn Se-iims. You should be for the telling."

Erin spent another moment letting the Starspeaker's sudden familiarity with her settle in. "Hang on," she said. "First off, call me Sar'ha. That's the name the Valley People gave me and it's probably a lot easier for you to say. Second, who the hell are you that I should tell you anything?"

Paar'ha was quiet for a moment and Erin was sure she saw that same amused smirk cross her face that she had seen earlier. Her eyes cut up then and took in Brinn'ha and Gratt'na. "Hunters of the Valley People Tribe, be for joining us," she said loud enough for them to hear. "Your wounds and skill are for having brought great pride to your tribe, but we should be for the tending of flesh now."

Brinn'ha and Gratt'na shared a nervous glance and then started toward them. Brinn'ha moved with a noticeable limp and Gratt'na's face was sheeted in thin, pale blood from the cut on his face. As they grew closer, though, they both stared at Paar'ha with growing confusion.

Erin looked at Paar'ha and saw that she had changed. It wasn't that her features had shifted or anything that dramatic, but she had pulled her loose hair back into two thick tails which she then knotted at the base of her skull to keep the hair from her face. Her stooped posture was gone, and she stood straight and tall, watching the trio with eyes that glittered with age and intelligence. The intricate tattoos that covered her face and body seemed to glisten in the firelight. If it weren't for the same ragged clothes and her walking stick, Erin would question whether or not this Paar'ha was the same person she had seen earlier.

When Gratt'na and Brinn'ha got close enough, they suddenly stopped and raised their open hands with the palms facing out next to their faces. Then they bowed their heads in respect.

"Be for the pardoning of we two, Paar'ha," Brinn'ha said. "We were for thinking that you were a Starspeaker to Cuts in Night Tribe. We were not for the knowing that you were of the Wise Wanderers."

"Be for showing your faces, hunters of the Valley People Tribe. There is being nothing to pardon. I was then being forced to live a not-truth so that I could be for keeping Raff'na from the power of this machine that has intruded on our world. Now, I am for showing the truth of my self."

Gratt'na and Brinn'ha raised their faces and looked at Erin. Erin knew her expression had to be nothing short of perplexed. "Anybody want to tell the woman from another planet what the hell's going on?"

"Paar'ha is for being of the Wise Wanderers, Sar'ha," Brinn'ha said. "Elder Barr'na was for the speaking of them before. Are you not for the recalling?"

Erin shook her head.

"There is being time for the telling," Parr'ha said. "First, I am for thinking that the grass has drunk its share of Valley Tribe blood. You," Paar'ha said, pointing at Gratt'na, "be for stepping forward and I will be for the mending of flesh."

Gratt'na did as he was told and Paar'ha held out her walking stick for Brinn'ha to take. Brinn'ha did so automatically and nodded in respect as she accepted it. Erin moved closer to her and said in a low tone, "Okay, who is she? You guys are treating her like the eldest of Elders."

"Elder Barr'na would be for doing no less, Sar'ha. Be for the watching and it may be that understanding will be for you," Brinn'ha said.

That took Erin back a step. She had not seen Barr'na treat anyone except the other Elders as equals and had never seen him defer to anyone. She tried to keep that in mind as she turned her attention on Paar'ha and Gratt'na.

Paar'ha was examining the cut on Gratt'na's face while turning his head this way or that with a gentle but determined hand. Gratt'na complied without a word, and after a moment, Paar'ha placed her right hand on his forehead and closed her eyes in concentration.

Her left hand rose, the three thick fingers and opposable thumb closed into a flat plane. Tattoos, the finest and most intricately detailed that Erin had ever seen, flared into life on her palm with a silver-gold glow. Lines as thin as silk thread curved and spiraled across her palm like a luminescent cobweb, then slowly spread to other tattoos that ran the length of her left arm. This light spread like water filling a network of pipes until it flowed through the markings on her face and then down her right shoulder and arm. When it connected with Gratt'na's skin, he gave a soft, surprised shudder.

Light sprang out from the cut and his other injuries in broken halos of metallic brilliance. Slowly, over the course of a minute or more, the light faded from Gratt'na's skin. When the last of it had diminished to nothing, Paar'ha spread the fingers of her left hand and the light blinked out as cleanly as if someone had flipped a switch. The Wise Wanderer took in a deep breath and said, "I am not for denying you your scars, hunter of the Valley Tribe. Be for the wearing of them as a sign of your courage and truth."

"I am for being in gratitude to you, Wise Paar'ha. Be for knowing that I am Gratt'na. My flesh-sister is for being called Brinn'ha. Be for knowing that we are for calling Sar'ha our heart-sister and are for standing with her in all things."

Paar'ha glanced at Erin with a look of appraisal. She said nothing, but kept her eyes on Erin as she gestured Brinn'ha forward. Brinn'ha stood stock still next to Gratt'na while Paar'ha repeated the healing process on her. When it was done, brother and sister both looked refreshed, if still bloody and dirty, and sported fresh pink scars where their injuries had been. Neither seemed distressed by this and proudly pointed out their new permanent adornments.

Paar'ha turned to Erin and said, "And what of you, Sar'ha? I was for seeing Raff'na attack with a mighty kick that laid you down. Are you for needing the mending of flesh?"

Erin would have been lying if she said her chest didn't

feel like someone had been jumping on it. Instead, she said, "In a minute, maybe. My body is different from theirs. I think we should talk first."

Paar'ha nodded. "It is for being so, then. I am for hearing your tale, Sar'ha, Starstrider and heart-sister of the Valley People Tribe."

"First, you tell me how you know my name. My real name, I mean. No offense intended, but I don't know you and that kind of thing makes me nervous."

"Sar'ha," Brinn'ha said, "she is for being a Wise Wanderer. She is for being among the highest seekers of truth. She is for the trusting."

"Yeah, I get that," Erin said. "She's also the first native I've met who could speak any kind of English."

"That is for being your native language?" Gratt'na asked.

"Yeah," Erin said. "I'd like to know how you worked that out, Paar'ha."

Paar'ha stood stock still as she studied the trio before her. Erin met her eyes without blinking. Finally, Paar'ha said, "You are not for being the first of your kind to come to this place, Sar'ha. I am for having studied the things they left, spoken with the other Starstriders, learned small pieces of their languages."

"You mean there are others like me? Here? Now?"

"No, Sar'ha. The last of them reached their all-truth many, many seasons ago."

Erin considered that. It was entirely plausible, she realized, that other humans had found ways through the barriers that separated one reality from another. According to what she remembered from her time with the Sentry Group, different organizations had been screwing around with just that sort of thing for decades, maybe even centuries. It was totally possible that someone could have pulled it off either accidentally or intentionally.

"Fine," she said, "but what about my name? Just because you learned some English back in the day doesn't mean you should know my real name."

"Are you not for seeing my Marks, Sar'ha? I am for the carrying of many Marks to your one." She gestured to the Marks of Understanding that curved around Erin's ears. "Among them are for being the Soonwatcher's Pattern. The pattern is for allowing me to see and hear pieces of truths not yet known. That is how I was for knowing to make my way to this place and this night. Season past, I was for seeing you, Sar'ha, standing on a low rise near the Valley People Tribe. They were for the speaking, but not the understanding. Many times you were for speaking your name and many times I was for hearing it."

Erin could remember that night in vivid detail. She was battered and bloodied from the fight in Leticia, Texas. Beyond that, she had teleported an aviation refueling truck over a thousand miles and nearly died from the effort. Feeling like that and trying to talk to a bunch of aliens with no common language was a level of frustration not easily forgotten.

"Fair enough, I guess."

"Are you for the mending of flesh, now?" Paar'ha said.

"I don't know. Like I said, my body doesn't always react to things here the same way as you guys."

"Wise Paar'ha," Brinn'ha said, "on the path to this place we were for stopping to have the Nala-fruit. Sar'ha was for having the wrong-mind and having her eyes filled with not-truth. She is for being correct about her re-actions."

Paar'ha looked at Erin. "The Nala is not being for your kind, Sar'ha. How much of the fruit were you for eating?"

"Just one of them."

Paar'ha gaped at her. "You were for having a whole of the Nala? Sar'ha, that you are not for being still lost within your mind is a great thing. I am for having witnessed a Starstrider from long past eat but a slice of the Nala and spending more than a day with their eyes filled with not-truth."

"If that's your way of saying the guy was tripping balls, then I'm with you. I saw some severe weirdness," Erin said.

Paar'ha seemed to be thinking over the statement. "I am for having forgotten the strangeness of a Starstrider's words," she said. "Be for knowing this, Sar'ha: You will not be the first of your kind whose flesh I have been for mending. You are for being safe under my hands."

Erin considered it. She was hurting and she knew that they still had the plane's wreckage to deal with. Doing that without a chest full of bruises might be worth the risk. "Okay," she said, "but take it slow and if I say stop, then back off. I don't want to end up dead from the procedure. Know what I mean?"

Paar'ha was staring at her with an expression that Erin read as something between curiosity and confusion. She knew the Marks of Understanding were not perfect translators and she often wondered if the way the Valley People heard things sounded as strange to them as the things they said to Erin did to her.

"Just be careful, Paar'ha," Erin said, hoping to simplify things.

"I am always for being just so," Paar'ha said.

Erin nodded, took a deep breath, and stepped forward. She watched closely as Paar'ha raised her left hand and brought the fingers together. Now that she was closer, Erin could see the tracery of lines on Paar'ha's palm much clearer. The lines seemed random until the fingers closed and the full pattern was revealed. It was an intricate tangle of curves and angles that completely covered her palm and fingers, but no two lines ever crossed. It was like one of those find a path puzzles she remembered from her childhood, but on so small a scale that it would take a magnifying glass to work it out.

The light started filling Paar'ha's palm and making its way across her body. Erin watched it coming toward Paar'ha's right hand and when the glow started coalescing in the marks on that palm, Erin could swear she felt it pressing on her eyes. Paar'ha reached out and placed her palm on Erin's chest.

Erin's body was suddenly suffused with a warmth that penetrated every cell in her body. It was like climbing into a hot tub after walking naked through a freezing night. Pain evaporated, weariness fled, and the sensation was one of the most wonderful Erin had ever felt – for about three seconds.

The first thing she felt was Paar'ha's hand trembling against her sternum. Then, in the space of a heartbeat, the warmth that suffused her grew into something like a fire that threatened to consume her whole. Paar'ha's palm continued to spasm against Erin's chest. Erin worked her mouth to speak, to tell Paar'ha to stop, but her jaw muscles refused to co-operate, instead spasming in time with Paar'ha's hand.

Erin wanted to knock that hand away, but her arms wouldn't move. The heat continued to grow and then, suddenly, she felt power rushing into her in a flood. Her awareness, her sense of here and there, suddenly spread out from her in a burst so thorough that she was certain she could use her power to take them all back to the valley if she chose. More than that, she could sense tendrils of that power shooting away from her, pulled through the air into a place of nothing and beyond.

Then it was all gone.

The night rushed back in on Erin as she staggered backward and away from Paar'ha. Gratt'na had pulled the Wise Wanderer's hand away from her chest and held it still. His other arm was under Paar'ha's shoulder, supporting her as she sagged against him. Her skin was lit slightly with the fading light of the power she had been channeling and she was gasping for breath.

Brinn'ha was next to Erin with one hand on her shoulder and a worried look in her eye. Erin nodded that she was okay and said, "What happened? Is she okay?"

"I am not for knowing," Brinn'ha said. "All was for seeming well until Paar'ha's body grew bright and the both of you were for the shuddering. Sar'ha, are you for being certain of your wellness?"

"I'm fine, Brinn. Really." Erin joined Gratt'na and Paar'ha. The older native had regained some of her composure and looked up at Erin with an expression of pure wonder.

"You are for truth being the one for who I am for seeking, Sar'ha. You are for being connected to power I was not for expecting. I am for the resting and the hearing of your tale. Come, let us be for the taking of warmth from the fire."

Gratt'na helped Paar'ha to a place next to the fire. Erin stayed with Paar'ha while Gratt'na and Brinn'ha spent a few minutes collecting the bodies of the fallen Starless and moving them away from the camp.

Erin and Paar'ha did not speak while the siblings worked. Paar'ha remained seated, staring into the fire with eyes that were no longer dulled by pain. Erin stood and watched her, wondering all the while where this night was taking her.

Brinn'ha and Gratt'na finished their unpleasant work and joined them by the fire. Once they were settled, Paar'ha looked up at Erin and said, "Be for the telling of it, Sar'ha."

Erin didn't see any reason to give Paar'ha the whole of her life story like she had when the Valley People had accepted her into their tribe. She considered everything that was going on and finally said, "Okay. It all started when I woke up in a basement."

She told Paar'ha her story, leaving out the most personal things, but giving her as much information as she could recall when it came to matters related to her Paragon nature, her power, and how she had ended up in a world that was not her own. The telling of it again after so long put a tiny ache of homesickness into her heart, a small ache that reminded her of things she loved about the world she knew and the friends she had made, some from her past, others she had known only briefly before being catapulted from one world to another. Israel Trent and his confident, easy nature was at the top of that list and Erin pointedly put the thought away.

The story took some time to tell, but Paar'ha listened to all of it in stoic silence. When it was done, she asked a few questions about things that were unfamiliar to her and then spent a long while thinking it all over. Eventually, she said, "Sar'ha, I am not for offering you insult, but I must be for the asking: This is all truth?"

Erin nodded. "Every word."

Paar'ha rose and then spent another long moment staring into the fire. "Never," she said without looking up, "has such a powerful Starstrider been for walking the paths of this world. Never in all the tales I am for knowing, and I am for knowing most. There is being far more to you and your tale than I was for expecting, Sar'ha."

"Yeah, I've gotten that a lot in the last year or so."

Paar'ha faced the trio and said, "I am for seeing that you are for having found a place and a tribe among the Valley People. I am for having great sorrow for that."

Erin and her heart-siblings exchanged looks before Brinn'ha said, "Sorrow, wise Paar'ha?"

"Yes, Brinn'ha. Your heart-sister must be for returning to her world. She must, or we are all for risking the all-truth."

CHAPTER TWENTY-FOUR

The declaration hung in the air for a time before anyone spoke.

"Why, wise Paar'ha?" Gratt'na said at last. "Sar'ha would never be for bringing the all-truth to the unde-serving. Why must such a thing be for the happening?"

Paar'ha gestured to the piles of aircraft debris scat-tered around them. "Be for the looking to these not-world things for your answer, Gratt'na. I am for being a Wise Wanderer; I am for watching all lands and all peoples. You are being of the Valley People and living in your place of beauty, but isolation. Much is for happening in the wider world that the Valley People Tribe is not for the knowing of."

"Hang on," Erin said. "What do you mean? Have there been other things like this?"

"Truth, Sar'ha. From your telling, I am for thinking the first of such things was for the coming not long after your own. I was for first hearing of it after a turning of moons from the time I was for seeing your coming. Strange animals appeared far to the north of your valley. They were for doing no harm, but were not for being known to any. Another Wise Wanderer, Stev'na, was for the examining of the animals and he declared them Worldwalkers, though they were for having no more intelligence than a Tarr-beast. Twice more was this for happening in places spread far from the first. Objects that were unknown were for the second and the third was a small collection of beings who had met their all-truth. Among the Wise Wanderer tribe, there are none who were for the knowing of what brought these things. Then there was for being a fourth event that was not for being so harmless.

"Beasts who were for having many legs and the cunning of a hunter appeared in the midst of Three Rivers settlement, much to the east of here. They were for attacking the tribes there, for feeding on their flesh, and making nests from vines that they were for making with their bodies. Many warriors and Wise Ones were for coming to the battle for Three Rivers. I was for being among them. I am now wishing for the day I will forget what I was for seeing there."

"What happened?" Erin said softly.

"We were for fighting them for two cycles of the moons, Sar'ha. When it was for being done, we had shown seven of the monsters their all-truth, but we were for having lost six and ten times again that many."

Erin closed her eyes against the image the words painted in her mind. If this Three Rivers place was anything like the Valley People settlement, then that meant whole families could have died at once. After a moment, she whispered, "Then what?"

"The Wise Wanderers were for the calling of an Assemblage."

"Which is what?" Erin said.

"A gathering of all the Wise Wanderers. It is only done when that which is not yet known has become a threat too great for any one of us to be for the facing. It is a time for which we are for the sharing of the known to find solutions not known. It was there I was for the telling of my seeing of you. The Assemblage was for the talking of it, the sharing the knowns, and we were for deciding the seeking of you was important."

"Well, what took so long? Why didn't you just come straight to me? You said you saw me when I got here."

"The seeing of things through the Soonwatcher's Pattern is not the same as the seeing of things through one's own eyes, Sar'ha. Details are for being lost and dull. I was for knowing you had come and that you had been for the finding by a peaceful tribe, but I was not for knowing which. Romanos'Ta is for being great in size–"

"What's that? Ro-whatever you said?"

"Romanos'Ta," Paar'ha said. "It is the place your path is for having brought you. It is here." She gestured in a general way to their surroundings. "It is the name that is for all the things surrounding us."

Romanos'Ta. Erin realized that she had been living there for over a year and never thought to ask if the planet had a name.

"There is for being a name for all the things of soil and plant?" Brinn'ha said. "I was never for knowing such a thing."

"You are for being a Valley Tribe hunter, Brinn'ha," Paar'ha said, "and a skilled one. You are for knowing things that aid your skill and path. I am for knowing things that aid mine."

"So, what then?" Erin asked. "How did you get here? I mean, this can't be a coincidence."

"There are ways that are for manipulating the Soonwatcher's Pattern. I am not for the controlling of it; it is for being a thing of power and such things are always for their own ways, but I am for being able to use its own ways to my purposes. I could not be for forcing it to show you or your location, but larger, broader events like this–" she gestured to the wreckage once more, "–are easier for the pattern to be discerning. I was for following those events as best I was able until I was for seeing you standing in battle against Raff'na. Once I was for knowing that, I tracked Raff'na and Cuts in Night so that I might be for the witnessing and the meeting."

"So you knew I was going to win that fight?"

Paar'ha hesitated, then said, "I was not for the knowing of that truth."

Erin took a moment with that and then said, "I guess it would have worked out either way for you, though, right? I kill him, you've got me and maybe a way to stop the breaches; he kills me, breaches die with me. Is that about right?"

Paar'ha met Erin's eyes and said, "Truth."

They held that gaze until Erin half smiled and shook her head. "Well, at least you're honest about it."

"Wise Paar'ha," Gratt'na said. "You are for saying that Sar'ha must be for the returning to her home-place. How can such a thing be for happening if she is not for the knowing of how she arrived here?"

"Gratt'na and Brinn'ha are for being of the same flesh in matters of seeking to know truth. Both are for asking the wise thing and listening more than seeking to be heard. The Valley Tribe is for being well to claim you. As for Sar'ha's return, the mending of flesh was for showing me more than the nature and way of Sar'ha's hurt. I was for the seeing of her power and the hurt that it endures."

"I don't understand," Erin said. "I'm sure that surprises all of you."

"It is for being well, Sar'ha," Paar'ha said. "The path to understanding is for being often long. What were you for seeing in the mending, Sar'ha? When my power was joining to your own?"

Erin thought about it and said, "I felt like I used to back on Earth. I could sense farther out from myself than

I've been able to since coming here. But there was something else, too; I felt like I was getting... pulled, maybe? Like my awareness was stretching away to..." The thought trailed off and she looked at Paar'ha with wide, understanding eyes. "No way," she said. "It can't be that easy."

Paar'ha nodded. "Do not be for thinking that which is for being simple is also for being done with ease. If you are for walking a path and come to large boulder that is for blocking the way, knowing that moving it will solve your problem is simple; the moving of the thing will not be done with ease."

"That's a fair point. Still, though, you're saying that all this time all I needed was an extra boost of energy to get me home? I thought my ability was all but gone."

"What I was for seeing in the mending, Sar'ha, was that in your coming to this place, your power created an unseen tunnel from the—" Paar'ha considered it for a moment, made an awkward face, and said, "Ur-eth... to Romanos'Ta. Your power is lessened because the tunnel remains open and is for the draining of your power to stay that way. Your path back to your home has always been for being open, Sar'ha, but it is that very path which makes you too weak to walk it."

"And all the breaches that brought these different things into Romanos'Ta, they somehow got swept up in this tunnel?"

"I am for thinking that is truth, Sar'ha."

Erin closed her eyes and shook her head. She tried not to think about the harm she had inadvertently done, but the story of the Three Rivers breach kept coming back to her. "Oh, God," she said, unbidden tears welling in her eyes. "I am so sorry. I had no idea. Please believe that."

"There are for being none here who are for thinking you sought to bring harm, Sar'ha," Brinn'ha said.

"Truth," Paar'ha replied. "I am for the believing of your telling. You are for coming here by an act of sacrifice for your heart-brother, the Tree-nt." Again, Paar'ha's face twisted awkwardly around the word, though she seemed to enjoy trying to speak the alien English.

Erin wiped her eyes and smiled. "Keep trying to talk like me and you might hurt yourself," she said.

Paar'ha's eyes shot up. "Is your world-tongue for holding power in its words, Sar'ha?"

"No, no," Erin said with a shake of her head. "It was a joke. I was just trying to lighten the moment."

Paar'ha looked at Erin with confusion simmering in her eyes. She looked to Gratt'na and Brinn'ha.

"It is her way," Brinn'ha said, "to be for inspiring laughter in times of knowing new truth."

"We are for having grown used to it," Gratt'na said.

Paar'ha seemed to accept this and turned back to Erin. "Truth."

"Okay, then," Erin said. "That all seems to make sense. So, what now? You do another mending thing and I hop on the Cross-Reality Express? How's this work?"

"As I am for having said, Sar'ha, simplicity is not for being of one with ease. The power I was for channeling to mend your flesh was great, but only enough to be for allowing us to observe the path of power. For you to be for the walking of that path will require greater power than ever I have been for channeling before. I would be for the resting for a time before we try."

"Fair enough," Erin said. There was slight tremble in her voice and she was suddenly angry at herself for letting it live there. "I guess we should rest, too."

"No, Sar'ha," Paar'ha said, a sudden softness in her eyes and words. "Now is for being the time you are for sitting with your heart-tribe. Now is for being the time of farewells."

Erin looked up at Brinn'ha and Gratt'na. Their large eyes looked back, moist but not tearful. Their faces were never as expressive as a human's, but she had learned to read them over time. Now, she saw resignation, sadness, and, more than anything, love.

It was the last one that broke her down and set her to crying.

They sat while Paar'ha slept. They talked, they wept, and they laughed. At one point after Erin had given them a message to convey back to Elder Barr'na, Gratt'na said, "What are you for thinking you are for the returning to, Sar'ha? Are you for having a shelter? A tribe?"

Erin thought about it and shrugged. "I'm not sure. I mean, I'm sure they all think I'm dead, so I could just get back and fade into the crowd. I don't know that they'd ever know the difference."

Brinn'ha looked at her with a curious tilt to her head. "You would be for walking this new path alone, Sar'ha?"

Again, Erin shrugged. "I don't know, Brinn. Things are different there. People have different expectations, treat each other differently. Honestly, I'm not sure what to expect."

"Sar'ha, were you not for the hearing of Paar'ha? This place, Romanos'Ta, is for being no different. You were for not the knowing of Raff'na and his Starless until you were far the path that was for leading here, but there are for being many like him in the wider world. I am for thinking that your world must have tribes that are for being like the ways of the Valley People. You should be for the finding of them. Do not be for the walking of the world alone."

Erin thought that over. She couldn't help but think of the people she had met in the Sentry Group. And Israel, of course. She didn't know what kind of reception Olivia Warburton would give her – Erin had given the head of Sentry a pretty hard time – but she was sure Israel would be glad to see her. Assuming he was alive, that is. She had been allowing herself some assumptions; for all she knew, the breach in Leticia, Texas, hadn't been closed by the explosion. If that was the case, she might be going home to a world she wouldn't recognize, one overrun with things straight out of some lunatic's nightmares.

Erin shook her head in resignation. It was what it was. There was no way she was staying there and further endangering the people of Romanos'Ta. She'd just as soon end it all.

"Sar'ha" Gratt'na said, "you are for being lost on the paths of your mind."

Erin looked up at him and smiled. "Yeah, I guess so. It's nothing, though. What about you guys? Are you going straight back to the valley?"

Brinn'ha and Gratt'na shared a look and then Gratt'na said, "We are for thinking not."

Erin was surprised. "Really? What are you going to do?"

"We are for walking the longer path from here, Sar'ha. We are for thinking that the world seems small when all you are for knowing is the truth of the place and ways of your birth and tribe. You have been for showing us that, though truth is all, there are many more truths than the Valley People are for knowing. We are for walking farther than any before us and bringing tales of these truths back to the Valley People."

Erin nodded and said, "Wow. Okay. I think that's a really good idea. Any idea where you're headed first?"

Another glance passed between the siblings and they said, "We were for thinking we would be for following a path to the Three Rivers settlement. If there is still for being need there, we would be for giving what help we could in the name of the Valley People Tribe."

Erin closed her eyes for a moment and beat back the regret simmering in her chest. After a moment, she said, "That would be a good thing to do."

They all looked up as Paar'ha stirred from her place by

the fire. She sat up and spent a few minutes taking in deep, measured breaths before asking Gratt'na to bring her some water. He did so without hesitation and she spent another few minutes taking long drinks from the water before she spoke to them.

"It is for being time, my young friends. Brinn'ha and Gratt'na, you must be for the leaving of this place."

"No, wise Paar'ha," Brinn'ha said. "We are for staying with our heart-sister until she is for leaving our sight."

"It cannot be, Brinn'ha. What we are for doing is not for having been done before to my knowing. There is for being much risk, both to we and to any near. If you are for the watching, then you must do so from the farthest distance. I am not for knowing what to expect."

"Wait, Wise One," Gratt'na said, "you were not for speaking of risk before. If there is for being danger to Sar'ha then we should be for more thinking on this."

"Your loyalty to your heart-sister shows your truth, Gratt'na. Be for the remembering, though: There is for being much risk, much danger, every moment she is for remaining in this place. It is for being present not as her choosing, but it is for being present all the same. One risk must outweigh another."

Erin put a hand on Gratt'na's arm and said, "It's my choice, Gratt, and she's right. The longer I'm here, the longer there's a chance of something terrible dropping through a breach. I'm endangering the tribe and everyone else. I have to go, Gratt'na. For the truth and the tribe, I have to go."

Gratt'na closed his eyes and whispered, "Truth, Sar'ha." He pulled her into a tight embrace that Erin was sure she would feel the rest of her life. Then, without a word, he turned and went to retrieve his pack.

Brinn'ha had already done so and was standing a few steps away when Erin looked up.

"I had always been for the wanting of a sister," she

said. "I was never for the thinking that she would be for falling from the stars."

Erin embraced Brinn'ha much as she had her brother. Tears welled once again in her eyes and she said, "Thank you for everything, Brinn. I really don't know if I could have survived without either of you. If I could, I'd stay."

"No, Sar'ha," Brinn'ha said. "I am for seeing now that your path was never to find its all-truth here. For truth and tribe, you must be for departing, but not only for the Valley People Tribe." Brinn'ha pulled away from the embrace and met Erin's eyes. "Be for the returning to your world. Be for seeking out the tribe who stood beside you when you were for fighting the darkness. They will be for embracing you again, Sar'ha. Be for standing with them. You are for being a daughter and a warrior of the Valley People Tribe and there will always be darkness to fight. Be for carrying our name and our truth with you."

Erin felt the knot of emotions in her gut tighten, but she nodded. "I will, Brinn'ha."

Brinn'ha raised a thick finger and brushed a tear from Erin's cheek. In a voice that was thick with its own emotion, she said, "Farewell, Sar'ha, sister of my heart. May your path be long." Then she turned and joined Gratt'na. They started walking east into a night that was growing steadily brighter. Neither looked back.

Erin watched them go until they were nearly out of sight. Paar'ha came to stand next to her and said, "We can be for the beginning when you are for being ready, Sar'ha."

Erin looked up at her, brushed the tears from her eyes with an angry swipe of her hand, and said, "Yeah. Let's get this shit over with."

CHAPTER TWENTY-FIVE

Bones

Deputy Justin "Bones" Wainwright wove between the groups of people making their way out of the administration building and into the gymnasium next door. Occasionally he would stop to try and answer a question or offer what little reassurance he could, but in the end always wound up pointing them toward an exit. The transfer was going well, but there was a person missing from the crowd who he'd started to wonder about, so he went from door to door in the administration building until he found her.

He spotted her through the small window on one of the classroom doors. She was standing in front of one of three large dry-erase boards that were hung side by side on the classroom's front wall and was writing something there that he couldn't make heads or tails of. In fact, it looked as though she had covered all three boards in some kind of complex math that Justin had never seen outside of movies about geniuses and the occasional science fiction epic.

He started to open the door and go in but hesitated, taking a moment to watch her. She would step in and scribble something onto the end of her – Equation? Proof? He wasn't sure what the hell to call it – and then step back and take in her work. From the way she stood when she did that, he was sure she was seeing all three boards at once and that it somehow made sense to her.

There was something about her, he decided. Sure, she was good-looking in that sexy teacher, naughty librarian kind of way, but it was more than that. There was something in her eyes; it was a kind of focus and no-nonsense intensity that he appreciated. He figured it was the kind of thing that some folks might find a little cold, but it seemed like strength to him. As far as Justin "Bones" Wainwright was concerned, strong women were sexy women. Of course, the naughty librarian thing didn't hurt, either.

He pushed open the door on silent hinges and slipped into the room. Michelle didn't notice. Bones got the impresssion he could have banged on the door and she wouldn't have heard him.

"Whole damned world coming to an end and you're in here working on math problems," he said, letting an easy smile slide onto his face.

Michelle looked over at him, though the look in her eyes said she was still seeing whatever she had scribbled across those three whiteboards. "The world isn't going to end from all this, Bones. Though I suppose this island is pretty much screwed."

Bones snorted a laugh. "Well, ain't you just a ray of sunshine," he said.

Michelle shrugged and turned back to the boards. "Just keeping it real. It's kind of my thing."

"Copy that," he said. "What are you doing anyway? What is all that?"

Michelle reached up to erase something from one of the lines near the top of the board and write something else in its place. She had to stretch to do it and Bones wasn't shy about enjoying the view it provided him. She kept working, but didn't answer his question.

"Hey, Doc," he said, waving a hand playfully in her direction.

Michelle looked back at him. "I'm sorry. What?"

Bones gestured toward the boards. "What is all that?"

"Oh," Michelle said, "right. It's just something Sheriff Holmes made me think of. I think she may have showed me where I made a mistake."

Bones looked the board over for a moment, then said, "Sheriff's a smart woman, but I'm fair to certain that kind of math would give her a headache."

"It was the rubber bands," she said, staring at the board as though he hadn't spoken.

"That thing she does when she's questioning folks? Yeah, I asked her about that once. She said it was a trick she picked up back in the Army. Says it distracts the suspect and gives her a chance to get a look at them when they can't concentrate on whatever lie they're trying to tell."

"Uh huh," Michelle said. "They stretch. Rubber bands stretch..." Michelle's voice trailed off as she seemed to disappear into the equation again.

Bones watched her for another minute, concentrating, stretching, erasing, and rewriting. He shook his head and smiled. Naughty librarian or not, she might be the oddest woman he'd ever met. It was working for him, though.

"Well, darlin', as much as I'm intrigued by whatever you've got going on here, we need to get you in position. Most everyone's in the gym now and–"

"Excuse me?" she said, looking up at him.

"I said we need to go. Everyone else–"

"No, not that. Did you call me 'darling'?"

Bones made a show of thinking about that. "Did I? Maybe so. Can't really recall."

"Why would you do that?"

Bones shrugged and said, "Well, you're pretty as a

sunset and seem smarter than any ten people I know, so I guess it just seemed like somebody should." He met her eyes and shot her a smile that had gotten him attention in more than a few countries around the world.

She didn't smile back. "You're cute," she said. "Got the whole soldier boy, southern gent thing going for you." She looked back at board. "Stretches..." she muttered.

"Doc, we need to go."

"Why 'Bones'?"

"What?"

"Your nickname. It's a little odd since you don't seem to have any medical training. Why do people call you that?"

Bones watched her staring at the board. The question hung between them like a challenge.

Without thinking, he said, "I was a Marine Corps Scout Sniper. Full blown P.I.G."

"Pig?"

"Professionally Instructed Gunman. Sometimes they called us H.O.Gs – Hunters of Gunmen. Anyway, a couple of weeks into my second tour through the sandbox, I got attached to a group that was supposed to take down known cells in rapid succession. The idea was to find a verified active insurgent cell, take it down with minimal casualties, interrogate the captives, and immediately move on whatever intel they gave us."

Michelle thought that over and said, "That seems a little weak as plans go."

"It was a total bullshit plan thought up by some ass-polisher sitting at a desk someplace who'd never seen the business end of an enemy's weapon. We could take cells, sure, but the intel part of that was a total waste of time. They either wouldn't talk, would give us old information, or they'd lie through their fundamentalist asses. Still, though, command wanted reportable results, so word came down to push the captives harder. So we go on this one mission, catch this real big fish – a bomb maker we knew for a fact had taken out a couple of our patrols with some particularly nasty IEDs."

"Sounds like a sweetheart," Michelle said with a smirk. She had turned from the board and seemed intent on his story now.

"Yeah, the guy was a real snake, nearly a Hollywood cliché. As bloodthirsty a zealot as you've ever heard about. So we've got this guy and we're holed up in an old shack way out in the field. Protocol was to interrogate on-site, so my lieutenant, he goes to work on him. I'm on sentry duty at the windows, but there's nothing but sand and sunlight as far as the eye can see.

"After a while, the L.T. starts getting a little flustered because this guy, he just ain't talking. L.T. comes out for a breather and, as a joke, asks me if I want a crack at him. I'd never interrogated anybody before, but I said, 'What the hell,' not even expecting the L.T. to take me up on it. He did, though, so I went for it."

Bones slipped into the memory and felt the smile leave his face. Some new feeling crawled through him, making his skin feel too small for the muscle and bone beneath it.

"What happened?" Michelle said.

Bones looked up, shaking off the memory and the sensation. "I've had a lot of hand-to-hand training," he said. "Even before the Corps I was into Krav Maga and jiujitsu. A lot of grappling work, joint locks, throws – that kind of thing. Now, my L.T., he was a good guy – good marine, respected the hell out of him – but he was a talker. I'm not. Long story short, after about a half hour, I convinced this guy to give up one of the biggest weapon caches in the area. It was a major score for our side."

"How did you do it?" Michelle asked. She was watching him closely, watching his eyes. Bones realized she was looking for a lie.

He didn't give her one to find. "I started by breaking

his fingers," he said. "By the time I got around to dislocating one of his elbows, he was singing like a canary."

Michelle nodded. "They call you Bones because you broke his."

"Yeah. I got kind of a reputation after that."

"They ask you to do it again?"

Bones frowned. "They did. I got the name after that first time, though."

"You're home now. Why keep using the name?"

He shrugged. That too-tight feeling was creeping over him again. "Before my mama passed, she used to say that a person can't really appreciate the picture of who they are without the frame of who they used to be. I guess that name is part of my frame, a reminder of lines I crossed and maybe don't want to cross again."

Michelle studied him for minute. It looked like she was thinking over his story. "You seem to be honest, at least."

"Not the trusting sort?"

"No. And the last guy who called me anything like 'darling' really reinforced the tendency."

"Sounds like a story."

"It is. Tell you what: We live through this, maybe I'll give you a chance to hear it. Maybe."

Bones flashed her another one of those smiles. "I can work with 'maybe.'"

"In the meantime," Michelle said, "how are you feeling? Noticed anything yet?"

Bones shrugged. "Not really. My skin seems to be tingling a bit, but that's probably just nerves, what with the island being screwed and all."

Michelle nodded, glanced at the whiteboards again, and then said, "I wasn't kidding. It could actually get worse."

Bones opened his mouth to speak, realized he didn't know what to say, and then just shook his head. "Lovely.

Simply goddamn lovely," he muttered.

Michelle had a soft smile on her face when he looked up at her. "Don't sweat it too much, Marine. Things getting worse is where the Sentry Group goes to work. Come on, let's find Stone. He needs to hear what I figured out."

Bones led Michelle out of the room and out the doors that were closest to the gym. The last of the Jasper Island survivors were moving inside in a slow but steady stream. Cars had been moved into position around the door in an attempt to create a choke point if it became necessary to defend the place. Bones knew the other two entrances had been blocked and barricaded both inside and outside – he'd overseen that himself – but he still wondered if it would be enough.

They took a right out the door and headed for the school's front wall. They reached it and found Stone standing alone on the roof of an SUV looking out at the island. They joined him, and when Bones saw the view, ice water seemed to suddenly flood through him.

There had to be more than a thousand of them. He recognized some of the faces even though they were gray and veined in dark shadows now, but most of them he did not. They were clustered together like cattle, all standing stock still in the mist. They made no sound, just stared with dead eyes and silently bared teeth. The yard beyond the wall and the driveway that bisected it were filled with them standing in loose ranks that extended back until they faded into the mist. Though he couldn't see them, Bones was sure there were even more hidden back there. It was like he could feel those gray, feral eyes watching him.

"That..." Michelle said, swallowing hard, "that is a lot of Necrophage."

"I stopped counting at nine hundred and thirty," Stone said in his deep voice. "Fighters to 'phage, I figure they've got about eleven to our one. That's just what we can see."

"Well," Bones said, trying to keep his voice even,

"that's a whole new level of suck for me."

"Sheriff's pretty sure we'll run out of ammo before we can kill them all," Stone said, "and that's assuming we even get a chance to make this a shooting fight. If they come all at once..." Stone let the statement trail off into a shrug.

"Then we pull back to the gym and that choke point we set up. Make our stand there." Bones realized he was rubbing his hands together. The tight feeling in his skin was getting worse. He swore it felt like his skin was getting colder.

"That's the plan," Stone said. "If the Gunderson woman sticks to her word, though, we still have some time. I'll stand watch until everyone else is in, then I'll fall back."

Bones stretched out his neck. It was suddenly aching like he'd overdone it at the gym. "I'll do you one better; let me get my rifle and I'll get up on the gym roof. I can keep overwatch with the scope and you can fall back and help out the sheriff with the fortifications."

Stone considered it and then nodded. "Nice thinking, mate. We'll do that."

"We need to talk about the Erin thing," Michelle said, her eyes still on the assembled monsters.

"What about it?" Stone asked.

"I was sort of wrong," Michelle said.

Stone looked over at her. "Did I just hear Doctor Michelle Brandt admit she was wrong?"

"No, you just heard me admit I was 'sort of' wrong. Don't be an ass."

Bones rolled his shoulders. The ache was spreading. At first he'd thought the sensation was like his skin was shrinking, but now it was like something cold was pushing out from his bones. "Erin? That's your friend you think went M.I.A?"

"That's the one," Stone said. He glanced at Bones and

said, "Are you all right, mate?"

Bones nodded. "It'll keep. I want to hear this."

"Remember how I said I had theorized that Erin had cut a hole through multiple realities and that was why we kept having the micro-breaches?"

Stone nodded.

"Well, there were a couple of things about that theory that didn't sit well with me, the biggest of which is that there weren't enough breaches."

"Say again?" Stone said.

"Look, if she had plowed through the fabric of everything leaving a bunch of holes in her wake, shouldn't things be able to just come pouring through all at once? It's a hole, after all? Right?"

"Okay," Stone said.

"Instead, things just kind of pop through either by accident or effort. So, it's not so much that there's a hole, but a thinning, a place where someone could push through more than fall through. Like walking through a doorway with a heavy curtain over it instead of a solid door. That's what she left behind."

"Why does that matter, Michelle? She's still there, we're still here, and the breaches keep coming."

"It matters because what I was wrong about was the nature of her effect on space-time. She didn't cut a conduit through to wherever she is, she just stretched it so thin that things ended up the way they are now."

"Like the sheriff's rubber bands," Bones said, massaging the knuckles of his left hand with his right. "That's what you meant back in the classroom."

"Exactly," Michelle said.

"Still waiting for the relevant bit," Stone said.

"She's stretched her way through space-time. Things that are stretched eventually snap back, right? So why didn't Erin?"

Stone mulled it over for a moment. "She's dead or

something's stopping her."

"Gunderson," Michelle said. "Whatever DGS did to her at that facility has allowed her to tap into previously unrecorded levels of ID energy. I mean, she's manipulating square miles worth of weather, for God's sake. That kind of thing is unheard of in recorded Veil history and only theorized about based on historical myth. Couple that with her ability to control Necrophage and you're looking at channeled power on a scale that would turn a normal Mage to cinders in a second or three."

"Mage? How do you know that?"

Michelle pointed at the assembled Necrophage horde. "That. It came to me while I was working – one of the rarest of all the Mage disciplines."

Stone closed his eyes and slowly shook his head. "Of course," he said. "She's a thrice-damned Necromancer. I should've seen it."

"That explains all this, how she could communicate with Israel, and how she managed to get into Carmine's head since he was apparently carrying around Necrophage DNA in that eye of his," Michelle said.

"Figured out how he's managing that yet?" Stone asked.

Michelle shook her head. "No. I'll need Allie for that, but that's not really what's relevant here. Somehow Gunderson is drawing this enormous power without killing herself, but she's doing it through the hole or dent or whatever it is that Erin left in space-time. If Erin is still alive and holding that conduit open, doesn't it stand to reason that Gunderson could be leaching power off of Erin too? It would take as much energy as Erin expressed to get wherever she is for her to get back, but if Gunderson is somehow stealing energy from her–" Michelle gestured toward Stone to finish the thought.

"Then that's why she hasn't returned on her own," he said.

"That's not all; if my theory holds then when she comes back, it won't be a subtle thing. She'll—"

Bones didn't hear the rest. Icy pressure exploded out from his spine and through his body like a bomb. He thought he screamed, but couldn't hear. Silver-white light popped in his eyes and he felt himself stagger, then fall, but there was no impact. There was just cold, white light that suddenly turned to cold, silent darkness.

CHAPTER TWENTY-SIX

Israel

Jordan's scent was a faint but still noticeable aroma in air that was choked with the scent of blood and rotting meat. Israel ran across the island as fast as he could manage, only stopping when he needed to reacquire the scent and adjust his course. It seemed that Jordan was also moving fast, but not in a straight line. Israel couldn't tell whether this was to avoid the undead or to throw Israel off his trail. Either way, the need to stop and adjust his course was slowing him down.

He thought about what he knew about Jordan as he ran. They were about the same age, but whereas Israel had spent his life getting educated and working – the average, middle-class American story – Jordan had spent his life with Carmine going in and out of foster care, juvenile detention, and eventually prison. Jordan and Carmine were career criminals to the bone and had spent a lot of their life on the run, so it made sense that Jordan might know how to cover his trail.

The gap in Israel's knowledge of the Screed brothers started when they had gone to work for the Progeny of the Inner Dark and been Awakened. After that, the Progeny had obviously used its resources to cover up the men's crimes and, when it didn't or couldn't, there wasn't a regular cop in the world who had a chance of arresting a pair of Paragons. The problem was that Israel had no idea exactly what bloodline the two men belonged to. He assumed they were the same since they were brothers, but their abilities seemed to vary somewhat.

He'd fought them both; Carmine was incredibly strong and tougher than hammered steel, while Jordan was fast, nimble, and had reflexes that Israel was pretty sure would allow him to dodge bullets so long as there weren't too many of them coming at him at once. Neither had given any indication of abilities outside of the obvious physical traits. Not until Jordan had told them the story of how Carmine had used his ruined eye to start the undead outbreak on the island.

Israel skidded to a halt and sniffed the air. The chill atmosphere was perfumed by the sweet tang of fresh death, but under it Israel could still sense the sweat and earthy musk that Jordan was giving off. There was another scent, though, a new one that seemed to join with Jordan's. It was familiar, he thought, something he had smelled recently. It came to him in a hard instant. The ferret-like creatures that had fallen through the micro-breach outside the school had carried that scent. He turned a slow circuit until he had the path where that musk was strongest and found himself facing what must be the small town of Emberoak, Massachusetts.

Through the ever-present mist, Israel could see that the town curved around a large bay in a rough semicircle. The buildings were all classical New England Coastal architecture – lots of wood and shaker-style siding painted in subdued tones ranging from barn-red to gray. Here and there a brick structure stood among the more classic buildings. Boats bobbed up and down in the bay, tugging against anchor lines and banging into piers as though the distant storms were reminding everyone they were still there by churning the normally calm waters.

On a normal day, the sight would have made for a postcard perfect view. Between the thick columns of smoke rising from various spots in the town, the heavy mist, and the distant black clouds with their constant spikes of lightning, though, it was more suited to perdition than postcards. Jordan seemed to be heading right for it.

At first, this confused Israel. Though small, Emberoak was still the densest population center on the island. It stood to reason that if everyone there had been turned, then that would be the absolute worst place to be. Then it clicked for him; Jordan must have seen the undead gathering outside the school grounds and figured out that Susan was massing them for an assault. If he had witnessed a Necrophage exodus from Emberoak, he was probably thinking that the town would be clear and provide him with supplies and lots of places to hide. It was a solid plan, Israel figured, but it wouldn't keep him from tracking Jordan down.

He started running again and within a few minutes had reached the road leading into town. The first thing that caught his eye was a minivan. It had run off the road and collided with a large stone sign welcoming people to Emberoak. The front of the vehicle was a mess. Israel could see where the air bags had deployed, but it was the bodies he noticed more than anything.

He had read accounts of zombie Necrophage out-breaks. It was always pointed out that not everyone who was attacked by an undead would rise as one. If the bodies suffered enough damage to the spine or brain, then the body did not rise. That was what had happened to these people.

The driver had been a woman. She had been pulled through the shattered driver's side window up to her hips and was hanging from it, facing up to the sky with a bowed back. Her face, head, torso, and arms were a bloody ruin of torn flesh and missing features. One eye hung motionless from a thin strip of tissue that led back into the ruined socket.

It looked as though the three preteen children who had been with her had tried to run but hadn't gotten more than a few feet. Their bodies were scattered around the van in gore-soaked piles. There wasn't enough of them left for Israel to tell if they had been boys or girls.

Cold, horrified tension washed through him as his eyes drifted up and took in the main street. It was a worn asphalt lane with wide, cobblestone sidewalks that ran past businesses with glass fronts and hanging signs advertising this pub or that shop. Some of the stores were smoldering wrecks, though. Glass littered the street from shattered windows. Bodies, dozens of them of all ages and sexes, were scattered up the lane. Blood filled the cracks between the cobblestones in wide pools, slowly congealing into rancid gel.

Israel wanted to turn away, wanted to scream and retch, but he couldn't move, couldn't think.

"This is your fault! You! All of this, all those dead people, all of it, Trent! It's all on you!"

"...you keep playing this stupid game where you pretend that you aren't what you are..."

The words of his enemy and his friend bounced through his mind like an endlessly ricocheting bullet. He stared down the length of that bloody street and saw his legacy. He might not have chosen this exact thing, but it was his blood, his twisted, horrific DNA that had given Carmine Screed the ability to do what he had done and lead these people and all the others to their nightmarish end.

Revulsion washed over him at the thought. They had been right – both his enemy and his friend. His actions, his very existence, had led to this. This was what his detractors among the Council of the Veil feared – this, but on a global scale. Israel couldn't help but imagine a world filled with scenes like this, a world where the undead outnumbered the living and people lived in hiding like frightened prey animals. He would be a king in a world like that, and the thought of it offended him on a level that might make a man go to war.

He stood like a statue, taking in the scene for a long time, forcing it into a relief carving in his memory that would never go away. He didn't want it to, didn't want to lose the image to the easy routine of everyday life that had fooled him into forgetting that this tapestry of horror was what he was capable of creating with just a few drops of his blood or tears. Michelle was right: He'd been playing a game of 'Let's pretend Israel's not a monster' with himself for over a year now and it needed to stop. He needed to make it stop.

A crash and a shout echoed from somewhere to his right and farther up the street. Israel slowly let his eyes close against the charnel avenue in front of him, but it was there in his mind and would be for the rest of his existence. Another shout then, the sound of a window breaking, a familiar voice cursing at the top of his lungs.

Eyes closed, Israel listened but kept still, frozen and lost in the death he had so unintentionally wrought.

Stone, Michelle, Sheriff Holmes, Bones, the rest of the survivors – they needed him to move. If he didn't deliver Jordan to the DGS facility, then they would all die. He latched onto that thought and held it like a light through the terrible darkness that was encroaching on his mind.

His eyes snapped open and he started running toward the sound. He didn't look at the carnage around him, didn't contemplate the tragedy, he just focused and sprinted toward the sounds of Jordan Screed fighting for his life.

He rushed up the street as fast as he could. A car was

in his path, but he jumped over it as easily as stepping off a curb. He wove between obstacles without noting any details because that's what they were – obstacles. Israel knew that if he let himself see the staring, dead eyes and the ruins that had once been human bodies, he might not be able to hold it together. So he focused on the sounds of the fighting and ran.

His path brought him to a church. It was a large, wooden structure with shaker-style siding, a short set of stairs leading to a porch, a gabled roof, and a front steeple and belfry that rose nearly a hundred feet into the air. Shards of stained glass littered the concrete walk leading up to the doors. A sign on the street read St. Ignatius Church of the Blessed. The crashes and thuds from within told Israel there was still a fight going on, but he couldn't hear Jordan shouting anymore.

He didn't even slow down as he barreled up the steps and through the front doors shouting "Screed!"

The interior of the church was a wreck of shattered windows and broken and strewn pews, but it was refreshingly free of corpses. Israel spotted Jordan behind a small barricade of pews up near the altar. He was staggering like a drunk and was bleeding from two long tears that ran in diagonal lines down the front of his shirt. The sources of those wounds were standing with their backs to Israel, but had turned their dozen-eyed faces to look when he had come in shouting.

In all the excitement since making it to the school, Israel had nearly forgotten about the semi-reptilian ferret things that had dropped out of the sky near the school, assuming they had all been killed when they ran afoul of the zombie masses that had tried to run down Israel and his friends. While that might have been true for the bulk of the pack, the three facing him were injured, but looked more than able to fend for themselves. Suddenly, Israel was regretting not bringing the gun that Michelle had suggested.

The monsters roared in unison. The sound was so loud that he felt the old wood around him tremble. When they suddenly surged forward, their claws scratched deep gouges in the floors and he felt the whole building shake.

Israel spent a split second assessing the situation and then started moving. He took one long step to his right and grabbed one end of a displaced pew and shoved it as hard as he could toward the closest creature. The pew shot across the floor like a javelin and collided with the creature at one of its backward-bending knees. Israel thought he heard a pop just before the thing roared in pain and flipped over the pew in a mass of fur, scales, and splintering wood.

The other two clambered over their packmate as though it weren't there and kept coming for Israel. Israel bolted outside, desperately seeking whatever weapon he could find. His feet touched the front walk just as he heard the two predators come crashing through the church doors.

Israel spun and saw the things launch themselves from the porch with all their claws and teeth pointed at him as they descended like angels of death. That would have been the last thing a normal man would have ever seen. Israel, though, reacted far faster than a normal man ever could.

He dove and rolled so fast to one side that he was already coming to his feet as the monsters hit the front walk and sent a small explosion of concrete chunks and dirt snapping into the air. One of them snapped jaws onto empty air and Israel swore he saw a look of surprise on the thing's alien face.

He sprinted for the back of the church. The monsters recovered quickly and were hot on his heels. A tall, wrought iron fence adjoined the back corner of the church and encircled a respectable-sized graveyard that was full of grave markers, some old, some newer, and two small mausoleums.

Israel skipped a step, timed it, and jumped. He cleared the seven-foot fence with ease. He hit the ground on the other side, tucked into a forward roll, and came up running.

The alien predators barreled into the fence like rampaging bulls. The fence actually held against the first impact, though it tilted dramatically and lifted bowling ball-sized divots from the soil where the concrete bases were buried. The predators started battering the fence out of their way, but it gave Israel a precious second to look around.

Up to the point Israel had arrived, the cemetery had been remarkably untouched by the tragedy that had befallen Jasper Island. Flowers still lay where loved ones had placed them on some of the fresher graves and everything seemed near to normal in this small corner of Emberoak. The groaning of wrought iron and the roar of twin monsters dispelled that illusion rather quickly, though.

A pair of matching tombstones, large and thick with foot-tall vases attached to the tops, caught Israel's eye and he sprinted for them. He didn't bother with the names on the markers, but instead wrapped one hand around each of the flower vases and pulled. The heavy marble adornments came free easier than he had expected and he looked up in time to see the predators tearing up the ground between him and the mangled fence.

Israel took three steps, hopped onto the top of another tombstone, and launched himself into a high backwards flip that carried him to the roof of one of the mausoleums. The nearest predator leaped just as he did and Israel felt claws tear through his jacket, his shirt, and then into his back. There was no pain, but the impact was enough to throw off his trajectory and cause him to land on his back instead of his feet.

Fortunately, the roof of the small structure was relatively flat and he managed not to fall back to the ground. He scrambled to his feet, managing to hang on to the vases while the two predators skidded in the dirt and started trying to climb to Israel's perch. That was exactly what he wanted.

The moment the first predator's head cleared the edge of the mausoleum, he raised his arm and slammed one of the marble vases between the rows of eyes that ran down the thing's face as hard and as fast as he could. Bone cracked under the impact and he saw the eyes suddenly bulge out of their sockets under the blow's pressure. The monster went limp and fell to the ground where it lay motionless. The hunger was gnawing at him but he had no time for it.

Israel spun as the remaining predator came at him from the other side, teeth bared and claws extended. This one didn't climb, though. It had gotten a short running start and was flying through the air in a leap that carried it over the mausoleum's edge and into Israel.

He shoved the marble vases into the thing's face as it struck him and felt one of them slide between hard, wet teeth as the impact knocked Israel off his feet and sent them both arching through the air and to the ground below.

They landed hard, but managed to do so between the rows of tombstones. Israel shoved the marble vase harder into the predator's mouth, holding it open and watching teeth crack against the stone. Claws raked at Israel's chest and shoulders, but he hardly noticed as he brought his free hand up and pressed against the thing's sternum. With a mighty shove, he sent the creature flying away from him and into an old grave marker.

The creature got back to its feet, but not as quickly as before. It was obviously in pain and Israel took advantage of the monster's hesitation, rolling to his feet and taking three long steps that ended with him landing a solid kick where the predator's jaw connected to its skull. He felt the joint pop and suddenly the monster staggered away on all fours as though confused or blind. Israel picked up one of the vases from where it had fallen and rushed the creature.

He jumped onto its back and brought his makeshift club down once, twice, and a third time to be sure. When he was done, the thing's head was a misshapen mass of ruined skin and protruding bone.

He knelt there for a time. The hunger was boiling in him like a living thing as his body burned energy to repair itself. Israel could feel his teeth grinding together against it as he fished into his pocket for one of the protein bars and shoved it into his mouth, barely taking the second he needed to tear the wrapper off with his teeth.

His jacket was pretty much ruined, and he noticed the silver outlines of some of his other protein bars where they had fallen in the grass next to the mausoleum. He pulled the last one from his jacket and stood up as he shoved it into his mouth. The edge was starting to come off his hunger, but the spilled blood and raw flesh laid out before him sent tremors of need through his body.

A grimace worked its way onto his face and he went to collect the rest of his rations.

CHAPTER TWENTY-SEVEN

Israel had four bars left.

The count seemed off – he was sure he'd had eleven of them at the school – but he figured he must have lost a few when he fought with Jordan or had been running after him. There really wasn't anything he could do about it, so he shoved them into his pants pockets, discarded his shredded jacket, and headed back inside the church to check on Jordan. The hunger had subsided to a strong tingle under his skin instead of the aching need it had been, but he didn't want to use another ration until he had to.

He found the predator he had crippled on the front steps where it had apparently dragged itself with its three good limbs. Despite it taking a few half-hearted swipes at him with claws and teeth, Israel managed to put the thing out of its misery after retrieving one of his makeshift weapons from the cemetery. As he dropped the bloody and cracked piece of marble to the ground, he made a silent vow to never get caught without a proper weapon again if he could at all avoid it.

Jordan was in the same spot Israel had left him. It

looked as though he had collapsed onto his side behind the barricade he had tried to make when the predators had come for him. For one dread-inducing moment, Israel thought the man had died, but as soon as he got closer he could hear him breathing and smell the sweat on his skin. There was something else in that scent, though. Something wrong.

Israel stepped over the makeshift wall of pews and small tables, calling out Jordan's name as he did so. The other man did not respond. Israel got close to him and checked his pulse. It was fairly strong, but Jordan showed no signs of consciousness. Whatever it was that smelled wrong was stronger now. Israel rolled Jordan onto his back and examined the wound on his chest. It didn't take a doctor to realize the puffy redness around the claw wounds was not a normal thing, and when Israel inhaled through his nose, the acrid scent he'd been getting was overwhelming.

"Frickin' venom," he said. "Those things weren't bad enough already?"

No one responded, of course. Israel just shook his head. He had no idea whether or not the venom would be fatal. For all he knew, it could just be some kind of anesthetic or paralytic that the predators had used to help bring down their prey. All that mattered was that Jordan was alive, Israel had him, and the clock was still ticking on the people back at the school.

When he had rolled Jordan onto his back, Israel had uncovered the weapon the elder Screed brother had taken from the dead guard back at the school. It was a well-worn Remington 870 12-gauge pump action with a polished walnut stock. The weapon looked well-maintained and smelled as though it had been recently fired. Israel picked it up and ejected the remaining shells; four red plastic cartridges fell to the floor. Israel did a quick search and found six more in Jordan's pockets. He loaded a cartridge into the ejection port, then put seven more into the magazine. The last two went into his front shirt pocket.

Freshly armed, Israel looked Jordan over again. It was possible he was faking unconsciousness again, but Israel's gut and the smell of the venom from the wounds told him that was unlikely. "If you're faking this, Jordan, I'm going to break your legs." That said, Israel threw the unconscious man over one shoulder and gripped the shotgun in the other. He did his best to ignore the scents coming off the other man – the venom smell helped – but his hunger started squirming at his skin all the same. Israel gritted his teeth against it and headed for the street.

He'd gotten directions to the DGS facility from Bones, but he doubted he could make it on foot in time carrying his captive and the shotgun. There was also the matter of the predators; though he thought it unlikely, it was possible there were more of them lurking around. He needed a vehicle.

Fortunately, he didn't have to go far to find one. He had carried Jordan a quarter mile down the main street when he spotted a Subaru Forester parked outside a shop. There were other cars around, but most of them looked to have been wrecked or were so damaged that he wasn't sure they were functional. This one, though, looked relatively untouched unless you counted the smears of blood on the outside of the driver's side door and window. The Forester was an older model and looked well-used. Stickers from all over the United States displayed the owner's love of the outdoors and any kind of thrill-seeking activity that came with that. A heavy bicycle rack was mounted on the rear and was currently holding a single mountain bike in one of its four slots.

What separated this vehicle from the others was the body lying next to it. It had been a man – late twenties, Israel guessed – and it looked as though he had died trying to get to the Subaru. He was wearing black bicycle shorts and a windbreaker with a North Face logo on the lapel. He was lying face down and the back of his head was a gaping hole of ruined flesh.

Israel walked over and deposited Jordan onto the sidewalk next to the vehicle. Then he started going through the corpse's jacket until he came out with a set of keys on a Subaru key chain. There was a black dongle on the key chain and he pressed the button with the picture of an unsecured padlock on it. The Forester's lights blinked once in time with an electronic chirp. Israel looked at the body and said, "Thanks, man. Sorry about all this."

He shook his head when he realized what he was doing and then stood up. The SUV was parked outside a shop with the words Emberoak Base Camp and Supplies stenciled onto the cracked window. It looked like the mountain biker had just stopped for some supply or another and was leaving the shop when he'd been killed. Israel had an idea, collected Jordan, and then went into the abandoned store.

A couple of minutes later, he exited the shop with Jordan, now bound at wrists and ankles with a generous amount of paracord, and a machete on his belt. He had hoped the place would be carrying firearms, but there was no luck there, though he did manage to eat a half a dozen bags of turkey jerky after he'd secured Jordan. It wasn't as effective at curtailing the hunger as his rations were, but it definitely helped.

He spent a few minutes clearing camping and biking gear out of the back of the Forester and then dumped Jordan into the spot it had all been in. He climbed into the driver's seat and laid the machete and shotgun across the passenger's side.

Insect tingles scurried across his spine and his head filled with Susan Gunderson's voice.

"Where are you? You're running out of time."

"I know," he said aloud, "I ran into a problem, but it's

all good now. I've got a car and I'm coming. You can tell Carmine I'll have his brother to him in just a few minutes."

"*Carmine's not here. He wanted to go to the school because he doesn't think you'll make it here in time.*"

"Susan, are you going to keep your word? I'm going to make it there."

"*Yes! I keep my promises, even if Carmine says I shouldn't. You get here soon, though, or I'll keep my other promise and everyone will be part of my clique from now on.*"

"Susan, don–" Israel started, but the tingle vanished from his spine along with her voice.

He cursed and used the dead man's keys to start the engine.

The drive was macabrely peaceful. Aside from having to weave around one abandoned car or another a few times, Israel made the trip without any trouble. The mist was still hanging over the island like a shroud and he watched the shadowed places for any kind of movement as he drove. There was nothing, though, and he allowed himself a moment to relax and go over things in his mind.

In retrospect, he almost wished he were driving through rows of undead. He didn't know how many of them had gathered outside the school, but he was sure it was far more than the defenders could handle. The more he thought about it, about the horde just standing there like a loaded gun aimed at the survivors, the more confusing it was. Why didn't Susan just cut them loose and order them to take the school and bring Jordan back to her? Why the whole hostage exchange scenario? It didn't make much sense to him, but when it came to the Screed brothers he could rarely find reason in their actions.

He kept thinking it over as he turned onto the long driveway marked with a large sign that read Darkarcher

Gaming Sciences Center for Idea Realization. As he guided the car along the winding, tree-lined road, he went over everything Jordan had told him. He had glimpsed his brother in the act of turning people and then ran. He'd had limited conversations with him. The more Israel thought about it, the more he realized that Jordan was making some assumptions.

He'd said that Carmine was under some sort of mind control, that Susan was controlling his actions. Obviously that was the case with the Necrophage, but Carmine hadn't turned after Israel had exposed him in Texas. Somehow – and he knew Allison would have a field day with this one – he had not only managed to resist the Necrophage transformation, but kept a pocket of it contained within his eye. So if he wasn't a Necrophage, how was Susan controlling him? If she could mind control normal people, why infect anyone at all? She could have just taken over the island through sheer willpower.

The alternative was that Carmine wasn't being controlled. Israel considered that and felt his teeth clench tighter. The pieces started coming together for him. It was entirely possible that Carmine had done the things he had of his own volition. The little bit of Necrophage DNA in his system might have given Susan a way into his head, a way to talk to him, but not enough to control him. If that was true, there was no reason to think this whole thing hadn't been his idea. Maybe he'd convinced Susan that she would be safer if she had a hold over the rest of the island, convinced her that the outbreak was necessary somehow. It was very possible that the whole thing – the outbreak, all the deaths – had been Carmine's plan all along. Israel thought about that and felt his hatred for the man spike.

He knew all too well the strength of the Necrophage hunger. It could be that if the former islanders got too close to a living thing that Susan couldn't control them. That made sense to him. She could direct them, tell them to go here, stand there, but once the feeding frenzy started she had no choice but to let it play out to its conclusion. That's why she was holding the undead so far back from the school. If they got too close, she'd lose control of them. That was why she couldn't tell them to just bring Jordan to her; he'd never have made it in one piece. That and the fact that Israel couldn't help but get the impression that Susan didn't really want to kill the people in the school. That thought was chased away, though, as he rounded a curve and got his first look at the DGS building.

The structure rose four stories above a well-manicured landscape that looked more like a garden than a lawn. Built from a combination of glass, steel, and dark wood, the DGS building was roughly a half moon-shaped structure with a gently flowing roof line that gave the impression of long ripples in an otherwise still body of water. It virtually reeked of corporate pretension and architectural expression. Israel shook his head and drove the Forester through the landscaping, over the sidewalk, and right up to the front door.

Closer, he could see the cracks in the glass and the bloody smears on the windows. It looked like a few bodies were on the floor inside and the place was scattered with broken or overturned furniture. Israel got out of the truck, collected his weapons, and retrieved Jordan from the cargo area. With the Screed brother over one shoulder and the shotgun in his other, he walked in through the shattered front doors.

"Susan!" he shouted. "I'm here! I've got Jordan!"

There was no reply mentally or otherwise. Israel spent a moment looking over the space. It was pretty torn up from whatever had happened there, but he could still see the modern architecture and furniture here and there. He figured in its normal state it would look the epitome of a high-tech, creativity-friendly environment. Israel didn't much care for that and instead studied the ceiling. Once he spotted what he wanted, he walked over and stood in plain view of the small, black half-dome that housed the security camera.

"Hey!" he shouted again. "I'm here!"

The tingle in his spine came almost immediately. *"I see you. You did make it."*

"With Jordan, so tell your monsters to back off from the school."

There was a long moment of silence. Israel could still feel the tingle in his spine and he said, "Susan? We had a deal."

"I know that! Don't call them monsters. They're my clique."

"Okay," Israel said, "whatever. Just pull them back."

"Why are you carrying him?"

"Long story, but he's alive and he's here, so keep your promise."

"You could be tricking me. Bring him here so I can make sure he's okay. Carmine will be really mad if he's not."

"He's alive, Susan, okay? Just don't do anything until I can get to you, all right? Tell me where to go."

"I won't do anything. Just follow Jerry. He'll show you where to go. Leave the guns and stuff, though. I don't like them."

"Jerry? Who the hell is–" Israel's words were cut off as one of the bodies on the floor started getting to its feet. It rose in slow, jerking motions accentuated by pops as it forced the rigor from its joints. The thing was dressed in a security guard uniform and when it turned its ash gray, black-veined face toward Israel, he saw the uniform's name tag: Jerry.

Israel scanned the rest of the reception area and saw more than a dozen other bodies. "Susan," he said, "are all these bodies in your clique?"

"Yeah, but they're on the down-low. They let me see if

anybody is trying to sneak up on me. Smart, right?"

Israel kept scanning the floor. None of the other bodies moved, but he saw at least three pairs of dead eyes looking his way. He'd assumed that Susan had seen him through the security cameras. He'd assumed wrong.

"How can I be sure they won't try to hurt Jordan?" he asked.

"It's okay. It's easier to control them when they're this close. Just follow Jerry; it'll be okay. Now get rid of the guns and stuff, Israel."

He nodded and gently placed the shotgun on the floor. He pulled the machete from his belt and dropped it next to the Remington.

The thing that had once been a security guard named Jerry started a slow shuffle toward an adjoining hallway.

Israel followed.

CHAPTER TWENTY-EIGHT

Bones

Justin Wainwright dreamed.

He floated and tumbled through an ocean of silver and gold light. It carried him, washed over him, warmed and caressed him. There was no pain, no grief, no sensation at all save that of gentle, flowing motion. He thought he might feel like dancers do, boneless and graceful. He rolled and tumbled through the light until he was suddenly floating motionless as the silver and gold luminescence flowed around him.

Images formed before his eyes, panoramic reliefs of his memories in full color, but always haloed in the gold and silver that seemed to be his world now. He saw himself as a young boy, his father in his uniform leaving to fight in the first Gulf War. It was the last time he'd ever seen him. The images swirled in the brilliant current: his first fistfight at school; his mother teaching him to shoot; finding out she was secretly spending time with Uncle Ray, his father's brother.

The image froze there, a shimmering still life of a young Justin, too young to understand, screaming at his mother for keeping secrets and his mother yelling back, her hand raised for the first and only time she would ever slap him for being disrespectful. The image hovered before him, but Justin felt nothing, merely observed as though watching a movie he had seen a hundred times.

The current of light swept it all away, fast-forwarded in a smear of glittering images that stretched past his sight until he saw himself in the desert wearing his uniform and having tense words with a taller man wearing the silver bar insignia of a Marine First Lieutenant.

Justin remembered this. He remembered the small woman who was handcuffed to the chair in the abandoned building they stood in front of. He remembered what the Lieutenant was ordering him to do, remembered what command had said she'd known, how his reputation as an interrogator would be enough, remembered him lecturing him about a Marine's duty.

Justin remembered doing his duty. He remembered the way she had screamed. He remembered fighting back his own tears and disgust.

A shift in the image: a woman broken on a chair, the Lieutenant telling him that the real target had been drawn out and killed when he'd heard the American they called Bones had captured her, that she wasn't involved and didn't know anything at all. Command had lied to get Bones to do his duty and tried to keep it secret. He remembered the way he had vomited when he realized what he'd done.

All because of secrets.

The light shuddered as the thought formed in Justin's mind. He reached for the light, felt it in his hand like a real thing, pulled a handful toward him and studied it. It spun and glowed and suddenly formed into a perfect sphere, like a tiny silver sun in the palm of his hand.

Some new instinct bloomed in his mind and he pictured the sphere changing shape – a cube, a pyramid, a beer can, one of those twenty-sided dice he'd rolled as a kid playing Dungeons and Dragons. They all formed like gently glowing sculptures.

He tossed the twenty-sider through the air and it arched from one hand to the other. As it did, it shifted and lengthened. When it slapped into his palm, solid and real, but still glowing silver-gold, it was a knife. He recognized the shape and the feel of it instantly. It was the Clip Point KA-BAR he had carried through every minute of his tours in the Middle East.

Another shudder rippled through the ocean of light: his fist time on Jasper Island, meeting Sheriff Holmes for the first time, long hours talking and drinking with her and her partner Karla, his first patrol as a deputy, the night the dead rose and came for them, him and Jan putting Karla down with tears in their eyes, the race for the school, and the deaths – all the sickening deaths he could do nothing about.

Shudder: Stone, Israel, and Michelle telling him lies and keeping secrets, then telling him the truth about all the other secrets and lies the world believed, Michelle stretching to erase a line of marker from a whiteboard.

It all suddenly washed away and Justin felt the Ocean of light sweeping him up again, but differently now. It no longer washed him along at its whim, but carried him as he directed, responded to him as it had when he'd held it in his hand. Now, his small ball of light was an ocean for him to mold and bend, to shape to his will, and he willed it to carry him forward toward a black point in the far distance.

In his dream, Justin flew toward the world of death and secrets.

CHAPTER TWENTY-NINE

Erin

She had expected more ceremony, but Paar'ha had simply instructed Erin to sit next to the fire with her legs crossed. Then, Paar'ha had sat facing her. They joined hands and leaned forward until their foreheads were resting against one another.

"Be for opening yourself to your power, Sar'ha. Be for opening yourself to the joining of powers."

Erin really didn't have a clue what that meant or what she was supposed to do, so she just expanded her senses for the sense of *here* and *there* that she always felt when she teleported. It was the same as it had been since she had arrived among the Valley People; where once she could stretch her senses over hundreds of miles, now she was doing well to cover hundreds of feet.

There was something, though, a kind of tingle that rode through her mind and seemed to push at the boundaries of her mental reach. She felt it blending with her senses and when Paar'ha spoke to her, it vibrated through the power and into her mind.

"Be patient, Sar'ha. We must be for the slow growth in this thing we are for doing. We must be for the patience and the precise knowing. If we are for the rushing of this thing, we will be for the risk of being forever lost to the Otherworlds."

Erin started to respond, but bit it back. The time for talk had passed.

She relaxed and slowly, so slowly, felt her power grow.

CHAPTER THIRTY

Israel

Jerry led them through the dark hallways that smelled of blood, meat, and fear. He stopped next to an elevator that had a sign next to it that read 'Authorized Personnel Only.' Israel didn't see the usual up or down buttons that were common to elevators. Instead, there was a thick card reader mounted on the wall next to the stainless steel doors.

"Jerry has a card on that necklace thing he's wearing that will open the doors," Susan said through Israel's mind. *"Just take it off his neck and swipe it. He's not so good with little movements like that."*

"Are you sure he won't try and take a bite out of Jordan?"

"Yes. God, Israel, don't be such a wuss. Jerry won't do anything I tell him not to."

Israel had been following a safe distance behind Jerry for their short walk and he closed that now, keeping his body angled so that it wouldn't be easy for the undead security guard to go for Jordan. Carefully, Israel reached out and lifted the bloody lanyard from around Jerry's neck. Jerry just stared at him with dead, dry eyes while he

did it. As soon as Israel had the card, Jerry turned with a
jerky motion and started shuffling back toward the lobby.

*"See? Easy peasey lemon squeezy. Just take the ele-
vator down. It only goes to one place, so it'll be easy."*

"Susan," Israel said, "Why don't you just come up
here?"

*"Oh, you'd like that, wouldn't you? Carmine said
you'd try to trick me like that, try and get me to come out
into the big world where you can hurt me. Well, I don't
think so. You come down here where I'm strong and you
can't hurt me and my clique will keep me safe."*

Israel swiped the card and thought over what Susan
had said. Something that had occurred to him earlier tip-
toed back into his thoughts. "Susan?" he said.

There was no reply. The insect tingle was gone from
his mind.

The doors opened and Israel got into the elevator.
There was another card reader with a single unmarked
button next to it. He ran Jerry's key-card through the reader and the button lit up. Israel pushed it and immediately
felt the elevator begin to descend.

The ride was a silent one and took a little longer that
Israel expected. He wasn't sure how far underground they
were, but he knew from Jordan's interrogation that there
were more than a few sub-levels to the DGS facility. He
didn't know how far underground he was, but it was pretty
obvious the buried part of DGS was much larger than the
visible portions.

The first thing that hit him when the doors opened
was the scent; the sickly sweet aroma of decayed flesh
washed into the elevator like a flood. To Israel's heightened senses, it was overwhelming, but he did not gag or react
in any way other than to wrinkle his nose. This he did
more out of habit than anything else. He knew that anyone
who was alive in the more traditional sense would most
likely be vomiting in the corner. He didn't find the aroma

repulsive, however; for him it was just another scent among the hundreds of others he came across on a daily basis.

As he stepped into the hall, the sources of the stink came into view. They shambled and shuffled from the doors that lined the long hallway, dozens of the dead, all looking at him with eyes that looked at the world as nothing more than potential food. Most were wearing lab coats, but there were more than a few who looked like security. Some of them still had weapons holstered on their hips. To a one, though, they stared his way with the focused gaze of a predator. Israel knew it wasn't him they studied, though, but rather the Jordan-sized slab of warm meat he was carrying over his shoulder.

"It's okay," Susan said, *"just follow the hall to the end. You'll have to swipe Jerry's card again to get into my room. These guys won't bother you, I promise. They'll act just like Jerry did."*

Israel didn't reply. He watched the dead faces looking his way and the way their mouths flexed and stretched in silent response to their overwhelming hunger. He knew there was no way he could fight off that many if they decided to come for Jordan.

"Are you sure you can hold back this many?" he said aloud.

"This is nothing, Israel. I'm holding back almost two thousand from your friends at the school. Just trust me, will you? I told you: Carmine wants Jordan here, but he doesn't want him to be part of a clique. He wants his brother the way he is. I promised him he could have him that way. Just come on already."

Israel tightened his jaw and started moving forward. The eyes of the dead never wavered from him. Faces leaned toward him, turned to follow his progress, and more than once hands rose to reach for Jordan, but then fell back to their owners' sides. He wondered if that meant

Susan's control was being stretched too thin.

Israel moved as quickly as he could, but not so much that he thought it would excite the zombies to give chase. It took more than a minute to traverse the hallway and in that time he counted twenty-seven undead watching him from doorways and adjoining corridors. When he reached the end of the hall, the dead had filled in behind him and were watching with stares so intense Israel could feel them.

There was another card reader on the wall next to a heavy steel door. A sign above the reader said 'Primary Conduit Containment S2-313' in raised plastic letters. There was a small slot beneath the words. Someone had written 'S. Gunderson' in red sharpie onto a piece of cardstock and slid it into the slot.

Israel spared another moment to glance back over his shoulder at the gathered dead and then swiped the plastic card through the reader. There was a loud click and then a hiss off cold air as he pushed the door open. He could feel the room's slightly negative pressure on his skin as he entered and quickly pushed the door closed behind him. With the door closed, he took a look at the room and immediately wanted to scream.

Emergency LED lights bathed the large space in an ice-blue glow. It was a lab or a surgery suite of some kind, and the cold hue glowed from the steel and white surfaces like luminescent frost. The air was cold and smelled sterile and plastic. Glass-front tool cabinets lined one wall along with a workbench that held a partially disassembled piece of electronic equipment the size of a football. Tools of varying sorts were scattered casually across the table next to a large, white coffee mug. Along the opposite wall were more glass-fronted cabinets that held large, plastic-wrapped packs of surgical supplies that were labeled and meticulously wrapped in some kind of heavy, blue material. The rest of the walls were a dizzying collection of computers, workstations, cables, and other electronic devices that Israel couldn't put names to. Monitors glowed, status lights blinked, and cables of varying sizes ran like petrified snakes to the dais at the center of the room.

It rose on a foot-high disk and held a single stainless steel table with dozens and dozens of those same cables running up its sides and center to connect with fist-sized connectors at either end. On the table was a woman – no, not a woman, but a girl, sixteen if she was a day. She was nude and hairless. Her body was pale and had hundreds of wires and tubes running into her flesh from the cables that were connected to the machines. Every limb was festooned with one intruding piece of machinery or another. Her head was especially violated; a huge cluster of tiny fiber-optic cables glowed softly in various shades of gold and blue. The colors faded and grew stronger in what seemed a random pattern to Israel and he could see the discoloration underneath her skin as they disappeared past the soft, shaved scalp and into the girl's skull.

Israel dropped Jordan next to the door. The man slumped there, but Israel hardly noticed as he stepped onto the dais and stood next to the table. Rage and revulsion boiled in his mind as he looked down at the girl and realized that he was looking at Susan Gunderson.

Her eyes fluttered opened and rolled toward him. From the way her head stayed still, Israel got the impression that was all the physical movement she was capable of. He looked into her gray-blue eyes and saw tiny capillaries of gold light running like cobwebs through the white orbs. As he watched, a single tear trailed from one eye past her temple to disappear into the curves of her ear.

"Hi," Susan said. "Nice to meet you."

Israel's voice was choked as he said, "My god, Susan. What did they do to you?"

"They made me strong. Stronger than any other

Para-gon ever."

Israel shook his head as he looked at the technological obscenity they had made of her body. "How?" he said, the question coming instinctively to his lips. "I don't—"

"They explained it to me. Well, one of them did. His name was Mark, but I just called him Pervy because of some of the other things he said to me. He explained about the bloodlines and Paragons and all that. You know this stuff, right?"

Israel nodded.

"Well, he said I was a like a fuse in a circuit. Like, a Mage can pull this weird energy from someplace and if he pulls too much, he burns out like a fuse. So long as he doesn't pull too much, though, and he learns how, he can do pretty much anything he wants with the energy he draws. Fireballs, levitation, all that Harry Potter kind of stuff."

Israel looked around. It didn't take a genius to figure it out. "All of this," he said, "they used all of this to amplify how much energy you could draw."

"Yeah. I heard Pervy say I was pulling more ID energy – whatever that is – than anyone else in the history of history."

"How'd you know what to do with it?"

"Some of that was Carmine, but most of it was from Pervy and his guys. They lied to me a lot, but they had this machine that just put stuff in my head. It hurt, but when the pain was gone I just knew things. Things about how to use the power I was getting. That was how I first figured out how to talk to Carmine. Then, I figured out how to move the clouds around. That was pretty easy, really. They were kind of like a top. I just set them spinning and now all I have to do is give them a little push once in a while to keep them moving."

Israel's mind reeled at the idea of manipulating the planet's weather being 'pretty easy.' From what he had learned from Allison and Michelle over the past year, that kind of power could only be measured on a continental scale. "Weren't they afraid you'd use it against them?" he asked.

"They said they could shut me down, kill me any time they wanted. These machines could do that. I'm pretty sure that they didn't lie about that. They lied a lot, though. They told me that because I was special the machines would keep me alive because my power would kill me; stuff like that. Carmine, though, couldn't lie to me and when I found him he told me the truth about things."

Israel closed his eyes against the sight and shook his head. "This, Susan, what they've done– Dammit, I am so sorry."

"Thanks, I guess. It's not your fault and, honestly, I've had time to get used to it and me and Carmine made Pervy and everybody else pay for what they did. Anyway, I don't visit this room very often, but I had to when you came in."

"What do you mean 'visit'?" Israel asked.

"Carmine said you'd ask a lot of questions."

"I used to be a journalist. Questions are second nature to me."

There was silence in Israel's mind for a minute. He looked back into the girl's eyes as she silently studied him.

"You aren't what I thought you'd be," she said.

"How do you mean?"

"Carmine made you sound all mean and violent, like all you cared about was hurting people and getting your way. I can't see that, though. You just look... sad, I guess."

Israel nodded. "I'm a little sad. More angry, though. They had no right to do this to you. That makes me sad and angry."

"I can't see into you the way I can Carmine, but I believe you. That's why he can't lie to me. I saw his memory of when you hurt him. Why'd you do that?"

"He was trying to kill me."

Again, an almost unfamiliar silence settled over Israel's mind.

"I believe that, too. He's got a lot of other memories that he tries to hide. He says he deserves privacy, but I've seen a little. I don't really like looking too hard at him."

"I don't know what all he's told you, Susan, but he's not a good man."

"I'm starting to see that. He keeps trying to tell me to just let my clique go on the school now that we know where Jordan is. He says that it'd be better if we're all in one clique. I don't think that's it, though. The longer I do this, the more I can see into people. I think Carmine just likes all the fighting. He's my friend, though. He's the one who made it so I could leave."

"I don't understand. You said 'visit' before and now 'leave.' What do you mean by that?"

"My clique. I can go anywhere through them. I can get into them and live in their happy places and see through their eyes. In fact, I was with Jerry when he was walking you over. We were in a race, see? A 5k, I think. He'd been training for it for months and he was so happy when we crossed the finish line."

Israel thought on that and then said, "Susan, you know Jerry's dead, right?"

"Well, kind of. He's not dead-dead; he's still walking around. I made him my clique so that he could always live in the best parts and the best days of his life. They all can, and I get to go from one to another and live it with them. I'm trying to figure a way to bring them all together in their happy places and–"

"Susan," Israel said, "that's not reality, not the here and now. Those are just memories."

"Don't say that!" Another tear escaped the eye. Susan's expressionless face did an admirable job of showing him her anger with nothing but her eyes.

"Don't you dare say that! What do you know? We live in their happy places! I've been to weddings and seen babies born and sailed on the ocean while the sun set and a hundred other wonderful things since Carmine helped me escape. They were as real as anything! They were better! Better than anything you're talking about because they can keep living them over and over! It's better than a drunk mother and a trailer park, which is all I had!"

"Is that what you do? Is that how you hold them back? By showing them their best memories?"

"Their happy places, yeah. It calms them down. Those parts are hard to get to, though, so I have to keep them in the front or the other thing pulls the person away. It's confusing sometimes."

"The other thing?"

The eyes went from angry to something else. *"You know,"* she said, *"the black thing. The hungry thing with all the mouths. I can feel it in you, too, but you're better at telling it what to do. My clique can't without my help. It just fills them up."*

Israel nodded. "Yeah, I know what you mean. Look, Susan, I held up my end of the deal. Will you tell your clique to leave the school now? Please? Just send them to the other side of the island or something. Then I can call for help. I can—"

Later, when the dust had settled and the reports were filed, Israel would say it was the sight of the horribly victimized teenage girl and the nature of the sterile room with its slightly negative pressure that had kept him from sensing the attack and, to some extent, that would be true. The larger truth was, though, that he was so rapt by the situation and Susan's terrible story that he had simply forgotten about the serial killer in the room.

Jordan barreled into him and shoved him hard enough to knock him off his feet and into a bank of computer servers. Israel was off-balance when he landed and rebounded off the server cabinet to land face-first on the floor. He looked up just as Jordan raised a tool of some kind, a long, heavy screwdriver, he thought, over Susan's chest.

"Nobody fucks with the Screeds!" he shouted as he plunged the weapon down.

"No!" Israel screamed.

CHAPTER THIRTY-ONE

One.

Two.

Three.

Israel pushed up from the floor and tackled Jordan before he could stab Susan a fourth time.

The two men flew from the dais under the force of Israel's tackle. He felt something violate the flesh of his shoulder and back – the screwdriver, he figured – but ignored it. They hit the floor hard. Israel was sure he had been in position to come up on top of Jordan, but somehow the smaller man had slipped from under him and was rolling away to Israel's left.

They came to their feet at the same time. Jordan came in with his hands raised in a boxer's stance, dancing on the balls of his feet and slightly bent at the waist.

Israel had gotten plenty of hand-to-hand training since he had joined Sentry. He didn't care about any of it. He balled his fists tight and walked toward Jordan like a man who didn't care about consequences. At that point, that was exactly what he was.

Jordan danced in faster than any normal man could

and slammed four lightning-fast blows into Israel's ribs. Bones cracked beneath the impacts. Israel ignored them and grabbed for Jordan, but he darted out of reach, knelt, and did a spinning kick designed to sweep Israel's front leg.

Israel had seen the move coming and shifted his weight to his back foot. He lifted his front foot so that the sweep passed under it with no effect. Jordan continued the spin and stood back up simultaneously.

Israel rushed him as he spun, swinging in tight arcs for his head. Jordan ducked low and stepped to Israel's left. Israel felt the kidney blows on his left side as little more than sudden bursts of pressure and responded with a sideways elbow strike that cut through the air without finding its mark.

Israel turned just as Jordan did a tight backflip that would have done any professional gymnast proud. Israel rushed forward as though to tackle him. Jordan moved to Israel's left again, which was just what the larger man wanted.

Predictable behavior is never a good thing in a fight. Israel had picked up on Jordan's tendency to move to his opponent's left when evading a blow and was counting on the move. At the last possible moment, Israel shifted his charge into a spin of his own that led into a sweeping move with his right arm that clotheslined Jordan across his neck and shoulders hard enough to flip the man over backward and deposit him face-down on the cold tile floor.

Jordan was fast and was already trying for his feet, but Israel was ready for that, too. He dropped onto the man's back like a wrestler and slammed him back to the floor. Pinned with no room to maneuver, Jordan shouted, "Okay, you got me, man! I give up!"

Israel shoved his face into the floor with one hand and positioned his knees over the backs of Jordan's arms just above the elbows. Jordan shouted and struggled, but

Israel's superior weight and position made it a pointless effort.

Israel reached out, grabbed one of Jordan's wrists in each of his hands, and said, "After what you just did, fuck you." He pulled his hands and Jordan's wrists toward his body.

The sound of Jordan's elbows dislocating was like the muffled snap of a wet towel, but Israel only had a heartbeat to hear it before Jordan started screaming like a man on fire.

"You brought her here!" Israel screamed, slamming his right fist into Jordan's back and feeling ribs collapse under the blow. "Just a little girl, you murdering bastard!" His left fist fell to the same effect for the ribs on that side.

Israel had more to say, but knew Jordan wouldn't hear him, so he just let his own rage come out in a bellow and punched Jordan twice in the back of the head. The man's face bounced off the tile and, suddenly, the room was silent again.

Hunger rippled through him like an aftershock. Despite the room's slightly negative atmosphere, he could smell the combination of Jordan and Susan and he felt his tongue quiver at the thought of it. He fished into his pockets for one of his protein bars. Still kneeling on Jordan, he ate one of the bars, then a second, and finally just finished them all.

The hunger retreated to the shadows of his mind. He stood up and looked down at Jordan Screed. He knew he could end the man right there and no one would ask him twice about it. He knew the man deserved it. Killing an unconscious and helpless man, though, was a particularly cold kind of murder and just the sort of thing Jordan would do.

Israel remembered watching TV with his dad on a night long past. There was a news story about soldiers who had humiliated prisoners of war in Afghanistan. Israel had asked why it was such a bad thing since the prisoners were supposed to be terrorists who would've done so much worse to the soldiers if they got the chance. Israel's dad had just looked at him and said, "Because we're supposed to be better than our enemies, not the same."

The memory drifted away and Israel turned from Jordan. He walked back onto the dais and looked down at Susan. To his surprise, she looked back.

"Susan?" he said, shock crackling in his voice.

"Israel? Oh, shit, Israel. What did he do? I feel strange."

"What do you mean 'what did he do'? Can't you feel it?"

"No. I haven't been able to feel this body since I got here. I think the machines messed that up. Is that blood? Did he hurt me? Oh, crap, it's getting harder to talk to them, Israel. The happy places are getting harder to see."

"Just hang on, Susan." Israel stepped over to the medical cabinets and starting ripping open packs of surgical supplies. Instruments clattered to the floor, but inside of a minute he returned to the table with handfuls of gauze and towels. There was a lot of blood pumping from the wounds Jordan had left in her skin. "Hey," he said, "you gotta stay with me, Susan."

"Why did he..." There was a pause then, and Israel felt something like disgust and horror fill his mind. "Oh my god oh my god oh my god..."

"Susan," Israel said, "what is it?"

"I can't see the happy places, Israel. I can see the school, though, and... I see them, Israel. I see the people from the happy places and... is that what we did? Are they what we made?"

"I thought you knew," Israel said.

"No! I stayed in the happy places. Carmine, he was the one who lived in the really real world. He told me they were just sleepwalking. Oh god, no no no..."

Blood ran in thin streams from under the towels. "Susan, I need you to focus. I've got to get some help here. You need to release the storm, break it apart or something so help can get to us."

Susan's eyes darted about now, panicked and frantic.

"Susan!" Israel said. "Let go of the storm! Use your power to help yourself."

"I can't. I've already let go of the storm and I'm holding back the clique, but I'm doing it without a happy place to take them to and they're fighting me, Israel. They're fighting so hard. I can see what they want to do to the people in the school, Israel! I can't let them do that."

Israel's mind raced. "I need to call for help," he said.

"Just turn the tower back on." Somehow, the words in his mind seemed weaker.

Israel pressed harder on the towels. "What?"

"The phone tower. Carmine was talking about how easy it was to turn it off. Just a big switch to cut the power. I think he felt smart for figuring it out. It's in the building someplace."

Israel looked around the room. He saw several rolls of white, silk tape that had fallen from the packs he had opened. Quickly, he left Susan's side and gathered them up along with a few more towels he had dropped. He pressed down on the towels and taped them down as tightly as he could, going so far as to secure some of the tape to the side of the table where there was no blood to interfere with the adhesive.

"Susan, I need you to be strong. I'm coming back, but I've got to get a call out to my people for help. I'll be back; you just keep doing what you're doing."

"Go, Israel."

Israel turned for the door and pulled it open. The twenty-seven dead things that had watched him in the hall were clustered closer to the door now, and when it opened they all took a halting step toward the room. The intensity in their dead faces was stronger now. The hunger was like a charge in the air. Israel quickly closed the door and heard the locks click into place.

He took the express elevator back to the lobby. Jerry and the rest of his undead watchers were all on their feet now and wandered about in aimless directions. Though a few of them looked his way with feral eyes and bared, black-stained teeth, none of them came at him. Israel ignored them and found a security room. It was locked, but a single, swift kick solved that problem.

The room was empty except for a small desk, a weapons locker with half a dozen Glocks and three shotguns, and a heavy, wire mesh cage for storing whatever they wanted to keep temporarily secure. A map of the facility was on the wall and cameras still showed various views on the assorted screens.

Between the map and the video screens, locating the Telecommunications Control Room was relatively simple. Israel contemplated breaking into the weapons locker and re-arming, but decided he didn't have time. The route firmly in mind, he set off for the communications room at a run.

He reached it in a couple of minutes, only pausing to kick his way through any locked doors he encountered, and found himself in the hall outside his destination. The door opened easily and he stepped in.

It was really more of a walk-in closet than a room. The icy emergency lights filled the space and it smelled of dust and ozone. It was filled with several banks of silent and inactive computer servers with wires running between them like multicolored vines. On the wall near the door were two large steel boxes with fist-sized switches on their sides. Both of them pointed to the 'Off' position.

Israel stared at them a moment and then said, "No

way it's this easy." He flipped both switches. The server banks lit up, lights flashed, machines beeped, and fans whirred. On the wall next to the right-hand switch, a large plastic button Israel hadn't noticed before lit up with a yellow light. The word 'Initialize' was printed in the center of the button. Israel shrugged and pushed it.

The light turned green and the computer's humming seemed to grow louder. He fished his phone from his pocket and checked the signal. He started to curse when he saw that there was nothing coming through, but then snapped a sharp "Yes!" when he saw the five tiny dots light up across the top of the small screen.

He pressed the first number on his speed dial and heard the call go through. There was static -- remnants of the storm, he figured – but the call was answered on the second ring.

"Israel?" Olivia Warburton said. "Are you there?" Her voice was distant and echoed electronically, but he could hear her.

"Olivia!" he said. "It's me! There's no time, so listen: We have a Valhalla-level outbreak event on this island. Say again: Valhalla-level outbreak situation! We need exfil and reinforcements immediately! There's a cluster of several hundred survivors at a school on the west side of the island, so focus there and come heavy because most of the island has been affected."

"I understand, Israel. The Council and the DGRI both have ships in the area, but the storm–"

"The storm will break soon. No time to explain how I know, just tell them to get here fast and to come loaded."

"Will do. It's good to hear your voice, young man. Stone and Michelle?"

"Fine last time I saw them, but we were separated. I've got to go, Olivia. Get those people moving." Israel hung up without waiting for a reply.

He tapped another button on his phone and Stone's

picture flashed on the screen while it dialed his number. There were several rings before his voicemail picked up. Israel hung up without leaving a message. He scrolled through his contacts and tapped the entry for Michelle. The phone rang while he pulled open the door and headed into the hall.

She answered on the third ring. "Israel?" she said.

"It's me. I got the cell tower back up. What's the situation there?"

"Pretty much how you left it – world's most terrifying staring contest. Are you with Gunderson?"

Israel moved through the halls, backtracking his steps as he gave Michelle the fast details of what had happened since they had parted company. "I'm on my way back to her now," he said as he rounded the corner that would take him to the express elevator.

"Shit, shit, shit," Michelle said, frustration bleeding from her words.

"What?" Israel said.

"Look, aside from the obvious undead horde looking at us, Susan cannot die, you hear me?"

"What is it?"

"I was wrong. Erin didn't cut through the fabric of space-time; she stretched it. Susan is a big part of what's holding that stretch taut. If Susan dies, then it will snap back violently."

"So?"

"Remember that scene in *Titanic* when DiCaprio tells Winslet that when the ship hits the water it's going to pull them under because of the difference in their masses?"

Israel stopped at the elevator and reached for Jerry's key-card. "Kind of. Get to the point."

"The point is all the math says that if that thing snaps closed like that it'll bring Erin back, but she won't come alone. It'll drag things from other places with it. An unpredictable number of micro–"

The unmistakable pops of gunfire came over the line, then shouts, screams, more gunfire.

"Michelle!"

"Israel! They're coming! They're coming over the walls!" The sound of a phone clattering to the ground, louder gunshots. Then the connection went dead.

Israel held his phone in front of him and stared at it like it had betrayed him. He barely felt the tickle of ants on his spine.

"Israel," Susan said, *"I'm so sorry... so sorry... I... tried... I re–"*

The sensation vanished from his mind. He yelled her name, but she was gone.

CHAPTER THIRTY-TWO

Erin

She could feel her reach expanding. It was starting to feel like it had back home, her sense of *here* and *there* widening out beyond the range of her normal vision. She couldn't quite sense the Valley People settlement yet, but she thought she could lock onto the Coldpass if she tried. More than that, what area she could feel seemed to come easier than it had before. Back when she'd first Awakened, she had to have a strong, emotional memory to a place before she was able to teleport there without seeing it. Now, though, it seemed to come with just a strong mental picture of the location.

"Be for the focusing, Sar'ha. Awareness grows, but it must not do so in the soil of impatience."

"I understand, Paar'ha. It's just nice to–"

Sensation exploded through Erin. It lit up every nerve in her body with a heat that bordered on pain and suddenly pushed her awareness up and out as power flooded into her like some kind of explosion blossoming out through her mind. She felt the Valley People settlement now, along with the cave where she had trained with her new family, the hilltop where she had first arrived, and the spot she had stood the night she had been inducted into the Valley People Tribe. She could even sense Brinn'ha and Gratt'na to the east. She felt all this so clearly, but the power kept coming and her senses reached out in a sudden jerk away from the here and into the morning sky.

The heat in her body became an aching burn. Someone let out an inhuman scream and Erin felt everything shift to black and cold.

CHAPTER THIRTY-THREE

Bones

His eyes fluttered as he left the ocean of light behind and came back into the world. He could still feel the ocean there like a warm sheen on his skin or the faint tickle of a warm draft in a chilly room. Things were confusing, though. For one thing, it was far too loud. People were shouting and screaming and someone was putting on a fireworks show way too close to where he was resting. He wanted the quiet back, the swirling, silent warmth of the silver-gold ocean.

Firecrackers popped and boomed and he closed his eyes tighter against the sound as though it might block out the pyrotechnic cacophony. There was another round of pops that suddenly blossomed into a cascade of sound that–

No. No, that wasn't fireworks he was hearing. He knew the sound, knew it well – it was the chaos of a lot of people firing a lot of guns all at once.

Bones opened his eyes and it all came rushing back. He remembered talking with Stone and Michelle on the wall, then he was dreaming about light, and now...

He sat up like he was coming off a weekend drinking

binge. His vision was slightly blurred, but cleared quickly and he realized that he was on one of the cots in the gymnasium where they had set up their fallback position. People were running about, gunfire was echoing through the large space and mixing with the screams of hundreds of terrified people.

Bones came to his feet in a rush. The lethargy was disappearing and his mind was clearing as he took in the scene. The roar of combat was at his back and he turned to see the defenders clustered near the door, using their makeshift barricade of cars and whatever else they could scrounge to hold back the dead that were clawing and rushing against it. Stone, Sheriff Holmes, and Michelle all stood side by side atop the cars with a dozen other people who were firing into the mass of monsters until they needed to reload. They handed weapons down for reload as a fresh one was held up to them by the people behind the barricade who kept the weapons primed.

It was a reasonable plan, Bones knew, that had one fatal flaw: At the rate they were shooting, they would run out of ammo really soon. The plan at that point was to close and further barricade the doors from the inside and then what? Wait for rescue? Hope the monsters got bored and went away? He'd never really been clear on that point.

He started toward the choke point, his strength returning with every step. The warmth on his skin seemed to be growing and the memory of his swim in the ocean of light was a presence that existed just behind his thoughts and seemed to cast a clarity over his mind that he'd never had before.

A young man he didn't know rushed up and bumped into him shoulder to shoulder. The man was carrying a crying little girl and was holding the hand of a pregnant young woman. Bones' hand snapped out to help steady the man and when he looked up at Bones, the man's eyes grew wide.

"Dude, are you okay? What the hell?" he said.

Bones looked at him in confusion. "What?"

The young woman spoke up. Her eyes were wide with shock and she pressed into her husband or boyfriend or whatever he was and said, "Why are you glowing like that?"

Bones shook his head. "I'm sorry? I don't--"

The man started backing away from him, pushing the woman in front of him so that he was between her and Bones. "Look at your skin, man. Look at your skin."

Bones held his hands up and watched the silver-gold glow dance and ripple over his skin like a heavy layer of sweat. It rolled up from his skin and drifted off it like some kind of illuminated smoke. He clenched his fists and swore he could feel the light like it was a solid thing pressing against his palms.

Bones remembered the dreams, remembered the shapes and the glowing KA-BAR. He took a deep breath and concentrated on the presence of the ocean that he felt in his mind. More of the light, more of the power, flowed into him. He could feel it all over his body now, like a second skin of glowing heat that responded to him far better than the flesh he had been born with. He focused, felt the light ripple against his skin, then pull tighter and stronger against him. He couldn't help but smile.

A thought occurred to him and he held up his right fist, pictured a scene from one of his favorite movies, and sent a mental command to the glow that enveloped the limb. There was no sound, no metal against metal hiss or click when three identical blades of luminescent power snapped up from the back of his hand. Bones felt his smile turn into a grin. He lowered his newly formed claws and then pressed them into a cot next to his leg. They cut through the cloth like it wasn't even there.

"Oh, hell yeah," he said, his grin growing even larger.

The screeching of metal and Stone shouting brought

him back to reality. The claws faded back into the layer of
light that surrounded him and Bones snapped his attention back to the defenders. The barricade still stood, but it
seemed pressed inward now. Beyond it, Bones could see a
sea of dead, frenzied faces scrambling over one another
and pressing against the steel as they clawed and bit at the
men and women who fought them. Some had actually
made it to the top of the barricade, and more than once in
a couple of seconds Bones saw a rifle or shotgun butt get
smashed into a zombie face before the shooter could get
the business end of the weapon into position.

They were being overrun. It was only a matter of time.

Bones rushed forward, shouldering his way through
the throng of escalating panic around him. Most of the
people recoiled from the glowing man who was suddenly
rushing through them. Some screamed, and one woman
dropped to her knees and started saying something about
Jesus. To a one, though, they got out of his way.

The defenders didn't notice him as he came up behind
them. The constant gunfire was deafening. Cordite stink
mixed with the tang of rotting flesh filled the air. He took a
moment to survey the defenses. They had parked three of
the school's panel vans around the entrance, effectively
creating a three-sided wall, and then piled or thrown
whatever they could find onto the ground outside the wall
until it was piled high enough that the defenders could fire
over it. Benches, lockers, furniture of all kind, sports
equipment – anything that might slow down or trip up the
zombies littered the ground beyond the makeshift wall.
The wall, though, wasn't the neat box it had been. It
canted slightly to the left as thousands of pounds of dead,
hungry flesh pressed against it.

He climbed to the top of the rightmost van and stood
up between two of the shooters, people he didn't really
know, and looked out over the school's courtyard. It was a
veritable sea of dead faces. There were so many of them

that they filled the courtyard and were still clambering over the wall and falling to the ground. More of them pressed through the bent and broken iron gates. Guns roared all around him, but he knew it was all in vain.

Dead hands came over the top of the wall and grabbed at Bones. Instinctively, he shoved them back. The sight of his luminescent skin reminded him what he had done in the gym and he put up his hands and watched the glowing blades suddenly appear on the backs of his hands. He made two quick downward swings with his hands and watched as dead hands separated from dead arms and dropped twitching to bounce off the car's top and onto the ground below.

A dead man's face appeared over the top of the barricade and years of hand-to-hand training kicked in as Bones automatically punched for the tip of the thing's nose. The blow landed, but instead of simply rocking its head back, the blades of light punched through its face and out the back of its head and neck. The thing dropped limply and slid down the barricade, stumbling a few of the other zombies that were coming up behind it.

Bones spared a glance at his newly weaponized fist and then at the shooter standing next to him. He was a middle-aged man with shaggy hair and a graying Van Dyke beard. He was staring at Bones with wide eyes and a slightly open mouth, the shotgun in his hands all but forgotten.

"Just shoot, goddammit!" Bones shouted.

The man suddenly blinked and then nodded, remembering with a jolt where he was. He turned his attention back to the horde and started firing again. Bones stood his ground, lashing out at anything that got within reach and slicing through his targets without fail. The biggest weakness he had, he realized, was his limited reach. He considered it for a moment and decided that as cool as it was to be imitating one of his favorite comic book characters, he needed to adapt if he was to overcome.

He sent another zombie tumbling backward with three holes in its forehead. He took the instant's respite to focus and merge the three blades on each hand into one longer one. With a deep breath, he reached for the ocean of light that he knew lived within him now and pulled more of it into his fists. The single blades lengthened and grew brighter until they glowed like four-foot-long blades of white hot steel.

Bones roared as the light's heat filled him and he started swinging at the encroaching enemies in alternating strokes of each hand that swept low and severed everything in their path. He was careful to keep the strokes narrow enough not to hit the shooters beside him, but he felt them edge away from him, all the same.

The dead kept coming. The shooters kept shooting. Bones kept swinging. There was a scream from the opposite side of the barricade as one of the shooters was pulled from her position and dragged into the horde. Her reloader, a boy of no more than fifteen, jumped into her place and started firing the weapon he had been reloading without so much as a pause. Bones saw the sheriff yell something at the boy, but it was lost in the cacophony.

Something hit Bones hard in the chest, exploding a wave of pain through his ribs and throat. He staggered backward, slipped off the edge of the van and fell to the ground. He hit hard, but managed to keep his breath in his lungs. Confused, he got up and brushed his weaponless hand across the spot on his chest where he'd been hit. A flattened piece of lead came away in his palm. Bones recognized it instantly as the round from a hunting rifle of some kind. Somebody had shot him, but the light that covered him, his second skin, had stopped the bullet from killing him, though it still hurt like a son of a bitch.

He gritted his teeth in anger and stood up, ignoring the wide-eyed stare he was getting from the reloaders.

Bones didn't bother climbing this time, but rather focused on his feet and created a column of light that lifted him to the van's roof. He ducked low and looked out over the top of the barricade, exposing just enough of his head to scan the courtyard. Gunfire continued to echo around him.

Bones spotted the shooter almost immediately. The man was big, well over six feet tall, and he was standing just inside the remains of the main gate. He held a rifle with a large scope mounted on it and was lining it up with the defenders manning the barricade. Though he had never met the man, from the way the undead ignored him Bones knew this had to be Carmine Screed.

Bones looked down the line. They were all focused on the undead assaulting the fortifications. No one was looking further out at the sniper who had suddenly taken the field.

Bones could almost see it in his mind's eye – Screed was lining up a shot on one of the defenders just like he had Bones. All he was waiting for was enough of a gap in the assaulting undead to take a clear shot.

Bones came to his feet and tried to determine where Screed was aiming through the clouds of gun smoke and the damned mist. He was aiming farther down the line toward the leftmost van. Stone and the Sheriff were both well within his sights, but Bones didn't know which–

A faint sound cut through the gunfire. Bones looked back toward the gate just as Carmine fired and a battered Subaru Forrester, horn blaring and lights flashing, came plowing through the encroaching undead and knocked the big man flat onto his face a good ten feet from his firing position.

The corner of the Subaru clipped the corner of the wall Carmine had been nested beside and jerked to a halt. Bones kept his eyes on it just long enough to see Israel Trent get out of the vehicle and start toward Carmine with a tactical shotgun in his hands and a face knotted with anger.

He felt like he was moving in slow motion as he looked down the line. Sheriff Holmes had dropped her weapon and had both hands pressed against a dark stain that was spreading through her uniform beneath her left breast. Her eyes came up and met his just as two sets of gray, dead hands latched onto her legs and waist and pulled her into the throng.

Bones screamed and the ocean within him surged.

CHAPTER THIRTY-FOUR

Erin

Water woke her. It was ice cold and tasted of salt, brine, and the faint, earthy tang of kelp. Erin let her eyes open slowly. She could see a beach of hard, grainy sand stretching out before her. It pressed into her cheekbone and puffed up in bitter clouds of grit when she coughed. Broken mist flowed across the beach in lazy drifts, thick then clear, like a tattered stage curtain.

Another gentle wash of icy water rushed up her legs and jolted her more awake. With slow, pained movements she pushed herself up to her knees. She decided that was far enough for the moment and remained there catching her breath and letting her head clear. Rocky cliffs rose up twenty feet from the beach. She studied them, trying hard to recall what had happened. She'd been with Paar'ha in the forest, they'd been doing something with their power and it had—

A dull, rhythmic thudding just loud enough to catch her attention came from her right. Erin turned her head and watched as the mist rolled past and she caught sight of the source. There was a long moment where she wasn't sure that what she was seeing was real. A little over a hundred feet from where Erin knelt, a boat dock extended out into the cold sea. There was a large fishing boat there that was bouncing against the wooden dock in time with the water's slow movement. Erin watched it rap against the worn, gray wood for three more repetitions before she noticed the lettering on the rear of the vessel: Harper's Gambit, Jasper Island, MA.

A knot suddenly formed in her throat. Tears welled in her eyes and she let out a single, choking sob.

Home. She was home.

She stared at the gently bobbing words, processing the sudden rush of emotion that was boiling through her. Something caught her eye, then – a shape roughly halfway between her and the dock. A shallow wave washed up over it and pulled at some kind of fabric that covered the shape. It took Erin a moment to realize it was a body; it took her another moment to realize whose body it was.

"Paar'ha!" she said, climbing quickly to her feet and rushing over.

The Wise Wanderer did not respond. As soon as Erin drew close, she could see why. Paar'ha's eyes, nose, and mouth were all blackened holes in her skull. Her skin was wet, but Erin could see darkly burned skin stretching over her long limbs. Her clothing was nothing but a mass of scorched and tattered rags. It looked like she had burned from the inside out.

Erin stepped back with a hand to her mouth. The tears and sobs returned in force and she whispered, "Oh, god, I'm sorry. I'm so sorry." She turned away from the sight and closed her eyes, hoping the darkness would ease the grief.

Paar'ha had said they had to go slow or they would burn. What had happened, though? Why had it suddenly gotten so intense? She was sure she hadn't done anything to make it happen. Had Paar'ha tried to draw too much power?

She had been standing there, weeping and confused for a nearly a minute before she felt the pressure behind her eyes and the tingle through her head. She recognized it, knew what it meant, but couldn't see anything beyond the cliff that was in front of her. Erin took a deep breath, focused on a spot near the top of the cliff, and Pulled.

It was as easy as exhaling. The struggles she had been living with for the past year whenever she tried to use her ability were gone. She appeared at the top of the cliff and looked out over the mist-shrouded island. There was a small town to her right that looked like every picture she had ever seen of a New England coastal village. Something had happened here, though, because she could see buildings smoldering from fires that didn't seem to have been put out by any human means. In fact, there weren't any people at all.

A sound came to her. It was distant and faint, but it sounded very familiar. Like someone was setting off whole packs of firecrackers. That wasn't it, though, and with a sickening realization she knew she was hearing the sound of multiple guns firing all at once.

The pressure in her eyes built and suddenly the sky lit up with bursts of silver-gold light like a fireworks display. Dozens and dozens of micro-breaches popped into existence all over the island at varying distances and altitudes. Erin saw things, some alive and some inanimate, fall from some of them while others merely popped into existence and then vanished.

It went on for nearly a minute and the whole time Erin kept repeating "No, no, no" as though the sound would somehow stop the punctures in space and time.

The boiling emotions in her mind were a storm now, and she blinked away tears as the last of the breaches faded out of existence. The pops of gunfire continued in the far distance. Things moved in the mist where the breaches had formed. Erin just stared and tried to reign in her confusion.

Two faces suddenly appeared in her mind; Israel Trent and Elder Gratt'na. Both visages encouraged her to focus, to pick a path for good or ill and move forward. The images lasted only an instant, but in that instant the confused, frightened girl Erin had once been gave way to the warrior she had become.

Erin focused on the farthest point she could see in the direction of the gunfire and Pulled.

CHAPTER THIRTY-FIVE

Israel

Israel exited the Subaru just in time to see Sheriff Holmes get pulled into a mass of undead. She disappeared under the clawing limbs and snapping teeth. For half a second, he considered running to help her, but he knew it was probably already too late to save her. As he finished the thought, though, he saw a man – a glowing man – launch himself from the barricade into the same spot the sheriff had vanished. Shafts of light shone between the undead bodies and he saw individual figures fall back as blows were struck.

"Israel fucking Trent!" a man shouted. Israel's grip tightened on the shotgun he'd taken from the security room on his way out of the DGS facility, but he didn't bother raising it.

Israel turned and faced Carmine. The younger Screed brother hadn't changed much since the last time he'd seen him – same facial tattoos and lean, muscular build. The only obvious difference was the oily black orb that filled his right eye socket. It was just like Jordan had described. Undead lumbered and ran between them as more and more filled the courtyard and tried to press into the gymnasium. They had spilled around the sides of the building now, but Israel knew there was nothing he could do about that. Gunfire kept echoing, and through it he could hear Stone shouting orders for the defenders to fall back into the building.

"I really thought you'd be dead by now," Israel shouted back.

"I know, right? Instead, you gave me this little gem." He gestured toward his right eye. Israel didn't see the rifle he'd been holding and figured Carmine had dropped it when the car had hit him.

"It let me create all this," Carmine said, spreading his arms to encompass the madness that was surrounding them.

"Create? All you did was kill people who had nothing to do with any of us!"

"I created a world the way it should be, Trent! Beautiful anarchy! A world where the strong rule the weak and take whatever they want!"

"Oh, screw you, man." Israel snapped the shotgun to his shoulder and fired at Carmine's head. The shot might have connected if a zombie hadn't taken that exact moment to pass between them and catch the blast in the side of its neck. The buckshot ripped through the dead flesh like tissue paper and nearly separated the head from the body completely. The back half of the thing's neck was ripped away along with the brain stem. The zombie pitched forward into the dirt and gravel lot, its head folded grotesquely against its chest and bent trachea.

Israel didn't pause as he worked the action and fired again, but Carmine was already moving. The weapon bucked in Israel's hands, but the barrel barely moved. Carmine was moving fast to the right and Israel tracked him, but the crowd of undead between them either interrupted his aim or blocked the shots entirely.

He fired off the last shell just as Carmine ducked

behind the fountain in the center of the courtyard. Israel threw the weapon aside and Carmine stepped out from cover.

"You ready to do this like a couple of men?" Carmine asked.

Israel nodded. "Yeah, I think I am."

They closed the distance between them, both of them shoving zombies out of their way as they moved. Fists lashed out as soon as they were within reach. Carmine struck first; he swung high for Israel's face, but then shifted his weight and kicked low for his leading knee. Israel expected that, though, and sidestepped the attack, then closed in for a lightning-fast rib shot. The blow connected, but Carmine was already turning away from the attack so the damage was minimal. Carmine came right back in, his fists flashing out like meaty hammers moving far faster than anything made of flesh and bone had a right to.

Israel met the attacks with a combination of blocks that slowly moved him inside Carmine's reach. He blocked a punch and then let one land hard against his cheek. He knew it was coming and had steadied himself for it, so in the instant that Carmine's arm was extended, he grabbed Carmine's wrist, ducked under and outside the arm, snapped his left elbow into Carmine's face, grabbed him by the belt, and threw him head-first at the toga-clad statue in the center of the fountain.

Carmine hit the statue face-first and fell into the water in a cloud of cracked stone and marble dust. Despite the force of the impact, Carmine was on his feet almost immediately, hands up and ready for more. Blood trickled from his nose and lips.

He spit into the fountain and said, "You didn't have moves like that in Texas. You've been practicing."

"Thanks for noticing," Israel said, his own hands up and ready. "Though I have to admit, I thought I'd finished you in Texas, so I was planning on doing this with Jordan."

Carmine stepped out of the fountain. "Where is he, anyway? Get away from you?"

"No, I left him back at DGS sleeping off a couple of broken arms."

For an instant, the shock on Carmine's face was so encompassing that it even showed in his blackened eye. "There were a lot of deaders in that place," he said, "and you just left him there? Hurt?"

Israel decided Carmine didn't need to know about the locked door between his brother and the remaining dead at DGS. "Yeah," he said with a smile, "that about sums it up."

"You mother fucker," Carmine hissed.

Israel shrugged. "Guess he shouldn't have killed Susan and set all these things loose. He had it coming and so do you."

Carmine's face twisted into a portrait of rage and he took one step forward before stopping and putting the palms of both hands to his eyes with a gasp of surprise.

Israel felt it, too, and closed his eyes against the sudden pressure and the electric tingle he felt all through his head. He knew what it was – he'd felt it when the meerkat things had breached in, but it hadn't been nearly so strong. He forced his eyes open and muttered, "And what fresh hell is this?"

The sky was blossoming with silver-gold light. Far up, near to the ground, close, in the distance – everywhere he looked he could see micro-breaches opening and closing.

The courtyard seemed to flare with light as Carmine hit him with a full body tackle that lifted Israel off his feet and sent both men tumbling. Undead tripped over them, collided with them, and continued on their way as they continued to assault the gymnasium. Carmine came out of the roll on top of Israel and started raining blows at his head, screaming curses at him with every strike. Israel knew Carmine was strong enough to crush his skull if he set his mind to it, and that definitely seemed to be what the man was in the mood for, so he threw his arms up and rolled back and forth to deflect the blows until he spotted an opening.

Israel let a blow to his jaw in so that he could land a punch of his own into Carmine's sternum. Israel felt his jaw shift unnaturally, but breath exploded from the larger man's lungs, stunning him momentarily. Israel took the opportunity to grab him by the belt again and half throw, half shove him far to one side.

Israel rolled to his feet and felt the hunger begin to quiver in him as the bones that Carmine had broken in his arms started to mend. He reached up and shoved his dislocated jaw back into place with a dull pop. Carmine was climbing to his feet, but still held one hand to his chest.

Carmine got his hands up just as Israel came at him with a series of fast palm strikes that would have shattered the bones in a normal man's face. Carmine managed to block most of them, but the few that got through snapped his head back to one side or the other.

Carmine roared and started swinging like a madman. Israel blocked the wildest of the blows, but a few got through and cracked more than a couple of his ribs. Carmine kept swinging wild, kept bellowing like an angry bull, and kept moving forward in a desperate attempt to bulldoze over his opponent.

That was what Israel had been waiting for. He matched Carmine's advancing pace with quick, backward steps. That Carmine would swing so wildly that it over-balanced him was inevitable. When it happened, Israel darted in behind the other man and grappled him with his left arm locked across Carmine's throat and his right arm hooked up under his right shoulder.

This was all leading to a single, brutal purpose and, when the moment came, Israel didn't think, didn't speak, and didn't hesitate. He merely shoved his right arm up and, with the thumb and first two fingers of that hand, dug in and tore the blackened eyeball from Carmine's skull.

Carmine went rigid with pain and screamed with a mourning, agonized wail that Israel had never heard from another human being. He shifted his grip with his left hand and flung Carmine away from him. The larger man staggered away and fell to his knees, both hands pressed hard against his bleeding eye socket.

"My eye!" he yelled. "You took my eye, you bastard! Give it back!"

"Give it–" Israel shook his head in disgust, not bothering to finish the question. Without looking away from Carmine's remaining eye, Israel dropped the ink-black orb of flesh to the ground and slowly crushed it under his boot.

Carmine wailed again, vile curses spilling from his lips like the blood from his ruined face. He stood up glaring fresh hate at Israel. He took a single step then stopped, his good eye growing wide.

The undead had thinned, most of the horde already in the courtyard and piling against the gymnasium walls. The stragglers that were closest to Israel and Carmine, though, had stopped and were turning toward Carmine. They seemed to be studying him in their own feral way. About ten had turned his direction and were starting to shuffle toward him as though unsure or surprised at his sudden change.

Israel glanced down at the mess under his boot and then at the newly distracted group of zombies. "Y'know," he said, "I don't think they like you anymore."

The zombies surged forward like sprinters at the sound of a starting pistol. Carmine flung another curse at Israel and started running. More zombies peeled off from the main body and soon Carmine had dozens of them hot on his heels.

There was an instant as the hunger rolled through him that Israel felt compelled to join the chase, to catch the sweet scent of fear and living flesh and chase it down and—

He shook it off and turned toward the gym and the horde of undead pressing against it. As he did so, he caught a flash of movement on top of the school administration building. It wasn't much, just a quick glimpse of someone walking from the edge of the roof, but it struck him as odd since everyone was supposed to be in the gym.

Israel decided to ignore it, figuring that someone had chosen to hide up there rather than with the rest of the survivors. For the first time, he realized that the gunfire had stopped. The defenders had fallen back into the building. The barricade was buried beneath undead trying to claw their way into the building. They clawed at the walls, pressed into the doors, and climbed over one another to get at the entrances. Israel didn't know how long the doors would hold. If Stone and the others could keep them secure long enough for the Council's reinforcements to arrive then—

Something crashed with a stony crack behind him. Israel spun in time to see the brick wall on the opposite side of the courtyard bulge inward as something battered it from the other side. Just over the top of the ten-foot-high wall he could see the shadow of something large moving, but couldn't make out any details through the mist. A second later, that was no longer a problem. There was another cracking boom and the wall exploded inward, revealing the monstrosity beyond.

It lumbered in on two legs like a giant, heavy-limbed crustacean. It was easily twelve feet tall with a thick, ridged exoskeleton the color of dark moss streaked with broken gray lines. Its legs were as thick as Israel's torso and ended in heavy, two-toed hooves that tore into the ground with every step it took. Its body was wide and slightly stooped, with long, black tentacles snaking out from under its shoulders to end in three smaller tentacles that gripped at the air as though anxious to throttle something. It had no head, but instead sported a large joint at the peak of its body that linked two massive and thick limbs which ended in heavy, jagged claws that reminded Israel of a lobster. A cluster of different shaped and sized eyes blinked out at the world from just beneath the joint at its top, and when it roared, a vertical mouth the size of a beer keg opened in its abdomen and revealed row after row of triangular teeth. It was like the maw of a shark born in the River Styx.

It seemed to pause for a moment, as though taking in its new surroundings, and then started charging straight for the gymnasium.

CHAPTER THIRTY-SIX

Bones

The ocean of light roared through him like a flood as Bones jumped into the undead mob after the sheriff. He hit the ground and started lashing out with his fists, once again shimmering with the glowing blades. His second skin was tight around him and even though teeth snapped against his skin and clawed hands grabbed at him, he felt no pain and took no wounds. Instead, he fought his way to the fallen woman and pulled the dead away from her, cutting and punching and shoving with all his strength until he had the opening he needed to kneel down and grab her.

He willed his second skin to expand out over the two of them. It flowed like quicksilver at his mental command and within seconds they both glowed like a candle in a dark room. Still, the dead came and grabbed and pulled at them with persistence born of the unending hunger that drove the monsters. He didn't know how long he knelt there, thinking frantically and trying to ignore the ravenous, crushing weight of the monsters that continued to pile onto them, clawing and biting. He redoubled his focus, willing his second skin not to bend or give way beneath the pressing throng, reaching deeper and deeper into the ocean of light to pull out the power he needed, but it was getting to be too much. The more they came at them, the more difficult it was to maintain his concentration against the crushing weight.

He thought frantically for an idea, anything that would get them clear. He could feel the ocean roaring inside him, could feel it on his skin enveloping them and ready to respond to anything he willed, but what could he –

A memory flashed in his mind of a painting that had hung above his mother's couch the whole time he'd been growing up. It was a cheap, framed print of a painting that depicted the Virgin Mary and the baby Jesus being watched over and protected by an angel who cradled them in his arms with its wings spread and gently folded to encompass them.

The image sparked an idea. Could he do that? Could he really do that?

He divided his focus, shifting his attention until he felt the second skin on his back and arms begin to ripple.

Sheriff Holmes's eyes fluttered open in a face that had become a blood-streaked mess. "Justin? What are you doing?"

He couldn't respond. He closed his eyes tight and poured every ounce of will he had into reaching for the ocean within until he could feel it pounding in him, waiting to be released. He kept reaching, drawing in more and more power from that infinite well until he felt his head pounding and heat building in his chest. Then, when he could take no more, he released and willed his second skin to respond.

Wings of light exploded out from Bones' back and unfurled with enough force to send dozens of undead flying backward through the air. He stood quickly, his newly formed wings spread wide, easily twenty feet or more tip to tip. His second skin blazed bright, lighting up the courtyard and staggering undead away from him. He lifted Holmes in front of him like a newlywed and sent a command to his second skin. The wings moved awkwardly at first, but after a moment of effort they flapped once and sent air and dirt rushing away from his feet.

The undead had recovered and started moving toward them again. Bones kept his focus on sending commands to his second skin and suddenly felt his feet leave the ground in a jerky up and down motion that coincided with the beating rhythm.

Up they went, slowly at first, but with greater speed as his mind and body grew used to the rhythm. Undead jumped for them, clawing and biting, but their rotted, bone-tipped fingers and teeth just slipped off Bones' second skin. Higher and higher they climbed until Bones could see the tops of the school buildings and the island beyond. He kept the rhythm, kept concentrating on feeling the wings and how they reacted to his thoughts.

Lights suddenly started flaring in the sky around him, but he didn't pay them any attention, his focus solely on maintaining his momentum. He saw things in his peripheral vision – shapes dropping from the light, someone on the roof of the administration building, a man running across the school lawn with a small pack of undead chasing him. None of it mattered to him enough for him to break his concentration.

He wanted to move forward now that they were clear of the ground and focused on adjusting the angle at which the wings hit the air, trying to push forward more than up. Within a couple of seconds, he was doing just that, moving out over the school wall in a bouncing, slightly lurching flight that carried them toward the back of the school and the fields beyond.

He spared a glance for Sheriff Holmes. She had passed out again and he saw that in addition to the gunshot wound, her arms and face were a collection of deep scratches and bloody bite marks. Lines of angry red and black were starting to form around the wounds.

Bones bit back a cry of grief and focused on flying faster.

CHAPTER THIRTY-SEVEN

Israel

"Well, shit, this might as well happen," Israel said, frustration creeping into his voice.

The clawed horror roared again as it charged, loose bricks flying ahead of it as it kicked them or exploding into dust if it stepped on them. Israel only had a few seconds before it was going to be on top of him and he thought frantically as he watched it coming.

It seemed to be charging toward the gymnasium and, from the state of the wall behind it, it wouldn't take much for it to crash right through the place. If that happened, the undead would pour into the hole it left and it would be game over for everyone inside. That was all assuming he was after the living flesh within the gymnasium walls. It could just as well be seeing the courtyard of undead bodies as an all you can eat buffet. If it got into a fracas with the zombies, though, the result could be the same. A wild swing from one of those claws could easily weaken or damage the gym walls enough for the undead to get in. He had to keep it away from the gym.

As he started running toward the beast, its scent rolled over him. It smelled like an ocean, but one choked with dead fish and sulfur. Still, it was enough that the hunger rose up in him like a choking vine that squeezed and constricted his reasoning. Others of the undead had caught the scent and by the time Israel reached the beast, he had a hundred zombies following his lead.

The thing was easily twice his height, but seemed to be top heavy, his body more suited to the buoyancy of an underwater world than the unforgiving gravity of dry land. Israel came in low and fast, intent on tackling the thing at its thick, armored knees and knocking it off-balance. He launched himself forward, throwing all his weight at the thing's legs.

One of the clawed appendages swept low and swatted Israel aside with a blow that sent him flying through the air and over dozens of the undead that trailed behind him. He felt bones break all throughout his body. The hunger welled in him like lava spilling over a volcano's rim.

The rest of the undead kept charging toward the thing as Israel struggled to climb to his feet. The crab-man swatted one group away with one clawed arm, chopped a heavyset undead cleanly in two with its other, and snatched up another with one of its tentacle arms and shoved it into the gaping maw in its abdomen center. It kept moving forward the whole time, though slowing considerably as more and more of the zombies grappled with it.

Israel forced himself up among the throng of dead rushing the creature. The smell of it, of the meat beneath the hard exoskeleton, was maddening. Israel tried to take a step away from it, tried to take a step at all, but his right leg wouldn't move. He looked down and saw his right hip joint was distorted as though it were a mass of clay that had been pushed back toward his butt by some inept sculptor of flesh. It was dislocated, he realized, and as he reached down to try and force it into place, a particularly heavy zombie came stomping up behind him in a lumbering run and knocked him back to the ground.

Israel tried to get up, but more and more of the un-dead were streaming toward the sweet scent of briny flesh now and they kept knocking him back to the ground. Every time he would get a few inches off the ground, a foot would land in the middle of his back or on his legs and force him back down. There was no pain, but every blow made the hunger rise up and choke the parts of him that wanted to think all that harder.

A booted foot came down on his left wrist and he watched it bend backward farther than it should have, felt the bones crack and break under the weight. Israel tried to curse, but it came out as a growl that dripped with hunger and menace. Another foot came down on his back as he pushed himself up, but this one bounced off and staggered to one side, then kept moving toward the crab-man. He was up on his good arm and right knee. The parts of him that were still aware of anything but his raging hunger and the smell of fresh meat thought he might actually get up this time, but a passing zombie kicked his right arm out from under him and he fell face-first to the gravel. Before he could move again, another heavy foot came down on his skull and any part of him that was still Israel Trent vanished.

When he came back to himself, the first thing he noticed was a greasy oil that coated his mouth and face. It tasted of chicken livers and honey and smelled like a city dump. There were tiny pieces of gelatinous meat stuck in his teeth, and when his vision returned he saw he was holding two handfuls of the bloody, white stuff as though he were just about to shove them in his mouth. With a groan of disgust, he threw them aside, spat out what residue he could, and looked around.

He was standing atop the fallen crab-man's chest. He

couldn't see much of the thing anymore as more undead than he could count were swarming over it and tearing at each other to get to the carcass. Israel stood watching with horror and revulsion at the monsters at his feet.

His broken bones seemed mended, but his hip was still distorted. He was about to try and correct that when he heard a sudden roar from overhead.

Three coal-black helicopters came roaring in overhead and circled the courtyard. As he followed their path with his eyes, he saw that they all had their side doors open with a gunner strapped in behind matching M60 machine guns. Israel watched somewhat confused as the three helicopters took up position around the gym. When they opened fire, he shouted, "No! Stop! NO!"

Bullets starting tearing through the horde of undead at a rate of 600 rounds a minute. Bodies started dropping nearly as fast, but that wasn't what had set Israel to shouting. The third chopper was hovering directly above the gym, firing straight through the roof skylights and into the building.

Israel kept shouting, kept waving his arms, but there was nothing for it. Stone, Michelle, and all the survivors were as good as dead. All the fighting, all the struggle and horror, and this was–

He felt a strong hand grab his shoulder from behind.

In the space of a blink, the courtyard was gone. He was standing a few feet from the edge of a cliff looking out over the cold Atlantic. The sun was a dull pastel glow behind thick clouds and the drifting remnants of a powerful storm. The ever-present mist was breaking apart in huge clouds and he could see the horizon as a gray line sprinkled with white-capped waves. He could still hear the machine guns roaring away, but it was distant.

"It's okay," a voice said from behind him, "I got them all out while you were tangling with the Kool-Aid man from Hell. Stone, Michelle – they're all safe."

Israel turned and faced the speaker. Erin stared back at him. "Get it?" she said. "Kool-Aid man because he crashed through the wall and from Hell because... well, obviously."

Israel stared. It was her, without a doubt, but different. Her hair was no longer the unnatural shade of red it had been when he'd last seen her. Now it was a dark, dusky blond that was braided down the sides and cut short. She was leaner and dressed in what looked like some kind of natural material he couldn't place. Dark, narrow arches – small tattoos, he thought – curved over her scalp and behind her ears.

"Erin?" he said, his voice breaking slightly.

She nodded. "It's me, Izzy."

Israel grabbed her in a tight embrace. He held it for a time before he said, "I missed you, girl. Thought you were dead."

"Yeah, I really missed you, too, Izzy, but whatever's on you smells like sweaty locker room ass, so could we hug later maybe?"

Israel barked out a laugh and broke the embrace, stepping away. "Where the hell have you been? What happened?"

Erin waved the questions away. "Too long a story for right now. What happened here?"

Israel shrugged. "What? You don't appreciate your welcome home party? Where is everybody, anyway?"

"Other side of the island. Once I saw the *Walking Dead* rejects trying to get into the gym, I figured I could get a look inside through the skylights and start getting people out before the doors gave way. Stone called the cavalry and they've set up a safe zone. It's all good, man."

Israel nodded. "I guess so. Carmine Screed's loose on the island somewhere."

"I thought I recognized that guy. What about his brother?"

"He's locked in a room with a whole bunch of hungry dead between him and the exit. He's not going anywhere."

"Nice. What's the story with the guy with the Day-Glo wings?"

Israel wrinkled his brow. "Who?"

"The glowing guy with the big fucking wings? Flew away with some woman? You didn't see that?"

Israel shook his head.

"Huh. That's too bad. I was kind of hoping you saw it, too."

"Why?"

"Well," she said, "it's kind of a long story, but I ate something I shouldn't have and I saw something like that and – you know what? Never mind. Let's go get your leg fixed."

Israel nodded. "Yeah, I can't seem to get the right angle to do it myself."

"Don't need the details, Izzy," Erin said as she reached for his shoulder.

"I do have one pressing question before we go," Israel said, his tone grave.

"Yeah? What's that?"

"What the hell are you wearing?"

CHAPTER THIRTY-EIGHT

Bones

Bones sat at the highest point on Jasper Island, his face to the Atlantic Ocean and the breaking storm in the distance. He had let his second skin recede, its glow retreating into the place where the wellspring of light lived within him now. The day was growing late and, even though the clouds and mist were dissipating, it was still enough to lower an early dark on the island. With it came the cold, but it couldn't match the chill that filled his heart.

On the ground next to him lay the corpse of his friend and mentor, Sheriff Janet Holmes. She had died in his arms as they flew over the island. She had risen as one of the things that had killed her not long after, but Bones had ended that existence in short order.

He felt like he should be crying or angry or something – anything, really – but the events of the previous days had drained him, left him haggard and tired in a way he had never known before. He had no fire left. No anger, no grief, no pity. So he just sat silently with his dead friend, his back to the place that had brought him to this, and listened to the surf washing up on the beach below. Occasionally he would hear a distant gunshot or the whup-

whup-whup of helicopter blades from behind him, but he really couldn't care less about that.

No, that wasn't completely true. He was glad that Israel and the others had found a way to get some help to the island; he even hoped that they had managed to rescue the people at the school, but it was a distant thought, like wishing for cold beer in the middle of the desert.

Instead, all he could think about was Jan. After he had come to the island, she had sensed in him a kindred spirit and befriended him even when he didn't really want to be anyone's friend. The night she had finally gotten him to tell her the story behind his name and what he had done to an innocent woman because of the secrets Marine Command was keeping, she'd told him her own story.

She'd spent her life keeping secrets. Not only secrets about the Army and what she had done for them, but secrets about who she loved, how she lived, and who she was. They had bonded over their secrets and now she was gone and Bones knew a secret that might break the world.

He leaned over and reached into his back pocket where he kept the small, leather-covered notebook he used when taking down statements and making notes. He pulled the small ink-pen from its leather loop and wrote three words in big, block letters in the center of the pad.

Bones tore the page from the notebook, then dropped the pen and the notebook to the grass next to Jan's body. He reached over and unpinned the sheriff's badge from her shirt, put the pin through his note, then returned the badge to its spot on her uniform. He knew that whoever was working rescue on the island would find the body along with his note once the sun came up. Bones clasped his hand over hers and watched as the small paper shifted in the persistent breeze. His goodbyes said, Bones stood up.

His second skin flowed out of him like sweat, covering him in an instant and flowing out to form the wings that

352 | C. Steven Manley

sprang from his back and stretched wide to catch the night's wind. He was getting the hang of the flying thing, so when he stepped off the edge of the cliff and let his wings catch the updraft that carried him into the night, he still held the image of the words he had written in his mind.

No More Secrets.

EPILOGUE

Silversky Mansion

Three Weeks Later

The whole thing went viral.

In retrospect, Israel realized it was probably his fault. From the images that were showing up on YouTube, Twitter, Instagram, and every other social media website, the recording had started before he had arrived on the island. Videos of the power going out, the first of the zombie attacks, the town of Emberoak being overrun – all the things that had happened prior to his plane crashing off the coast were the first to show up. After that, it was zombie attack after zombie attack, scenes from the school siege, the meerkat things fighting with the undead, and even some footage of the mass micro-breaches that had followed in the wake of Erin's return. Those had been taken by a family that had chosen to ride the disaster out holed up in their home.

Hundreds of cell phones and who knew how many images and pictures had been sitting silently stored in their owners' phones and cameras while the Jasper Island incident played itself out. Silently stored, that is, until

354 | C. Steven Manley

Israel had turned the cell service back on and allowed it all to go streaming through space and into the mass data collective that is the Internet.

The Council, the DGRI, and every politician in the know about the Veiled world was in a complete frenzy of information manipulation and spin control. They pulled what they could, lied about what they couldn't, and laughed off the rest as nonsense. The Council went so far as to spend millions of dollars on a big budget horror film and claim that much of what was being seen was just leaked test footage and stock or publicity photos. So-called experts took to the talk show circuit explaining how none of it was possible and just had to be a hoax. Lots of people believed all the cover stories, but there was a strong, quieter minority that seemed to be hoarding the videos and asking questions no one behind the Veil wanted asked.

The Jasper Island survivors were all given a cover story about weapons-grade hallucinogens being released on the island by a domestic terrorist group that had gotten caught in its own attack. They were given large payouts in exchange for their signatures on ironclad non-disclosure agreements that cited national security and promised pro-secution for treason if they were ever violated. The amount of money on the table ensured that everyone signed and went along with whatever cover story the DGRI provided them with. By the time it was all said and done, there were so many carefully crafted lies and half-truths woven a-round the story of Jasper Island that it would take decades for anyone to take it all apart.

Special Agent Namura and Council Delegate Black had both raised a cry for Israel's arrest and execution. Despite the official reports filed by everyone involved, they stood fast to the claim that without his existence none of the tragedies in Jasper Island would have been possible. They even went so far as to accuse him of working with the

Screed brothers since he had let Carmine get away and disappear for a second time. One of the things that kept them from getting what they wanted, though, was the fact that Israel was directly responsible for the lives that were saved on the island, as well as the capture of Jordan Screed who, as far as the world at large was concerned, was confirmed among the Jasper Island casualties. When Jordan had gotten a look at the secret DGRI prison where he was going to spend the rest of his life, he had immediately started laying the blame for the whole affair at his brother's feet. On top of that, he helped the DGRI obtain encrypted files from the computers at the DGS facility that were producing leads to other Progeny of the Inner Dark projects and interests scattered throughout the country. With these facts in play, no one expected Israel to suffer any official fallout.

That was what he thought had earned him a summons to Olivia's office as he stepped through the door. He had expected Olivia to be alone and waiting for him. Instead, he saw that Stone, Erin, and Allison were in the room as well. They were clustered around the large monitor that Olivia used for teleconferences, and though they all looked up as he came in, none of them smiled. Allison looked near tears and looked away as soon as he entered. Stone and Olivia both wore stern expressions that bordered on angry. Erin sat on a couch with an expression that was cold and focused.

"What's going on?" Israel said.

Olivia swallowed and said, "This came in to the general e-mail account about thirty minutes ago. You need to see it."

Israel walked over and stood next to Stone. The shorter man didn't look at him as Olivia pointed a remote at the monitor and pressed a button.

The video was good quality and showed a corridor of some kind in what looked like a standard grade hotel. The only light, though, was the light that shone from the camera and it illuminated such a narrow space that Israel couldn't make out too many details. Still, there was something familiar about the space that Israel couldn't quite place.

The cameraman continued down the dark corridor until he reached a door that was ajar. No light showed from inside the room, but there was small placard on the wall next to the door that held a handwritten name that sent a shot of panic through Israel.

"What is this?" he said

Stone reached up and placed a firm hand on Israel's shoulder. "Steady, mate. Steady."

On the screen, a hand came into frame and pushed the door open. With slow steps, the cameraman entered the room. Israel knew it immediately. It was small like a studio apartment. The furnishings were sparse but comfortable. Pictures hung on the walls, photos and paintings alike. Israel knew them all. He was in many of the photos.

"No, no, no," he whispered. "God, no."

Maxwell Trent, Israel's father, was seated in the middle of his room at the assisted living facility where he lived. Duct tape showed at his feet and ankles where they were secured to the plastic chair. More tape covered his eyes and mouth. His bald head reflected the camera's light and patches of gray whiskers stuck out around the tape that covered his mouth. Standing behind him, Carmine Screed stared into the camera's light with his good left eye. A black leather patch covered the right one.

"You take my brother, I take your father," he said.

In one smooth motion, Carmine reached down and wrenched Maxwell's head around so hard and fast that the sound of snapping vertebra came clearly through the audio. The old man's head snapped back and lolled unnaturally loose against his chest.

"Be seeing you, Trent," Carmine said.

The video went black.

It was a long time before Israel stopped screaming.

THE END

AUTHOR'S NOTE

They say that if a writer was to ever meet one of his main characters in the real world and not immediately get punched in the face by said character, then he didn't do his job as a storyteller. I think it's safe to say that if through some cosmic circumstance I ever meet Israel, he'll beat the hell out of me.

This book was a bit of a challenge. It was the first time I'd ever written the second book of a series or the middle book of a trilogy. A lot of times, the middle books tend to be a bit of a slog in the action department since so much of the middle part of a story is compiling complications without much resolution. I didn't want that. I wanted a middle book that moved at a quick pace while still raising the stakes. It was a challenge, but I think – I hope – I met it with some level of success.

The next and final book in the Paragons trilogy is on the horizon and will bring the story of Israel and Erin to something of a close. Are there still stories that can be told in the Veiled universe? Sure, but this one has just about run its course.

For the curious, the next book will be called *Unveiled*. Why that particular title? Well, I think Bones summed it up best: No More Secrets.